THE REVIEW *of* CONTEMPORARY FICTION

SPECIAL FICTION ISSUE
; OR THE WHALE

SUMMER 2009 | VOL. XXIX, NO. 2

EDITOR

JOHN O'BRIEN

ASSOCIATE EDITORS

MARTIN RIKER

IRVING MALIN

MANAGING EDITOR

JEREMY M. DAVIES

PRODUCTION

DANIELLE DUTTON

PROOFREADER

JESSICA HENRICHS

INTERN

SARAH LINDENBAUM

REVIEW OF CONTEMPORARY FICTION
Summer 2009
Vol. XXIX, No. 2

The *Review of Contemporary Fiction* is published three times each year
(January, June, September). Subscription prices are as follows:

Single volume (three issues):
Individuals: $17.00 U.S.; $22.60 Canada; $32.60 all other countries
Institutions: $26.00 U.S.; $31.60 Canada; $41.60 all other countries

ISSN: 0276-0045
ISBN: 978-1-56478-590-9

Partially funded by a grant from the Illinois Arts Council, a state agency, and by
the University of Illinois at Urbana-Champaign

Indexed in *Humanities International Complete, International Bibliography of Periodical Literature, International Bibliography of Book Reviews, MLA Bibliography*, and *Book Review Index.*
Abstracted in *Abstracts of English Studies.*

The *Review of Contemporary Fiction* is also available on 16mm microfilm, 35mm microfilm, and
105mm microfiche from University Microfilms International, 300 North Zeeb Road, Ann Arbor,
MI 48106-1346.

Address all correspondence to:
Review of Contemporary Fiction
University of Illinois
1805 S. Wright Street, MC-011
Champaign, IL 61820

www.dalkeyarchive.com

THE REVIEW OF CONTEMPORARY FICTION

BACK ISSUES AVAILABLE

Back issues are still available for the following numbers of the *Review of Contemporary Fiction* ($8 each unless otherwise noted):

Douglas Woolf / Wallace Markfield
William Eastlake / Aidan Higgins
Camilo José Cela
Chandler Brossard
Samuel Beckett
Claude Ollier / Carlos Fuentes
Joseph McElroy
John Barth / David Markson
Donald Barthelme / Toby Olson
William H. Gass / Manuel Puig
Robert Walser
José Donoso / Jerome Charyn
William T. Vollmann / Susan Daitch /
  David Foster Wallace
Djuna Barnes
Angela Carter / Tadeusz Konwicki
Stanley Elkin / Alasdair Gray
Brigid Brophy / Robert Creeley /
  Osman Lins
Edmund White / Samuel R. Delany
Mario Vargas Llosa / Josef Škvorecký
Wilson Harris / Alan Burns
Raymond Queneau / Carole Maso
Richard Powers / Rikki Ducornet
Edward Sanders
Writers on Writing: The Best of The *Review of
  Contemporary Fiction*
Bradford Morrow
Jean Rhys / John Hawkes /
  Paul Bowles / Marguerite Young

Henry Green / James Kelman /
  Ariel Dorfman
Janice Galloway / Thomas Bernhard /
  Robert Steiner / Elizabeth Bowen
Gilbert Sorrentino / William Gaddis /
  Mary Caponegro / Margery Latimer
Italo Calvino / Ursule Molinaro /
  B. S. Johnson
Louis Zukofsky / Nicholas Mosley /
  Coleman Dowell
Casebook Study of Gilbert
  Sorrentino's *Imaginative Qualities of
  Actual Things*
Rick Moody / Ann Quin /
  Silas Flannery
Diane Williams / Aidan Higgins /
  Patricia Eakins
Douglas Glover / Blaise Cendrars /
  Severo Sarduy
Robert Creeley / Louis-Ferdinand Céline /
  Janet Frame
William H. Gass
Gert Jonke / Kazuo Ishiguro /
  Emily Holmes Coleman
William H. Gass / Robert Lowry /
  Ross Feld
Flann O'Brien / Guy Davenport /
  Aldous Huxley
Steven Millhauser
William Eastlake / Julieta Campos /
  Jane Bowles

NOVELIST AS CRITIC: Essays by Garrett, Barth, Sorrentino, Wallace, Ollier, Brooke-Rose, Creeley, Mathews, Kelly, Abbott, West, McCourt, McGonigle, and McCarthy
NEW FINNISH FICTION: Fiction by Eskelinen, Jäntti, Kontio, Krohn, Paltto, Sairanen, Selo, Siekkinen, Sund, and Valkeapää
NEW ITALIAN FICTION: Interviews and fiction by Malerba, Tabucchi, Zanotto, Ferrucci, Busi, Corti, Rasy, Cherchi, Balduino, Ceresa, Capriolo, Carrera, Valesio, and Gramigna
GROVE PRESS NUMBER: Contributions by Allen, Beckett, Corso, Ferlinghetti, Jordan, McClure, Rechy, Rosset, Selby, Sorrentino, and others
NEW DANISH FICTION: Fiction by Brøgger, Høeg, Andersen, Grøndahl, Holst, Jensen, Thorup, Michael, Sibast, Ryum, Lynggaard, Grønfeldt, Willumsen, and Holm
NEW LATVIAN FICTION: Fiction by Ikstena, Bankovskis, Berelis, Kolmanis, Ziedonis, and others
THE FUTURE OF FICTION: Essays by Birkerts, Caponegro, Franzen, Galloway, Maso, Morrow, Vollmann, White, and others ($15)
NEW JAPANESE FICTION: Interviews and fiction by Ohara, Shimada, Shono, Takahashi, Tsutsui, McCaffery, Gregory, Kotani, Tatsumi, Koshikawa, and others
NEW CUBAN FICTION: Fiction by Ponte, Mejides, Aguilar, Bahr, Curbelo, Plasencia, Serova, and others
SPECIAL FICTION ISSUE: JUAN EMAR: Fiction and illustrations by Juan Emar, translated by Daniel Borzutzky
NEW AUSTRALIAN FICTION: Fiction by Murnane, Tsiolkas, Falconer, Wilding, Bird, Yu, and others
NEW CATALAN FICTION: Fiction by Rodoreda, Espriu, Ibarz, Monsó, Serra, Moliner, Serés, and others
WRITERS ON WRITING: Essays by Gail Scott, William H. Gass, Gert Jonke, Nicholas Delbanco, and others
GEORGES PEREC ISSUE: Essays by Perec, Harry Mathews, David Bellos, Marcel Bénabou, and others

Individuals receive a 10% discount on orders of one issue and a
20% discount on orders of two or more issues. To place an order,
use the form on the last page of this issue.

CONTENTS

THE REVIEW *of* CONTEMPORARY FICTION

Introduction

; or The Whale is a lost work from Herman Melville's major period (1851), never before published, which was unknown—quite literally could not have been known—until 2007. It is thus both a classic and a contemporary work of fiction, avant-garde even, in its typographical experimentation and radical narrative elisions. In fact, in today's environment after the end of widespread cultural literacy* and arguably facing the end of modern civilization itself,** *; or The Whale*'s engagement with the tradition of American fiction is the most contemporary thing about it.

2007 was a crucial year in Melville's creation of *; or The Whale* because it marked the publication by Orion Books of *Moby-Dick in Half the Time,* one of their first six Compact Editions of canonical works. Abridged by Anonymous, these editions were "sympathetically edited" to "retain all the elements of the originals: the plot, the characters, the social, historical, and local backgrounds and the authors' language and style."***

Missing from this list of "all the elements," however, are digression, texture, and weirdness, three of the literary values most characteristic of Melville's work. As Adam Gopnik writes:

> The Orion "Moby-Dick" is not defaced; it is, by conventional contemporary standards of good editing and critical judgment,

---

*   "I see a high point of reading in the United States from around 1850 to about 1950—call it the century of the book" (Ursula K. LeGuin, "Staying Awake: Notes on the Alleged Decline of Reading," *Harper's,* Feb. 2008, 33–38), p. 34.

**   "If we are indeed at the end, let us make our work a fitting coda to what came before us. That is as worthy a goal as any we writers have left" (Damion Searls, "Apocalypse Then," *n+1,* Fall 2008, 215–17), p. 217.

***   www.orionbooks.co.uk/extras/bookBlurbs/Classics_Compact_Editions.pdf, p. 2.

improved. The compact edition adheres to a specific idea of what a good novel ought to be: the contemporary aesthetic of the realist psychological novel. . . . [It] cut[s] out the self-indulgent stuff and present[s] a clean story, inhabited by plausible characters—the "taut, spare, driving" narrative beloved of Sunday reviewers. . . . You think, Nice job—what were the missing bits again? And when you go back to find them you remember why the book isn't just a thrilling adventure with unforgettable characters but a great book. The subtraction does not turn a good work into hackwork; it turns a hysterical, half-mad masterpiece into a sound, sane book. It still has its phallic reach and point, but lacks its flaccid, anxious self-consciousness: it is all Dick and no Moby. (*The New Yorker,* 10/22/2007, p. 68)

; or The Whale, in contrast, may fairly and logically be stated to be all Moby, no Dick. While just as conveniently compact as *Moby-Dick in Half the Time, ; or The Whale* preserves "all" the "other" "elements" of Melville's original *Moby-Dick; or The Whale,* by including every chapter, sentence, word, and punctuation mark that Anonymous removed to produce the Orion edition. To express the relationship in scholarly, mathematical form:

$$(\, ; \text{edition} \,) \; = \; (M \text{ text}) - (\tfrac{1}{2} \text{ edition})$$

; or The Whale thus forms a vital complement to the ½ edition. It also is, like the other abridgment, a self-standing work in its own right.

■

This introduction does not provide enough space to discuss *; or The Whale* in full, but the editor would like to call the reader's attention to a few moments in the text, to provide at least some ways into its particular, contemporary fictional mode.

Like the more famous first sentence of the M text ("Call me Ishmael"),*
the ; edition's abrupt first sentence presents the book's dominant poetic form,
while the rest of the paragraph preserves M's emphasis on the companionable
relationship between narrator and reader. Even before Chapter 1, however,
the preliminary material—unaccountably omitted from Orion's Compact
Edition, and hence seemingly identical in ; and M—takes on additional layers of meaning in ; , from the ironical first etymology ("While . . . leaving out
[that] which almost alone maketh up the signification . . . you deliver that
which is not true") through the extracts which foreshadow Melville's methods
in ; or *The Whale* as a whole. One might go so far as to call the ; text an Extract
Edition.

Melville's ability to preserve the Moby in this edition is probably the most
remarkable thing about ; or *The Whale*. In Chapter 6 of the M text, for example, Melville emphasizes New Bedford as a meeting point for the world:
"actual cannibals stand chatting at street corners; savages outright . . . Fee-
geeans, Tongatabooans, Erromanggoans, Pannangians, and Brighggians," and
"still more curious, certainly more comical," the "scores of green Vermonters
and New Hampshire men, all athirst for gain and glory in the fishery"—and at
the same time describes it as a place created solely by the whale fishery (M, p.
37). The ; text streamlines this account to say that New Bedford is "brilliant"
and "reckless," incomparable even to a famous German magician. Likewise,
Chapter 21 in the ; text is atmospheric, suspenseful, and fully characterizes
Queequeg despite its concision; Chapter 62, compared to the 566 words of the
M text or the 565 words of the ½ text, is a model of condensation and force;
and the exquisitely smooth Chapter 111 is almost as calm and lovely in ; as the
beautiful chapter in M, with its "milky-ways of coral isles, and low-lying, endless, unknown Archipelagoes, and impenetrable Japans" (M, p. 525, another
foreshadowing perhaps of the archipelagic poetics of ;).

The metaphors your editor has been using, of concision, streamlining, and
extraction, do not, however, capture the remarkably fluid feel of melting or

---

*   The Northwestern–Newberry edition (1988) republished by Penguin Books
(1992) was used in the making of ; or *The Whale*.

dissolving which is characteristic of *; or The Whale.* ; is, astonishingly, an even more watery book than *Moby-Dick*. See, for example, Chapter 4, where the phantom hand on the counterpane dissolves syntax itself in the rest of the chapter, or the last paragraph of Chapter 28 leading into the second paragraph of Chapter 29, which introduces the deeply moving distillation which will culminate in the last three chapters of the book.

Finally, it is in the chapters omitted entirely from ½ that we can best see the wisdom of ; . "Etymology" and "Extracts" have already been mentioned; in Chapters 8–9, the first such chapters in the body of the text, we have Father Mapple's memorable pulpit, with its rope ladder and vanguard prow, and the sermon which ends in the credo of the experimental writer ("Woe to him who seeks to please rather than to appal!" etc.) and begins with the credo of the reader of *; or The Whale* ("And taken with the context, this is full of meaning").

■

The present volume does not, unfortunately, present a scholarly text of *; or The Whale*. The British and American editions of the M text have not been collated; the ½ edition is based on the British text of *Moby-Dick* while the ; edition is based on the American text, and variations in spelling, in the hyphenation of compound words, and in single/double quotation marks have been neither listed in an appendix nor otherwise taken into account. Typos in ½, missing or added italics, and at least one miscorrection[*] have been disregarded and a list of emendations foregone. In one instance, Chapter 80 of the ½ edition, a descriptive phrase from the otherwise omitted M Chapter 112 ("the begrimed, blistered old blacksmith") is *moved* into the *middle* of M Chapter 113, *out of order!* It was difficult to know how best to react to this lapse in principle. Finally, there are two classes of textual artifact from the M text which appear in *both* the ; text and the ½ text:

---

[*]   ½, p. 220, line 22, and M, p. 434, line 24: "defendants" is changed to "plaintiffs," garbling the sense of the paragraph and the argument of the chapter as a whole.

- Chapter titles extant in ½ are repeated in ;
- When part but not "all" of a piece of dialogue is in ½, the quotation marks extant in ½ are repeated in the ; text to indicate that someone is speaking

We trust that the reader will appreciate how vitally important these exceptions are and will keep them firmly in mind.

In short, ; or *The Whale* awaits a critical edition. The present volume is a reader's edition, designed to introduce ; to a general audience. If it is, perhaps, of some service nevertheless to the scholars who will come after him, its editor will be humbly grateful.

HERMAN MELVILLE
EDITED BY DAMION SEARLS

;

or The Whale

IN TOKEN
OF MY ADMIRATION FOR HIS GENIUS,
This Book is Inscribed
TO
NATHANIEL HAWTHORNE

ETYMOLOGY

(Supplied by a Late Consumptive Usher to a Grammar School)

[The pale Usher—threadbare in coat, heart, body, and brain; I see him now. He was ever dusting his old lexicons and grammars, with a queer handkerchief, mockingly embellished with all the gay flags of all the known nations of the world. He loved to dust his old grammars; it somehow mildly reminded him of his mortality.]

Etymology

"While you take in hand to school others, and to teach them by what name a whale-fish is to be called in our tongue leaving out, through ignorance, the letter H, which almost alone maketh the signification of the word, you deliver that which is not true." —*Hackluyt*

"WHALE. * * * Sw. and Dan. *hval.* This animal is named from roundness or rolling; for in Dan. *hvalt* is arched or vaulted." —*Webster's Dictionary*

"WHALE. * * * It is more immediately from the Dut. and Ger. *Wallen;* A.S. *Walw-ian*, to roll, to wallow." —*Richardson's Dictionary*

ח,	*Hebrew.*
κετος,	*Greek.*
CETUS,	*Latin.*
WHÆL,	*Anglo-Saxon.*
HVAL,	*Danish.*
WAL,	*Dutch.*
HWAL,	*Swedish.*
HVALUR,	*Icelandic.*
WHALE,	*English.*
BALEINE,	*French.*

BALLENA,	*Spanish.*
PEKEE-NUEE-NUEE,	*Fegee.*
PEKEE-NUEE-NUEE,	*Erromangoan.*

Extracts

(Supplied by a Sub-Sub-Librarian.)

[It will be seen that this mere painstaking burrower and grub-worm of a poor devil of a Sub-Sub appears to have gone through the long Vaticans and street-stalls of the earth, picking up whatever random allusions to whales he could anyways find in any book whatsoever, sacred or profane. Therefore you must not, in every case at least, take the higgledy-piggledy whale statements, however authentic, in these extracts, for veritable gospel cetology. Far from it. As touching the ancient authors generally, as well as the poets here appearing, these extracts are solely valuable or entertaining, as affording a glancing bird's eye view of what has been promiscuously said, thought, fancied, and sung of Leviathan, by many nations and generations, including our own.

So fare thee well, poor devil of a Sub-Sub, whose commentator I am. Thou belongest to that hopeless, sallow tribe which no wine of this world will ever warm; and for whom even Pale Sherry would be too rosy-strong; but with whom one sometimes loves to sit, and feel poor-devilish, too; and grow convivial upon tears; and say to them bluntly, with full eyes and empty glasses, and in not altogether unpleasant sadness—Give it up, Sub-Subs! For by how much the more pains ye take to please the world, by so much the more shall ye for ever go thankless! Would that I could clear out Hampton Court and the Tuileries for ye! But gulp down your tears and hie aloft to the royal-mast with your hearts; for your friends who have gone before are clearing out the seven-storied heavens, and making refugees of long-pampered Gabriel, Michael, and Raphael, against your coming. Here ye strike but splintered hearts together—there, ye shall strike unsplinterable glasses!]

Extracts

"And God created great whales."

—Genesis.

"Leviathan maketh a path to shine after him;
One would think the deep to be hoary."

—Job.

"Now the Lord had prepared a great fish to swallow up Jonah." —*Jonah.*

"There go the ships; there is that Leviathan whom thou hast made to play therein." —*Psalms.*

"In that day, the Lord with his sore, and great, and strong sword, shall punish Leviathan the piercing serpent, even Leviathan that crooked serpent; and he shall slay the dragon that is in the sea." —*Isaiah*

"And what thing soever besides cometh within the chaos of this monster's mouth, be it beast, boat, or stone, down it goes all incontinently that foul great swallow of his, and perisheth in the bottomless gulf of his paunch."
—*Holland's Plutarch's Morals.*

"The Indian Sea breedeth the most and the biggest fishes that are: among which the Whales and Whirlpooles called Balaene, take up as much in length as four acres or arpens of land." —*Holland's Pliny.*

"Scarcely had we proceeded two days on the sea, when about sunrise a great many Whales and other monsters of the sea, appeared. Among the former, one was of a most monstrous size. * * This came towards us, open-mouthed, raising the waves on all sides, and beating the sea before him into a foam." —*Tooke's Lucian. "The True History."*

"He visited this country also with a view of catching horse-whales, which had bones of very great value for their teeth, of which he brought some to the king. * * * The best whales were catched in his own country, of which some were forty-eight, some fifty yards long. He said that he was one of six who had killed sixty in two days." —*Other or Octher's verbal narrative taken down from his mouth by King Alfred, A.D. 890.*

"And whereas all the other things, whether beast or vessel, that enter into the dreadful gulf of this monster's (whale's) mouth, are immediately lost and swallowed up, the sea-gudgeon retires into it in great security, and there sleeps." —MONTAIGNE.—*Apology for Raimond Sebond.*

"Let us fly, let us fly! Old Nick take me if is not Leviathan described by the noble prophet Moses in the life of patient Job." —*Rabelais.*

"This whale's liver was two cartloads." —*Stowe's Annals.*

"The great Leviathan that maketh the seas to seethe like boiling pan." —*Lord Bacon's Version of the Psalms.*

"Touching that monstrous bulk of the whale or ork we have received nothing certain. They grow exceeding fat, insomuch that an incredible quantity of oil will be extracted out of one whale." —*Ibid. "History of Life and Death."*

"The sovereignest thing on earth is parmacetti for an inward bruise." —*King Henry.*

"Very like a whale." —*Hamlet.*

> "Which to secure, no skill of leach's art
> Mote him availle, but to returne againe
> To his wound's worker, that with lowly dart,
> Dinting his breast, had bred his restless paine,

Like as the wounded whale to shore flies thro' the maine."
—*The Faerie Queen.*

"Immense as whales, the motion of whose vast bodies can in a peaceful calm trouble the ocean til it boil." —*Sir William Davenant. Preface to Gondibert.*

"What spermacetti is, men might justly doubt, since the learned Hosmannus in his work of thirty years, saith plainly, Nescio quid sit." —*Sir T. Browne. Of Sperma Ceti and the Sperma Ceti Whale. Vide his V. E.*

> "Like Spencer's Talus with his modern flail
> He threatens ruin with his ponderous tail.
>   *   *   *   *   *
> Their fixed jav'lins in his side he wears,
> And on his back a grove of pikes appears."
> —*Waller's Battle of the Summer Islands.*

"By art is created that great Leviathan, called a Commonwealth or State—(in Latin, Civitas) which is but an artificial man." —*Opening Sentence of Hobbes's Leviathan.*

"Silly Mansoul swallowed it without chewing, as if it had been a sprat in the mouth of a whale." —*Pilgrim's Progress.*

> "That sea beast Leviathan, which God of all his works Created
> hugest that swim the ocean stream." —*Paradise Lost.*

> ——"There Leviathan,
> Hugest of living creatures, in the deep
> Stretched like a promontory sleeps or swims,
> And seems a moving land; and at his gills
> Draws in, and at his breath spouts out a sea." —*Ibid.*

"The mighty whales which swim in a sea of water, and have a sea of oil swimming in them." —*Fuller's Profane and Holy State.*

> "So close behind some promontory lie
> The huge Leviathan to attend their prey,
> And give no chance, but swallow in the fry,
> Which through their gaping jaws mistake the way."
> —*Dryden's Annus Mirabilis.*

"While the whale is floating at the stern of the ship, they cut off his head, and tow it with a boat as near the shore as it will come; but it will be aground in twelve or thirteen feet water." —*Thomas Edge's Ten Voyages to Spitzbergen, in Purchas.*

"In their way they saw many whales sporting in the ocean, and in wantonness fuzzing up the water through their pipes and vents, which nature has placed on their shoulders." —*Sir T. Herbert's Voyages into Asia and Africa. Harris Coll.*

"Here they saw such huge troops of whales, that they were forced to proceed with a great deal of caution for fear they should run their ship upon them." —*Schouten's Sixth Circumnavigation.*

"We set sail from the Elbe, wind N.E. in the ship called The Jonas-in-the-Whale. * * *

Some say the whale can't open his mouth, but that is a fable. * * *

They frequently climb up the masts to see whether they can see a whale, for the first discoverer has a ducat for his pains. * * *

I was told of a whale taken near Shetland, that had above a barrel of herrings in his belly. * * *

One of our harpooneers told me that he caught once a whale in Spitzbergen that was white all over." —*A Voyage to Greenland, A.D. 1671. Harris Coll.*

"Several whales have come in upon this coast (Fife) Anno 1652, one eighty feet in length of the whale-bone kind came in, which (as I was informed), besides a vast quantity of oil, did afford 500 weight of baleen. The jaws of it stand for a gate in the garden of Pitferren." —*Sibbald's Fife and Kinross.*

"Myself have agreed to try whether I can master and kill this Sperma-ceti whale, for I could never hear of any of that sort that was killed by any man, such is his fierceness and swiftness." —*Richard Strafford's Letter from the Bermudas. Phil. Trans. A.D. 1668.*

"Whales in the sea
God's voice obey." —*N. E. Primer.*

"We saw also abundance of large whales, there being more in those southern seas, as I may say, by a hundred to one; than we have to the northward of us." —*Captain Cowley's Voyage round the Globe. A.D. 1729.*

* * * * * "and the breath of the whale is frequendy attended with such an insupportable smell, as to bring on a disorder of the brain." —*Ulloa's South America.*

"To fifty chosen sylphs of special note,
We trust the important charge, the petticoat.
Oft have we known that seven-fold fence to fail,
Tho' stuffed with hoops and armed with ribs of whale."
—*Rape of the Lock.*

"If we compare land animals in respect to magnitude, with those that take up their abode in the deep, we shall find they will appear contemptible in the comparison. The whale is doubtless the largest animal in creation." —*Goldsmith, Nat. Hist.*

"If you should write a fable for little fishes, you would make them speak like great whales." —*Goldsmith to Johnson.*

"In the afternoon we saw what was supposed to be a rock, but it was found to be a dead whale, which some Asiatics had killed, and were then towing ashore. They seemed to endeavor to conceal themselves behind the whale, in order to avoid being seen by us." —*Cook's Voyages.*

"The larger whales, they seldom venture to attack. They stand in so great dread of some of them, that when out at sea they are afraid to mention even their names, and carry dung, lime-stone, juniper-wood, and some other articles of the same nature in their boats, in order to terrify and prevent their too near approach." —*Uno Von Troil's Letters on Banks's and Solander's Voyage to Iceland in 1772.*

"The Spermacetti Whale found by the Nantuckois, is an active, fierce animal, and requires vast address and boldness in the fishermen." —*Thomas Jefferson's Whale Memorial to the French minister in 1778.*

"And pray, sir, what in the world is equal to it?" —*Edmund Burke's reference in Parliament to the Nantucket Whale-Fishery.*

"Spain——a great whale stranded on the shores of Europe." —*Edmund Burke. (somewhere.)*

"A tenth branch of the king's ordinary revenue, said to be grounded on the consideration of his guarding and protecting the seas from pirates and robbers, is the right to *royal* fish, which are whale and sturgeon. And these, when either thrown ashore or caught near the coast, are the property of the king." —*Blackstone.*

"Soon to the sport of death the crews repair:

Rodmond unerring o'er his head suspends
The barbed steel, and every turn attends." —*Falconer's Shipwreck*.

"Bright shone the roofs, the domes, the spires,
   And rockets blew self driven,
To hang their momentary fire
   Around the vault of heaven.

"So fire with water to compare,
   The ocean serves on high,
Up-spouted by a whale in air,
   To express unwieldy joy."
                     —*Cowper, on the Queen's Visit to London*.

"Ten or fifteen gallons of blood are thrown out of the heart at a stroke, with immense velocity." —*John Hunter's account of the dissection of a whale. (A small sized one.)*

"The aorta of a whale is larger in the bore than the main pipe of the water-works at London Bridge, and the water roaring in its passage through that pipe is inferior in impetus and velocity to the blood gushing from the whale's heart." —*Paley's Theology*.

"The whale is a mammiferous animal without hind feet." —*Baron Cuvier*.

"In 40 degrees south, we saw Spermacetti Whales, but did not take any till the first of May, the sea being then covered with them." —*Colnett's Voyage for the Purpose of Extending the Spermaceti Whale Fishery*.

"In the free element beneath me swam,
Floundered and dived, in play, in chace, in battle,
Fishes of every color, form, and kind;

Which language cannot paint, and mariner
Had never seen; from dread Leviathan
To insect millions peopling every wave:
Gather'd in shoals immense, like floating islands,
Led by mysterious instincts through that waste
And trackless region, though on every side
Assaulted by voracious enemies,
Whales, sharks, and monsters, arm'd in front or jaw,
With swords, saws, spiral horns, or hooked fangs."

—Montgomery's World before the Flood.

"Io! Pæan! Io! sing.
To the finny people's king.
Not a mightier whale than this
In the vast Atlantic is;
Not a fatter fish than he,
Flounders round the Polar Sea."

—Charles Lamb's Triumph of the Whale.

"In the year 1690 some persons were on a high hill observing the whales spouting and sporting with each other, when one observed: there—pointing to the sea—is a green pasture where our children's grand-children will go for bread." *—Obed Macy's History of Nantucket.*

"I built a cottage for Susan and myself and made a gateway in the form of a Gothic Arch, by setting up a whale's jaw bones." *—Hawthorne's Twice Told Tales.*

"She came to bespeak a monument for her first love, who had been killed by a whale in the Pacific ocean, no less than forty years ago." *—Ibid.*

"No, Sir, 'tis a Right Whale," answered Tom; "I saw his sprout; he threw up a pair of as pretty rainbows as a Christian would wish to look at. He's a raal oil-butt, that fellow!" —*Cooper's Pilot.*

"The papers were brought in, and we saw in the Berlin Gazette that whales had been introduced on the stage there." —*Eckermann's Conversations with Goethe.*

"My God! Mr. Chace, what is the matter?" I answered, "we have been stove by a whale." —"*Narrative of the Shipwreck of the Whale Ship Essex of Nantucket, which was attacked and finally destroyed by a large Sperm Whale in the Pacific Ocean." By Owen Chace of Nantucket, first mate of said vessel. New York, 1821.*

> "A mariner sat in the shrouds one night,
>   The wind was piping free;
> Now bright, now dimmed, was the moonlight pale,
> And the phospher gleamed in the wake of the whale,
>   As it floundered in the sea." —*Elizabeth Oakes Smith.*

"The quantity of line withdrawn from the boats engaged in the capture of this one whale, amounted altogether to 10,440 yards or nearly six English miles." * * *
"Sometimes the whale shakes its tremendous tail in the air, which, cracking like a whip, resounds to the distance of three or four miles." —*Scoresby.*

"Mad with the agonies he endures from these fresh attacks, the infuriated Sperm Whale rolls over and over; he rears his enormous head, and with wide expanded jaws snaps at everything around him; he rushes at the boats with his head; they are propelled before him with vast swiftness, and sometimes utterly destroyed.

　　　* * * It is a matter of great astonishment that the consideration of the habits of so interesting, and, in a commercial point of view, so important

an animal (as the Sperm Whale) should have been so entirely neglected, or should have excited so little curiosity among the numerous, and many of them competent observers, that of late years, must have possessed the most abundant and the most convenient opportunities of witnessing their habitudes." —*Thomas Beale's History of the Sperm Whale, 1839.*

"The Cachalot" (Sperm Whale) "is not only better armed than the True Whale" (Greenland or Right Whale) "in possessing a formidable weapon at either extremity of its body, but also more frequently displays a disposition to employ these weapons offensively and in manner at once so artful, bold, and mischievous, as to lead to its being regarded as the most dangerous to attack of all the known species of the whale tribe." —*Frederick Debell Bennett's Whaling Voyage Round the Globe, 1840.*

October 13. "There she blows," was sung out from the mast-head.
  "Where away?" demanded the captain.
  "Three points off the lee bow, sir."
  "Raise up your wheel. Steady!"
  "Steady, sir."
  "Mast-head ahoy! Do you see that whale now?"
  "Ay ay, sir! A shoal of Sperm Whales! There she blows! There she breaches!"
  "Sing out! sing out every time!"
  "Ay Ay, sir! There she blows! there—there—*thar* she blows—bowes—bo-o-os!"
  "How far off?"
  "Two miles and a half."
  "Thunder and lightning! so near! Call all hands." —*J. Ross Browne's Etchings of a Whaling Cruise. 1846.*

"The Whale-ship Globe, on board of which vessel occurred the horrid transactions we are about to relate, belonged to the island of Nantucket." —*"Narrative of the Globe Mutiny," by Lay and Hussey, Survivors. A.D. 1828.*

"Being once pursued by a whale which he had wounded, he parried the assault for some time with a lance; but the furious monster at length rushed on the boat; himself and comrades only being preserved by leaping into the water when they saw the onset was inevitable." —*Missionary Journal of Tyerman and Bennett.*

"Nantucket itself," said Mr. Webster, "is a very striking and peculiar portion of the National interest. There is a population of eight or nine thousand persons living here in the sea, adding largely every year to the National wealth by the boldest and most persevering industry." —*Report of Daniel Webster's Speech in the U. S. Senate, on the application for the Erection of a Breakwater at Nantucket. 1828.*

"The whale fell directly over him, and probably killed him in a moment." —*"The Whale and his Captors, or The Whaleman's Adventures and the Whale's Biography, as gathered on the Homeward Cruise of the Commodore Preble." By Rev. Henry T. Cheever.*

"If you make the least damn bit of noise," replied Samuel, "I will send you to hell." —*Life of Samuel Comstock (the mutineer), by his brother, William Comstock. Another Version of the whale-ship Globe narrative.*

"The voyages of the Dutch and English to the Northern Ocean, in order, if possible, to discover a passage through it to India, though they failed of their main object, laid-open the haunts of the whale." —*McCulloch's Commercial Dictionary.*

"These things are reciprocal; the ball rebounds, only to bound forward again; for now in laying open the haunts of the whale, the whalemen seem to have indirectly hit upon new clews to that same mystic North-West Passage." —*From "Something" unpublished.*

"It is impossible to meet a whale-ship on the ocean without being struck by her near appearance. The vessel under short sail, with look-outs at the mast-heads, eagerly scanning the wide expanse around them, has a totally different air from those engaged in regular voyage." —*Currents and Whaling. U.S. Ex. Ex.*

"Pedestrians in the vicinity of London and elsewhere may recollect having seen large curved bones set upright in the earth, either to form arches over gateways, or entrances to alcoves, and they may perhaps have been told that these were the ribs of whales." —*Tales of a Whale Voyager to the Arctic Ocean.*

"It was not till the boats returned from the pursuit of these whales, that the whites saw their ship in bloody possession of the savages enrolled among the crew." —*Newspaper Account of the Taking and Retaking of the Whale-ship Hobomack.*

"It is generally well known that out of the crews of Whaling vessels (American) few ever return in the ships on board of which they departed." —*Cruise in a Whale Boat.*

"Suddenly a mighty mass emerged from the water, and shot up perpendicularly into the air. It was the while." —*Miriam Coffin or the Whale Fisherman.*

"The Whale is harpooned to be sure; but bethink you, how you would manage a powerful unbroken colt, with the mere appliance of a rope tied to the root of his tail." —*A Chapter on Whaling in Ribs and Trucks.*

"On one occasion I saw two of these monsters (whales) probably male and female, slowly swimming, one after the other, within less than a stone's throw of the shore" (Terra Del Fuego), "over which the beech tree extended its branches." —*Darwin's Voyage of a Naturalist.*

"'Stern all!' exclaimed the mate, as upon turning his head, he saw the distended jaws of a large Sperm Whale close to the head of the boat, threatening it with instant destruction;—'Stern all, for your lives!'" —*Wharton the Whale Killer.*

"So be cheery, my lads, let your hearts never fail,
While the bold harpooneer is striking the whale!"

—*Nantucket Song.*

"Oh, the rare old Whale, mid storm and gale
  In his ocean home will be
A giant in might, where might is right,
  And King of the boundless sea." —*Whale Song.*

CHAPTER 1

Loomings

methodically. With a philosophical flourish Cato throws himself upon his sword; I quietly take to the ship. There is nothing surprising in this. If they but knew it, almost all men in their degree, some time or other, cherish very nearly the same feelings towards the ocean with me

There now is your insular city of the Manhattoes, belted round by wharves as Indian isles by coral reefs—commerce surrounds it with her surf. Right and left, the streets take you waterward. Its extreme downtown is the battery, where that noble mole is washed by waves, and cooled by breezes, which a few hours previous were out of sight of land. Look at the crowds of water-gazers there.

Circumambulate the city of a dreamy Sabbath afternoon. Go from Corlears Hook to Coenties Slip, and from thence, by Whitehall, northward. What do you see?—Posted like silent sentinels all around the town, stand thousands upon thousands of mortal men fixed in ocean reveries. Some leaning against the spiles; some seated upon the pier-heads; some looking over the bulwarks of ships from China; some high aloft in the rigging, as if striving to get a still better seaward peep. But these are all landsmen; of week days pent up in lath and plaster—tied to counters, nailed to benches, clinched to desks. How then is this? Are the green fields gone? What do they here?

But look! here come more crowds, pacing straight for the water, and seemingly bound for a dive. Strange! Nothing will content them but the extremest limit of the land; loitering under the shady lee of yonder warehouses will not suffice. No. They must get just as nigh the water as they possibly can without falling in. And there they stand—miles of them—leagues. Inlanders all, they come from lanes and alleys, streets and avenues—north, east, south, and west. Yet here they all unite. Tell me, does the magnetic virtue of the needles of the compasses of all those ships attract them thither?

Once more. Say you are in the country; in some high land of lakes. Take almost any path you please, and ten to one it carries you down in a dale, and leaves you there by a pool in the stream. There is magic in it. Let the most absent-minded of men be plunged in his deepest reveries—stand that man on his legs, set his feet a-going, and he will infallibly lead you to water, if water there be in all that region. Should you ever be athirst in the great American desert, try this experiment, if your caravan happen to be supplied with a metaphysical professor. Yes, as every one knows, meditation and water are wedded for ever.

But here is an artist. He desires to paint you the dreamiest, shadiest, quietest, most enchanting bit of romantic landscape in all the valley of the Saco. What is the chief element he employs? There stand his trees, each with a hollow trunk, as if a hermit and a crucifix were within; and here sleeps his meadow, and there sleep his cattle; and up from yonder cottage goes a sleepy smoke. Deep into distant woodlands winds a mazy way, reaching to overlapping spurs of mountains bathed in their hill-side blue. But though the picture lies thus tranced, and though this pine-tree shakes down its sighs like leaves upon this shepherd's head, yet all were vain, unless the shepherd's eye were fixed upon the magic stream before him. Go visit the Prairies in June, when for scores on scores of miles you wade knee-deep among Tiger-lilies—what is the one charm wanting?—Water—there is not a drop of water there! Were Niagara but a cataract of sand, would you travel your thousand miles to see it? Why did the poor poet of Tennessee, upon suddenly receiving two hand-fuls of silver, deliberate whether to buy him a coat, which he sadly needed, or invest his money in a pedestrian trip to Rockaway Beach? Why is almost every robust healthy boy with a robust healthy soul in him, at some time or other crazy to go to sea? Why upon your first voyage as a passenger, did you yourself feel such a mystical vibration, when first told that you and your ship were now out of sight of land? Why did the old Persians hold the sea holy? Why did the Greeks give it a separate deity, and own brother of Jove? Surely all this is not without meaning. And still deeper the meaning of that story of Narcissus, who because he could not grasp the tormenting, mild image he saw in the fountain, plunged into it and was drowned. But that same image, we ourselves see in all rivers and oceans. It is the image of the ungraspable phantom of life; and this is the key to it all.

For my part, I abominate all honorable respectable toils, trials, and tribula-tions of every kind whatsoever.   , not to say reverentially,   It is out of the idolatrous dotings of the old Egyptians upon broiled ibis and roasted river horse, that you see the mummies of those creatures in their huge bake-houses the pyramids.

and respectfully   and punch   that it is all right   one way or other

that I ever heard of   The act of paying is perhaps the most uncomfortable infliction that the two orchard thieves entailed upon us.

(that is, if you never violate the Pythagorean maxim)   He thinks he breathes it first; but not so. has the constant surveillance of me, and

With other men, perhaps, such things would not have been inducements; but as for me, I am tormented with an everlasting itch for things remote. I love to sail forbidden seas, and land on barbarous coasts. Not ignoring what is good, I am quick to perceive a horror, and could still be social with it—would they let me—since it is but well to be on friendly terms with all the inmates of the place one lodges in.

By reason of these things, then, the whaling voyage was welcome; the great flood-gates of the wonder-world swung open, and in the wild conceits that swayed me to my purpose, two and two there floated into my inmost soul, endless processions of the whale, and, mid most of them all, one grand hooded phantom, like a snow hill in the air.

CHAPTER 2

The Carpet-Bag

for my destined port,   a very dubious-looking, nay,   shouldering my bag, and   be sure to inquire the price, and

,—rather weary for me, when I struck my foot against the flinty projections, because from hard, remorseless service the soles of my boots were in a most miserable plight   don't you hear?   by instinct

, like a candle moving about in a tomb

"In judging of that tempestuous wind called Euroclydon," says an old writer— of whose works I possess the only copy extant—"it maketh a marvellous dif- ference, whether thou lookest out at it from a glass window where the frost is all on the outside, or whether thou observest it from that sashless window, where the frost is on both sides, and of which the wight Death is the only glazier." True enough, thought I, as this passage occurred to my mind—old black-letter, thou reasonest well. Yes, these eyes are windows, and this body of mine is the house. What a pity they didn't stop up the chinks and the crannies though, and thrust in a little lint here and there. But it's too late to make any improvements now. The universe is finished; the copestone is on, and the chips were carted off a million years ago. Poor Lazarus there, chattering his teeth against the curbstone for his pillow, and shaking off his tatters with his shiverings, he might plug up both ears with rags, and put a corn-cob into his mouth, and yet that would not keep out the tempestuous Euroclydon. Euroclydon! says old Dives, in his red silken wrapper—(he had a redder one afterwards) pooh, pooh! What a fine frosty night; how Orion glitters; what northern lights! Let them talk of their oriental summer climes of everlasting conservatories; give me the privilege of making my own summer with my own coals.

But what thinks Lazarus? Can he warm his blue hands by holding them up to the grand northern lights? Would not Lazarus rather be in Sumatra than here? Would he not far rather lay him down lengthwise along the line of the equator; yea, ye gods! go down to the fiery pit itself, in order to keep out this frost?

Now, that Lazarus should lie stranded there on the curbstone before the door of Dives, this is more wonderful than that an iceberg should be moored to one of the Moluccas. Yet Dives himself, he too lives like a Czar in an ice palace made of frozen sighs, and being a president of a temperance society, he only drinks the tepid tears of orphans.

But no more of this blubbering now, we are going a-whaling, and there is plenty of that yet to come.

CHAPTER 3

The Spouter-Inn

every way in the unequal crosslights by which you viewed it,   and a series of systematic visits to it, and careful inquiry of the neighbors, Such unaccountable masses of shades and shadows, that at first you almost thought some ambitious young artist, in the time of the New England hags, had endeavored to delineate chaos bewitched. But by dint of much and earnest contemplation, and oft repeated ponderings, and especially by throwing open the little window towards the back of the entry, you at last come to the conclusion that such an idea, however wild, might not be altogether unwarranted.

But what most puzzled and confounded you was a long, limber, portentous, black mass of something hovering in the centre of the picture over three blue, dim, perpendicular lines floating in a nameless yeast. —It's a blasted heath.— It's a Hyperborean winter scene.—It's the breaking-up of the icebound stream of Time. But at last all these fancies yielded to that one portentous something in the picture's midst. *That* once found out, and all the rest were plain.

In fact, the artist's design seemed this: a final theory of my own, partly based upon the aggregated opinions of many aged persons with whom I conversed upon the subject.

original

, when this corner-anchored old ark rocked so furiously

—not a bed unoccupied

I never liked to sleep two in a bed; that if I should ever do so, about a strange town

like a bench on the Battery

Nothing but two dismal tallow candles, each in a winding sheet.

"he don't"

"Is he here?"

, when, knowing not what else to do with myself, I resolved to spend the rest of the evening as a looker on

A tramping of sea boots was heard in the entry;   enough   there officiating whatsoever, never mind of how long standing, or

held somewhat aloof, and though he seemed desirous not to spoil the hilarity of his shipmates by his own sober face, yet upon the whole he. This man interested me at once; and since the sea-gods had ordained that he should soon become my shipmate (though but a sleeping-partner one, so far as this narrative is concerned), I will here venture upon a little description of him. He stood full six feet in height, with noble shoulders, and a chest like a cofferdam. I have seldom seen such brawn in a man. His face was deeply brown and burnt, making his white teeth dazzling by the contrast;   His voice at once announced that he was a Southerner, and from his fine stature, I thought he must be one of those tall mountaineers from the Alleghanian Ridge in Virginia.   and I saw no more of him till he became my comrade on the sea. he was missed by, and being, it seems, for some reason a huge favorite with them, they "Bulkington!"

Nor was there any earthly reason why I as a sailor should sleep two in a bed, more than anybody else; for sailors no more sleep two in a bed at sea, than bachelor Kings do ashore. To be sure they all sleep together in one apartment, but you have your own hammock, and cover yourself with your own blanket, and sleep in your own skin.

It was fair to presume that being a harpooneer, his linen or woollen, as the case might be, would not be of the tidiest, certainly none of the finest. I began to twitch all over.   it was getting late, and

", and it's a plaguy rough board here"—feeling of the knots and notches. "But wait a bit, Skrimshander; I've got a carpenter's plane there in the bar—wait, I say, and I'll make ye snug enough"   he procured the plane; and with his old silk handkerchief first dusting the bench, vigorously set to planing away at my bed, the while grinning like an ape. The shavings flew right and left; till at last the plane-iron came bump against an indestructible knot. The landlord was near spraining his wrist, and I told him for heaven's sake to quit—the bed was soft enough to suit me, and I did not know how all the planing in the world could make eider down of a pine plank. So gathering up the shavings with an-other grin, and throwing them into the great stove in the middle of the room,
    and left me in a brown study.

than the planed one,   , especially as another current from the rickety door met the one from the window, and both together formed a series of small whirlwinds in the immediate vicinity of the spot where I had thought to spend the night

but stop, couldn't I steal a march on him—bolt his door inside, and jump into his bed, not to be wakened by the most violent knockings? It seemed no bad idea; but upon second thoughts I dismissed it. For who could tell but what the next morning, so soon as I popped out of the room, the harpooneer might be standing in the entry, all ready to knock me down!

I'll have a good look at him then, and perhaps we may become jolly good bedfellows after all—there's no telling.

by ones, twos, and threes,

again with his lean chuckle,

"What sort of a bamboozingly story is this you are telling me?" getting into a towering rage.

"Broke," said I—"*broke*, do you mean?"

"Sartain"

"I come to your house and want a bed; you tell me you can only give me half a one; that the other half belongs to a certain harpooneer. And about this harpooneer, whom I have not yet seen, you persist in telling me the most mystifying and exasperating stories tending to beget in me an uncomfortable feeling towards the man whom you design for my bedfellow—a sort of connexion, landlord, which is an intimate and confidential one in the highest degree. *You* I mean, landlord, *you*, sir,"

"He wanted to, last Sunday, but I stopped him just as he was goin' out of the door with four heads strung on a string, for all the airth like a string of inions."

"Why, afore we give it up, Sal used to put our Sam and little Johnny in the foot of it. But I got a dreaming and sprawling about one night, and somehow, Sam got pitched on the floor, and came near breaking his arm. Arter that, Sal said it wouldn't do."

on the bed-side, half undressed as I was, and remembering what the landlord said about the harpooneer's not coming home at all that night, it being so very late, made no more ado, but then

light and had pretty nearly made a good offing towards the land of Nod,

Yes, it's just as I thought, he's a terrible bedfellow; he's been in a fight, got dreadfully cut, and here he is, just from the surgeon. But at that moment he chanced to turn his face so towards the light, that I plainly saw they could not be sticking-plasters at all, those black squares on his cheeks. They were stains of some sort or other. an inkling of the truth occurred to me too that part of it, I mean, lying round about, and completely independent of the squares of tattooing To be sure, it might be nothing but a good coat of tropical tanning;

but   all   after some difficulty   commenced fumbling in it, and   enough
—none to speak of at least

Even as it was, I thought something of slipping out of the window, but it was
the second floor back.   and being completely nonplussed and confounded
about the stranger   In fact, I was so afraid of him that I was not game enough
just then to address him, and demand a satisfactory answer concerning what
seemed inexplicable in him.

; he seemed to have been in a Thirty Years' War, and just escaped from it with
a sticking-plaster shirt   or other   —perhaps the heads of his own brothers

completely fascinated my attention, and   previously   at length

feeling but ill at ease meantime—

queer   before the light was put out

to myself

Chapter 4

The Counterpane

about daylight,   they so blended their hues together

My sensations were strange. Let me try to explain them. When I was a child,
I well remember a somewhat similar circumstance that befell me; whether it
was a reality or a dream, I never could entirely settle. The circumstance was
this. I had been cutting up some caper or other—I think it was trying to crawl
up the chimney, as I had seen a little sweep do a few days previous; and my
stepmother who, somehow or other, was all the time whipping me, or sending
me to bed supperless,—my mother dragged me by the legs out of the chimney

and packed me off to bed, though it was only two o'clock in the afternoon of the 21st June, the longest day in the year in our hemisphere. I felt dreadfully. But there was no help for it, so up stairs I went to my little room in the third floor, undressed myself as slowly as possible so as to kill time, and with a bitter sigh got between the sheets.

I lay there dismally calculating that sixteen entire hours must elapse before I could hope for a resurrection. Sixteen hours in bed! the small of my back ached to think of it. And it was so light too; the sun shining in at the window, and a great rattling of coaches in the streets, and the sound of gay voices all over the house. I felt worse and worse—at last I got up, dressed, and softly going down in my stockinged feet, sought out my stepmother, and suddenly threw myself at her feet, beseeching her as a particular favor to give me a good slippering for my misbehavior; anything indeed but condemning me to lie abed such an unendurable length of time. But she was the best and most conscientious of stepmothers, and back I had to go to my room. For several hours I lay there broad awake, feeling a great deal worse than I have ever done since, even from the greatest subsequent misfortunes. At last I must have fallen into a troubled nightmare of a doze; and slowly waking from it—half steeped in dreams—I opened my eyes, and the before sun-lit room was now wrapped in outer darkness. Instantly I felt a shock running through all my frame; nothing was to be seen, and nothing was to be heard; but a supernatural hand seemed placed in mine. My arm hung over the counterpane, and the nameless, unimaginable, silent form or phantom, to which the hand belonged, seemed closely seated by my bed-side. For what seemed ages piled on ages, I lay there, frozen with the most awful fears, not daring to drag away my hand; yet ever thinking that if I could but stir it one single inch, the horrid spell would be broken. I knew not how this consciousness at last glided away from me; but waking in the morning, I shudderingly remembered it all, and for days and weeks and months afterwards I lost myself in confounding attempts to explain the mystery. Nay, to this very hour, I often puzzle myself with it.

Now, take away the awful fear, and my sensations at feeling the supernatural hand in mine were very similar, in their strangeness, to those which I expe-

rienced on waking up and seeing Queequeg's pagan arm thrown round me.
one by one, in fixed reality,   as though naught but death should part us
twain. in a strange house in the broad day   and incessant   though a dim
consciousness of knowing something about me seemed slowly dawning over
him,   and bent upon narrowly observing so curious a creature. When, his
mind seemed made up touching the character of his bedfellow, and he became, as it were, reconciled to the fact;   say what you will, he and his ways
were well worth unusual regarding.

His education was not yet completed. He was an undergraduate. If he had
not been a small degree civilized, he very probably would not have troubled
himself with boots at all; but then, if he had not been still a savage, he never
would have dreamt of getting under the bed to put them on.   his pair of
damp, wrinkled cowhide ones—probably not made to order either—rather
pinched and tormented him at the first go off of a bitter cold morning.

as well as I could, to accelerate his toilet somewhat, and particularly

CHAPTER 5

Breakfast

I say, Still, for the most part, that sort of thing is to be had anywhere.

—all of the same calling, all of kindred tastes—

I cannot say much for his breeding.

CHAPTER 6

The Street

in this town

Can Herr Alexander perform a feat like that?

You must go to New Bedford to see a brilliant wedding; for, they say, they have reservoirs of oil in every house, and every night recklessly burn their lengths in spermaceti candles.

CHAPTER 7

The Chapel

sympathetically

What despair in those immovable inscriptions!   As well might those tablets stand in the cave of Elephanta as here.

In what census of living creatures, the dead of mankind are included; why it is that a universal proverb says of them, that they tell no tales, though containing more secrets than the Goodwin Sands; how it is that to his name who yesterday departed for the other world, we prefix so significant and infidel a word, and yet do not thus entitle him, if he but embarks for the remotest Indies of this living earth; why the Life Insurance Companies pay death-forfeitures upon immortals; in what eternal, unstirring paralysis, and deadly, hopeless trance, yet lies antique Adam who died sixty round centuries ago; how it is that we still refuse to be comforted for those who we nevertheless maintain are dwelling in unspeakable bliss; why all the living so strive to hush all the dead; wherefore but the rumor of a knocking in a tomb will terrify a whole city. All these things are not without their meanings.

But Faith, like a jackal, feeds among the tombs, and even from these dead doubts she gathers her most vital hope.

Chapter 8

The Pulpit

I had not been seated very long ere a man of a certain venerable robustness entered; immediately as the storm-pelted door flew back upon admitting him, a quick regardful eyeing of him by all the congregation, sufficiently attested that this fine old man was the chaplain. Yes, it was the famous Father Mapple, so called by the whalemen, among whom he was a very great favorite. He had been a sailor and a harpooneer in his youth, but for many years past had dedicated his life to the ministry. At the time I now write of, Father Mapple was in the hardy winter of a healthy old age; that sort of old age which seems merging into a second flowering youth, for among all the fissures of his wrinkles, there shone certain mild gleams of a newly developing bloom—the spring verdure peeping forth even beneath February's snow. No one having previously heard his history, could for the first time behold Father Mapple without the utmost interest, because there were certain engrafted clerical peculiarities about him, imputable to that adventurous maritime life he had led. When he entered I observed that he carried no umbrella, and certainly had not come in his carriage, for his tarpaulin hat ran down with melting sleet, and his great pilot cloth jacket seemed almost to drag him to the floor with the weight of the water it had absorbed. However, hat and coat and overshoes were one by one removed, and hung up in a little space in an adjacent corner; when, arrayed in a decent suit, he quietly approached the pulpit.

Like most old fashioned pulpits, it was a very lofty one, and since a regular stairs to such a height would, by its long angle with the floor, seriously contract the already small area of the chapel, the architect, it seemed, had acted upon the hint of Father Mapple, and finished the pulpit without a stairs, substituting a perpendicular side ladder, like those used in mounting a ship from a boat at sea. The wife of a whaling captain had provided the chapel with a handsome pair of red worsted man-ropes for this ladder, which, being itself nicely headed, and stained with a mahogany color, the whole contrivance, considering what manner of chapel it was, seemed by no means in bad taste. Halting for an instant at the foot of the ladder, and with both hands grasping the ornamental knobs of the man-ropes, Father Mapple cast a look upwards, and then with a truly sailor-like but still reverential dexterity, hand over hand, mounted the steps as if ascending the main-top of his vessel.

The perpendicular parts of this side ladder, as is usually the case with swinging ones, were of cloth-covered rope, only the rounds were of wood, so that at every step there was a joint. At my first glimpse of the pulpit, it had not escaped me that however convenient for a ship, these joints in the present instance seemed unnecessary. For I was not prepared to see Father Mapple after gaining the height, slowly turn round, and stooping over the pulpit, deliberately drag up the ladder step by step, till the whole was deposited within, leaving him impregnable in his little Quebec.

I pondered some time without fully comprehending the reason for this. Father Mapple enjoyed such a wide reputation for sincerity and sanctity, that I could not suspect him of courting notoriety by any mere tricks of the stage. No, thought I, there must be some sober reason for this thing; furthermore, it must symbolize something unseen. Can it be, then, that by that act of physical isolation, he signifies his spiritual withdrawal for the time, from all outward worldly ties and connexions? Yes, for replenished with the meat and wine of the word, to the faithful man of God, this pulpit, I see, is a self-containing stronghold—a lofty Ehrenbreitstein, with a perennial well of water within the walls.

But the side ladder was not the only strange feature of the place, borrowed from the chaplain's former sea-farings. Between the marble cenotaphs on either hand of the pulpit, the wall which formed its back was adorned with a large painting representing a gallant ship beating against a terrible storm off a lee coast of black rocks and snowy breakers. But high above the flying scud and dark-rolling clouds, there floated a little isle of sunlight, from which beamed forth an angel's face; and this bright face shed a distinct spot of radiance upon the ship's tossed deck, something like that silver plate now inserted into the Victory's plank where Nelson fell. "Ah, noble ship," the angel seemed to say, "beat on, beat on, thou noble ship, and bear a hardy helm; for lo! the sun is breaking through; the clouds are rolling off—serenest azure is at hand."

Nor was the pulpit itself without a trace of the same sea-taste that had achieved the ladder and the picture. Its panelled front was in the likeness of a ship's bluff bows, and the Holy Bible rested on a projecting piece of scroll work, fashioned after a ship's fiddle-headed beak.

What could be more full of meaning?—for the pulpit is ever this earth's foremost part; all the rest comes in its rear; the pulpit leads the world. From thence it is the storm of God's quick wrath is first descried, and the bow must bear the earliest brunt. From thence it is the God of breezes fair or foul is first invoked for favorable winds. Yes, the world's a ship on its passage out, and not a voyage complete; and the pulpit is its prow.

CHAPTER 9

The Sermon

Father Mapple rose, and in a mild voice of unassuming authority ordered the scattered people to condense. "Starboard gangway, there! side away to larboard—larboard gangway to starboard! Midships! midships!"

There was a low rumbling of heavy sea-boots among the benches, and a still slighter shuffling of women's shoes, and all was quiet again, and every eye on the preacher.

He paused a little; then kneeling in the pulpit's bows, folded his large brown hands across his chest, uplifted his closed eyes, and offered a prayer so deeply devout that he seemed kneeling and praying at the bottom of the sea.

This ended, in prolonged solemn tones, like the continual tolling of a bell in a ship that is foundering at sea in a fog—in such tones he commenced reading the following hymn; but changing his manner towards the concluding stanzas, burst forth with a pealing exultation and joy—

> "The ribs and terrors in the whale,
>   Arched over me a dismal gloom,
> While all God's sun-lit waves rolled by,
>   And lift me deepening down to doom.
>
> "I saw the opening maw of hell,
>   With endless pains and sorrows there;
> Which none but they that feel can tell—
>   Oh, I was plunging to despair.
>
> "In black distress, I called my God,
>   When I could scarce believe him mine,
> He bowed his ear to my complaints—
>   No more the whale did me confine.
>
> "With speed he flew to my relief,
>   As on a radiant dolphin borne;
> Awful, yet bright, as lightning shone
>   The face of my Deliverer God.
>
> "My song for ever shall record
>   That terrible, that joyful hour;
> I give the glory to my God,
>   His all the mercy and the power."

Nearly all joined in singing this hymn, which swelled high above the howling of the storm. A brief pause ensued; the preacher slowly turned over the leaves of the Bible, and at last, folding his hand down upon the proper page, said: "Beloved shipmates, clinch the last verse of the first chapter of Jonah—'And God had prepared a great fish to swallow up Jonah.'

"Shipmates, this book, containing only four chapters—four yarns—is one of the smallest strands in the mighty cable of the Scriptures. Yet what depths of the soul does Jonah's deep sealine sound! what a pregnant lesson to us is this prophet! What a noble thing is that canticle in the fish's belly! How billow-like and boisterously grand! We feel the floods surging over us; we sound with him to the kelpy bottom of the waters; sea-weed and all the slime of the sea is about us! But *what* is this lesson that the book of Jonah teaches? Shipmates, it is a two-stranded lesson; a lesson to us all as sinful men, and a lesson to me as a pilot of the living God. As sinful men, it is a lesson to us all, because it is a story of the sin, hard-heartedness, suddenly awakened fears, the swift punishment, repentance, prayers, and finally the deliverance and joy of Jonah. As with all sinners among men, the sin of this son of Amittai was in his wilful disobedience of the command of God—never mind now what that command was, or how conveyed—which he found a hard command. But all the things that God would have us do are hard for us to do—remember that—and hence, he oftener commands us than endeavors to persuade. And if we obey God, we must disobey ourselves; and it is in this disobeying ourselves, wherein the hardness of obeying God consists.

"With this sin of disobedience in him, Jonah still further flouts at God, by seeking to flee from Him. He thinks that a ship made by men will carry him into countries where God does not reign, but only the Captains of this earth. He skulks about the wharves of Joppa, and seeks a ship that's bound for Tarshish. There lurks, perhaps, a hitherto unheeded meaning here. By all accounts Tarshish could have been no other city than the modern Cadiz. That's the opinion of learned men. And where is Cadiz, shipmates? Cadiz is in Spain; as far by water, from Joppa, as Jonah could possibly have sailed in those ancient days, when the Atlantic was an almost unknown sea. Because Joppa, the modern Jaffa, shipmates, is on the most easterly coast of the Mediterranean, the Syrian; and Tarshish or Cadiz more than two thousand miles to the westward from that, just outside the Straits of Gibraltar. See ye not then, shipmates, that Jonah sought to flee world-wide from God? Miserable man! Oh! most contemptible and worthy of all scorn; with slouched hat and guilty eye, skulking from his God; prowling among the shipping like a vile burglar hastening to cross the seas. So disordered, self-condemning is his look, that had there been policemen in those days, Jonah, on the mere suspicion of something wrong, had been arrested ere he touched a deck. How plainly he's a fugitive! no baggage, not a hat-box, valise, or carpet-bag,—no friends accompany him to the wharf with their adieux. At last, after much dodging search, he finds the Tarshish ship receiving the last items of her cargo; and as he steps on board to see its Captain in the cabin, all the sailors for the moment desist from hoisting in the goods, to mark the stranger's evil eye. Jonah sees this; but in vain he tries to look all ease and confidence; in vain essays his wretched smile. Strong intuitions of the man assure the mariners he can be no innocent. In their gamesome but still serious way, one whispers to the other—'Jack, he's robbed a widow;' or, 'Joe, do you mark him; he's a bigamist;' or, 'Harry lad, I guess he's the adulterer that broke jail in old Gomorrah, or belike, one of the missing murderers from Sodom.' Another runs to read the bill that's stuck against the spile upon the wharf to which the ship is moored, offering five hundred gold coins for the apprehension of a parricide, and containing a description of his person. He reads, and looks from Jonah to the bill; while all his sympathetic shipmates now crowd round Jonah, prepared to lay their hands upon him. Frighted Jonah trembles, and summoning all his boldness to his face, only looks so much the more a coward. He will not confess himself suspected; but that itself is strong suspicion. So he makes the best of it; and when the sailors find him not to be the man that is advertised, they let him pass, and he descends into the cabin.

"'Who's there?' cries the Captain at his busy desk, hurriedly making out his papers for the Customs—'Who's there?' Oh! how that harmless question mangles Jonah! For the instant he almost turns to flee again. But he rallies. 'I seek a passage in this ship to Tarshish; how soon sail ye, sir?' Thus far the busy Captain had not looked up to Jonah, though the man now stands before him; but no sooner does he hear that hollow voice, than he darts a scrutinizing glance. 'We sail with the next coming tide,' at last he slowly answered, still intently eyeing him. 'No sooner, sir?'—'Soon enough for any honest man that goes a passenger.' Ha! Jonah, that's another stab. But he swiftly calls away the Captain from that scent. 'I'll sail with ye,'—he says,—'the passage money how much is that?—I'll pay now.' For it is particularly written, shipmates, as if it were a thing not to be overlooked in this history, 'that he paid the fare thereof' ere the craft did sail. And taken with the context, this is full of meaning.

"Now Jonah's Captain, shipmates, was one whose discernment detects crime in any, but whose cupidity exposes it only in the penniless. In this world, shipmates, sin that pays its way can travel freely, and without a passport; whereas Virtue, if a pauper, is stopped at all frontiers. So Jonah's Captain prepares to test the length of Jonah's purse, ere he judge him openly. He charges him thrice the usual sum; and it's assented to. Then the Captain knows that Jonah is a fugitive; but at the same time resolves to help a flight that paves its rear with gold. Yet when Jonah fairly takes out his purse, prudent suspicions still molest the Captain. He rings every coin to find a counterfeit. Not a forger, any way, he mutters; and Jonah is put down for his passage. 'Point out my state-room, Sir,' says Jonah now, 'I'm travel-weary; I need sleep.' 'Thou lookest like it,' says the Captain, 'there's thy room.' Jonah enters, and would lock the door, but the lock contains no key. Hearing him foolishly fumbling there, the Captain laughs lowly to himself, and mutters something about the doors of convicts' cells being never allowed to be locked within. All dressed and dusty as he is, Jonah throws himself into his berth, and finds the little state-room ceiling almost resting on his forehead. The air is close, and Jonah gasps. Then, in that contracted hole, sunk, too, beneath the ship's water-line, Jonah feels the heralding presentiment of that stifling hour, when the whale shall hold him in the smallest of his bowels' wards.

"Screwed at its axis against the side, a swinging lamp slightly oscillates in Jonah's room; and the ship, heeling over towards the wharf with the weight of the last bales received, the lamp, flame and all, though in slight motion, still maintains a permanent obliquity with reference to the room; though, in truth, infallibly straight itself, it but made obvious the false, lying levels among which it hung. The lamp alarms and frightens Jonah; as lying in his berth his tormented eyes roll round the place, and this thus far successful fugitive finds no refuge for his restless glance. But that contradiction in the lamp more and more appals him. The floor, the ceiling, and the side, are all awry. 'Oh! so my conscience hangs in me!' he groans, 'straight upwards, so it burns; but the chambers of my soul are all in crookedness!'

"Like one who after a night of drunken revelry hies to his bed, still reeling, but with conscience yet pricking him, as the plungings of the Roman race-horse but so much the more strike his steel tags into him; as one who in that miserable plight still turns and turns in giddy anguish, praying God for annihilation until the fit be passed; and at last amid the whirl of woe he feels, a deep stupor steals over him, as over the man who bleeds to death, for conscience is the wound, and there's naught to staunch it; so, after sore wrestlings in his berth, Jonah's prodigy of ponderous misery drags him drowning down to sleep.

"And now the time of tide has come; the ship casts off her cables; and from the deserted wharf the uncheered ship for Tarshish, all careening, glides to sea. That ship, my friends, was the first of recorded smugglers! the contraband was Jonah. But the sea rebels; he will not bear the wicked burden. A dreadful storm comes on, the ship is like to break. But now when the boatswain calls all hands to lighten her; when boxes, bales, and jars are clattering overboard; when the wind is shrieking, and the men are yelling, and every plank thunders with trampling feet right over Jonah's head; in all this raging tumult,

Jonah sleeps his hideous sleep. He sees no black sky and raging sea, feels not the reeling timbers, and little hears he or heeds he the far rush of the mighty whale, which even now with open mouth is cleaving the seas after him. Aye, shipmates, Jonah was gone down into the sides of the ship—a berth in the cabin as I have taken it, and was fast asleep. But the frightened master comes to him, and shrieks in his dead ear, 'What meanest thou, O, sleeper! arise!' Startled from his lethargy by that direful cry, Jonah staggers to his feet, and stumbling to the deck, grasps a shroud, to look out upon the sea. But at that moment he is sprung upon by a panther billow leaping over the bulwarks. Wave after wave thus leaps into the ship, and finding no speedy vent runs roaring fore and aft, till the mariners come nigh to drowning while yet afloat. And ever, as the white moon shows her affrighted face from the steep gullies in the blackness overhead, aghast Jonah sees the rearing bowsprit pointing high upward, but soon beat downward again towards the tormented deep.

"Terrors upon terrors run shouting through his soul. In all his cringing attitudes, the God-fugitive is now too plainly known. The sailors mark him; more and more certain grow their suspicions of him, and at last, fully to test the truth, by referring the whole matter to high Heaven, they fall to casting lots, to see for whose cause this great tempest was upon them. The lot is Jonah's; that discovered, then how furiously they mob him with their questions. 'What is thine occupation? Whence comest thou? Thy country? What people? But mark now, my shipmates, the behavior of poor Jonah. The eager mariners but ask him who he is, and where from; whereas, they not only receive an answer to those questions, but likewise another answer to a question not put by them, but the unsolicited answer is forced from Jonah by the hard hand of God that is upon him.

"'I am a Hebrew,' he cries—and then—'I fear the Lord the God of Heaven who hath made the sea and the dry land!' Fear him, O Jonah? Aye, well mightest thou fear the Lord God *then!* Straightway, he now goes on to make a full confession; whereupon the mariners became more and more appalled, but still are pitiful. For when Jonah, not yet supplicating God for mercy, since he but too well knew the darkness of his deserts,—when wretched Jonah cries out to them to take him and cast him forth into the sea, for he knew that for *his* sake this great tempest was upon them; they mercifully turn from him, and seek by other means to save the ship. But all in vain; the indignant gale howls louder; then, with one hand raised invokingly to God, with the other they not unreluctantly lay hold of Jonah.

"And now behold Jonah taken up as an anchor and dropped into the sea; when instantly an oily calmness floats out from the east, and the sea is still, as Jonah carries down the gale with him, leaving smooth water behind. He goes down in the whirling heart of such a masterless commotion that he scarce heeds the moment when he drops seething into the yawning jaws awaiting him; and the whale shoots-to all his ivory teeth, like so many white bolts, upon his prison. Then Jonah prayed unto the Lord out of the fish's belly. But observe his prayer, and learn a weighty lesson. For sinful as he is, Jonah does not weep and wail for direct deliverance. He feels that his dreadful punishment is just. He leaves all his deliverance to God, contenting himself with this, that spite of all his pains and pangs, he will still look towards His holy temple. And here, shipmates, is true and faithful repentance; not clamorous for pardon, but grateful for punishment. And how pleasing to God was this conduct in Jonah, is shown in the eventual deliverance of him from the sea and the whale. Shipmates, I do not place Jonah before you to be copied for his sin but I do place him before you as a model for repentance. Sin not; but if you do, take heed to repent of it like Jonah."

While he was speaking these words, the howling of the shrieking, slanting storm without seemed to add new power to the preacher, who, when describing Jonah's sea-storm, seemed tossed by a storm himself. His deep chest heaved as with a ground-swell; his tossed arms seemed the warring elements at work; and the thunders that rolled away from off his swarthy brow, and the light leaping from his eye, made all his simple hearers look on him with a quick fear that was strange to them.

There now came a lull in his look, as he silently turned over the leaves of the Book once more; and, at last, standing motionless, with closed eyes, for the moment, seemed communing with God and himself.

But again he leaned over towards the people, and bowing his head lowly, with an aspect of the deepest yet manliest humility, he spake these words:

"Shipmates, God has laid but one hand upon you; both his hands press upon me. I have read ye by what murky light may be mine the lesson that Jonah teaches to all sinners; and therefore to ye, and still more to me, for I am a greater sinner than ye. And now how gladly would I come down from this mast-head and sit on the hatches there where you sit, and listen as you listen, while some one of you reads *me* that other and more awful lesson which Jonah teaches to *me*, as a pilot of the living God. How being an anointed pilot-prophet, or speaker of true things, and bidden by the Lord to sound those unwelcome truths in the ears of a wicked Nineveh, Jonah, appalled at the hostility he should raise, fled from his mission, and sought to escape his duty and his God by taking ship at Joppa. But God is everywhere; Tarshish he never reached. As we have seen, God came upon him in the whale, and swallowed him down to living gulfs of doom, and with swift slantings tore him along 'into the midst of the seas,' where the eddying depths sucked him ten thousand fathoms down, and 'the weeds were wrapped about his head,' and all the watery world of woe bowled over him. Yet even then beyond the reach of any plummet—'out of the belly of hell'—when the whale grounded upon the ocean's utmost bones, even then, God heard the engulphed, repenting prophet when he cried. Then God spake unto the fish; and from the shuddering cold and blackness of the sea, the whale came breeching up towards the warm and pleasant sun, and all the delights of air and earth; and 'vomited out Jonah upon the dry land;' when the word of the Lord came a second time; and Jonah, bruised and beaten—his ears, like two sea-shells, still multitudinously murmuring of the ocean—Jonah did the Almighty's bidding. And what was that, shipmates? To preach the Truth to the face of Falsehood! That was it!

"This, shipmates, this is that other lesson; and woe to that pilot of the living God who slights it. Woe to him whom this world charms from Gospel duty! Woe to him who seeks to pour oil upon the waters when God has brewed them into a gale! Woe to him who seeks to please rather than to appal! Woe to him whose good name is more to him than goodness! Woe to him who, in this world, courts not dishonor! Woe to him who would not be true, even though to be false were salvation! Yea, woe to him who, as the great Pilot Paul has it, while preaching to others is himself a castaway!"

He dropped and fell away from himself for a moment; then lifting his face to them again, showed a deep joy in his eyes, as he cried out with a heavenly enthusiasm,—"But oh! shipmates! on the starboard hand of every woe, there is a sure delight; and higher the top of that delight, than the bottom of the woe is deep. Is not the main-truck higher than the kelson is low? Delight is to him—a far, far upward, and inward delight—who against the proud gods and commodores of this earth, ever stands forth his own inexorable self. Delight is to him whose strong arms yet support him, when the ship of this base treacherous world has gone down beneath him. Delight is to him, who gives no quarter in the truth, and kills, burns, and destroys all sin though he pluck it out from under the robes of Senators and Judges. Delight,—top-gallant delight is to him, who acknowledges no law or lord, but the Lord his God, and is only a patriot to heaven. Delight is to him, whom all the waves of the billows of the seas of the boisterous mob can never shake from this sure Keel of the Ages. And eternal delight and deliciousness will be his, who coming to lay him down, can say with his final breath—O Father!—chiefly known to me by Thy rod—mortal or immortal, here I die. I have striven to be Thine, more than to be this world's, or mine own. Yet this is nothing: I leave eternity to Thee; for what is man that he should live out the lifetime of his God?"

He said no more, but slowly waving a benediction, covered his face with his hands, and so remained kneeling, till all the people had departed, and he was left alone in the place.

CHAPTER 10

A Bosom Friend

long-drawn

It may seem ridiculous, but

He made no advances whatever; appeared to have no desire to enlarge the circle of his acquaintances.

If there yet lurked any ice of indifference towards me in the Pagan's breast, soon thawed it out, and

CHAPTER 11

Nightgown

what little nappishness remained in us altogether departed, and

imposed and   I no more felt unduly concerned for the landlord's policy of insurance.

CHAPTER 12

Biographical

when she quitted the island.   still afloat,   with its prow seaward,   backward

and his wild desire to visit Christendom,   relented, and   like Czar Peter content to toil in the shipyards of foreign cities,

Hence the queer ways about him, though now some time from home.

, he said,   They had made a harpooneer of him, and that barbed iron was in lieu of a sceptre now.

though well acquainted with the sea, as known to merchant seamen

CHAPTER 13

Wheelbarrow

and by turns revealing his brawny shoulders   at the grand and glorious fellow,
    seeming to see just how matters were,

CHAPTER 14

Nantucket

that they have to plant weeds there, they don't grow naturally; that they import Canada thistles; that they have to send beyond seas for a spile to stop a leak in an oil cask;

Look now at the wondrous traditional story of how this island was settled by the red-men. Thus goes the legend. In olden times an eagle swooped down upon the New England coast, and carried off an infant Indian in his talons. With loud lament the parents saw their child borne out of sight over the wide waters. They resolved to follow in the same direction. Setting out in their canoes, after a perilous passage they discovered the island, and there they found an empty ivory casket,—the poor little Indian's skeleton.

fearless and

And thus have these naked Nantucketers, these sea hermits, issuing from their ant-hill in the sea, overrun and conquered the watery world like so many Alexanders; parcelling out among them the Atlantic, Pacific, and Indian oceans, as the three pirate powers did Poland. Let America add Mexico to Texas, and pile Cuba upon Canada; let the English overswarm all India, and hang out their blazing banner from the sun; two thirds of this terraqueous globe are the Nantucketer's. For the sea is his; he owns it, as Emperors own empires; other seamen having but a right of way through it. Merchant ships are but extension bridges; armed ones but floating forts; even pirates and privateers, though following the sea as highwaymen the road, they but plunder other ships, other fragments of the land like themselves, without seeking to draw their living from the bottomless deep itself. The Nantucketer, he alone resides and riots on the sea; he alone, in Bible language, goes down to it in ships; to and fro ploughing it as his own special plantation. *There* is his home; *there* lies his business, which a Noah's flood would not interrupt, though it overwhelmed all the millions in China. He lives on the sea, as prairie cocks in the prairie; he hides among the waves, he climbs them as chamois hunters climb the Alps. For years he knows not the land; so that when he comes to it at last, it smells like another world, more strangely than the moon would to an Earthsman. With the landless gull, that at sunset folds her wings and is rocked to sleep between billows; so at nightfall, the Nantucketer, out of sight of land, furls his sails, and lays him to his rest, while under his very pillow rush herds of walruses and whales.

Chapter 15

Chowder

In short, he plainly hinted that we could not possibly do better than try pot-luck at the Try Pots. —our first point of departure— at last

Perhaps I was over sensitive to such impressions at the time, but postponing further scolding for the present,

who was waiting for it in the entry,

with great emphasis,

among some fishermen's boats

"every true whaleman sleeps with his harpoon—but why not?" (for she had learned his name)

CHAPTER 16

The Ship

told him two or three times over, and   upon it everyway,   for all the world as though it had turned out by chance;

I have forgotten to mention that, in many things, Queequeg placed great confidence in the excellence of Yojo's judgment and surprising forecast of things; and cherished Yojo with considerable esteem, as a rather good sort of god, who perhaps meant well enough upon the whole, but in all cases did not succeed in his benevolent designs.

this plan of Queequeg's, or rather Yojo's, touching the selection of our craft; and accordingly prepared to set about this business with a determined rushing sort of energy and vigor, that should quickly settle that trifling little affair.
   how it was I never could find out, for, though I applied myself to it several times, I never could master his liturgies and XXXIX Articles—

You may have seen many a quaint craft in your day, for aught I know;—square-toed luggers; mountainous Japanese junks; butter-box galliots, and what not;

but take my word for it, you never saw such a rare old craft as this same rare old Pequod. a thing of trophies. The helmsman who steered by that tiller in a tempest, felt like the Tartar, when he holds back his fiery steed by clutching its jaw.

There was nothing so very particular, perhaps, about the appearance of; he

advancing to the door of the tent.

"think that—"

and rather distrustful of all aliens, unless they hailed from Cape Cod or the Vineyard.

"Aye, aye, I thought so."

"—that's who ye are speaking to.

perhaps also a little touched at the hearty grief in his concluding exclamation,

"I thought so. back to me and"

For a moment I stood a little puzzled by this curious request, not knowing exactly how to take it, whether humorously or in earnest. But concentrating all his crow's feet into one scowl, Captain Peleg started me on the errand.

, as is sometimes the case in these ports,

indeed

with a globular brain and a ponderous heart;   But, as yet we have not to do with such an one, but with quite another; and still a man, who, if indeed peculiar, it only results again from another phase of the Quaker, modified by individual circumstances.

, and indeed deemed those self-same serious things the veriest of all trifles,
had not so much as altered one angle of his vest   , from conscientious scruples,   in his straight-bodied coat,   This world pays dividends. Rising from a little cabin-boy in short clothes of the drabbest drab, to a harpooneer in a broad shad-bellied waistcoat; from that becoming boat-header, chief-mate, and captain, and finally a ship owner; Bildad, as I hinted before, had concluded his adventurous career by wholly retiring from active life at the goodly age of sixty, and dedicating his remaining days to the quiet receiving of his well-earned income.

They told me in Nantucket, though it certainly seems a curious story, that when he sailed the old Categut whaleman, his crew, upon arriving home, were mostly all carried ashore to the hospital, sore exhausted and worn out.   He never used to swear, though, at his men, they said; but somehow he got an in-ordinate quantity of cruel, unmitigated hard work out of them.   When Bildad was a chief-mate, to have his drab-colored eye intently looking at you, made you feel completely nervous, till you could clutch something—a hammer or a marling-spike, and go to work like mad, at something or other, never mind what.   Indolence and idleness perished before him.

without noticing his present irreverence,

, and turning round to me

what they call a

would not have been surprised had I been offered the 200th, considering I was of a broad-shouldered make.

But one thing, nevertheless, that made me a little distrustful about receiving a generous share of the profits was this: Ashore, I had heard something of both Captain Peleg and his unaccountable old crony Bildad; how that they being the principal proprietors of the Pequod, therefore the other and more inconsiderable and scattered owners, left nearly the whole management of the ship's affairs to these two. And   especially as I now found him on board the Pequod, quite at home there in the cabin, and reading his Bible as if at his own fireside.   while Peleg was vainly trying to mend a pen with his jack-knife

Lay, indeed, thought I, and such a lay! the seven hundred and seventy-seventh! Well, old Bildad, you are determined that I, for one, shall not *lay* up many *lays* here below, where moth and rust do corrupt. It was an exceedingly *long lay* that, indeed; and though from the magnitude of the figure it might at first deceive a landsman, yet the slightest consideration will show that though seven hundred and seventy-seven is a pretty large number, yet, when you come to make a *teenth* of it, you will then see, I say, that the seven hundred and seventy-seventh part of a farthing is a good deal less than seven hundred and seventy-seven gold doubloons; and so I thought at the time.

"Seven hundred and seventy-seventh," again said Bildad, without lifting his eyes; and then went on mumbling—"for where your treasure is, there will your heart be also."

said Peleg,

"Captain Peleg," said Bildad steadily, "thy conscience may be drawing ten inches of water, or ten fathoms, I can't tell; but as thou art still an impenitent man, Captain Peleg, I greatly fear lest thy conscience be but a leaky one; and will in the end sink thee foundering down to the fiery pit, Captain Peleg."

"Fiery pit! fiery pit! ye insult me, man; past all natural bearing, ye insult me. It's an all-fired outrage to tell any human creature that he's bound to hell.

Flukes and flames! Bildad, say that again to me, and start my soul-bolts, but I'll—I'll—yes, I'll swallow a live goat with all his hair and horns on. Out of the cabin, ye canting, drab-colored son of a wooden gun—a straight wake with ye!"

As he thundered out this he made a rush at Bildad, but with a marvellous oblique, sliding celerity, Bildad for that time eluded him.

Alarmed at this terrible outburst between the two principal and responsible owners of the ship, and feeling half a mind to give up all idea of sailing in a vessel so questionably owned and temporarily commanded, I stepped aside from the door to give egress to Bildad, who, I made no doubt, was all eagerness to vanish from before the awakened wrath of Peleg. But to my astonishment, he sat down again on the transom very quietly, and seemed to have not the slightest intention of withdrawing. He seemed quite used to impenitent Peleg and his ways. As for Peleg, after letting off his rage as he had, there seemed no more left in him, and he, too, sat down like a lamb, though he twitched a little as if still nervously agitated.   "the squall's gone off to leeward, I think. Bildad, thou used to be good at sharpening a lance, mend that pen, will ye. My jack-knife here needs the grindstone. That's he; thank ye, Bildad."

"What lay does he want?" groaned Bildad, glancing up from the book in which he had again been burying himself.

"Oh! never thee mind about that, Bildad," said Peleg.   turning to me

; nothing doubting but that I had done a good morning's work, and that the Pequod was the identical ship that Yojo had provided to carry Queequeg and me round the Cape.

by arriving to take command

I know that he was never very jolly; and   a kind of moody—

As I walked away, I was full of thoughtfulness; what had been incidentally revealed to me of Captain Ahab, filled me with a certain wild vagueness of painfulness concerning him. And somehow, at the time, I felt a sympathy and a sorrow for him, but for I don't know what, unless it was the cruel loss of his leg. And yet I also felt a strange awe of him; but that sort of awe, which I cannot at all describe, was not exactly awe; I do not know what it was. But I felt it; and it did not disincline me towards him; though I felt impatience at what seemed like mystery in him, so imperfectly as he was known to me then. However, my thoughts were at length carried in other directions, so that for the present dark Ahab slipped my mind.

CHAPTER 17

The Ramadan

never mind how comical,

thought he knew what he was about, I suppose; he

Towards evening, when I felt assured that all his performances and rituals must be over, I went up to his room and knocked at the door; but no answer. I tried to open it, but it was fastened inside. "Queequeg," said I softly through the key-hole:—all silent. "I say, Queequeg! why don't you speak? It's I— Ishmael." But all remained still as before. I began to grow alarmed. I had allowed him such abundant time; I thought he might have had an apoplectic fit. I looked through the key-hole; but the door opening into an odd corner of the room, the key-hole prospect was but a crooked and sinister one. I could only see part of the foot-board of the bed and a line of the wall, but nothing more. I was surprised to behold resting against the wall the wooden shaft of Queequeg's harpoon, which the landlady the evening previous had taken from him, before our mounting to the chamber. That's strange, thought I;

but at any rate, since the harpoon stands yonder, and he seldom or never goes abroad without it, therefore he must be inside here, and no possible mistake.

"Queequeg!—Queequeg!"—all still. Something must have happened. Apoplexy! I tried to burst open the door; but it stubbornly resisted. Running down stairs, I quickly stated my suspicions to the first person I met—the chamber-maid. "La! la!" she cried, "I thought something must be the matter. I went to make the bed after breakfast, and the door was locked; and not a mouse to be heard; and it's been just so silent ever since. But I thought, may be, you had both gone off and locked your baggage in for safe keeping. La! la, ma'am!—Mistress! murder! Mrs. Hussey! apoplexy!"—and with these cries, she ran towards the kitchen, I following.

Mrs. Hussey soon appeared, with a mustard-pot in one hand and a vinegar-cruet in the other, having just broken away from the occupation of attending to the castors, and scolding her little black boy meantime.

"Wood-house!" cried I, "which way to it? Run for God's sake, and fetch something to pry open the door—the axe!—the axe! he's had a stroke; depend upon it!"—and so saying I was unmethodically rushing up stairs again empty-handed, when Mrs. Hussey interposed the mustard-pot and vinegar-cruet, and the entire castor of her countenance.

"What's the matter with you, young man?"

"Get the axe! For God's sake, run for the doctor, some one, while I pry it open!"

"Look here," said the landlady, quickly putting down the vinegar-cruet, so as to have one hand free; "look here; are you talking about prying open any of my doors?"—and with that she seized my arm. "What's the matter with you? What's the matter with you, shipmate?"

In as calm, but rapid a manner as possible, I gave her to understand the whole case. Unconsciously clapping the vinegar-cruet to one side of her nose, she ruminated for an instant; then exclaimed—"No! I haven't seen it since I put it there." Running to a little closet under the landing of the stairs, she glanced in, and returning, told me that Queequeg's harpoon was missing. "He's killed himself," she cried. "It's unfort'nate Stiggs done over again there goes another counterpane—God pity his poor mother!—it will be the ruin of my house. Has the poor lad a sister? Where's that girl?—there, Betty, go to Snarles the Painter, and tell him to paint me a sign, with—'no suicides permitted here, and no smoking in the parlor;'—might as well kill both birds at once. Kill? The Lord be merciful to his ghost! What's that noise there? You, young man, avast there!"

And running up after me, she caught me as I was again trying to force open the door.

"I don't allow it; I won't have my premises spoiled. Go for the locksmith, there's one about a mile from here. But avast!" putting her hand in her side-pocket, "here's a key that'll fit, I guess; let's see." And with that, she turned it in the lock; but, alas! Queequeg's supplemental bolt remained unwithdrawn within.

"Have to burst it open," said I, and was running down the entry a little, for a good start, when the landlady caught at me, again vowing I should not break down her premises; but I tore from her, and with a sudden bodily rush dashed myself full against the mark.

With a prodigious noise the door flew open, and the knob slamming against the wall, sent the plaster to the ceiling; and there, good heavens! there sat Queequeg, altogether cool and self-collected; right in the middle of the room; squatting on his hams, and holding Yojo on top of his head. He looked neither one way nor the other way, but sat like a carved image with scarce a sign of active life.

"Queequeg," said I, going up to him, "Queequeg, what's the matter with you?"

"He hain't been a sittin' so all day, has he?" said the landlady.

But all we said, not a word could we drag out of him; I almost felt like pushing him over, so as to change his position, for it was almost intolerable, it seemed so painfully and unnaturally constrained; especially, as in all probability he had been sitting so for upwards of eight or ten hours, going too without his regular meals.

"Mrs. Hussey," said I, "he's *alive* at all events; so leave us, if you please, and I will see to this strange affair myself."

Closing the door upon the landlady, I endeavored to prevail upon Queequeg to take a chair; but in vain. There he sat; and all he could do—for all my polite arts and blandishments—he would not move a peg, nor say a single word, nor even look at me, nor notice my presence in the slightest way.

I wonder, thought I, if this can possibly be a part of his Ramadan; do they fast on their hams that way in his native island. It must be so; yes, it's part of his creed, I suppose; well, then, let him rest; he'll get up sooner or later, no doubt. It can't last for ever, thank God, and his Ramadan only comes once a year; and I don't believe it's very punctual then.

I went down to supper. After sitting a long time listening to the long stories of some sailors who had just come from a plum-pudding voyage, as they called it (that is, a short whaling-voyage in a schooner or brig, confined to the north of the line, in the Atlantic Ocean only); after listening to these plum-puddingers till nearly eleven o'clock, I went up stairs to go to bed, feeling quite sure by this time Queequeg must certainly have brought his Ramadan to a termination. But no; there he was just where I had left him; he had not stirred an inch. I began to grow vexed with him; it seemed so downright senseless and insane to be sitting there all day and half the night on his hams in a cold room, holding a piece of wood on his head.

"For heaven's sake, Queequeg, get up and shake yourself; get up and have some supper. You'll starve; you'll kill yourself, Queequeg." But not a word did he reply.

Despairing of him, therefore, I determined to go to bed and to sleep; and no doubt, before a great while, he would follow me. But previous to turning in, I took my heavy bearskin jacket, and threw it over him, as it promised to be a very cold night; and he had nothing but his ordinary round jacket on. For some time, do all I would, I could not get into the faintest doze. I had blown out the candle; and the mere thought of Queequeg—not four feet off—sitting there in that uneasy position, stark alone in the cold and dark; this made me really wretched. Think of it; sleeping all night in the same room with a wide awake pagan on his hams in this dreary, unaccountable Ramadan!

But somehow I dropped off at last, and knew nothing more till break of day; when, looking over the bedside, there squatted Queequeg, as if he had been screwed down to the floor. But as soon as the first glimpse of sun entered the window, up he got, with stiff and grating joints, but with a cheerful look; limped towards me where I lay; pressed his forehead again against mine; and said his Ramadan was over.

Now, as I before hinted, I have no objection to any person's religion, be it what it may, so long as that person does not kill or insult any other person, because that other person don't believe it also. But when a man's religion becomes really frantic; when it is a positive torment to him; and, in fine, makes this earth of ours an uncomfortable inn to lodge in; then I think it high time to take that individual aside and argue the point with him.

And just so I now did with Queequeg. "Queequeg," said I, "get into bed now, and lie and listen to me." I then went on, beginning with the rise and progress of the primitive religions, and coming down to the various religions of the present time, during which time I labored to show Queequeg that all these Lents, Ramadans, and prolonged ham-squattings in cold, cheerless rooms were stark nonsense; bad for the health; useless for the soul; opposed, in short, to the obvious laws of Hygiene and common sense. I told him, too, that he being in other things such an extremely sensible and sagacious savage, it pained me, very badly pained me, to see him now so deplorably foolish about this ridiculous Ramadan of his. Besides, argued I, fasting makes the body cave in; hence the spirit caves in; and all thoughts born of a fast must necessarily be half-starved. This is the reason why most dyspeptic religionists cherish such melancholy notions about their hereafters. In one word, Queequeg, said I, rather digressively; hell is an idea first born on an undigested apple-dumpling; and since then perpetuated through the hereditary dyspepsias nurtured by Ramadans.

I then asked Queequeg whether he himself was ever troubled with dyspepsia; expressing the idea very plainly, so that he could take it in. He said no; only upon one memorable occasion. It was after a great feast given by his father the king, on the gaining of a great battle wherein fifty of the enemy had been killed by about two o'clock in the afternoon, and all cooked and eaten that very evening.

"No more, Queequeg," said I, shuddering; "that will do;" for I knew the inferences without his further hinting them. I had seen a sailor who had visited that very island, and he told me that it was the custom, when a great battle had been gained there, to barbecue all the slain in the yard or garden of the victor; and then, one by one, they were placed in great wooden trenchers, and garnished round like a pilau, with breadfruit and cocoanuts; and with some parsley in their mouths, were sent round with the victor's compliments to all his friends, just as though these presents were so many Christmas turkeys.

After all, I do not think that my remarks about religion made much impression upon Queequeg. Because, in the first place, he somehow seemed dull of hearing on that important subject, unless considered from his own point of view; and, in the second place, he did not more than one third understand me, couch my ideas simply as I would; and, finally, he no doubt thought he knew a good deal more about the true religion than I did. He looked at me with a sort of condescending concern and compassion, as though he thought it a great pity that such a sensible young man should be so hopelessly lost to evangelical pagan piety.

At last we rose and dressed; and Queequeg, taking a prodigiously hearty breakfast of chowders of all sorts, so that the landlady should not make much profit by reason of his Ramadan, we sallied out to board the Pequod, sauntering along, and picking our teeth with halibut bones.

Chapter 18

His Mark

he had not suspected my friend was a cannibal, and furthermore announcing that   that craft

taking out his spectacles, he rubbed them with his great yellow bandana handkerchief, and putting them on very carefully,

"No," said Peleg, "and he hasn't been baptized right either, or it would have washed some of that devil's blue off his face."

"Deacon Deuteronomy—why Father Mapple himself couldn't beat it, and he's reckoned something."

"Bildad," his partner,

same   to which I myself belonged

so that through Captain Peleg's obstinate mistake touching his appellative, it stood something like this:—

Quohog.
his ✠ mark.

Meanwhile Captain Bildad sat earnestly and steadfastly eyeing Queequeg, and at last rising solemnly and fumbling in the huge pockets of his broadskirted drab coat, took out a bundle of tracts, and selecting one entitled "The Latter Day Coming; or No Time to Lose," placed it in Queequeg's hands, and then grasping them and the book with both his, looked earnestly into his eyes, and said, "Son of darkness, I must do my duty by thee; I am part owner of this ship, and feel concerned for the souls of all its crew; if thou still clingest to thy Pagan ways, which I sadly fear, I beseech thee, remain not for aye a Belial bondsman. Spurn the idol Bell, and the hideous dragon; turn from the wrath to come; mind thine eye, I say; oh! goodness gracious! steer clear of the fiery pit!"

Something of the salt sea yet lingered in old Bildad's language, heterogeneously mixed with Scriptural and domestic phrases.

"Avast there, avast there, Bildad, avast now spoiling our harpooneer," Peleg. "Pious harpooneers never make good voyagers—it takes the shark out of 'em; no harpooneer is worth a straw who aint pretty sharkish. There was young Nat Swaine, once the bravest boat-header out of all Nantucket and the Vineyard; he joined the meeting, and never came to good. He got so frightened about his plaguy soul, that he shrinked and sheered away from whales, for fear of after-claps, in case he got stove and went to Davy Jones."

"Peleg! Peleg!" said Bildad, lifting his eyes and hands, "thou thyself, as I myself, hast seen many a perilous time; thou knowest, Peleg, what it is to have the fear of death; how, then, can'st thou prate in this ungodly guise. Thou beliest thine own heart, Peleg. Tell me, when this same Pequod here had her three masts overboard in that typhoon on Japan, that same voyage when thou went mate with Captain Ahab, did'st thou not think of Death and the Judgment then?"

"Hear him, hear him now," cried Peleg, marching across the cabin, and thrusting his hands far down into his pockets,—"hear him, all of ye. Think of that! When every moment we thought the ship would sink! Death and the Judgment then? What? With all three masts making such an everlasting thundering against the side; and every sea breaking over us, fore and aft. Think of Death and the Judgment then? No! no time to think about Death then. Life was what Captain Ahab and I was thinking of; and how to save all hands— how to rig jury-masts—how to get into the nearest port; that was what I was thinking of."

Bildad said no more, but buttoning up his coat, stalked on deck, where we followed him. There he stood, very quietly overlooking some sailmakers who were mending a top-sail in the waist. Now and then he stooped to pick up a patch, or save an end of tarred twine, which otherwise might have been wasted.

CHAPTER 19

The Prophet

, for the moment each occupied with his own thoughts, , pausing before us,

drawing back his whole arm, and then rapidly shoving it straight out from him, with the fixed bayonet of his pointed finger darted full at the object.

"What! the captain of our ship, the Pequod?"

"Aye,"

solemnly

"—yes, both true enough.   mayhap,   aye, ye have heard of that,"

"what all this gibberish of yours is about, I don't know, and I don't much care; for it seems to me that you must be a little damaged in the head. But"

beggar-like , as if in a troubled reverie   turned and —

"that's all I have to say."

"And it's said very well, and I like to hear a chap talk up that way; you are just the man for him—the likes of ye. Morning to ye, shipmates, morning! Oh! when ye get there, tell 'em I've concluded not to make one of 'em."

"Ah, my dear fellow, you can't fool us that way—you can't fool us."

"Morning to ye, shipmates, morning."

"Morning it is," said I.

nothing but   But we had not gone perhaps above a hundred yards, when chancing to turn a corner, and looking back as I did so, who should be seen but Elijah following us, though at a distance. Somehow, the sight of him struck me so, that I said nothing to Queequeg of his being behind, but passed on with my comrade, anxious to see whether the stranger would turn the same corner that we did. He did; and then it seemed to me that he was dogging us, but with what intent I could not for the life of me imagine. This circumstance, coupled with his ambiguous, half-hinting, half-revealing, shrouded sort of talk, now begat in me all kinds of vague wonderments and half-apprehensions, and all connected with the Pequod; and Captain Ahab; and the leg he had lost; and the Cape Horn fit; and the silver calabash; and what Captain Peleg had said of him, when I left the ship the day previous; and the prediction of the squaw Tistig; and the voyage we had bound ourselves to sail; and a hundred other shadowy things.

I was resolved to satisfy myself whether this ragged Elijah was really dogging us or not, and with that intent crossed the way with Queequeg, and on that side of it retraced our steps. But Elijah passed on, without seeming to notice us. This relieved me; and once more, and finally as it seemed to me, I pronounced him in my heart, a humbug.

CHAPTER 20

All Astir

but sat in his wigwam keeping a sharp look-out upon the hands:

On the day following Queequeg's signing the articles, word was given at all the inns where the ship's company were stopping, that their chests must be on board before night, for there was no telling how soon the vessel might be sailing. So Queequeg and I got down our traps, resolving, however, to sleep ashore till the last. But it seems they always give very long notice in these cases, and the ship did not sail for several days. But no wonder; there was a good deal to be done, and there is no telling how many things to be thought of, before the Pequod was fully equipped.

comprising her beef, bread, water, fuel, and iron hoops and staves.   as before hinted,   both large and small, who seemed resolved that, if *she* could help it, nothing should be found wanting in the Pequod, after once fairly getting to sea.   And like a sister of charity did this charitable Aunt Charity bustle about hither and thither, ready to turn her hand and heart to anything that promised to yield safety, comfort, and consolation to all on board a ship in which her beloved brother Bildad was concerned, and in which she herself owned a score or two of well-saved dollars.

it was startling to see this excellent hearted Quakeress coming on board, as she did the last day, with a long oil-ladle in one hand, and a still longer whaling lance in the other. Nor was Bildad himself nor Captain Peleg at all backward. As for Bildad, he carried about with him a long list of the articles needed, and at every fresh arrival, down went his mark opposite that article upon the paper. Every once in a while Peleg came hobbling out of his whalebone den, roaring at the men down the hatchways, roaring up to the riggers at the mast-head, and then concluded by roaring back into his wigwam.

During these days of preparation, Queequeg and I often visited the craft, and as often I asked about Captain Ahab, and how he was, and when he was going to come on board his ship. To these questions they would answer, that he was getting better and better, and was expected aboard every day; meantime, the two captains, Peleg and Bildad, could attend to everything necessary to fit the vessel for the voyage. If I had been downright honest with myself, I would have seen very plainly in my heart that I did but half fancy being committed this way to so long a voyage, without once laying my eyes on the man who was to be the absolute dictator of it, so soon as the ship sailed out upon the open sea. But when a man suspects any wrong, it sometimes happens that if he be already involved in the matter, he insensibly strives to cover up his suspicions even from himself. And much this way it was with me. I said nothing, and tried to think nothing.

some time   certainly

CHAPTER 21

Going Aboard

"it can't be shadows;"

shaking himself,

looking from me to Queequeg, with the most unaccountable glances.

and touching my shoulder again, said,

;   again marking the sleeper, jocularly hinted to Queequeg that perhaps we had best sit up with the body; telling him to establish himself accordingly. He put his hand upon the sleeper's rear, as though feeling if it was soft enough; and then,   there

"Gracious! Queequeg, don't sit there," said I.

"Oh! perry dood seat," said Queequeg, "my country way; won't hurt him face."

"Face!" said I, "call that his face? very benevolent countenance then; but how hard he breathes, he's heaving himself; get off, Queequeg, you are heavy, it's grinding the face of the poor. Get off, Queequeg! Look, he'll twitch you off soon. I wonder he don't wake."

Meanwhile, upon questioning him in his broken fashion, Queequeg gave me to understand that, in his land, owing to the absence of settees and sofas of all sorts, the king, chiefs, and great people generally, were in the custom of fattening some of the lower orders for ottomans; and to furnish a house comfortably in that respect, you had only to buy up eight or ten lazy fellows, and lay them round in the piers and alcoves. Besides, it was very convenient on an excursion; much better than those garden-chairs which are convertible into walking-sticks; upon occasion, a chief calling his attendant, and desiring him to make a settee of himself under a spreading tree, perhaps in some damp marshy place.

While narrating these things, every time Queequeg received the tomahawk from me, he flourished the hatchet-side of it over the sleeper's head.

"What's that for, Queequeg?"

"Perry easy, kill-e; oh! perry easy!"

He was going on with some wild reminiscences about his tomahawk-pipe, which, it seemed, had in its two uses both brained his foes and soothed his soul, when we were directly attracted to the sleeping rigger.   completely filling the contracted hole, it   breathed with a sort of muffledness; then seemed troubled in the nose; then

"ye are going in her, be ye?"

some

And

Meanwhile Captain Ahab remained invisibly enshrined within his cabin.

Chapter 22

Merry Christmas

and after the ever-thoughtful Charity had come off in a whale-boat, with her last gift—a night-cap for Stubb, the second mate, her brother-in-law, and a spare Bible for the steward—after all this,

"are you sure everything is right?"

; only, they said he was in the cabin   ; and as he was not yet completely re-covered   ; especially as in the merchant service many captains never show themselves on deck for a considerable time after heaving up the anchor, but remain over the cabin table, having a farewell merry-making with their shore friends, before they quit the ship for good with the pilot.

He seemed to do most of the talking and commanding, and not Bildad.

for thirty years,

with hearty good will. Nevertheless, not three days previous, Bildad had told them that no profane songs would be allowed on board the Pequod, particu-larly in getting under weigh; and Charity, his sister, had placed a small choice copy of Watts in each seaman's berth.

involuntarily I paused on my handspike, and told Queequeg to do the same, thinking of the perils we both ran, in starting on the voyage with such a devil for a pilot. I was comforting myself, however, with the thought that in pi-ous Bildad might be found some salvation, spite of his seven hundred and seventy-seventh lay; when I felt a sudden sharp poke in my rear, and turning round, was horrified at the apparition of Captain Peleg in the act of withdraw-ing his leg from my immediate vicinity. That was my first kick.

"Is that the way they heave in the marchant service?" he roared. "Spring, thou sheep-head; spring, and break thy backbone! Why don't ye spring, I say, all of ye—spring! Quohog! spring, thou chap with the red whiskers; spring there, Scotch-cap; spring, thou green pants. Spring, I say, all of ye, and spring your eyes out!" And so saying, he moved along the windlass, here and there using his leg very freely, while imperturbable Bildad kept leading off with his psalmody. Thinks I, Captain Peleg must have been drinking something to-day.

; and meads and glades so eternally vernal, that the grass shot up by the spring, untrodden, unwilted, remains at midsummer.

once more starting to encounter all the terrors of the pitiless jaw;   ran down into the cabin to speak another farewell word there; again came on deck,   looked towards the land; looked aloft; looked right and left; looked everywhere and nowhere; and at last, mechanically coiling a rope upon its pin, convulsively grasped stout Peleg by the hand, and holding up a lantern, for a moment stood gazing heroically in his face, as much as to say, "Neverthe-less, friend Peleg, I can stand it; yes, I can."

he took it more like a philosopher; but for all his philosophy,   And he, too, did not a little run from cabin to deck—now a word below, and now a word with Starbuck, the chief mate.

"boy—say your last."

"twenty cents the pound it was, and mind ye, if—"

CHAPTER 23

The Lee Shore

Some chapters back, one Bulkington was spoken of, a tall, newlanded mariner, encountered in New Bedford at the inn.

When on that shivering winter's night, the Pequod thrust her vindictive bows into the cold malicious waves, who should I see standing at her helm but Bulkington! I looked with sympathetic awe and fearfulness upon the man, who in mid-winter just landed from a four years' dangerous voyage, could so unrestingly push off again for still another tempestuous term. The land seemed scorching to his feet. Wonderfullest things are ever the unmentionable; deep memories yield no epitaphs; this six-inch chapter is the stoneless grave of Bulkington. Let me only say that it fared with him as with the storm-tossed ship, that miserably drives along the leeward land. The port would fain give succor; the port is pitiful; in the port is safety, comfort, hearthstone, supper, warm blankets, friends, all that's kind to our mortalities. But in that gale, the port, the land, is that ship's direst jeopardy; she must fly all hospitality; one touch of land, though it but graze the keel, would make her shudder through and through. With all her might she crowds all sail off shore; in so doing, fights 'gainst the very winds that fain would blow her homeward; seeks all the lashed sea's landlessness again; for refuge's sake forlornly rushing into peril; her only friend her bitterest foe!

Know ye now, Bulkington? Glimpses do ye seem to see of that mortally intolerable truth; that all deep, earnest thinking is but the intrepid effort of the soul to keep the open independence of her sea; while the wildest winds of heaven and earth conspire to cast her on the treacherous, slavish shore?

But as in landlessness alone resides highest truth, shoreless, indefinite as God—so, better is it to perish in that howling infinite, than be ingloriously dashed upon the lee, even if that were safety! For worm-like, then, oh! who would craven crawl to land! Terrors of the terrible! is all this agony so vain? Take heart, take heart, O Bulkington! Bear thee grimly, demigod! Up from the spray of thy ocean-perishing—straight up, leaps thy apotheosis!

CHAPTER 24

The Advocate

and that when actively engaged therein, we are surrounded by all manner of defilements.   quickly

taken in one aggregate,   She has explored seas and archipelagoes which had no chart, where no Cook or Vancouver had ever sailed.   Often, adventures which Vancouver dedicates three chapters to, these men accounted unworthy of being set down in the ship's common log.

distinctly   at last

primitive

aesthetically

The whale has no famous author, and whaling no famous chronicler, you will say.

The whale no famous author, and whaling no famous chronicler? Who wrote the first account of our Leviathan? Who but mighty Job! And who composed the first narrative of a whaling-voyage? Who, but no less a prince than Alfred the Great, who, with his own royal pen, took down the words from Other, the Norwegian whale-hunter of those times! And who pronounced our glowing eulogy in Parliament? Who, but Edmund Burke!

True enough, but then whalemen themselves are poor devils; they have no good blood in their veins.

No good blood in their veins? They have something better than royal blood there. The grandmother of Benjamin Franklin was Mary Morrel; afterwards, by marriage, Mary Folger, one of the old settlers of Nantucket, and the ancestress to a long line of Folgers and harpooneers—all kith and kin to noble Benjamin—this day darting the barbed iron from one side of the world to the other.

Good again; but then all confess that somehow *

Oh, that's only nominal! The whale himself has never figured in any grand imposing way.

The whale never figured in any grand imposing way? In one of the mighty triumphs given to a Roman general upon his entering the world's capital, the bones of a whale, brought all the way from the Syrian coast, were the most conspicuous object in the cymballed procession.**

Grant it, since you cite it; but, say what you will,

prospectively

CHAPTER 25

Postscript

In behalf of the dignity of whaling, I would fain advance naught but substantiated facts. But after embattling his facts, an advocate who should wholly

---

* See subsequent chapters for something more on this head.
** See subsequent chapters for something more on this head.

suppress a not unreasonable surmise, which might tell eloquently upon his cause—such an advocate, would he not be blameworthy?

It is well known that at the coronation of kings and queens, even modern ones, a certain curious process of seasoning them for their functions is gone through. There is a saltcellar of state, so called, and there may be a castor of state. How they use the salt, precisely—who knows? Certain I am, however, that a king's head is solemnly oiled at his coronation, even as a head of salad. Can it be, though, that they anoint it with a view of making its interior run well, as they anoint machinery? Much might be ruminated here, concerning the essential dignity of this regal process, because in common life we esteem but meanly and contemptibly a fellow who anoints his hair, and palpably smells of that anointing. In truth, a mature man who uses hair-oil, unless medicinally, that man has probably got a quoggy spot in him somewhere. As a general rule, he can't amount to much in his totality.

But the only thing to be considered here, is this—what kind of oil is used at coronations? Certainly it cannot be olive oil, nor macassar oil, nor castor oil, nor bear's oil, nor train oil, nor cod-liver oil. What then can it possibly be, but sperm oil in its unmanufactured, unpolluted state, the sweetest of all oils?

Think of that, ye loyal Britons! we whalemen supply your kings and queens with coronation stuff!

CHAPTER 26

Knights and Squires

Transported to the Indies, his live blood would not spoil like bottled ale.   or upon one of those fast days for which his state is famous.   ; quite the contrary , and to endure always, as now; for be it Polar snow or torrid sun, like a patent chronometer, his interior vitality was warranted to do well in all climates. not only that the most reliable and useful courage was that which arises from the fair estimation of the encountered peril, but

But it was not in reasonable nature that a man so organized, and with such terrible experiences and remembrances as he had; it was not in nature that these things should fail in latently engendering an element in him, which, under suitable circumstances, would break out from its confinement, and burn all his courage up. And brave as he might be, it was that sort of bravery chiefly, visible in some intrepid men, which, while generally abiding firm in the conflict with seas, or winds, or whales, or any of the ordinary irrational horrors of the world, yet cannot withstand those more terrific, because more spiritual terrors, which sometimes menace you from the concentrating brow of an enraged and mighty man.

But were the coming narrative to reveal in any instance, the complete abasement of poor Starbuck's fortitude, scarce might I have the heart to write it; for it is a thing most sorrowful, nay shocking, to expose the fall of valor in the soul. Men may seem detestable as joint stock-companies and nations; knaves, fools, and murderers there may be; men may have mean and meagre faces; but man, in the ideal, is so noble and so sparkling, such a grand and glowing creature, that over any ignominious blemish in him all his fellows should run to throw their costliest robes. That immaculate manliness we feel within ourselves, so far within us, that it remains intact though all the outer character seem gone; bleeds with keenest anguish at the undraped spectacle of a valor-ruined man. Nor can piety itself, at such a shameful sight, completely stifle her upbraidings against the permitting stars. But this august dignity I treat of, is not the dignity of kings and robes, but that abounding dignity which has no robed investiture. Thou shalt see it shining in the arm that wields a pick or drives a spike; that democratic dignity which, on all hands, radiates without end from God; Himself! The great God absolute! The centre and circumference of all democracy! His omnipresence, our divine equality!

If, then, to meanest mariners, and renegades and castaways, I shall hereafter ascribe high qualities, though dark; weave round them tragic graces; if
even the most mournful, perchance the most abased, among them all, shall
at times lift himself to the exalted mounts; if I shall touch that workman's
arm with some ethereal light; if I shall spread a rainbow over his disastrous
set of sun; then against all mortal critics bear me out in it, thou Just Spirit
of Equality, which hast spread one royal mantle of humanity over all my
kind! Bear me out in it, thou great democratic God! who didst not refuse
to the swart convict, Bunyan, the pale, poetic pearl; Thou who didst clothe
with doubly hammered leaves of finest gold, the stumped and paupered
arm of old Cervantes; Thou who didst pick up Andrew Jackson from the
pebbles; who didst hurl him upon a war-horse; who didst thunder him
higher than a throne! Thou who, in all Thy mighty, earthly marchings, ever
cullest Thy selectest champions from the kingly commons; bear me out in
it, O God!

CHAPTER 27

Knights and Squires

, according to local usage,   , as a whistling tinker his hammer   after a
comfortable dinner,

, all bowed to the ground with their packs; what helped to bring about that
almost impious good-humor of his; that thing   lighting one from the other
to the end of the chapter;

I say this continual smoking must have been one cause, at least, of his peculiar
disposition; for every one knows that this earthly air, whether ashore or afloat,
is terribly infected with the nameless miseries of the numberless mortals who
have died exhaling it; and as in time of the cholera, some people go about with
a camphorated handkerchief to their mouths; so, likewise, against all mortal

tribulations, Stubb's tobacco smoke might have operated as a sort of disinfecting agent.

—Starbuck, Stubb, and Flask,   Or, being armed with their long keen whaling spears, they were as a picked trio of lancers; even as the harpooneers were flingers of javelins.

the second mate

and having now led for many years the bold life of the fishery in the ships of owners uncommonly heedful of what manner of men they shipped;   Curious to tell,   Poor Alabama boy!

CHAPTER 28

Ahab

This was strangely heightened at times by the ragged Elijah's diabolical incoherences uninvitedly recurring to me, with a subtle energy I could not have before conceived of. But poorly could I withstand them, much as in other moods I was almost ready to smile at the solemn whimsicalities of that outlandish prophet of the wharves.   colorless   Reality outran apprehension;

By some tacit consent, throughout the voyage little or no allusion was made to it, especially by the mates.   , the immemorial credulities, popularly

from his first visit in the air,   indeed, began to grow a little genial,   as ever all clouds choose the loftiest peaks to pile themselves upon

soon

CHAPTER 29

Enter Ahab; to him, Stubb

and the band on deck sentinelled the slumbers of the band below; and when if a rope was to be hauled upon the forecastle, the sailors flung it not rudely down, as by day, but with some cautiousness dropt it to its place for fear of disturbing their slumbering shipmates; when this sort of steady quietude would begin to prevail, habitually, to help his crippled way   at times like these,
 with heavy, lumber-like pace

"—"

of the so suddenly scornful old man

"How he flashed at me!—his eyes like powder-pans!   Anyway there's something on his mind, as sure as there must be something on a deck when it cracks.
 either, He's full of riddles;   But there's no telling, it's the old game—Here goes for a snooze. Damn me, it's worth a fellow's while to be born into the world, if only to fall right asleep. And now that I think of it, that's about the first thing babies do, and that's a sort of queer, too. Damn me, but all things are queer, come to think of 'em. But that's against my principles. Think not, is my eleventh commandment; and sleep when you can, is my twelfth—So here goes again. But how's that? didn't he call me a dog? blazes! he called me ten times a donkey, and piled a lot of jackasses on top of *that*! He might as well have kicked me, and done with it. Maybe he *did* kick me, and I didn't observe it, I was so taken all aback with his brow, somehow. It flashed like a bleached bone. What the devil's the matter with me? I don't stand right on my legs. Coming afoul of that old man has a sort of turned me wrong side out. By the Lord, I must have been dreaming, though—How? how? how?—but the only way's to stash it; so here goes to hammock again; and in the morning, I'll see how this plaguey juggling thinks over by daylight."

CHAPTER 30

The Pipe

When Stubb had departed, Ahab stood for a while leaning over the bulwarks; and then, as had been usual with him of late, calling a sailor of the watch, he sent him below for his ivory stool, and also his pipe. Lighting the pipe at the binnacle lamp and planting the stool on the weather side of the deck, he sat and smoked.

In old Norse times, the thrones of the sea-loving Danish kings were fabricated, saith tradition, of the tusks of the narwhale. How could one look at Ahab then, seated on that tripod of bones, without bethinking him of the royalty it symbolized? For a Khan of the plank, and a king of the sea, and a great lord of Leviathans was Ahab.

Some moments passed, during which the thick vapor came from his mouth in quick and constant puffs, which blew back again into his face. "How now," he soliloquized at last, withdrawing the tube, "this smoking no longer soothes. Oh, my pipe! hard must it go with me if thy charm be gone! Here have I been unconsciously toiling, not pleasuring—aye, and ignorantly smoking to windward all the while; to windward, and with such nervous whiffs, as if, like the dying whale, my final jets were the strongest and fullest of trouble. What business have I with this pipe? This thing that is meant for sereneness, to send up mild white vapors among mild white hairs, not among torn iron-grey locks like mine. I'll smoke no more—"

He tossed the still lighted pipe into the sea. The fire hissed in the waves; the same instant the ship shot by the bubble the sinking pipe made. With slouched hat, Ahab lurchingly paced the planks.

CHAPTER 31

Queen Mab

Next morning Stubb accosted Flask.

"Such a queer dream, King-Post, I never had. You know the old man's ivory leg, well I dreamed he kicked me with it; and when I tried to kick back, upon my soul, my little man, I kicked my leg right off! And then, presto! Ahab seemed a pyramid, and I, like a blazing fool, kept kicking at it. But what was still more curious, Flask—you know how curious all dreams are—through all this rage that I was in, I somehow seemed to be thinking to myself, that after all, it was not much of an insult, that kick from Ahab. 'Why,' thinks I, 'what's the row? It's not a real leg, only a false leg.' And there's a mighty difference between a living thump and a dead thump. That's what makes a blow from the hand, Flask, fifty times more savage to bear than a blow from a cane. The living member—that makes the living insult, my little man. And thinks I to myself all the while, mind, while I was stubbing my silly toes against that cursed pyramid—so confoundedly contradictory was it all, all the while, I say, I was thinking to myself, 'what's his leg now, but a cane—a whalebone cane. Yes,' thinks I, 'it was only a playful cudgelling—in fact, only a whaleboning that he gave me—not a base kick. Besides,' thinks I, 'look at it once; why, the end of it—the foot part—what a small sort of end it is; whereas, if a broad footed farmer kicked me, *there's* a devilish broad insult. But this insult is whittled down to a point only.' But now comes the greatest joke of the dream, Flask. While I was battering away at the pyramid, a sort of badger-haired old merman, with a hump on his back, takes me by the shoulders, and slews me round. 'What are you 'bout?' says he. Slid! man, but I was frightened. Such a phiz! But, somehow, next moment I was over the fright. 'What am I about?' says I at last. 'And what business is that of yours, I should like to know, Mr. Humpback? Do *you* want a kick?' By the lord, Flask, I had no sooner said that, than he turned round his stern to me, bent over, and dragging up a lot of seaweed he had for a clout—what do you think, I saw?—why thunder alive, man, his stern was stuck full of mar- linspikes, with the points out. Says I, on second thoughts, 'I guess I won't kick you, old fellow.' 'Wise Stubb,' said he, 'wise Stubb;' and kept muttering it all the time, a sort of eating of his own gums like a chimney hag. Seeing he wasn't going to stop saying over his 'wise Stubb, wise Stubb,' I thought I might as well fall to kicking the pyramid again. But I had only just lifted my foot for it, when he roared out, 'Stop that kicking!' 'Halloa,' says I, 'what's the matter now, old fellow?' 'Look ye here,' says he; 'let's argue the insult. Captain Ahab kicked ye, didn't he?' 'Yes, he did,' says I—'right *here* it was.' 'Very good,' says he—'he used his ivory leg, didn't he?' 'Yes, he did,' says I. 'Well then,' says he, 'wise Stubb, what have you to complain of? Didn't he kick with right good will? it wasn't a common pitch pine leg he kicked with, was it? No, you were kicked by a great man, and with a beautiful ivory leg, Stubb. It's an honor; I consider it an honor. Listen, wise Stubb. In old England the greatest lords think it great glory to be slapped by a queen, and made garter-knights of; but, be *your* boast, Stubb, that ye were kicked by old Ahab, and made a wise man of. Remember what I say; *be* kicked by him; account his kicks honors; and on no account kick back; for you can't help yourself, wise Stubb. Don't you see that pyramid?' With that, he all of a sudden seemed somehow, in some queer fashion, to swim off into the air. I snored; rolled over; and there I was in my hammock! Now, what do you think of that dream, Flask?"

"I don't know; it seems a sort of foolish to me, tho.'"

"May be; may be. But it's made a wise man of me, Flask. D'ye see Ahab stand- ing there, sideways looking over the stern? Well, the best thing you can do, Flask, is to let the old man alone; never speak to him, whatever he says. Hal- loa! What's that he shouts? Hark!"

"Mast-head, there! Look sharp, all of ye! There are whales hereabouts! If ye see a white one, split your lungs for him!"

"What do you think of that now, Flask? ain't there a small drop of something queer about that, eh? A white whale—did ye mark that, man? Look ye— there's something special in the wind. Stand by for it, Flask. Ahab has that that's bloody on his mind. But, mum; he comes this way."

CHAPTER 32

Cetology

Already we are boldly launched upon the deep; but soon we shall be lost in its unshored, harborless immensities. Ere that come to pass; ere the Pequod's weedy hull rolls side by side with the barnacled hulls of the leviathan; at the outset it is but well to attend to a matter almost indispensable to a thorough appreciative understanding of the more special leviathanic revelations and al- lusions of all sorts which are to follow.

It is some systematized exhibition of the whale in his broad genera, that I would now fain put before you. Yet is it no easy task. The classification of the constituents of a chaos, nothing less is here essayed. Listen to what the best and latest authorities have laid down.

"No branch of Zoology is so much involved as that which is entitled Cetol- ogy," says Captain Scoresby, A.D. 1820.

"It is not my intention, were it in my power, to enter into the inquiry as to the true method of dividing the cetacea into groups and families. * * * Utter confusion exists among the historians of this animal" (sperm whale), says Sur- geon Beale, A.D. 1839.

"Unfitness to pursue our research in the unfathomable waters." "Impenetrable veil covering our knowledge of the cetacea." "A field strewn with thorns." "All these incomplete indications but serve to torture us naturalists."

Thus speak of the whale, the great Cuvier, and John Hunter, and Lesson, those lights of zoology and anatomy. Nevertheless, though of real knowledge there be little, yet of books there are a plenty; and so in some small degree, with cetology, or the science of whales. Many are the men, small and great, old and new, landsmen and seamen, who have at large or in little, written of the whale. Run over a few:—The Authors of the Bible; Aristotle; Pliny; Aldrovandi; Sir Thomas Browne; Gesner; Ray; Linnæus; Rondeletius; Willoughby; Green; Artedi; Sibbald; Brisson; Marten; Lacepede; Bonneterre; Desmarest; Baron Cuvier; Frederick Cuvier; John Hunter; Owen; Scoresby; Beale; Bennett; J. Ross Browne; the Author of Miriam Coffin; Olmstead; and the Rev. T. Cheever. But to what ultimate generalizing purpose all these have written, the above cited extracts will show.

Of the names in this list of whale authors, only those following Owen ever saw living whales; and but one of them was a real professional harpooneer and whaleman. I mean Captain Scoresby. On the separate subject of the Greenland or right-whale, he is the best existing authority. But Scoresby knew nothing and says nothing of the great sperm whale, compared with which the Greenland whale is almost unworthy mentioning. And here be it said, that the Greenland whale is an usurper upon the throne of the seas. He is not even by any means the largest of the whales. Yet, owing to the long priority of his claims, and the profound ignorance which, till some seventy years back, invested the then fabulous or utterly unknown sperm-whale, and which ignorance to this present day still reigns in all but some few scientific retreats and whale-ports; this usurpation has been every way complete. Reference to nearly all the leviathanic allusions in the great poets of past days, will satisfy you that the Greenland whale, without one rival, was to them the monarch of the seas. But the time has at last come for a new proclamation. This is Charing Cross; hear ye! good people all,—the Greenland whale is deposed,—the great sperm whale now reigneth!

There are only two books in being which at all pretend to put the living sperm whale before you, and at the same time, in the remotest degree succeed in the attempt. Those books are Beale's and Bennett's; both in their time surgeons to English South-Sea whale-ships, and both exact and reliable men. The original matter touching the sperm whale to be found in their volumes is necessarily small; but so far as it goes, it is of excellent quality, though mostly confined to scientific description. As yet, however, the sperm whale, scientific or poetic, lives not complete in any literature. Far above all other hunted whales, his is an unwritten life.

Now the various species of whales need some sort of popular comprehensive classification, if only an easy outline one for the present, hereafter to be filled in all its departments by subsequent laborers. As no better man advances to take this matter in hand, I hereupon offer my own poor endeavors. I promise nothing complete; because any human thing supposed to be complete, must for that very reason infallibly be faulty. I shall not pretend to a minute anatomical description of the various species, or—in this place at least—to much of any description. My object here is simply to project the draught of a systematization of cetology. I am the architect, not the builder.

But it is a ponderous task; no ordinary letter-sorter in the Post-Office is equal to it. To grope down into the bottom of the sea after them; to have one's hands among the unspeakable foundations, ribs, and very pelvis of the world; this is a fearful thing. What am I that I should essay to hook the nose of this leviathan! The awful tauntings in Job might well appal me. "Will he (the leviathan) make a covenant with thee? Behold the hope of him is vain!" But I have swam through libraries and sailed through oceans; I have had to do with whales with these visible hands; I am in earnest; and I will try. There are some preliminaries to settle.

First: The uncertain, unsettled condition of this science of Cetology is in the very vestibule attested by the fact, that in some quarters it still remains a moot point whether a whale be a fish. In his System of Nature, A.D. 1776, Linnæus declares, "I hereby separate the whales from the fish." But of my own knowledge, I know that down to the year 1850, sharks and shad, alewives and herring, against Linnæus's express edict, were still found dividing the possession of the same seas with the Leviathan.

The grounds upon which Linnæus would fain have banished the whales from the waters, he states as follows: "On account of their warm bilocular heart, their lungs, their movable eyelids, their hollow ears, penem intrantem feminam mammis lactantem," and finally, "ex lege naturae jure meritoque." I submitted all this to my friends Simeon Macey and Charley Coffin, of Nantucket, both messmates of mine in a certain voyage, and they united in the opinion that the reasons set forth were altogether insufficient. Charley profanely hinted they were humbug.

Be it known that, waiving all argument, I take the good old fashioned ground that the whale is a fish, and call upon holy Jonah to back me. This fundamental thing settled, the next point is, in what internal respect does the whale differ from other fish. Above, Linnæus has given you those items. But in brief, they are these: lungs and warm blood; whereas, all other fish are lungless and cold blooded.

Next: how shall we define the whale, by his obvious externals, so as conspicuously to label him for all time to come? To be short, then, a whale is *a spouting fish with a horizontal tail.* There you have him. However contracted, that definition is the result of expanded meditation. A walrus spouts much like a whale, but the walrus is not a fish, because he is amphibious. But the last term of the definition is still more cogent, as coupled with the first. Almost any one must have noticed that all the fish familiar to landsmen have not a flat, but a vertical, or up-and-down tail. Whereas, among spouting fish the tail, though it may be similarly shaped, invariably assumes a horizontal position.

By the above definition of what a whale is, I do by no means exclude from the leviathanic brotherhood any sea creature hitherto identified with the whale by the best informed Nantucketers; nor, on the other hand, link with it any fish hitherto authoritatively regarded as alien.* Hence, all the smaller, spouting, and horizontal tailed fish must be included in this ground-plan of Cetology. Now, then, come the grand divisions of the entire whale host.

First: According to magnitude I divide the whales into three primary BOOKS (subdivisible into CHAPTERS), and these shall comprehend them all, both small and large.

I. THE FOLIO WHALE; II. the OCTAVO WHALE; III. the DUODECIMO WHALE.

As the type of the FOLIO I present the *Sperm Whale*; of the OCTAVO, the *Grampus*; of the DUODECIMO, the *Porpoise*.

FOLIOS. Among these I here include the following chapters:—I. The *Sperm Whale*; II. the *Right Whale*; III. the *Fin-Back Whale*; IV. the *Hump-Backed Whale*; V. the *Razor-Back Whale*; VI. the *Sulphur-Bottom Whale*.

BOOK I. (*Folio*), CHAPTER I. (*Sperm Whale*).—This whale, among the English of old vaguely known as the Trumpa whale, and the Physeter whale, and the Anvil Headed whale, is the present Cachalot of the French, and the Pottsfich of the Germans, and the Macrocephalus of the Long Words. He is, without doubt, the largest inhabitant of the globe; the most formidable of all whales to encounter; the most majestic in aspect; and lastly, by far the most valuable in commerce; he being the only creature from which that valuable substance, spermaceti, is obtained. All his peculiarities will, in many other places, be enlarged upon. It is chiefly with his name that I now have to do. Philologically considered, it is absurd. Some centuries ago, when the Sperm whale was

---

* I am aware that down to the present time, the fish styled Lamatins and Dugongs (Pig-fish and Sow-fish of the Coffins of Nantucket) are included by many naturalists among the whales. But as these pig-fish are a noisy, contemptible set, mostly lurking in the mouths of rivers, and feeding on wet hay, and especially as they do not spout, I deny their credentials as whales; and have presented them with their passports to quit the Kingdom of Cetology.

almost wholly unknown in his own proper individuality, and when his oil was only accidentally obtained from the stranded fish; in those days spermaceti, it would seem, was popularly supposed to be derived from a creature identical with the one then known in England as the Greenland or Right Whale. It was the idea also, that this same spermaceti was that quickening humor of the Greenland Whale which the first syllable of the word literally expresses. In those times, also, spermaceti was exceedingly scarce, not being used for light, but only as an ointment and medicament. It was only to be had from the druggists as you nowadays buy an ounce of rhubarb. When, as I opine, in the course of time, the true nature of spermaceti became known, its original name was still retained by the dealers; no doubt to enhance its value by a notion so strangely significant of its scarcity. And so the appellation must at last have come to be bestowed upon the whale from which this spermaceti was really derived.

BOOK I. (*Folio*), CHAPTER II. (*Right Whale*).—In one respect this is the most venerable of the leviathans, being the one first regularly hunted by man. It yields the article commonly known as whalebone or baleen; and the oil specially known as "whale oil," an inferior article in commerce. Among the fishermen, he is indiscriminately designated by all the following titles: The Whale; the Greenland Whale; the Black Whale; the Great Whale; the True Whale; the Right Whale. There is a deal of obscurity concerning the identity of the species thus multitudinously baptized. What then is the whale, which I include in the second species of my Folios? It is the Great Mysticetus of the English naturalists; the Greenland Whale of the English whalemen; the Baliene Ordinaire of the French whalemen; the Growlands Walfish of the Swedes. It is the whale which for more than two centuries past has been hunted by the Dutch and English in the Arctic seas; it is the whale which the American fishermen have long pursued in the Indian ocean, on the Brazil Banks, on the Nor' West Coast, and various other parts of the world, designated by them Right Whale Cruising Grounds.

Some pretend to see a difference between the Greenland whale of the English and the right whale of the Americans. But they precisely agree in all their grand features; nor has there yet been presented a single determinate fact upon which to ground a radical distinction. It is by endless subdivisions based upon the most inconclusive differences, that some departments of natural history become so repellingly intricate. The right whale will be elsewhere treated of at some length, with reference to elucidating the sperm whale.

BOOK I. (*Folio*), CHAPTER III. (*Fin-Back*).—Under this head I reckon a monster which, by the various names of Fin-Back, Tall-Spout, and Long-John, has been seen almost in every sea and is commonly the whale whose distant jet is so often descried by passengers crossing the Atlantic, in the New York packet-tracks. In the length he attains, and in his baleen, the Fin-back resembles the right whale, but is of a less portly girth, and a lighter color, approaching to olive. His great lips present a cable-like aspect, formed by the intertwisting, slanting folds of large wrinkles. His grand distinguishing feature, the fin, from which he derives his name, is often a conspicuous object. This fin is some three or four feet long, growing vertically from the hinder part of the back, of an angular shape, and with a very sharp pointed end. Even if not the slightest other part of the creature be visible, this isolated fin will, at times, be seen plainly projecting from the surface. When the sea is moderately calm, and slightly marked with spherical ripples, and this gnomon-like fin stands up and casts shadows upon the wrinkled surface, it may well be supposed that the watery circle surrounding it somewhat resembles a dial, with its style and wavy hour-lines graved on it. On that Ahaz-dial the shadow often goes back. The Fin-Back is not gregarious. He seems a whale-hater, as some men are man-haters. Very shy; always going solitary; unexpectedly rising to the surface in the remotest and most sullen waters; his straight and single lofty jet rising like a tall misanthropic spear upon a barren plain; gifted with such wondrous power and velocity in swimming, as to defy all present pursuit from man; this leviathan seems the banished and unconquerable Cain of his race, bearing for his mark that style upon his back. From having the baleen in his mouth, the Fin-Back is sometimes included with the right whale, among a theoretic species denominated *Whalebone whales,* that is, whales with baleen. Of these so called Whalebone whales, there would seem to be several varieties, most of which, however, are little known. Broad-nosed whales and beaked whales; pike-headed whales; bunched whales; under-jawed whales and rostrated whales, are the fishermen's names for a few sorts.

In connection with this appellative of "Whalebone whales," it is of great importance to mention, that however such a nomenclature may be convenient in facilitating allusions to some kind of whales, yet it is in vain to attempt a clear classification of the Leviathan, founded upon either his baleen, or hump, or fin, or teeth; notwithstanding that those marked parts or features very obviously seem better adapted to afford the basis for a regular system of Cetology than any other detached bodily distinctions, which the whale, in his kinds, presents. How then? The baleen, hump, back-fin, and teeth; these are things whose peculiarities are indiscriminately dispersed among all sorts of whales, without any regard to what may be the nature of their structure in other and more essential particulars. Thus, the sperm whale and the humpbacked whale, each has a hump; but there the similitude ceases. Then, this same humpbacked whale and the Greenland whale, each of these has baleen; but there again the similitude ceases. And it is just the same with the other parts above mentioned. In various sorts of whales, they form such irregular combinations; or, in the case of any one of them detached, such an irregular isolation; as utterly to defy all general methodization formed upon such a basis. On this rock every one of the whale-naturalists has split.

But it may possibly be conceived that, in the internal parts of the whale, in his anatomy—there, at least, we shall be able to hit the right classification. Nay; what thing, for example, is there in the Greenland whale's anatomy more striking than his baleen? Yet we have seen that by his baleen it is impossible correctly to classify the Greenland whale. And if you descend into the bowels of the various leviathans, why there you will not find distinctions a fiftieth part as available to the systematizer as those external ones already enumerated. What then remains? nothing but to take hold of the whales bodily, in their entire liberal volume, and boldly sort them that way. And this is the Bibliographical system here adopted; and it is the only one that can possibly succeed, for it alone is practicable. To proceed.

BOOK I. (*Folio*), CHAPTER IV. (*Hump-Back*).—This whale is often seen on the northern American coast. He has been frequently captured there, and towed into harbor. He has a great pack on him like a peddler; or you might call him the Elephant and Castle whale. At any rate, the popular name for him does not sufficiently distinguish him, since the sperm whale also has a hump though a smaller one. His oil is not very valuable. He has baleen. He is the most gamesome and light-hearted of all the whales, making more gay foam and white water generally than any other of them.

BOOK I. (*Folio*), CHAPTER V. (*Razor-Back*).—Of this whale little is known but his name. I have seen him at a distance off Cape Horn. Of a retiring nature, he eludes both hunters and philosophers. Though no coward, he has never yet shown any part of him but his back, which rises in a long sharp ridge. Let him go. I know little more of him, nor does anybody else.

BOOK I. (*Folio*), CHAPTER VI. (*Sulphur-Bottom*).—Another retiring gentleman, with a brimstone belly, doubtless got by scraping along the Tartarian tiles in some of his profounder divings. He is seldom seen; at least I have never seen him except in the remoter southern seas, and then always at too great a distance to study his countenance. He is never chased; he would run away with rope-walks of line. Prodigies are told of him. Adieu, Sulphur Bottom! I can say nothing more that is true of ye, nor can the oldest Nantucketer.

Thus ends BOOK I. (*Folio*), and now begins BOOK II. (*Octavo*).

OCTAVOES.*—These embrace the whales of middling magnitude, among which present may be numbered:—I., the *Grampus*; II., the *Black Fish*; III., the *Narwhale*; IV., the *Killer*; V., the *Thrasher*.

BOOK II. (*Octavo*), CHAPTER I. (*Grampus*).—Though this fish, whose loud sonorous breathing, or rather blowing, has furnished a proverb to landsmen, is so well known a denizen of the deep, yet is he not popularly classed among whales. But possessing all the grand distinctive features of the leviathan, most naturalists have recognized him for one. He is of moderate octavo size, varying from fifteen to twenty-five feet in length, and of corresponding dimensions round the waist. He swims in herds; he is never regularly hunted, though his oil is considerable in quantity, and pretty good for light. By some fishermen his approach is regarded as premonitory of the advance of the great sperm whale.

BOOK II. (*Octavo*), CHAPTER II. (*Black Fish*).—I give the popular fishermen's names for all these fish, for generally they are the best. Where any name happens to be vague or inexpressive, I shall say so, and suggest another. I do so now, touching the Black Fish, so-called, because blackness is the rule among almost all whales. So, call him the Hyena Whale, if you please. His voracity is well known, and from the circumstance that the inner angles of his lips are curved upwards, he carries an everlasting Mephistophelean grin on his face. This whale averages some sixteen or eighteen feet in length. He is found in almost all latitudes. He has a peculiar way of showing his dorsal hooked fin in swimming, which looks something like a Roman nose. When not more profitably employed, the sperm whale hunters sometimes capture the Hyena whale, to keep up the supply of cheap oil for domestic employment—as some frugal housekeepers, in the absence of company, and quite alone by them-

---

* Why this book of whales is not denominated the Quarto is very plain. Because, while the whales of this order, though smaller than those of the former order, nevertheless retain a proportionate likeness to them in figure, yet the bookbinder's Quarto volume in its dimensioned form does not preserve the shape of the Folio volume, but the Octavo volume does.

selves, burn unsavory tallow instead of odorous wax. Though their blubber is very thin, some of these whales will yield you upwards of thirty gallons of oil.

BOOK II. (*Octavo*), CHAPTER III. (*Narwhale*), that is, *Nostril whale.*— Another instance of a curiously named whale, so named I suppose from his peculiar horn being originally mistaken for a peaked nose. The creature is some sixteen feet in length, while its horn averages five feet, though some exceed ten, and even attain to fifteen feet. Strictly speaking, this horn is but a lengthened tusk, growing out from the jaw in a line a little depressed from the horizontal. But it is only found on the sinister side, which has an ill effect, giving its owner something analogous to the aspect of a clumsy left-handed man. What precise purpose this ivory horn or lance answers, it would be hard to say. It does not seem to be used like the blade of the sword-fish and bill-fish; though some sailors tell me that the Narwhale employs it for a rake in turning over the bottom of the sea for food. Charley Coffin said it was used for an ice-piercer; for the Narwhale, rising to the surface of the Polar Sea, and finding it sheeted with ice, thrusts his horn up, and so breaks through. But you cannot prove either of these surmises to be correct. My own opinion is, that however this one-sided horn may really be used by the Narwhale—however that may be—it would certainly be very convenient to him for a folder in reading pamphlets. The Narwhale I have heard called the Tusked whale, the Horned whale, and the Unicorn whale. He is certainly a curious example of the Unicornism to be found in almost every kingdom of animated nature. From certain cloistered old authors I have gathered that this same sea-unicorn's horn was in ancient days regarded as the great antidote against poison, and as such, preparations of it brought immense prices. It was also distilled to a volatile salts for fainting ladies, the same way that the horns of the male deer are manufactured into hartshorn. Originally it was in itself accounted an object of great curiosity. Black Letter tells me that Sir Martin Frobisher on his return from that voyage, when Queen Bess did gallantly wave her jewelled hand to him from a window of Greenwich Palace, as his bold ship sailed down the Thames; "when Sir Martin returned from that voyage," saith Black Letter, "on bended knees he presented to her highness a prodigious long horn of the Narwhale, which for a long period after hung in the castle at Windsor." An Irish author avers that the Earl of Leicester, on bended knees, did likewise present to her highness another horn, pertaining to a land beast of the unicorn nature.

The Narwhale has a very picturesque, leopard-like look, being of a milk-white ground color, dotted with round and oblong spots of black. His oil is very superior, clear and fine; but there is little of it, and he is seldom hunted. He is mostly found in the circumpolar seas.

BOOK II. (*Octavo*), CHAPTER IV. (*Killer*).—Of this whale little is precisely known to the Nantucketer, and nothing at all to the professed naturalist. From what I have seen of him at a distance, I should say that he was about the bigness of a grampus. He is very savage—a sort of Feegee fish. He sometimes takes the great Folio whales by the lip, and hangs there like a leech, till the mighty brute is worried to death. The Killer is never hunted. I never heard what sort of oil he has. Exception might be taken to the name bestowed upon this whale, on the ground of its indistinctness. For we are all killers, on land and on sea; Bonapartes and Sharks included.

BOOK II. (*Octavo*), CHAPTER V. (*Thrasher*).—This gentleman is famous for his tail, which he uses for a ferule in thrashing his foes. He mounts the Folio whale's back, and as he swims, he works his passage by flogging him; as some schoolmasters get along in the world by a similar process. Still less is known of the Thrasher than of the Killer. Both are outlaws, even in the lawless seas.

Thus ends BOOK II. (*Octavo*), and begins BOOK III. (*Duodecimo*).

DUODECIMOES.—These include the smaller whales. I. The Huzza Porpoise. II. The Algerine Porpoise. III. The Mealy-mouthed Porpoise.

To those who have not chanced specially to study the subject, it may possibly seem strange, that fishes not commonly exceeding four or five feet should be marshalled among WHALES—a word, which, in the popular sense, always conveys an idea of hugeness. But the creatures set down above as Duodecimoes are infallibly whales, by the terms of my definition of what a whale is— i.e. a spouting fish, with a horizontal tail.

BOOK III. (*Duodecimo*), CHAPTER I. (*Huzza Porpoise*).—This is the common porpoise found almost all over the globe. The name is of my own bestowal; for there are more than one sort of porpoises, and something must be done to distinguish them. I call him thus, because he always swims in hilarious shoals, which upon the broad sea keep tossing themselves to heaven like caps in a Fourth-of-July crowd. Their appearance is generally hailed with delight by the mariner. Full of fine spirits, they invariably come from the breezy billows to windward. They are the lads that always live before the wind. They are accounted a lucky omen. If you yourself can withstand three cheers at beholding these vivacious fish, then heaven help ye; the spirit of godly gamesomeness is not in ye. A well-fed, plump Huzza Porpoise will yield you one good gallon of good oil. But the fine and delicate fluid extracted from his jaws is exceedingly valuable. It is in request among jewellers and watchmakers. Sailors put it on their hones. Porpoise meat is good eating, you know. It may never have occurred to you that a porpoise spouts. Indeed, his spout is so small that it is not very readily discernible. But the next time you have a chance, watch him; and you will then see the great Sperm whale himself in miniature.

BOOK III. (*Duodecimo*), CHAPTER II. (*Algerine Porpoise*).—A pirate. Very savage. He is only found, I think, in the Pacific. He is somewhat larger than the Huzza Porpoise, but much of the same general make. Provoke him, and he will buckle to a shark. I have lowered for him many times, but never yet saw him captured.

BOOK III. (*Duodecimo*), CHAPTER III. (*Mealy-Mouthed Porpoise*).—The largest kind of Porpoise; and only found in the Pacific, so far as it is known. The only English name, by which he has hitherto been designated, is that of the fishers—Right-Whale Porpoise, from the circumstance that he is chiefly found in the vicinity of that Folio. In shape, he differs in some degree from the Huzza Porpoise, being of a less rotund and jolly girth; indeed, he is of quite a neat and gentleman-like figure. He has no fins on his back (most other porpoises have), he has a lovely tail, and sentimental Indian eyes of a hazel hue. But his mealy-mouth spoils all. Though his entire back down to his side fins is of a deep sable, yet a boundary line, distinct as the mark in a ship's hull, called the "bright waist," that line streaks him from stem to stern, with two separate colors, black above and white below. The white comprises part of his head, and the whole of his mouth, which makes him look as if he had just escaped from a felonious visit to a meal-bag. A most mean and mealy aspect! His oil is much like that of the common porpoise.

* * * * *

Beyond the DUODECIMO, this system does not proceed, inasmuch as the Porpoise is the smallest of the whales. Above, you have all the Leviathans of note. But there are a rabble of uncertain, fugitive, half-fabulous whales, which, as an American whaleman, I know by reputation, but not personally. I shall enumerate them by their fore-castle appellations; for possibly such a list may be valuable to future investigators, who may complete what I have here but begun. If any of the following whales, shall hereafter be caught and marked, then he can readily be incorporated into this System, according to his Folio, Octavo, or Duodecimo magnitude:—The Bottle-Nose Whale; the Junk Whale; the Pudding-Headed Whale; the Cape Whale; the Leading Whale; the Cannon Whale; the Scragg Whale; the Coppered Whale; the Elephant Whale;

the Iceberg Whale; the Quog Whale; the Blue Whale; etc. From Icelandic, Dutch, and old English authorities, there might be quoted other lists of uncertain whales, blessed with all manner of uncouth names. But I omit them as altogether obsolete; and can hardly help suspecting them for mere sounds, full of Leviathanism, but signifying nothing.

Finally: It was stated at the outset, that this system would not be here, and at once, perfected. You cannot but plainly see that I have kept my word. But I now leave my cetological System standing thus unfinished, even as the great Cathedral of Cologne was left, with the crane still standing upon the top of the uncompleted tower. For small erections may be finished by their first architects; grand ones, true ones, ever leave the copestone to posterity. God keep me from ever completing anything. This whole book is but a draught—nay, but the draught of a draught. Oh, Time, Strength, Cash, and Patience!

CHAPTER 33

The Specksynder

, a class unknown of course in any other marine than the whale-fleet

At present he ranks simply as senior Harpooneer; and as such, is but one of the captain's more inferior subalterns. ,

nay, extorting almost as much outward homage as if he wore the imperial purple, and not the shabbiest of pilot-cloth

, ,

, ,

CHAPTER 34

The Cabin Table

by a dexterous sleight,   reversing all other processions, by bringing up the rear with music

and defyingly   deprecatory and   Wherefore this difference? A problem? Perhaps not. To have been Belshazzar, King of Babylon; and to have been Belshazzar, not haughtily but courteously, therein certainly must have been some touch of mundane grandeur. But he who in the rightly regal and intelligent spirit presides over his own private dinner-table of invited guests, that man's unchallenged power and dominion of individual influence for the time; that man's royalty of state transcends Belshazzar's, for Belshazzar was not the greatest. Who has but once dined his friends, has tasted   Now, if to this consideration you superadd the official supremacy of a ship-master, then, by inference, you will derive the cause of that peculiarity of sea-life just mentioned.

and a little started if, perchance, the knife grazed against the plate;   somehow solemn meals,   youngest son, and   in the first degree

For hereby Flask's dinner was badly jammed in point of time. Starbuck and Stubb both had the start of him; and yet they also have the privilege of lounging in the rear.   even   For what he ate did not so much relieve his hunger, as keep it immortal in him.

They made a sort of temporary servants' hall of the high and mighty cabin.

if he did not go with a nimble hop-skip-and-jump,

But for all this, the great negro was wonderfully abstemious, not to say dainty. It seemed hardly possible that by such comparatively small mouthfuls he could keep up the vitality diffused through so broad, baronial, and superb a person.

But, doubtless, this noble savage fed strong and drank deep of the abounding element of air; and through his dilated nostrils snuffed in the sublime life of the worlds. Not by beef or by bread, are giants made or nourished. But Que-equeg, he had a mortal, barbaric smack of the lip in eating—an ugly sound enough—so much so, that the trembling Dough-Boy almost looked to see whether any marks of teeth lurked in his own lean arms. And when he would hear Tashtego singing out for him to produce himself, that his bones might be picked, the simple-witted steward all but shattered the crockery hanging round him in the pantry, by his sudden fits of the palsy.

But, though these barbarians dined in the cabin, and nominally lived there; still, being anything but sedentary in their habits, they were scarcely ever in it except at mealtimes, and just before sleeping-time, when they passed through it to their own peculiar quarters.

In this one matter, Ahab seemed no exception to most American whale cap-tains, who, as a set, rather incline to the opinion that by rights the ship's cabin belongs to them; and that it is by courtesy alone that anybody else is, at any time, permitted there. So that, in real truth, the mates and harpooneers of the Pequod might more properly be said to have lived out of the cabin than in it. For when they did enter it, it was something as a street-door enters a house; turning inwards for a moment, only to be turned out the next; and, as a permanent thing, residing in the open air. Nor did they lose much hereby; in the cabin was no companionship; socially, Ahab was inaccessible. Though nominally included in the census of Christendom, he was still an alien to it. He lived in the world, as the last of the Grisly Bears lived in settled Missouri. And as when Spring and Summer had departed, that wild Logan of the woods, burying himself in the hollow of a tree, lived out the winter there, sucking his own paws; so, in his inclement, howling old age, Ahab's soul, shut up in the caved trunk of his body, there fed upon the sullen paws of its gloom!

CHAPTER 35

The Mast-Head

as the business of standing mast-heads, ashore or   , is a very ancient and in-teresting one, let us in some measure expatiate here. I take it, that the earliest standers of mast-heads were the old Egyptians; because, in all my researches, I find none prior to them. For though their progenitors, the builders of Babel, must doubtless, by their tower, have intended to rear the loftiest mast-head in all Asia, or Africa either; yet (ere the final truck was put to it) as that great stone mast of theirs may be said to have gone by the board, in the dread gale of God's wrath; therefore, we cannot give these Babel builders priority over the Egyptians. And that the Egyptians were a nation of mast-head standers, is an assertion based upon the general belief among archaeologists, that the first pyramids were founded for astronomical purposes: a theory singularly sup-ported by the peculiar stair-like formation of all four sides of those edifices; whereby, with prodigious long upliftings of their legs, those old astronomers were wont to mount to the apex, and sing out for new stars; even as the look-outs of a modern ship sing out for a sail, or a whale just bearing in sight. In Saint Stylites, the famous Christian hermit of old times, who built him a lofty stone pillar in the desert and spent the whole latter portion of his life on its summit, hoisting his food from the ground with a tackle; in him we have a remarkable instance of a dauntless stander-of-mast-heads; who was not to be driven from his place by fogs or frosts, rain, hail, or sleet; but valiantly facing everything out to the last, literally died at his post. Of modern standers-of-mast-heads we have but a lifeless set; mere stone, iron, and bronze men; who, though well capable of facing out a stiff gale, are still entirely incompetent to the business of singing out upon discovering any strange sight. There is Napoleon; who, upon the top of the column of Vendome, stands with arms folded, some one hundred and fifty feet in the air; careless, now, who rules the decks below; whether Louis Philippe, Louis Blanc, or Louis the Devil. Great Washington, too, stands high aloft on his towering main-mast in Baltimore, and like one of Hercules' pillars, his column marks that point of human gran-deur beyond which few mortals will go. Admiral Nelson, also, on a capstan of gun-metal, stands his mast-head in Trafalgar Square; and ever when most obscured by that London smoke, token is yet given that a hidden hero is there; for where there is smoke, must be fire. But neither great Washington, nor Napoleon, nor Nelson, will answer a single hail from below, however madly invoked to befriend by their counsels the distracted decks upon which they gaze; however it may be surmised, that their spirits penetrate through the thick haze of the future, and descry what shoals and what rocks must be shunned.

It may seem unwarrantable to couple in any respect the mast-head standers of the land with those of the sea; but that in truth it is not so, is plainly evinced by an item for which Obed Macy, the sole historian of Nantucket, stands account-able. The worthy Obed tells us, that in the early times of the whale fishery, ere ships were regularly launched in pursuit of the game, the people of that island erected lofty spars along the sea-coast, to which the look-outs ascended by means of nailed cleats, something as fowls go upstairs in a hen-house. A few years ago this same plan was adopted by the Bay whalemen of New Zealand, who, upon descrying the game, gave notice to the ready-manned boats nigh the beach. But this custom has now become obsolete; turn we then to the one proper mast-head, that of a whale-ship at sea.

nor even move out of it, without running great risk of perishing (like an igno-rant pilgrim crossing the snowy Alps in winter);   You cannot put a shelf or chest of drawers in your body, and no more can you make a convenient closet of your watch-coat.

, and holding that if we call our own children after our own names (we fathers being the original inventors and patentees), so likewise should we denominate after ourselves any other apparatus we may beget.   When Captain Sleet in person stood his mast-head in this crow's-nest of his, he tells us that he always had a rifle with him (also fixed in the rack), together with a powder flask and shot, for the purpose of popping off the stray narwhales, or vagrant sea unicorns infesting those waters; for you cannot successfully shoot at them from the deck owing to the resistance of the water, but to shoot down upon them is a very dif-ferent thing. Now, it was plainly a labor of love for Captain Sleet to describe, as he does, all the little detailed conveniences of his crow's-nest; but though he so enlarges upon many of these, and though he treats us to a very scientific account of his experiments in this crow's-nest, with a small compass he kept there for the purpose of counteracting the errors resulting from what is called the "local attraction" of all binnacle magnets; an error ascribable to the horizontal vicinity of the iron in the ship's planks, and in the Glacier's case, perhaps, to there having been so many broken-down blacksmiths among her crew; I say, that though the Captain is very discreet and scientific here, yet, for all his learned "binnacle deviations," "azimuth compass observations," and "approximate errors," he knows very well, Captain Sleet, that he was not so much immersed in those profound magnetic meditations, as to fail being attracted occasionally towards   in on one side of his crow's nest,   of his hand. Though, upon the whole, I greatly admire and even love the brave, the honest, and learned Captain; yet I take it very ill of him that he should so utterly ignore that case-bottle, seeing   , while with mittened fingers and hooded head he was studying the mathematics aloft there in that bird's nest within three or four perches of the pole.

; then ascending a little way further, and throwing a lazy leg over the top-sail yard, take a preliminary view of the watery pastures, and so at last mount to my ultimate destination

; and who offers to ship with the Phaedon instead of Bowditch in his head   , melancholy,   carking

Very often do the captains of such ships take those absent-minded young philosophers to task, upbraiding them with not feeling sufficient "interest" in the voyage; half-hinting that they are so hopelessly lost to all honorable ambition, as that in their secret souls they would rather not see whales than otherwise. But all in vain; those young Platonists have a notion that their vision is imperfect; they are short-sighted; what use, then, to strain the visual nerve? They have left their opera-glasses at home.

"Why, thou monkey," said a harpooneer to one of these lads, "we've been cruising now hard upon three years, and thou hast not raised a whale yet.

Whales are scarce as hen's teeth whenever thou art up here." Perhaps they were; or perhaps there might have been shoals of them in the far horizon; but lulled into such an opium-like listlessness of vacant, unconscious reverie is this absent-minded youth by the blending cadence of waves with thoughts, that at last he loses his identity; takes the mystic ocean at his feet for the visible image of that deep, blue, bottomless soul, pervading mankind and nature; and every strange, half-seen, gliding, beautiful thing that eludes him; every dimly-discovered, uprising fin of some undiscernible form, seems to him the embodiment of those elusive thoughts that only people the soul by continually flitting through it. In this enchanted mood, thy spirit ebbs away to whence it came; becomes diffused through time and space; like Crammer's sprinkled Pantheistic ashes, forming at last a part of every shore the round globe over.

There is no life in thee, now, except that rocking life imparted by a gently rolling ship; by her, borrowed from the sea; by the sea, from the inscrutable tides of God. But while this sleep, this dream is on ye, move your foot or hand an inch; slip your hold at all; and your identity comes back in horror. Over Descartian vortices you hover. And perhaps, at mid-day, in the fairest weather, with one half-throttled shriek you drop through that transparent air into the summer sea, no more to rise for ever. Heed it well, ye Pantheists!

CHAPTER 36

The Quarter-Deck

(Enter Ahab: Then, all)

It was not a great while after the affair of the pipe, that

as to and fro he paced his old rounds,

now at the main-mast and now at the binnacle, so completely possessing him, indeed, that it all but seemed the inward mould of every outer movement with the same intense bigotry of purpose in his aspect

;   as though not a soul were nigh him   and half-slouched hat   —

observing the hearty animation into which his unexpected question had so magnetically thrown them

,

tightly,   —

with a high raised voice

", men"

"even for a parmacetty,"

as though uncorking a bottle

"after the great annual sheep-shearing"

thus far

"Madness!"

Ah, ye admonitions and warnings! why stay ye not when ye come? But rather are ye predictions than warnings, ye shadows! Yet not so much predictions from without, as verifications of the foregoing things within. For with little external to constrain us, the innermost necessities in our being, these still drive us on.

slowly going from one officer to the other,

CHAPTER 37

Sunset

(The cabin; by the stern windows; Ahab sitting alone, and gazing out.)

I leave a white and turbid wake; pale waters, paler cheeks, where'er I sail. The envious billows sidelong swell to whelm my track; let them; but first I pass.

Yonder, by ever-brimming goblet's rim, the warm waves blush like wine. The gold brow plumbs the blue. The diver sun—slow dived from noon—goes down; my soul mounts up! she wearies with her endless hill. Is, then, the crown too heavy that I wear? this Iron Crown of Lombardy. Yet is it bright with many a gem; I the wearer, see not its far flashings; but darkly feel that I wear that, that dazzlingly confounds. 'Tis iron—that I know—not gold. 'Tis split, too—that I feel; the jagged edge galls me so, my brain seems to beat against the solid metal; aye, steel skull, mine; the sort that needs no helmet in the most brain-battering fight!

Dry heat upon my brow? Oh! time was, when as the sunrise nobly spurred me, so the sunset soothed. No more. This lovely light, it lights not me; all loveliness is anguish to me, since I can ne'er enjoy. Gifted with the high perception, I lack the low, enjoying power; damned, most subtly and most malignantly! damned in the midst of Paradise! Good night—good night! *(waving his hand, he moves from the window.)*

'Twas not so hard a task. I thought to find one stubborn, at the least; but my one cogged circle fits into all their various wheels, and they revolve. Or, if you will, like so many ant-hills of powder, they all stand before me; and I their match. Oh, hard! that to fire others, the match itself must needs be wasting! What I've dared, I've willed; and what I've willed, I'll do! They think me mad—Starbuck does; but I'm demoniac, I am madness maddened! That wild madness that's only calm to comprehend itself! The prophecy was that I should be dismembered; and—Aye! I lost this leg. I now prophesy that I will dismember my dismemberer. Now, then, be the prophet and the fulfiller one. That's more than ye, ye great gods, ever were. I laugh and hoot at ye, ye cricket-players, ye pugilists, ye deaf Burkes and blinded Bendigoes! I will not say as schoolboys do to bullies—Take some one of your own size; don't pommel *me!* No, ye've knocked me down, and I am up again; but YE have run and hidden. Come forth from behind your cotton bags! I have no long gun to reach ye. Come, Ahab's compliments to ye; come and see if ye can swerve me. Swerve me? ye cannot swerve me, else ye swerve yourselves! man has ye there. Swerve me? The path to my fixed purpose is laid with iron rails, whereon my soul is grooved to run. Over unsounded gorges, through the rifled hearts of mountains, under torrents' beds, unerringly I rush! Naught's an obstacle, naught's an angle to the iron way!

CHAPTER 38

Dusk

CHAPTER 39

First Night-Watch

CHAPTER 40

Midnight, Forecastle

*   *   *   *   *

Chapter 41

Moby Dick

, though at intervals only,   of them   knowingly seen him; while the number who as yet had actually and   him, was small indeed. For, owing
to the large number of whale-cruisers; the disorderly way they were sprinkled
over the entire watery circumference, many of them adventurously pushing
their quest along solitary latitudes, so as seldom or never for a whole twelvemonth or more on a stretch, to encounter a single news-telling sail of any sort;
the inordinate length of each separate voyage; the irregularity of the times of
sailing from home; all these, with other circumstances, direct and indirect,
long obstructed the spread through the whole world-wide whaling-fleet of
the special individualizing tidings concerning   It was hardly to be doubted,
that   , at such or such a time, or on such or such a meridian,   to some
minds it was not an unfair presumption, I say, that the whale in question must
have been no other than Moby Dick.   as of late the Sperm Whale fishery
had been   and not unfrequent   ; therefore it was, that   for the most
part,   , as it were,   In that way, mostly, the disastrous encounter between
Ahab and the whale had hitherto been popularly regarded.

And as for those who, previously hearing of the White Whale, by chance
caught sight of him;   eventually

—as the smitten tree gives birth to its fungi; but, in maritime life, far more
than in that of terra firma, wild rumors abound, wherever there is any adequate reality for them to cling to. And as the sea surpasses the land in this
matter, so the whale fishery surpasses every other sort of maritime life, in
the wonderfulness and fearfulness of the rumors which sometimes circulate
there. For not only are whalemen as a body unexempt from that ignorance
and superstitiousness hereditary to all sailors; but of all sailors, they are by
all odds the most directly brought into contact with whatever is appallingly
astonishing in the sea; face to face they not only eye its greatest marvels, but,

hand to jaw, give battle to them. Alone, in such remotest waters, that though you sailed a thousand miles, and passed a thousand shores, you would not come to any chiseled hearth-stone, or aught hospitable beneath that part of the sun; in such latitudes and longitudes, pursuing too such a calling as he does, the whaleman is wrapped by influences all tending to make his fancy pregnant with many a mighty birth.

No wonder, then, that ever gathering volume from the mere transit over the widest watery spaces, the outblown rumors of the White Whale did in the end incorporate with themselves all manner of morbid hints, and half-formed foetal suggestions of supernatural agencies, which eventually invested Moby Dick with new terrors unborrowed from anything that visibly appears. So that in many cases such a panic did he finally strike, that few who by those rumors, at least, had heard of the White Whale, few of those hunters were willing to encounter the perils of his jaw.

But there were still other and more vital practical influences at work. Not even at the present day has the original prestige of the Sperm Whale, as fearfully distinguished from all other species of the leviathan, died out of the minds of the whalemen as a body. There are those this day among them, who, though intelligent and courageous enough in offering battle to the Greenland or Right whale, would perhaps—either from professional inexperience, or incompetency, or timidity, decline a contest with the Sperm Whale; at any rate, there are plenty of whalemen, especially among those whaling nations not sailing under the American flag, who have never hostilely encountered the Sperm Whale, but whose sole knowledge of the leviathan is restricted to the ignoble monster primitively pursued in the North; seated on their hatches, these men will hearken with a childish fireside interest and awe, to the wild, strange tales of Southern whaling. Nor is the pre-eminent tremendousness of the great Sperm Whale anywhere more feelingly comprehended, than on board of those prows which stem him.

And as if the now tested reality of his might had in former legendary times thrown its shadow before it; we find some book naturalists—Olassen and Povelson—declaring the Sperm Whale not only to be a consternation to every other creature in the sea, but also to be so incredibly ferocious as continually to be athirst for human blood. Nor even down to so late a time as Cuvier's, were these or almost similar impressions effaced. For in his Natural History, the Baron himself affirms that at sight of the Sperm Whale, all fish (sharks included) are "struck with the most lively terrors," and "often in the precipitancy of their flight dash themselves against the rocks with such violence as to cause instantaneous death." And however the general experiences in the fishery may amend such reports as these; yet in their full terribleness, even to the bloodthirsty item of Povelson, the superstitious belief in them is, in some vicissitudes of their vocation, revived in the minds of the hunters.

So that overawed by the rumors and portents concerning him, not a few of the fishermen recalled, in reference to Moby Dick, the earlier days of the Sperm Whale fishery, when it was oftentimes hard to induce long practised Right whalemen to embark in the perils of this new and daring warfare; such men protesting that although other leviathans might be hopefully pursued, yet to chase and point lance at such an apparition as the Sperm Whale was not for mortal man. That to attempt it, would be inevitably to be torn into a quick eternity. On this head, there are some remarkable documents that may be consulted.

Nevertheless, some there were, who even in the face of these things were ready to give chase to Moby Dick; and a still greater number who, chancing only to hear of him distantly and vaguely, without the specific details of any certain calamity, and without superstitious accompaniments, were sufficiently hardy not to flee from the battle if offered.

One of the wild suggestions referred to, as at last coming to be linked with the White Whale in the minds of the superstitiously inclined, was the unearthly conceit that Moby Dick was ubiquitous; that he had actually been encountered in opposite latitudes at one and the same instant of time.

Nor, credulous as such minds must have been, was this conceit altogether without some faint show of superstitious probability. For as the secrets of the currents in the seas have never yet been divulged, even to the most erudite research; so the hidden ways of the Sperm Whale when beneath the surface remain, in great part, unaccountable to his pursuers; and from time to time have originated the most curious and contradictory speculations regarding them, especially concerning the mystic modes whereby, after sounding to a great depth, he transports himself with such vast swiftness to the most widely distant points.

It is a thing well known to both American and English whale-ships, and as well a thing placed upon authoritative record years ago by Scoresby, that some whales have been captured far north in the Pacific, in whose bodies have been found the barbs of harpoons darted in the Greenland seas. Nor is it to be gainsaid, that in some of these instances it has been declared that the interval of time between the two assaults could not have exceeded very many days. Hence, by inference, it has been believed by some whalemen, that the Nor' West Passage, so long a problem to man, was never a problem to the whale. So that here, in the real living experience of living men, the prodigies related in old times of the inland Strello mountain in Portugal (near whose top there was said to be a lake in which the wrecks of ships floated up to the surface); and that still more wonderful story of the Arethusa fountain near Syracuse (whose waters were believed to have come from the Holy Land by an underground passage); these fabulous narrations are almost fully equalled by the realities of the whalemen.

Forced into familiarity, then, with such prodigies as these; and knowing that after repeated, intrepid assaults, the White Whale had escaped alive; it cannot be much matter of surprise that some whalemen should go still further in their superstitions; declaring Moby Dick not only ubiquitous, but immortal (for immortality is but ubiquity in time); that though groves of spears should be planted in his flanks, he would still swim away unharmed; or if indeed he should ever be made to spout thick blood, such a sight would be but a ghastly deception; for again in unensanguined billows hundreds of leagues away, his unsullied jet would once more be seen.

But   supernatural

, in most instances,

intangible   which has been from the beginning; to whose dominion even the modern Christians ascribe one-half of the worlds; which the ancient Ophites of the east reverenced in their statue devil;—   did not fall down and worship it like them; but   its idea

It is not probable that this monomania in him took its instant rise at the precise time of his bodily dismemberment. Then, in darting at the monster, knife in hand, he had but given loose to a sudden, passionate, corporal animosity; and when he received the stroke that tore him, he probably but felt the agonizing bodily laceration, but nothing more. Yet, when by this collision forced to turn towards home, and for long months of days and weeks, Ahab and anguish lay stretched together in one hammock, rounding in mid winter that dreary, howling Patagonian Cape; then it was, that his torn body and gashed soul bled into one another; and so interfusing, made him mad. That it was only then, on the homeward voyage, after the encounter, that the final monomania seized him, seems all but certain from the fact that, at intervals during the passage, he was a raving lunatic; and, though unlimbed of a leg, yet such vital strength yet lurked in his Egyptian chest, and was moreover intensified by his delirium, that his mates were forced to lace him fast, even there, as he sailed, raving in his hammock. In a strait-jacket, he swung to the mad rockings of the gales. And, when running into more sufferable latitudes, the ship, with mild stun'sails spread, floated across the tranquil tropics, and, to all appearances, the old man's delirium seemed left behind him with the Cape Horn swells, and he came forth from his dark den into the blessed light and air; even then, when he bore that firm, collected front, however pale, and issued his calm orders once again; and his mates thanked God the direful madness was now gone; even then, Ahab, in his hidden self, raved on. Human madness is oftentimes a cunning and most feline thing. When you think it fled, it may have but become transfigured into some still subtler form. Ahab's full lunacy subsided not, but deepeningly contracted; like the unabated Hudson, when that noble Northman flows narrowly, but unfathomably through the Highland gorge. But, as in his narrow-flowing monomania, not one jot of Ahab's broad madness had been left behind; so in that broad madness, not one jot of his great natural intellect had perished. That before living agent, now became the living instrument. If such a furious trope may stand, his special lunacy stormed his general sanity, and carried it, and turned all its concentred cannon upon its own mad mark; so that far from having lost his strength, Ahab, to that one end, did now possess a thousand fold more potency than ever he had sanely brought to bear upon any one reasonable object.

This is much; yet Ahab's larger, darker, deeper part remains unhinted. But vain to popularize profundities, and all truth is profound. Winding far down from within the very heart of this spiked Hotel de Cluny where we here stand—however grand and wonderful, now quit it;—and take your way, ye nobler, sadder souls, to those vast Roman halls of Thermes; where far beneath the fantastic towers of man's upper earth, his root of grandeur, his whole awful essence sits in bearded state; an antique buried beneath antiquities, and throned on torsoes! So with a broken throne, the great gods mock that captive king; so like a Caryatid, he patient sits, upholding on his frozen brow the piled entablatures of ages. Wind ye down there, ye prouder, sadder souls! question that proud, sad king! A family likeness! aye, he did beget ye, ye young exiled royalties; and from your grim sire only will the old State-secret come.

Now, in his heart, Ahab had some glimpse of this, namely: all my means are sane, my motive and my object mad. Yet without power to kill, or change, or shun the fact; he likewise knew that to mankind he did long dissemble; in some sort, did still. But that thing of his dissembling was only subject to his perceptibility, not to his will determinate. Nevertheless, so well did he succeed in that dissembling, that when with ivory leg he stepped ashore at last, no Nantucketer thought him otherwise than but naturally grieved, and that to the quick, with the terrible casualty which had overtaken him.

The report of his undeniable delirium at sea was likewise popularly ascribed to a kindred cause. And so too, all the added moodiness which always afterwards, to the very day of sailing in the Pequod on the present voyage, sat brooding on his brow. Nor is it so very unlikely, that far from distrusting his fitness for another whaling voyage, on account of such dark symptoms, the calculating people of that prudent isle were inclined to harbor the conceit, that for those very reasons he was all the better qualified and set on edge, for a pursuit so full of rage and wildness as the bloody hunt of whales. Gnawed within and scorched without, with the infixed, unrelenting fangs of some incurable idea; such an one, could he be found, would seem the very man to dart his iron and lift his lance against the most appalling of all brutes. Or, if for any reason thought to be corporeally incapacitated for that, yet such an one would seem superlatively competent to cheer and howl on his underlings to the attack. But be all this as it may, certain it is, that with the mad secret of his unabated rage bolted up and keyed in him, Ahab had purposely sailed upon the present voyage with the one only and all-engrossing object of hunting the White Whale. Had any one of his old acquaintances on shore but half dreamed of what was lurking in him then, how soon would their aghast and righteous souls have wrenched the ship from such a fiendish man! They were bent on profitable cruises, the profit to be counted down in dollars from the mint. He was intent on an audacious, immitigable, and supernatural revenge.

Here, then, was this grey-headed, ungodly old man, chasing with curses a Job's whale round the world, at the head of a crew, too, chiefly made up of mongrel renegades, and castaways, and cannibals—morally enfeebled also, by the incompetence of mere unaided virtue or right-mindedness in Starbuck, the invunerable jollity of indifference and recklessness in Stubb, and the pervading mediocrity in Flask. Such a crew, so officered, seemed specially picked and packed by some infernal fatality to help him to his monomaniac revenge. How it was that they so aboundingly responded to the old man's ire—by what evil magic their souls were possessed, that at times his hate seemed almost theirs; the White Whale as much their insufferable foe as his; how all this came to be—what the White Whale was to them, or how to their unconscious understandings, also, in some dim, unsuspected way, he might have seemed the gliding great demon of the seas of life,—all this to explain, would be to dive deeper than Ishmael can go. The subterranean miner that works in us all, how can one tell whither leads his shaft by the ever shifting, muffled sound of his pick? Who does not feel the irresistible arm drag? What skiff in tow of a seventy-four can stand still? For one, I gave myself up to the abandonment of the time and the place; but while yet all a-rush to encounter the whale, could see naught in that brute but the deadliest ill.

Chapter 42

The Whiteness of the Whale

What the white whale was to Ahab, has been hinted; what, at times, he was to me, as yet remains unsaid.

Aside from those more obvious considerations touching Moby Dick, which could not but occasionally awaken in any man's soul some alarm, there was another thought, or rather vague, nameless horror concerning him, which at times by its intensity completely overpowered all the rest; and yet so mystical and well nigh ineffable was it, that I almost despair of putting it in a comprehensible form. It was the whiteness of the whale that above all things appalled me. But how can I hope to explain myself here; and yet, in some dim, random way, explain myself I must, else all these chapters might be naught.

Though in many natural objects, whiteness refiningly enhances beauty, as if imparting some special virtue of its own, as in marbles, japonicas, and pearls; and though various nations have in some way recognized a certain royal pre-eminence in this hue; even the barbaric, grand old kings of Pegu placing the title "Lord of the White Elephants" above all their other magniloquent ascriptions of dominion; and the modern kings of Siam unfurling the same snow-white quadruped in the royal standard; and the Hanoverian flag bearing the one figure of a snow-white charger; and the great Austrian Empire, Caesarian, heir to overlording Rome, having for the imperial color the same imperial hue; and though this pre-eminence in it applies to the human race itself, giving the white man ideal mastership over every dusky tribe; and though, besides, all this, whiteness has been even made significant of gladness, for among the Romans a white stone marked a joyful day; and though in other mortal sympathies and symbolizings, this same hue is made the emblem of many touching, noble things—the innocence of brides, the benignity of age; though among the Red Men of America the giving of the white belt of wampum was the deepest pledge of honor; though in many climes, whiteness typifies the majesty of Justice in the ermine of the Judge, and contributes to the daily state of kings and queens drawn by milk-white steeds; though even in the higher mysteries of the most august religions it has been made the symbol of the divine spotlessness and power; by the Persian fire worshippers, the white forked flame being held the holiest on the altar; and in the Greek mythologies, Great Jove himself being made incarnate in a snow-white bull; and though to the noble Iroquois, the midwinter sacrifice of the sacred White Dog was by far the holiest festival of their theology, that spotless, faithful creature being held the purest envoy they could send to the Great Spirit with the annual tidings of their own fidelity; and though directly from the Latin word for white, all Christian priests derive the name of one part of their sacred vesture, the alb or tunic, worn beneath the cassock; and though among the holy pomps of the Romish faith, white is specially employed in the celebration of the Passion of our Lord; though in the Vision of St. John, white robes are given to the redeemed, and the four-and-twenty elders stand clothed in white before the great-white throne, and the Holy One that sitteth there white like wool; yet for all these accumulated associations, with whatever is sweet, and honorable, and sublime, there yet lurks an elusive something in the innermost idea of this hue, which strikes more of panic to the soul than that redness which affrights in blood.

This elusive quality it is, which causes the thought of whiteness, when divorced from more kindly associations, and coupled with any object terrible in itself, to heighten that terror to the furthest bounds. Witness the white bear of the poles, and the white shark of the tropics; what but their smooth, flaky whiteness makes them the transcendent horrors they are? That ghastly whiteness it is which imparts such an abhorrent mildness, even more loathsome than terrific, to the dumb gloating of their aspect. So that not the fierce-fanged tiger in his heraldic coat can so stagger courage as the white-shrouded bear or shark.*

---

* With reference to the Polar bear, it may possibly be urged by him who would fain go still deeper into this matter, that it is not the whiteness, separately regarded, which heightens the intolerable hideousness of that brute; for, analysed, that heightened hideousness, it might be said, only rises from the circumstance, that the irresponsible ferociousness of the creature stands invested in the fleece of celestial innocence and love; and hence, by bringing together two such opposite emotions in our minds, the Polar bear frightens us with so unnatural a contrast. But even assuming all this to be true; yet, were it not for the whiteness, you would not have that intensified terror.

As for the white shark, the white gliding ghostliness of repose in that creature, when beheld in his ordinary moods, strangely tallies with the same quality in the Polar quadruped. This peculiarity is most vividly hit by the French in the name they bestow upon that fish. The Romish mass for the dead begins with "Requiem eternam" (eternal rest), whence *Requiem* denominating the mass itself, and any other funeral music. Now, in allusion to the white, silent stillness of death in this shark, and the mild deadliness of his habits, the French call him *Requin*.

Bethink thee of the albatross, whence come those clouds of spiritual wonderment and pale dread, in which that white phantom sails in all imaginations? Not Coleridge first threw that spell; but God's great, unflattering laureate, Nature.*

Most famous in our Western annals and Indian traditions is that of the White Steed of the Prairies; a magnificent milk-white charger, large-eyed, small-headed, bluff-chested, and with the dignity of a thousand monarchs in his lofty, overscorning carriage. He was the elected Xerxes of vast herds of wild horses, whose pastures in those days were only fenced by the Rocky Moun-

---

* I remember the first albatross I ever saw. It was during a prolonged gale, in waters hard upon the Antarctic seas. From my forenoon watch below, I ascended to the over-clouded deck; and there, dashed upon the main hatches, I saw a regal, feathery thing of unspotted whiteness, and with a hooked, Roman bill sublime. At intervals, it arched forth its vast archangel wings, as if to embrace some holy ark. Wondrous flutterings and throbbings shook it. Though bodily unharmed, it uttered cries, as some king's ghost in supernatural distress. Through its inexpressible, strange eyes, methought I peeped to secrets which took hold of God. As Abraham before the angels, I bowed myself; the white thing was so white, its wings so wide, and in those for ever exiled waters, I had lost the miserable warping memories of traditions and of towns. Long I gazed at that prodigy of plumage. I cannot tell, can only hint, the things that darted through me then. But at last I awoke; and turning, asked a sailor what bird was this. A goney, he replied. Goney! never had heard that name before; is it conceivable that this glorious thing is utterly unknown to men ashore! never! But some time after, I learned that goney was some seaman's name for albatross. So that by no possibility could Coleridge's wild Rhyme have had aught to do with those mystical impressions which were mine, when I saw that bird upon our deck. For neither had I then read the Rhyme, nor knew the bird to be an albatross. Yet, in saying this, I do but indirectly burnish a little brighter the noble merit of the poem and the poet.

I assert, then, that in the wondrous bodily whiteness of the bird chiefly lurks the secret of the spell; a truth the more evinced in this, that by a solecism of terms there are birds called grey albatrosses; and these I have frequently seen, but never with such emotions as when I beheld the Antarctic fowl.

But how had the mystic thing been caught? Whisper it not, and I will tell; with a treacherous hook and line, as the fowl floated on the sea. At last the Captain made a postman of it; tying a lettered, leathern tally round its neck, with the ship's time and place; and then letting it escape. But I doubt not, that leathern tally, meant for man, was taken off in Heaven, when the white fowl flew to join the wing-folding, the invoking, and adoring cherubim!

tains and the Alleghanies. At their flaming head he westward trooped it like that chosen star which every evening leads on the hosts of light. The flashing cascade of his mane, the curving comet of his tail, invested him with housings more resplendent than gold and silver-beaters could have furnished him. A most imperial and archangelical apparition of that unfallen, western world, which to the eyes of the old trappers and hunters revived the glories of those primeval times when Adam walked majestic as a god, bluff-browed and fearless as this mighty steed. Whether marching amid his aides and marshals in the van of countless cohorts that endlessly streamed it over the plains, like an Ohio; or whether with his circumambient subjects browsing all around at the horizon, the White Steed gallopingly reviewed them with warm nostrils reddening through his cool milkiness; in whatever aspect he presented himself, always to the bravest Indians he was the object of trembling reverence and awe. Nor can it be questioned from what stands on legendary record of this noble horse, that it was his spiritual whiteness chiefly, which so clothed him with divineness; and that this divineness had that in it which, though commanding worship, at the same time enforced a certain nameless terror.

But there are other instances where this whiteness loses all that accessory and strange glory which invests it in the White Steed and Albatross.

What is it that in the Albino man so peculiarly repels and often shocks the eye, as that sometimes he is loathed by his own kith and kin! It is that whiteness which invests him, a thing expressed by the name he bears. The Albino is as well made as other men—has no substantive deformity—and yet this mere aspect of all-pervading whiteness makes him more strangely hideous than the ugliest abortion. Why should this be so?

Nor, in quite other aspects, does Nature in her least palpable but not the less malicious agencies, fail to enlist among her forces this crowning attribute of the terrible. From its snowy aspect, the gauntleted ghost of the Southern Seas has been denominated the White Squall. Nor, in some historic instances, has the art of human malice omitted so potent an auxiliary. How wildly it heightens the effect of that passage in Froissart, when, masked in the snowy symbol of their faction, the desperate White Hoods of Ghent murder their bailiff in the market-place!

Nor, in some things, does the common, hereditary experience of all mankind fail to bear witness to the supernaturalism of this hue. It cannot well be doubted, that the one visible quality in the aspect of the dead which most appals the gazer, is the marble pallor lingering there; as if indeed that pallor were as much like the badge of consternation in the other world, as of mortal trepidation here. And from that pallor of the dead, we borrow the expressive hue of the shroud in which we wrap them. Nor even in our superstitions do we fail to throw the same snowy mantle round our phantoms; all ghosts rising in a milk-white fog—Yea, while these terrors seize us, let us add, that even the king of terrors, when personified by the evangelist, rides on his pallid horse.

Therefore, in his other moods, symbolize whatever grand or gracious thing he will by whiteness, no man can deny that in its profoundest idealized significance it calls up a peculiar apparition to the soul.

But though without dissent this point be fixed, how is mortal man to account for it? To analyse it, would seem impossible. Can we, then, by the citation of some of those instances wherein this thing of whiteness—though for the time either wholly or in great part stripped of all direct associations calculated to impart to it aught fearful, but nevertheless, is found to exert over us the same sorcery, however modified;—can we thus hope to light upon some chance clue to conduct us to the hidden cause we seek?

Let us try. But in a matter like this, subtlety appeals to subtlety, and without imagination no man can follow another into these halls. And though, doubtless, some at least of the imaginative impressions about to be presented may have been shared by most men, yet few perhaps were entirely conscious of them at the time, and therefore may not be able to recall them now.

Why to the man of untutored ideality, who happens to be but loosely acquainted with the peculiar character of the day, does the bare mention of Whitsuntide marshal in the fancy such long, dreary, speechless processions of slow-pacing pilgrims, down-cast and hooded with new-fallen snow? Or, to the unread, unsophisticated Protestant of the Middle American States, why does the passing mention of a White Friar or a White Nun, evoke such an eyeless statue in the soul?

Or what is there apart from the traditions of dungeoned warriors and kings (which will not wholly account for it) that makes the White Tower of London tell so much more strongly on the imagination of an untravelled American, than those other storied structures, its neighbors—the Byward Tower, or even the Bloody? And those sublimer towers, the White Mountains of New Hampshire, whence, in peculiar moods, comes that gigantic ghostliness over the soul at the bare mention of that name, while the thought of Virginia's Blue Ridge is full of a soft, dewy, distant dreaminess? Or why, irrespective of all latitudes and longitudes, does the name of the White Sea exert such a spectralness over the fancy, while that of the Yellow Sea lulls us with mortal thoughts of long lacquered mild afternoons on the waves, followed by the gaudiest and yet sleepiest of sunsets? Or, to choose a wholly unsubstantial instance, purely addressed to the fancy, why, in reading the old fairy tales of Central Europe, does "the tall pale man" of the Hartz forests, whose changeless pallor unrustlingly glides through the green of the groves—why is this phantom more terrible than all the whooping imps of the Blocksburg?

Nor is it, altogether, the remembrance of her cathedral-toppling earthquakes; nor the stampedoes of her frantic seas; nor the tearlessness of arid skies that never rain; nor the sight of her wide field of leaning spires, wrenched copestones, and crosses all adroop (like canted yards of anchored fleets); and her suburban avenues of house-walls lying over upon each other, as a tossed pack of cards;—it is not these things alone which make tearless Lima, the strangest, saddest city thou can'st see. For Lima has taken the white veil; and there is a higher horror in this whiteness of her woe. Old as Pizarro, this whiteness keeps her ruins for ever new; admits not the cheerful greenness of complete decay; spreads over her broken ramparts the rigid pallor of an apoplexy that fixes its own distortions.

I know that, to the common apprehension, this phenomenon of whiteness is not confessed to be the prime agent in exaggerating the terror of objects otherwise terrible; nor to the unimaginative mind is there aught of terror in those appearances whose awfulness to another mind almost solely consists in this one phenomenon, especially when exhibited under any form at all approaching to muteness or universality. What I mean by these two statements may perhaps be respectively elucidated by the following examples.

First: The mariner, when drawing nigh the coasts of foreign lands, if by night he hear the roar of breakers, starts to vigilance, and feels just enough of trepidation to sharpen all his faculties; but under precisely similar circumstances, let him be called from his hammock to view his ship sailing through a midnight sea of milky whiteness—as if from encircling headlands shoals of combed white bears were swimming round him, then he feels a silent, superstitious dread; the shrouded phantom of the whitened waters is horrible to him as a real ghost; in vain the lead assures him he is still off soundings; heart and helm they both go down; he never rests till blue water is under him again. Yet where is the mariner who will tell thee, "Sir, it was not so much the fear of striking hidden rocks, as the fear of that hideous whiteness that so stirred me?"

Second: To the native Indian of Peru, the continual sight of the snowhowdahed Andes conveys naught of dread, except, perhaps, in the mere fancying of the eternal frosted desolateness reigning at such vast altitudes, and the natural conceit of what a fearfulness it would be to lose oneself in such inhuman solitudes. Much the same is it with the backwoodsman of the West, who with comparative indifference views an unbounded prairie sheeted with driven snow, no shadow of tree or twig to break the fixed trance of whiteness. Not so the sailor, beholding the scenery of the Antarctic seas; where at times, by some infernal trick of legerdemain in the powers of frost and air, he, shivering and half shipwrecked, instead of rainbows speaking hope and solace to his misery, views what seems a boundless churchyard grinning upon him with its lean ice monuments and splintered crosses.

But thou sayest, methinks that white-lead chapter about whiteness is but a white flag hung out from a craven soul; thou surrenderest to a hypo, Ishmael.

Tell me, why this strong young colt, foaled in some peaceful valley of Vermont, far removed from all beasts of prey—why is it that upon the sunniest day, if you but shake a fresh buffalo robe behind him, so that he cannot even see it, but only smells its wild animal muskiness—why will he start, snort, and with bursting eyes paw the ground in phrensies of affright? There is no remembrance in him of any gorings of wild creatures in his green northern home, so that the strange muskiness he smells cannot recall to him anything associated with the experience of former perils; for what knows he, this New England colt, of the black bisons of distant Oregon?

No; but here thou beholdest even in a dumb brute, the instinct of the knowledge of the demonism in the world. Though thousands of miles from Oregon, still when he smells that savage musk, the rending, goring bison herds are as present as to the deserted wild foal of the prairies, which this instant they may be trampling into dust.

Thus, then, the muffled rollings of a milky sea; the bleak rustlings of the festooned frosts of mountains; the desolate shiftings of the windrowed snows of prairies; all these, to Ishmael, are as the shaking of that buffalo robe to the frightened colt!

Though neither knows where lie the nameless things of which the mystic sign gives forth such hints; yet with me, as with the colt, somewhere those things must exist. Though in many of its aspects this visible world seems formed in love, the invisible spheres were formed in fright.

But not yet have we solved the incantation of this whiteness, and learned why it appeals with such power to the soul; and more strange and far more portentous—why, as we have seen, it is at once the most meaning symbol of spiritual things, nay, the very veil of the Christian's Deity; and yet should be as it is, the intensifying agent in things the most appalling to mankind.

Is it that by its indefiniteness it shadows forth the heartless voids and immensities of the universe, and thus stabs us from behind with the thought of annihilation, when beholding the white depths of the milky way? Or is it, that as in essence whiteness is not so much a color as the visible absence of color; and at the same time the concrete of all colors; is it for these reasons that there is such a dumb blankness, full of meaning, in a wide landscape of snows—a colorless, all-color of atheism from which we shrink? And when we consider that other theory of the natural philosophers, that all other earthly hues—every stately or lovely emblazoning—the sweet tinges of sunset skies and woods; yea, and the gilded velvets of butterflies, and the butterfly cheeks of young girls; all these are but subtile deceits, not actually inherent in substances, but only laid on from without; so that all deified Nature absolutely paints like the harlot, whose allurements cover nothing but the charnel-house within; and when we proceed further, and consider that the mystical cosmetic which produces every one of her hues, the great principle of light, for ever remains white or colorless in itself, and if operating without medium upon matter, would touch all objects, even tulips and roses, with its own blank tinge—pondering all this, the palsied universe lies before us a leper; and like wilful travellers in Lapland, who refuse to wear colored and coloring glasses upon their eyes, so the wretched infidel gazes himself blind at the monumental white shroud that wraps all the prospect around him. And of all these things the Albino whale was the symbol. Wonder ye then at the fiery hunt?

CHAPTER 43

Hark!

CHAPTER 44

The Chart

,

So assured, indeed, is the fact concerning the periodicalness of the sperm whale's resorting to given waters, that many hunters believe that, could he be closely observed and studied throughout the world; were the logs for one voyage of the entire whale fleet carefully collated, then the migrations of the sperm whale would be found to correspond in invariability to those of the herring-shoals or the flights of swallows. On this hint, attempts have been made to construct elaborate migratory charts of the sperm whale.*

undeviating   Though,   the direction taken by any one whale be straight as a surveyor's parallel, and though the line of advance be strictly confined to its own unavoidable, straight wake, yet   arbitrary   (more or less, as the vein is presumed to expand or contract)

There was a circumstance which at first sight seemed to entangle his delirious but still methodical scheme. But not so in the reality, perhaps.   gregarious

---

*   Since the above was written, the statement is happily borne out by an official circular, issued by Lieutenant Maury, of the National Observatory, Washington, April 16th,
1851. By that circular, it appears that precisely such a chart is in course of completion;
and portions of it are presented in the circular. "This chart divides the ocean into districts of five degrees of latitude by five degrees of longitude; perpendicularly through
each of which districts are twelve columns for the twelve months; and horizontally
through each of which districts are three lines; one to show the number of days that
have been spent in each month in every district, and the two others to show the number of days in which whales, sperm or right, have been seen."

peculiar and   In general, the same remark, only within a less wide limit, applies to the solitaries and hermits among the matured, aged sperm whales. So that though Moby Dick had in a former year been seen, for example, on what is called the Seychelle ground in the Indian ocean, or Volcano Bay on the Japanese Coast; yet it did not follow, that were the Pequod to visit either of those spots at any subsequent corresponding season, she would infallibly encounter him there. So, too, with some other feeding grounds, where he had at times revealed himself. But all these seemed only his casual stopping-places and ocean-inns, so to speak, not his places of prolonged abode.   where

hitherto been spoken of, allusion has only been made to whatever wayside, antecedent, extra prospects were his, ere   particular set time or place were attained, when all possibilities would become probabilities, and, as Ahab fondly thought, every possibility the next thing to a certainty. That   were

But in the cautious comprehensiveness and unloitering vigilance with which Ahab threw his brooding soul into this unfaltering hunt, he would not permit himself to rest all his hopes upon the one crowning fact above mentioned, however flattering it might be to those hopes; nor in the sleeplessness of his vow could he so tranquillize his unquiet heart as to postpone all intervening quest.

devious

own

Often, when forced from his hammock by exhausting and intolerably vivid dreams of the night, which, resuming his own intense thoughts through the day, carried them on amid a clashing of phrensies, and whirled them round and round and round in his blazing brain, till the very throbbing of his life-spot became insufferable anguish; and when, as was sometimes the case, these spiritual throes in him heaved his being up from its base, and a chasm seemed opening in him, from which forked flames and lightnings shot up, and accursed fiends beckoned him to leap down among them; when this hell in himself yawned beneath him, a wild cry would be heard through the ship; and with glaring eyes Ahab would burst from his state room, as though escaping from a bed that was on fire. Yet these, perhaps, instead of being the unsuppressable symptoms of some latent weakness, or fright at his own resolve, were but the plainest tokens of its intensity. For, at such times,   the   ; this Ahab that had gone to his hammock, was not the agent that so caused him to burst from it in horror again. The latter was the eternal, living principle or soul in him; and in sleep, being for the time dissociated from the characterizing mind, which at other times employed it for its outer vehicle or agent, it spontaneously sought escape from the scorching contiguity of the frantic thing, of which, for the time, it was no longer an integral. But as the mind does not exist unless leagued with the soul, therefore it must have been that, in Ahab's case, yielding up all his thoughts and fancies to his one supreme purpose; that purpose, by its own sheer inveteracy of will, forced itself against gods and devils into a kind of self-assumed, independent being of its own. Nay, could grimly live and burn, while the common vitality to which it was conjoined, fled horror-stricken from the unbidden and unfathered birth. Therefore, the tormented spirit that glared out of bodily eyes, when what seemed Ahab rushed from his room, was for the time but a vacated thing, a formless somnambulistic being, a ray of living light, to be sure, but without an object to color, and therefore a blankness in itself

CHAPTER 45

The Affidavit

So far as what there may be of a narrative in this book; and, indeed, as indirectly touching one or two very interesting and curious particulars in the habits of sperm whales, the foregoing chapter, in its earlier part, is as important a one as will be found in this volume; but the leading matter of it requires to be still further and more familiarly enlarged upon, in order to be adequately understood, and moreover to take away any incredulity which a profound ignorance of the entire subject may induce in some minds, as to the natural verity of the main points of this affair.

I care not to perform this part of my task methodically; but shall be content to produce the desired impression by separate citations of items, practically or reliably known to me as a whaleman; and from these citations, I take it—the conclusion aimed at will naturally follow of itself.

First: I have personally known three instances where a whale, after receiving a harpoon, has effected a complete escape; and, after an interval (in one instance of three years), has been again struck by the same hand, and slain; when the two irons, both marked by the same private cypher, have been taken from the body. In the instance where three years intervened between the flinging of the two harpoons; and I think it may have been something more than that; the man who darted them happening, in the interval, to go in a trading ship on a voyage to Africa, went ashore there, joined a discovery party, and penetrated far into the interior, where he travelled for a period of nearly two years, often endangered by serpents, savages, tigers, poisonous miasmas, with all the other common perils incident to wandering in the heart of unknown regions. Meanwhile, the whale he had struck must also have been on its travels; no doubt it had thrice circumnavigated the globe, brushing with its flanks all the coasts of Africa; but to no purpose. This man and this whale again came together, and the one vanquished the other. I say I, myself, have known three instances similar to this; that is in two of them I saw the whales struck; and, upon the second attack, saw the two irons with the respective marks cut in them, afterwards taken from the dead fish. In the three-year instance, it so fell out that I was in the boat both times, first and last, and the last time distinctly recognized a peculiar sort of huge mole under the whale's eye, which I had observed there three years previous. I say three years, but I am pretty sure it was more than that. Here are three instances, then, which I personally know the truth of; but I have heard of many other instances from persons whose veracity in the matter there is no good ground to impeach.

Secondly: It is well known in the Sperm Whale Fishery, however ignorant the world ashore may be of it, that there have been several memorable historical instances where a particular whale in the ocean has been at distant times and places popularly cognisable. Why such a whale became thus marked was not altogether and originally owing to his bodily peculiarities as distinguished from other whales; for however peculiar in that respect any chance whale may be, they soon put an end to his peculiarities by killing him, and boiling him down into a peculiarly valuable oil. No: the reason was this: that from the fatal experiences of the fishery there hung a terrible prestige of perilousness about such a whale as there did about Rinaldo Rinaldini, insomuch that most fishermen were content to recognize him by merely touching their tarpaulins when he would be discovered lounging by them on the sea, without seeking to cultivate a more intimate acquaintance. Like some poor devils ashore that happen to know an irascible great man, they make distant unobtrusive saluta- tions to him in the street, lest if they pursued the acquaintance further, they might receive a summary thump for their presumption.

But not only did each of these famous whales enjoy great individual celeb- rity—Nay, you may call it an ocean-wide renown; not only was he famous in life and now is immortal in forecastle stories after death, but he was admitted into all the rights, privileges, and distinctions of a name; had as much a name indeed as Cambyses or Caesar. Was it not so, O Timor Tom! thou famed le- viathan, scarred like an iceberg, who so long did'st lurk in the Oriental straits of that name, whose spout was oft seen from the palmy beach of Ombay? Was it not so, O New Zealand Jack! thou terror of all cruisers that crossed their wakes in the vicinity of the Tattoo Land? Was it not so, O Morquan! King of Japan, whose lofty jet they say at times assumed the semblance of a snow- white cross against the sky? Was it not so, O Don Miguel! thou Chilian whale, marked like an old tortoise with mystic hieroglyphics upon the back! In plain prose, here are four whales as well known to the students of Cetacean History as Marius or Sylla to the classic scholar.

But this is not all. New Zealand Tom and Don Miguel, after at various times creating great havoc among the boats of different vessels, were finally gone in quest of, systematically hunted out, chased and killed by valiant whaling captains, who heaved up their anchors with that express object as much in view, as in setting out through the Narragansett Woods, Captain Butler of old had it in his mind to capture that notorious murderous savage Annawon, the headmost warrior of the Indian King Philip.

I do not know where I can find a better place than just here, to make mention of one or two other things, which to me seem important, as in printed form establishing in all respects the reasonableness of the whole story of the White Whale, more especially the catastrophe. For this is one of those disheartening instances where truth requires full as much bolstering as error. So ignorant are most landsmen of some of the plainest and most palpable wonders of the world, that without some hints touching the plain facts, historical and other-wise, of the fishery, they might scout at Moby Dick as a monstrous fable, or still worse and more detestable, a hideous and intolerable allegory.

First: Though most men have some vague flitting ideas of the general perils of the grand fishery, yet they have nothing like a fixed, vivid conception of those perils, and the frequency with which they recur. One reason perhaps is, that not one in fifty of the actual disasters and deaths by casualties in the fishery, ever finds a public record at home, however transient and immediately forgot-ten that record. Do you suppose that that poor fellow there, who this moment perhaps caught by the whale-line off the coast of New Guinea, is being carried down to the bottom of the sea by the sounding leviathan—do you suppose that that poor fellow's name will appear in the newspaper obituary you will read to-morrow at your breakfast? No: because the mails are very irregular between here and New Guinea. In fact, did you ever hear what might be called regular news direct or indirect from New Guinea? Yet I tell you that upon one particular voyage which I made to the Pacific, among many others we spoke thirty different ships, every one of which had had a death by a whale, some of them more than one, and three that had each lost a boat's crew. For God's sake, be economical with your lamps and candles! not a gallon you burn, but at least one drop of man's blood was spilled for it.

Secondly: People ashore have indeed some indefinite idea that a whale is an enormous creature of enormous power; but I have ever found that when narrating to them some specific example of this two-fold enormousness, they have significantly complimented me upon my facetiousness; when, I declare upon my soul, I had no more idea of being facetious than Moses, when he wrote the history of the plagues of Egypt.

But fortunately the special point I here seek can be established upon testimony entirely independent of my own. That point is this: The Sperm Whale is in some cases sufficiently powerful, knowing, and judiciously malicious, as with direct aforethought to stave in, utterly destroy, and sink a large ship; and what is more, the Sperm Whale *has* done it.

First: In the year 1820 the ship Essex, Captain Pollard, of Nantucket, was cruising in the Pacific Ocean. One day she saw spouts, lowered her boats, and gave chase to a shoal of sperm whales. Ere long, several of the whales were wounded; when, suddenly, a very large whale escaping from the boats, issued from the shoal, and bore directly down upon the ship. Dashing his forehead against her hull, he so stove her in, that in less than "ten minutes" she settled down and fell over. Not a surviving plank of her has been seen since. After the severest exposure, part of the crew reached the land in their boats. Being returned home at last, Captain Pollard once more sailed for the Pacific in command of another ship, but the gods shipwrecked him again upon unknown rocks and breakers; for the second time his ship was utterly lost, and forthwith forswearing the sea, he has never tempted it since. At this day Captain Pollard is a resident of Nantucket. I have seen Owen Chace, who was chief mate of the Essex at the time of the tragedy; I have read his plain and faithful narrative; I have conversed with his son; and all this within a few miles of the scene of the catastrophe.*

Secondly: The ship Union, also of Nantucket, was in the year 1807 totally lost off the Azores by a similar onset, but the authentic particulars of this catastrophe I have never chanced to encounter, though from the whale hunters I have now and then heard casual allusions to it.

Thirdly: Some eighteen or twenty years ago Commodore J——, then commanding an American sloop-of-war of the first class, happened to be dining with a party of whaling captains, on board a Nantucket ship in the harbor of Oahu, Sandwich Islands. Conversation turning upon whales,

---

*   The following are extracts from Chace's narrative: "Every fact seemed to warrant me in concluding that it was anything but chance which directed his operations; he made two several attacks upon the ship, at a short interval between them, both of which, according to their direction, were calculated to do us the most injury, by being made ahead, and thereby combining the speed of the two objects for the shock; to effect which, the exact manoeuvres which he made were necessary. His aspect was most horrible, and such as indicated resentment and fury. He came directly from the shoal which we had just before entered, and in which we had struck three of his companions, as if fired with revenge for their sufferings." Again: "At all events, the whole circumstances taken together, all happening before my own eyes, and producing, at the time, impressions in my mind of decided, calculating mischief, on the part of the whale (many of which impressions I cannot now recall), induce me to be satisfied that I am correct in my opinion."

Here are his reflections some time after quitting the ship, during a black night an open boat, when almost despairing of reaching any hospitable shore. "The dark ocean and swelling waters were nothing; the fears of being swallowed up by some dreadful tempest, or dashed upon hidden rocks, with all the other ordinary subjects of fearful contemplation, seemed scarcely entitled to a moment's thought; the dismal looking wreck, and *the horrid aspect and revenge of the whale*, wholly engrossed my reflections, until day again made its appearance."

In another place—p. 45,—he speaks of "*the mysterious and mortal attack of the animal.*"

*   *   *   *   *   *   *   *   *   *   *   *   *

*   *   *   *   *   *   *   *   *   *   *   *   *

the Commodore was pleased to be sceptical touching the amazing strength ascribed to them by the professional gentlemen present. He peremptorily denied for example, that any whale could so smite his stout sloop-of-war as to cause her to leak so much as a thimbleful. Very good; but there is more coming. Some weeks after, the Commodore set sail in this impregnable craft for Valparaiso. But he was stopped on the way by a portly sperm whale, that begged a few moments' confidential business with him. That business consisted in fetching the Commodore's craft such a thwack, that with all his pumps going he made straight for the nearest port to heave down and repair. I am not superstitious, but I consider the Commodore's interview with that whale as providential. Was not Saul of Tarsus converted from unbelief by a similar fright? I tell you, the sperm whale will stand no nonsense.

I will now refer you to Langsdorff's Voyages for a little circumstance in point, peculiarly interesting to the writer hereof. Langsdorff, you must know by the way, was attached to the Russian Admiral Krusenstern's famous Discovery Expedition in the beginning of the present century. Captain Langsdorff thus begins his seventeenth chapter:

"By the thirteenth of May our ship was ready to sail, and the next day we were out in the open sea, on our way to Ochotsh. The weather was very clear and fine, but so intolerably cold that we were obliged to keep on our fur clothing. For some days we had very little wind; it was not till the nineteenth that a brisk gale from the northwest sprang up. An uncommon large whale, the body of which was larger than the ship itself, lay almost at the surface of the water, but was not perceived by any one on board till the moment when the ship, which was in full sail, was almost upon him, so that it was impossible to prevent its striking against him. We were thus placed in the most imminent danger, as this gigantic creature, setting up its back, raised the ship three feet at least out of the water. The masts reeled, and the sails fell altogether, while we who were below all sprang instantly upon the deck, concluding that we had struck upon some rock; instead of this we saw the monster sailing off with the utmost gravity and solemnity. Captain D'Wolf applied immediately to the pumps to examine whether or not the vessel had received any damage from the shock, but we found that very happily it had escaped entirely uninjured."

Now, the Captain D'Wolf here alluded to as commanding the ship in question, is a New Englander, who, after a long life of unusual adventures as a sea-captain, this day resides in the village of Dorchester near Boston. I have the honor of being a nephew of his. I have particularly questioned him concerning this passage in Langsdorff. He substantiates every word. The ship, however, was by no means a large one: a Russian craft built on the Siberian coast, and purchased by my uncle after bartering away the vessel in which he sailed from home.

In that up and down manly book of old-fashioned adventure, so full, too, of honest wonders—the voyage of Lionel Wafer, one of ancient Dampier's old chums—I found a little matter set down so like that just quoted from Langsdorff, that I cannot forbear inserting it here for a corroborative example, if such be needed.

Lionel, it seems, was on his way to "John Ferdinando," as he calls the modern Juan Fernandes. "In our way thither," he says, "about four o'clock in the morning, when we were about one hundred and fifty leagues from the Main of America, our ship felt a terrible shock, which put our men in such consternation that they could hardly tell where they were or what to think; but every one began to prepare for death. And, indeed, the shock was so sudden and violent, that we took it for granted the ship had struck against a rock; but when the amazement was a little over, we cast the lead, and sounded, but found no ground. * * * * * The suddenness of the shock made the guns leap in their carriages, and several of the men were shaken out of their hammocks. Captain Davis, who lay with his head on a gun, was thrown out of his cabin!" Lionel then goes on to impute the shock to an earthquake, and seems to substantiate the imputation by stating that a great earthquake, somewhere about that time, did actually do great mischief along the Spanish land. But I should not much wonder if, in the darkness of that early hour of the morning, the shock was after all caused by an unseen whale vertically bumping the hull from beneath.

I might proceed with several more examples, one way or another known to me, of the great power and malice at times of the sperm whale. In more than one instance, he has been known, not only to chase the assailing boats back to their ships, but to pursue the ship itself, and long withstand all the lances hurled at him from its decks. The English ship Pusie Hall can tell a story on that head; and, as for his strength, let me say, that there have been examples where the lines attached to a running sperm whale have, in a calm, been transferred to the ship, and secured there; the whale towing her great hull through the water, as a horse walks off with a cart. Again, it is very often observed that, if the sperm whale, once struck, is allowed time to rally, he then acts, not so often with blind rage, as with wilful, deliberate designs of destruction to his pursuers; nor is it without conveying some eloquent indication of his character, that upon being attacked he will frequently open his mouth, and retain it in that dread expansion for several consecutive minutes. But I must be content with only one more and a concluding illustration; a remarkable and most significant one, by which you will not fail to see, that not only is the most marvellous event in this book corroborated by plain facts of the present day, but that these marvels (like all marvels) are mere repetitions of the ages; so that for the millionth time we say amen with Solomon—Verily there is nothing new under the sun.

In the sixth Christian century lived Procopius, a Christian magistrate of Constantinople, in the days when Justinian was Emperor and Belisarius general. As many know, he wrote the history of his own times, a work every way of uncommon value. By the best authorities, he has always been considered a most trustworthy and unexaggerating historian, except in some one or two particulars, not at all affecting the matter presently to be mentioned.

Now, in this history of his, Procopius mentions that, during the term of his prefecture at Constantinople, a great sea-monster was captured in the neighboring Propontis, or Sea of Marmora, after having destroyed vessels at intervals in those waters for a period of more than fifty years. A fact thus set down in substantial history cannot easily be gainsaid. Nor is there any reason it should be. Of what precise species this sea-monster was, is not mentioned. But as he destroyed ships, as well as for other reasons, he must have been a whale; and I am strongly inclined to think a sperm whale. And I will tell you why. For a long time I fancied that the sperm whale had been always unknown in the Mediterranean and the deep waters connecting with it. Even now I am certain that those seas are not, and perhaps never can be, in the present constitution of things, a place for his habitual gregarious resort. But further investigations have recently proved to me, that in modern times there have been isolated instances of the presence of the sperm whale in the Mediterranean. I am told, on good authority, that on the Barbary coast, a Commodore Davis of the British navy found the skeleton of a sperm whale. Now, as a vessel of war readily passes through the Dardanelles, hence a sperm whale could, by the same route, pass out of the Mediterranean into the Propontis.

In the Propontis, as far as I can learn, none of that peculiar substance called *brit* is to be found, the aliment of the right whale. But I have every reason to believe that the food of the sperm whale—squid or cuttle-fish—lurks at the bottom of that sea, because large creatures, but by no means the largest of that sort, have been found at its surface. If, then, you properly put these statements together, and reason upon them a bit, you will clearly perceive that, according to all human reasoning, Procopius's sea-monster, that for half a century stove the ships of a Roman Emperor, must in all probability have been a sperm whale.

Chapter 46

Surmises

and impetuously   savage

and others perhaps too analytic to be verbally developed here,

Chapter 47

The Mat-Maker

: I say   strange   , that it seemed as if this were the Loom of Time, and I myself were a shuttle mechanically weaving and weaving away at the Fates. There lay the fixed threads of the warp subject to but one single, ever returning, unchanging vibration, and that vibration merely enough to admit of the crosswise interblending of other threads with its own. This warp seemed necessity; and here, thought I, with my own hand I ply my own shuttle and weave my own destiny into these unalterable threads. Meantime, Queequeg's impulsive, indifferent sword, sometimes hitting the woof slantingly, or crookedly, or strongly, or weakly, as the case might be; and by this difference in the concluding blow producing a corresponding contrast in the final aspect of the completed fabric; this savage's sword, thought I, which thus finally shapes and fashions both warp and woof; this easy, indifferent sword must be chance—aye, chance, free will, and necessity—nowise incompatible—all interweavingly working together. The straight warp of necessity, not to be swerved from its ultimate course—its every alternating vibration, indeed, only tending to that; free will still free to ply her shuttle between given threads; and chance, though restrained in its play within the right lines of necessity, and sideways in its motions directed by free will, though thus prescribed to by both, chance by turns rules either, and has the last featuring blow at events.

*   *   *   *   *

like a wand,   brief sudden   To be sure the same sound was that very moment perhaps being heard all over the seas, from hundreds of whalemen's look-outs perched as high in the air; but from few of those lungs could that accustomed old cry have derived such a marvellous cadence as from Tashtego the Indian's.

"she blows!"

CHAPTER 48

The First Lowering

—   ragamuffin

curiously

for a minute or so

"larboard boat there, ahoy!"

Though truly vivacious, tumultuous, ostentatious little Flask would now and then stamp with impatience; but not one added heave did he thereby give to the negro's lordly chest. So have I seen Passion and Vanity stamping the living magnanimous earth, but the earth did not alter her tides and her seasons for that.

,

lowest possible but

unlighted

—

;

Chapter 49

The Hyena

There are certain queer times and occasions in this strange mixed affair we call life when a man takes this whole universe for a vast practical joke, though the wit thereof he but dimly discerns, and more than suspects that the joke is at nobody's expense but his own. However, nothing dispirits, and nothing seems worth while disputing. He bolts down all events, all creeds, and beliefs, and persuasions, all hard things visible and invisible, never mind how knobby; as an ostrich of potent digestion gobbles down bullets and gun flints. And as for small difficulties and worryings, prospects of sudden disaster, peril of life and limb; all these, and death itself, seem to him only sly, good-natured hits, and jolly punches in the side bestowed by the unseen and unaccountable old joker. That odd sort of wayward mood I am speaking of, comes over a man only in some time of extreme tribulation; it comes in the very midst of his earnestness, so that what just before might have seemed to him a thing most momentous, now seems but a part of the general joke. There is nothing like the perils of whaling to breed this free and easy sort of genial, desperado philosophy; and with it I now regarded this whole voyage of the Pequod, and the great White Whale its object.

"Queequeg," said I, when they had dragged me, the last man, to the deck, and I was still shaking myself in my jacket to fling off the water; "Queequeg, my fine friend, does this sort of thing often happen?" Without much emotion, though soaked through just like me, he gave me to understand that such things did often happen.

"Mr. Stubb," said I, turning to that worthy, who, buttoned up in his oil-jacket, was now calmly smoking his pipe in the rain; "Mr. Stubb, I think I have heard you say that of all whalemen you ever met, our chief mate, Mr. Starbuck, is by far the most careful and prudent. I suppose then, that going plump on a flying whale with your sail set in a foggy squall is the height of a whaleman's discretion?"

"Certain. I've lowered for whales from a leaking ship in a gale off Cape Horn."

"Mr. Flask," said I, turning to little King-Post, who was standing close by; "you are experienced in these things, and I am not. Will you tell me whether it is an unalterable law in this fishery, Mr. Flask, for an oarsman to break his own back pulling himself back-foremost into death's jaws?"

"Can't you twist that smaller?" said Flask. "Yes, that's the law. I should like to see a boat's crew backing water up to a whale face foremost. Ha, ha! the whale would give them squint for squint, mind that!"

Here then, from three impartial witnesses, I had a deliberate statement of the entire case. Considering, therefore, that squalls and capsizings in the water and consequent bivouacks on the deep, were matters of common occurrence in this kind of life; considering that at the superlatively critical instant of going on to the whale I must resign my life into the hands of him who steered the boat—oftentimes a fellow who at that very moment is in his impetuousness upon the point of scuttling the craft with his own frantic stampings; considering that the particular disaster to our own particular boat was chiefly to be imputed to Starbuck's driving on to his whale almost in the teeth of a squall, and considering that Starbuck, notwithstanding, was famous for his great heedfulness in the fishery; considering that I belonged to this uncommonly prudent Starbuck's boat; and finally considering in what a devil's chase I was implicated, touching the White Whale: taking all things together, I say, I thought I might as well go below and make a rough draft of my will. "Queequeg," said I, "come along, you shall be my lawyer, executor, and legatee."

It may seem strange that of all men sailors should be tinkering at their last wills and testaments, but there are no people in the world more fond of that diversion. This was the fourth time in my nautical life that I had done the same thing. After the ceremony was concluded upon the present occasion, I felt all the easier; a stone was rolled away from my heart. Besides, all the days I should now live would be as good as the days that Lazarus lived after his resurrection; a supplementary clean gain of so many months or weeks as the case might be. I survived myself; my death and burial were locked up in my chest. I looked round me tranquilly and contentedly, like a quiet ghost with a clean conscience sitting inside the bars of a snug family vault.

Now then, thought I, unconsciously rolling up the sleeves of my frock, here goes for a cool, collected dive at death and destruction, and the devil fetch the hindmost.

CHAPTER 50

Ahab's Boat and Crew • Fedallah

*   *   *   *   *

So Tamerlane's soldiers often argued with tears in their eyes, whether that invaluable life of his ought to be carried into the thickest of the fight.

Considering that with two legs man is but a hobbling wight in all times of danger;

CHAPTER 51

The Spirit-Spout

distinct

Even when wearied nature seemed demanding repose he would not seek that
repose in his hammock.   ,   *

CHAPTER 52

The Albatross

"— —"

,

,

CHAPTER 53

The Gam

Though, to be sure, from the small number of English whalers, such meetings
do not very often occur, and when they do occur there is too apt to be a sort
of shyness between them; for your Englishman is rather reserved, and your
Yankee, he does not fancy that sort of thing in anybody but himself. Besides,
the English whalers sometimes affect a kind of metropolitan superiority over
the American whalers; regarding the long, lean Nantucketer, with his non-

---

* The cabin-compass is called the tell-tale, because without going to the compass at
the helm, the Captain, while below, can inform himself of the course of the ship.

descript provincialisms, as a sort of sea-peasant. But where this superiority in the English whalemen does really consist, it would be hard to say, seeing that the Yankees in one day, collectively, kill more whales than all the English, collectively, in ten years. But this is a harmless little foible in the English whale-hunters, which the Nantucketer does not take much to heart; probably, because he knows that he has a few foibles himself.

; and if by chance they should hear of it, they only grin at it, and repeat gamesome stuff about "spouters" and "blubber-boilers," and such like pretty exclamations Why it is that all Merchant-seamen, and also all Pirates and Man-of-War's men, and Slave-ship sailors, cherish such a scornful feeling towards Whale-ships; this is a question it would be hard to answer. Because, in the case of pirates, say, I should like to know whether that profession of theirs has any peculiar glory about it. It sometimes ends in uncommon elevation, indeed; but only at the gallows. And besides, when a man is elevated in that odd fashion, he has no proper foundation for his superior altitude. Hence, I conclude, that in boasting himself to be high lifted above a whaleman, in that assertion the pirate has no solid basis to stand on.

CHAPTER 54

The Town-Ho's Story

(As told at the Golden Inn)

The Cape of Good Hope, and all the watery region round about there, is much like some noted four corners of a great highway, where you meet more travellers than in any other part.

It was not very long after speaking the Goney that another homeward-bound whaleman, the Town-Ho,* was encountered. She was manned almost wholly

---

* The ancient whale-cry upon first sighting a whale from the mast-head, still used by whalemen in hunting the famous Gallipagos terrapin.

by Polynesians. In the short gam that ensued she gave us strong news of Moby Dick. To some the general interest in the White Whale was now wildly heightened by a circumstance of the Town-Ho's story, which seemed obscurely to involve with the whale a certain wondrous, inverted visitation of one of those so called judgments of God which at times are said to overtake some men. This latter circumstance, with its own particular accompaniments, forming what may be called the secret part of the tragedy about to be narrated, never reached the ears of Captain Ahab or his mates. For that secret part of the story was unknown to the captain of the Town-Ho himself. It was the private property of three confederate white seamen of that ship, one of whom, it seems, communicated it to Tashtego with Romish injunctions of secrecy, but the following night Tashtego rambled in his sleep, and revealed so much of it in that way, that when he was wakened he could not well withhold the rest. Nevertheless, so potent an influence did this thing have on those seamen in the Pequod who came to the full knowledge of it, and by such a strange delicacy, to call it so, were they governed in this matter, that they kept the secret among themselves so that it never transpired abaft the Pequod's main-mast. Interweaving in its proper place this darker thread with the story as publicly narrated on the ship, the whole of this strange affair I now proceed to put on lasting record.

For my humor's sake, I shall preserve the style in which I once narrated it at Lima, to a lounging circle of my Spanish friends, one saint's eve, smoking upon the thick-gilt tiled piazza of the Golden Inn. Of those fine cavaliers, the young Dons, Pedro and Sebastian, were on the closer terms with me; and hence the interluding questions they occasionally put, and which are duly answered at the time.

"Some two years prior to my first learning the events which I am about rehearsing to you, gentlemen, the Town-Ho, Sperm Whaler of Nantucket, was cruising in your Pacific here, not very many days' sail eastward from the eaves of this good Golden Inn. She was somewhere to the northward of the Line. One morning upon handling the pumps, according to daily usage, it was observed that she made more water in her hold than common. They supposed a sword-fish had stabbed her, gentlemen. But the captain, having some unusual reason for believing that rare good luck awaited him in those latitudes; and therefore being very averse to quit them, and the leak not being then considered at all dangerous, though, indeed, they could not find it after searching the hold as low down as was possible in rather heavy weather, the ship still continued her cruisings, the mariners working at the pumps at wide and easy intervals; but no good luck came; more days went by, and not only was the leak yet undiscovered, but it sensibly increased. So much so, that now taking some alarm, the captain, making all sail, stood away for the nearest harbor among the islands, there to have his hull hove out and repaired.

"Though no small passage was before her, yet, if the commonest chance favored, he did not at all fear that his ship would founder by the way, because his pumps were of the best, and being periodically relieved at them, those six-and-thirty men of his could easily keep the ship free; never mind if the leak should double on her. In truth, well nigh the whole of this passage being attended by very prosperous breezes, the Town-Ho had all but certainly arrived in perfect safety at her port without the occurrence of the least fatality, had it not been for the brutal overbearing of Radney, the mate, a Vineyarder, and the bitterly provoked vengeance of Steelkilt, a Lakeman and desperado from Buffalo."

"Lakeman!—Buffalo! Pray, what is a Lakeman, and where is Buffalo?" said Don Sebastian, rising in his swinging mat of grass.

"On the eastern shore of our Lake Erie, Don; but—I crave your courtesy—may be, you shall soon hear further of all that. Now, gentlemen, in square-sail brigs and three-masted ships, well-nigh as large and stout as any that ever sailed out of your old Callao to far Manilla; this Lakeman, in the land-locked heart of our America, had yet been nurtured by all those agrarian freebooting impressions popularly connected with the open ocean. For in their interflowing aggregate, those grand fresh-water seas of ours,—Erie, and Ontario, and

Huron, and Superior, and Michigan,—possess an ocean-like expansiveness, with many of the ocean's noblest traits; with many of its rimmed varieties of races and of climes. They contain round archipelagoes of romantic isles, even as the Polynesian waters do; in large part, are shored by two great contrasting nations, as the Atlantic is; they furnish long maritime approaches to our numerous territorial colonies from the East, dotted all round their banks; here and there are frowned upon by batteries, and by the goat-like craggy guns of lofty Mackinaw; they have heard the fleet thunderings of naval victories; at intervals, they yield their beaches to wild barbarians, whose red painted faces flash from out their peltry wigwams; for leagues and leagues are flanked by ancient and unentered forests, where the gaunt pines stand like serried lines of kings in Gothic genealogies; those same woods harboring wild Afric beasts of prey, and silken creatures whose exported furs give robes to Tartar Emperors; they mirror the paved capitals of Buffalo and Cleveland, as well as Winnebago villages; they float alike the full-rigged merchant ship, the armed cruiser of the State, the steamer, and the beech canoe; they are swept by Borean and dismasting blasts as direful as any that lash the salted wave; they know what shipwrecks are, for out of sight of land, however inland, they have drowned full many a midnight ship with all its shrieking crew. Thus, gentlemen, though an inlander, Steelkilt was wild-ocean born, and wild-ocean nurtured; as much of an audacious mariner as any. And for Radney, though in his infancy he may have laid him down on the lone Nantucket beach, to nurse at his maternal sea; though in after life he had long followed our austere Atlantic and your contemplative Pacific; yet was he quite as vengeful and full of social quarrel as the backwoods seaman, fresh from the latitudes of buck-horn handled bowie-knives. Yet was this Nantucketer a man with some good-hearted traits; and this Lakeman, a mariner, who though a sort of devil indeed, might yet by inflexible firmness, only tempered by that common decency of human recognition which is the meanest slave's right; thus treated, this Steelkilt had long been retained harmless and docile. At all events, he had proved so thus far; but Radney was doomed and made mad, and Steelkilt—but, gentlemen, you shall hear.

"It was not more than a day or two at the furthest after pointing her prow for her island haven, that the Town-Ho's leak seemed again increasing, but only so as to require an hour or more at the pumps every day. You must know that in a settled and civilized ocean like our Atlantic, for example, some skippers think little of pumping their whole way across it; though of a still, sleepy night, should the officer of the deck happen to forget his duty in that respect, the probability would be that he and his shipmates would never again remember it, on account of all hands gently subsiding to the bottom. Nor in the solitary and savage seas far from you to the westward, gentlemen, is it altogether unusual for ships to keep clanging at their pump-handles in full chorus even for a voyage of considerable length; that is, if it lie along a tolerably accessible coast, or if any other reasonable retreat is afforded them. It is only when a leaky vessel is in some very out of the way part of those waters, some really landless latitude, that her captain begins to feel a little anxious.

"Much this way had it been with the Town-Ho; so when her leak was found gaining once more, there was in truth some small concern manifested by several of her company; especially by Radney the mate. He commanded the upper sails to be well hoisted, sheeted home anew, and every way expanded to the breeze. Now this Radney, I suppose, was as little of a coward, and as little inclined to any sort of nervous apprehensiveness touching his own person as any fearless, unthinking creature on land or on sea that you can conveniently imagine, gentlemen. Therefore when he betrayed this solicitude about the safety of the ship, some of the seamen declared that it was only on account of his being a part owner in her. So when they were working that evening at the pumps, there was on this head no small gamesomeness slily going on among them, as they stood with their feet continually overflowed by the rippling clear water; clear as any mountain spring, gentlemen—that bubbling from the pumps ran across the deck, and poured itself out in steady spouts at the lee scupper-holes.

"Now, as you well know, it is not seldom the case in this conventional world of ours—watery or otherwise; that when a person placed in command over his fellow-men finds one of them to be very significantly his superior in general pride of manhood, straightway against that man he conceives an unconquerable dislike and bitterness; and if he have a chance he will pull down and pulverize that subaltern's tower, and make a little heap of dust of it. Be this conceit of mine as it may, gentlemen, at all events Steelkilt was a tall and noble animal with a head like a Roman, and a flowing golden beard like the tasseled housings of your last viceroy's snorting charger; and a brain, and a heart, and a soul in him, gentlemen, which had made Steelkilt Charlemagne, had he been born son to Charlemagne's father. But Radney, the mate, was ugly as a mule; yet as hardy, as stubborn, as malicious. He did not love Steelkilt, and Steelkilt knew it.

"Espying the mate drawing near as he was toiling at the pump with the rest, the Lakeman affected not to notice him, but unawed, went on with his gay banterings.

"'Aye, aye, my merry lads, it's a lively leak this; hold a cannikin, one of ye, and let's have a taste. By the Lord, it's worth bottling! I tell ye what, men, old Rad's investment must go for it! he had best cut away his part of the hull and tow it home. The fact is, boys, that sword-fish only began the job; he's come back again with a gang of ship-carpenters, saw-fish, and file-fish, and what not; and the whole posse of 'em are now hard at work cutting and slashing at the bottom; making improvements, I suppose. If old Rad were here now, I'd tell him to jump overboard and scatter 'em. They're playing the devil with his estate, I can tell him. But he's a simple old soul,—Rad, and a beauty too. Boys, they say the rest of his property is invested in looking-glasses. I wonder if he'd give a poor devil like me the model of his nose.'

"'Damn your eyes! what's that pump stopping for?' roared Radney, pretending not to have heard the sailors' talk. 'Thunder away at it!'

"'Aye, aye, sir,' said Steelkilt, merry as a cricket. 'Lively, boys, lively, now!' And with that the pump clanged like fifty fire-engines; the men tossed their hats off to it, and ere long that peculiar gasping of the lungs was heard which denotes the fullest tension of life's utmost energies.

"Quitting the pump at last, with the rest of his band, the Lakeman went forward all panting, and sat himself down on the windlass; his face fiery red, his eyes bloodshot, and wiping the profuse sweat from his brow. Now what cozening fiend it was, gentlemen, that possessed Radney to meddle with such a man in that corporeally exasperated state, I know not; but so it happened. Intolerably striding along the deck, the mate commanded him to get a broom and sweep down the planks, and also a shovel, and remove some offensive matters consequent upon allowing a pig to run at large.

"Now, gentlemen, sweeping a ship's deck at sea is a piece of household work which in all times but raging gales is regularly attended to every evening; it has been known to be done in the case of ships actually foundering at the time. Such, gentlemen, is the inflexibility of sea-usages and the instinctive love of neatness in seamen; some of whom would not willingly drown without first washing their faces. But in all vessels this broom business is the prescriptive province of the boys, if boys there be aboard. Besides, it was the stronger men in the Town-Ho that had been divided into gangs, taking turns at the pumps; and being the most athletic seaman of them all, Steelkilt had been regularly assigned captain of one of the gangs; consequently he should have been freed from any trivial business not connected with truly nautical duties, such being the case with his comrades. I mention all these particulars so that you may understand exactly how this affair stood between the two men.

"But there was more than this: the order about the shovel was almost as plainly meant to sting and insult Steelkilt, as though Radney had spat in his face. Any man who has gone sailor in a whale-ship will understand this; and all this and doubtless much more, the Lakeman fully comprehended when the mate uttered his command. But as he sat still for a moment, and as he steadfastly looked into the mate's malignant eye and perceived the stacks of powder-casks heaped up in him and the slow-match silently burning along towards them; as he instinctively saw all this, that strange forbearance and unwillingness to stir up the deeper passionateness in any already ireful being—a repugnance most felt, when felt at all, by really valiant men even when aggrieved—this nameless phantom feeling, gentlemen, stole over Steelkilt.

"Therefore, in his ordinary tone, only a little broken by the bodily exhaustion he was temporarily in, he answered him saying that sweeping the deck was not his business, and he would not do it. And then, without at all alluding to the shovel, he pointed to three lads as the customary sweepers; who, not being billeted at the pumps, had done little or nothing all day. To this, Radney replied with an oath, in a most domineering and outrageous manner unconditionally reiterating his command; meanwhile advancing upon the still seated Lakeman, with an uplifted cooper's club hammer which he had snatched from a cask near by.

"Heated and irritated as he was by his spasmodic toil at the pumps, for all his first nameless feeling of forbearance the sweating Steelkilt could but ill brook this bearing in the mate; but somehow still smothering the conflagration within him, without speaking he remained doggedly rooted to his seat, till at last the incensed Radney shook the hammer within a few inches of his face, furiously commanding him to do his bidding.

"Steelkilt rose, and slowly retreating round the windlass, steadily followed by the mate with his menacing hammer, deliberately repeated his intention not to obey. Seeing, however, that his forbearance had not the slightest effect, by an awful and unspeakable intimation with his twisted hand he warned off the foolish and infatuated man; but it was to no purpose. And in this way the two went once slowly round the windlass; when, resolved at last no longer to retreat, bethinking him that he had now forborne as much as comported with his humor, the Lakeman paused on the hatches and thus spoke to the officer:

"'Mr. Radney, I will not obey you. Take that hammer away, or look to yourself.' But the predestinated mate coming still closer to him, where the Lakeman stood fixed, now shook the heavy hammer within an inch of his teeth; meanwhile repeating a string of insufferable maledictions. Retreating not the thousandth part of an inch; stabbing him in the eye with the unflinching poniard of his glance, Steelkilt, clenching his right hand behind him and creepingly drawing it back, told his persecutor that if the hammer but grazed his cheek he (Steelkilt) would murder him. But, gentlemen, the fool had been branded for the slaughter by the gods. Immediately the hammer touched the cheek; the next instant the lower jaw of the mate was stove in his head; he fell on the hatch spouting blood like a whale.

"Ere the cry could go aft Steelkilt was shaking one of the backstays leading far aloft to where two of his comrades were standing their mastheads. They were both Canallers."

"Canallers!" cried Don Pedro. "We have seen many whale-ships in our harbors, but never heard of your Canallers. Pardon: who and what are they?"

"Canallers, Don, are the boatmen belonging to our grand Erie Canal. You must have heard of it."

"Nay, Senor; hereabouts in this dull, warm, most lazy, and hereditary land, we know but little of your vigorous North."

"Aye? Well then, Don, refill my cup. Your chicha's very fine; and ere proceeding further I will tell ye what our Canallers are; for such information may throw side-light upon my story.

"For three hundred and sixty miles, gentlemen, through the entire breadth of the state of New York; through numerous populous cities and most thriving villages; through long, dismal, uninhabited swamps, and affluent, cultivated fields, unrivalled for fertility; by billiard-room and bar-room; through the holy-of-holies of great forests; on Roman arches over Indian rivers; through sun and shade; by happy hearts or broken; through all the wide contrasting scenery of those noble Mohawk counties; and especially, by rows of snow-white chapels, whose spires stand almost like milestones, flows one continual stream of Venetianly corrupt and often lawless life. There's your true Ashantee, gentlemen; there howl your pagans; where you ever find them, next door to you; under the long-flung shadow, and the snug patronising lee of churches. For by some curious fatality, as it is often noted of your metropolitan freebooters that they ever encamp around the halls of justice, so sinners, gentlemen, most abound in holiest vicinities."

"Is that a friar passing?" said Don Pedro, looking downwards into the crowded plazza, with humorous concern.

"Well for our northern friend, Dame Isabella's Inquisition wanes in Lima," laughed Don Sebastian. "Proceed, Senor."

"A moment! Pardon!" cried another of the company. "In the name of all us Limeese, I but desire to express to you, sir sailor, that we have by no means overlooked your delicacy in not substituting present Lima for distant Venice in your corrupt comparison. Oh! do not bow and look surprised; you know the proverb all along this coast—'Corrupt as Lima.' It but bears out your saying, too; churches more plentiful than billiard-tables, and for ever open—and 'Corrupt as Lima.' So, too, Venice; I have been there; the holy city of the blessed evangelist, St. Mark!—St. Dominic, purge it! Your cup! Thanks: here I refill; now, you pour out again."

"Freely depicted in his own vocation, gentlemen, the Canaller would make a fine dramatic hero, so abundantly and picturesquely wicked is he. Like Mark

Antony, for days and days along his green-turfed, flowery Nile, he indolently floats, openly toying with his red-cheeked Cleopatra, ripening his apricot thigh upon the sunny deck. But ashore, all this effeminacy is dashed. The brigandish guise which the Canaller so proudly sports; his slouched and gaily-ribboned hat betoken his grand features. A terror to the smiling innocence of the villages through which he floats; his swart visage and bold swagger are not unshunned in cities. Once a vagabond on his own canal, I have received good turns from one of these Canallers; I thank him heartily; would fain be not ungrateful; but it is often one of the prime redeeming qualities of your man of violence, that at times he has as stiff an arm to back a poor stranger in a strait, as to plunder a wealthy one. In sum, gentlemen, what the wildness of this canal life is, is emphatically evinced by this; that our wild whale-fishery contains so many of its most finished graduates, and that scarce any race of mankind, except Sydney men, are so much distrusted by our whaling captains. Nor does it at all diminish the curiousness of this matter, that to many thousands of our rural boys and young men born along its line, the probationary life of the Grand Canal furnishes the sole transition between quietly reaping in a Christian corn-field, and recklessly ploughing the waters of the most barbaric seas."

"I see! I see!" impetuously exclaimed Don Pedro, spilling his chicha upon his silvery ruffles. "No need to travel! The world's one Lima. I had thought, now, that at your temperate North the generations were cold and holy as the hills.—But the story."

"I left off, gentlemen, where the Lakeman shook the backstay. Hardly had he done so, when he was surrounded by the three junior mates and the four harpooneers, who all crowded him to the deck. But sliding down the ropes like baleful comets, the two Canallers rushed into the uproar, and sought to drag their man out of it towards the forecastle. Others of the sailors joined with them in this attempt, and a twisted turmoil ensued; while standing out of harm's way, the valiant captain danced up and down with a whale-pike, calling upon his officers to manhandle that atrocious scoundrel, and smoke him along to the quarter-deck. At intervals, he ran close up to the revolving border of the confusion, and prying into the heart of it with his pike, sought to prick out the object of his resentment. But Steelkilt and his desperadoes were too much for them all; they succeeded in gaining the forecastle deck, where, hastily slewing about three or four large casks in a line with the windlass, these sea-Parisians entrenched themselves behind the barricade.

"'Come out of that, ye pirates!' roared the captain, now menacing them with a pistol in each hand, just brought to him by the steward. 'Come out of that, ye cut-throats!'

"Steelkilt leaped on the barricade, and striding up and down there, defied the worst the pistols could do; but gave the captain to understand distinctly, that his (Steelkilt's) death would be the signal for a murderous mutiny on the part of all hands. Fearing in his heart lest this might prove but too true, the captain a little desisted, but still commanded the insurgents instantly to return to their duty.

"'Will you promise not to touch us, if we do?' demanded their ringleader.

"'Turn to! turn to!—I make no promise;—to your duty! Do you want to sink the ship, by knocking off at a time like this? Turn to!' and he once more raised a pistol.

"'Sink the ship?' cried Steelkilt. 'Aye, let her sink. Not a man of us turns to, unless you swear not to raise a rope-yarn against us. What say ye, men?' turning to his comrades. A fierce cheer was their response.

"The Lakeman now patrolled the barricade, all the while keeping his eye on the Captain, and jerking out such sentences as these:—'It's not our fault; we didn't want it; I told him to take his hammer away; it was boy's business; he might have known me before this; I told him not to prick the buffalo; I believe I have broken a finger here against his cursed jaw; ain't those mincing knives down in the forecastle there, men? look to those handspikes, my hearties. Captain, by God, look to yourself; say the word; don't be a fool; forget it all; we are ready to turn to; treat us decently, and we're your men; but we won't be flogged.'

"'Turn to! I make no promises, turn to, I say!'

"'Look ye, now,' cried the Lakeman, flinging out his arm towards him, 'there are a few of us here (and I am one of them) who have shipped for the cruise, d'ye see; now as you well know, sir, we can claim our discharge as soon as the anchor is down; so we don't want a row; it's not our interest; we want to be peaceable; we are ready to work, but we won't be flogged.'

"'Turn to!' roared the Captain.

"Steelkilt glanced round him a moment, and then said:—'I tell you what it is now, Captain, rather than kill ye, and be hung for such a shabby rascal, we won't lift a hand against ye unless ye attack us; but till you say the word about not flogging us, we don't do a hand's turn.'

"'Down into the forecastle then, down with ye, I'll keep ye there till ye're sick of it. Down ye go.'

"'Shall we?' cried the ringleader to his men. Most of them were against it; but at length, in obedience to Steelkilt, they preceded him down into their dark den, growlingly disappearing, like bears into a cave.

"As the Lakeman's bare head was just level with the planks, the Captain and his posse leaped the barricade, and rapidly drawing over the slide of the scuttle, planted their group of hands upon it, and loudly called for the steward to bring the heavy brass padlock belonging to the companionway. Then opening the slide a little, the Captain whispered something down the crack, closed it, and turned the key upon them—ten in number—leaving on deck some twenty or more, who thus far had remained neutral.

"All night a wide-awake watch was kept by all the officers, forward and aft, especially about the forecastle scuttle and fore hatchway; at which last place it was feared the insurgents might emerge, after breaking through the bulkhead below. But the hours of darkness passed in peace; the men who still remained at their duty toiling hard at the pumps, whose clinking and clanking at intervals through the dreary night dismally resounded through the ship.

"At sunrise the Captain went forward, and knocking on the deck, summoned the prisoners to work; but with a yell they refused. Water was then lowered down to them, and a couple of handfuls of biscuit were tossed after it; when again turning the key upon them and pocketing it, the Captain returned to the quarter-deck. Twice every day for three days this was repeated; but on the fourth morning a confused wrangling, and then a scuffling was heard, as the customary summons was delivered; and suddenly four men burst up from the forecastle, saying they were ready to turn to. The fetid closeness of the air, and a famishing diet, united perhaps to some fears of ultimate retribution, had constrained them to surrender at discretion. Emboldened by this, the Captain reiterated his demand to the rest, but Steelkilt shouted up to him a terrific hint to stop his babbling and betake himself where he belonged. On the fifth morning three others of the mutineers bolted up into the air from the desperate arms below that sought to restrain them. Only three were left.

"'Better turn to, now?' said the Captain with a heartless jeer.

"'Shut us up again, will ye!' cried Steelkilt.

"'Oh! certainly,' the Captain, and the key clicked.

"It was at this point, gentlemen, that enraged by the defection of seven of his former associates, and stung by the mocking voice that had last hailed him, and maddened by his long entombment in a place as black as the bowels of despair; it was then that Steelkilt proposed to the two Canallers, thus far apparently of one mind with him, to burst out of their hole at the next summoning of the garrison; and armed with their keen mincing knives (long, crescentic, heavy implements with a handle at each end) run amuck from the bowsprit to the taffrail; and if by any devilishness of desperation possible, seize the ship. For himself, he would do this, he said, whether they joined him or not. That was the last night he should spend in that den. But the scheme met with no opposition on the part of the other two; they swore they were ready for that, or for any other mad thing, for anything in short but a surrender. And what was more, they each insisted upon being the first man on deck, when the time to make the rush should come. But to this their leader as fiercely objected, reserving that priority for himself; particularly as his two comrades would not yield, the one to the other, in the matter; and both of them could not be first, for the ladder would but admit one man at a time. And here, gentlemen, the foul play of these miscreants must come out.

"Upon hearing the frantic project of their leader, each in his own separate soul had suddenly lighted, it would seem, upon the same piece of treachery, namely: to be foremost in breaking out, in order to be the first of the three, though the last of the ten, to surrender; and thereby secure whatever small chance of pardon such conduct might merit. But when Steelkilt made known his determination still to lead them to the last, they in some way, by some subtle chemistry of villany, mixed their before secret treacheries together; and when their leader fell into a doze, verbally opened their souls to each other in three sentences; and bound the sleeper with cords, and gagged him with cords; and shrieked out for the Captain at midnight.

"Thinking murder at hand, and smelling in the dark for the blood, he and all his armed mates and harpooneers rushed for the forecastle. In a few minutes the scuttle was opened, and, bound hand and foot, the still struggling ring-leader was shoved up into the air by his perfidious allies, who at once claimed the honor of securing a man who had been fully ripe for murder. But all these were collared, and dragged along the deck like dead cattle; and, side by side, were seized up into the mizzen rigging, like three quarters of meat, and there they hung till morning. 'Damn ye,' cried the Captain, pacing to and fro before them, 'the vultures would not touch ye, ye villains!'

"At sunrise he summoned all hands; and separating those who had rebelled from those who had taken no part in the mutiny, he told the former that he had a good mind to flog them all round—thought, upon the whole, he would do so—he ought to—justice demanded it; but for the present, considering their timely surrender, he would let them go with a reprimand, which he accordingly administered in the vernacular.

"'But as for you, ye carrion rogues,' turning to the three men in the rigging—'for you, I mean to mince ye up for the try-pots;' and, seizing a rope, he applied it with all his might to the backs of the two traitors, till they yelled no more, but lifelessly hung their heads sideways, as the two crucified thieves are drawn.

"'My wrist is sprained with ye!' he cried, at last; 'but there is still rope enough left for you, my fine bantam, that wouldn't give up. Take that gag from his mouth, and let us hear what he can say for himself.'

"For a moment the exhausted mutineer made a tremulous motion of his cramped jaws, and then painfully twisting round his head, said in a sort of hiss, 'What I say is this—and mind it well—if you flog me, I murder you!'

"'Say ye so? then see how ye frighten me'—and the Captain drew off with the rope to strike.

"'Best not,' hissed the Lakeman.

"'But I must,'—and the rope was once more drawn back for the stroke.

"Steelkilt here hissed out something, inaudible to all but the Captain; who, to the amazement of all hands, started back, paced the deck rapidly two or three times, and then suddenly throwing down his rope, said, 'I won't do it—let him go—cut him down: d'ye hear?'

But as the junior mates were hurrying to execute the order, a pale man, with a bandaged head, arrested them—Radney the chief mate. Ever since the blow, he had lain in his berth; but that morning, hearing the tumult on the deck, he had crept out, and thus far had watched the whole scene. Such was the state of his mouth, that he could hardly speak; but mumbling something about his being willing and able to do what the captain dared not attempt, he snatched the rope and advanced to his pinioned foe.

"'You are a coward!' hissed the Lakeman.

"'So I am, but take that.' The mate was in the very act of striking, when another hiss stayed his uplifted arm. He paused: and then pausing no more, made good his word, spite of Steelkilt's threat, whatever that might have been. The three men were then cut down, all hands were turned to, and, sullenly worked by the moody seamen, the iron pumps clanged as before.

"Just after dark that day, when one watch had retired below, a clamor was heard in the forecastle; and the two trembling traitors running up, besieged the cabin door, saying they durst not consort with the crew. Entreaties, cuffs, and kicks could not drive them back, so at their own instance they were put down in the ship's run for salvation. Still, no sign of mutiny reappeared among the rest. On the contrary, it seemed, that mainly at Steelkilt's instigation, they had resolved to maintain the strictest peacefulness, obey all orders to the last, and, when the ship reached port, desert her in a body. But in order to insure the speediest end to the voyage, they all agreed to another thing—namely, not to sing out for whales, in case any should be discovered. For, spite of her leak, and spite of all her other perils, the Town-Ho still maintained her mast-heads, and her captain was just as willing to lower for a fish that moment, as on the day his craft first struck the cruising ground; and Radney the mate was quite as ready to change his berth for a boat, and with his bandaged mouth seek to gag in death the vital jaw of the whale.

"But though the Lakeman had induced the seamen to adopt this sort of passiveness in their conduct, he kept his own counsel (at least till all was over) concerning his own proper and private revenge upon the man who had stung him in the ventricles of his heart. He was in Radney the chief mate's watch; and as if the infatuated man sought to run more than half way to meet his doom, after the scene at the rigging, he insisted, against the express counsel of the captain, upon resuming the head of his watch at night. Upon this, and one or two other circumstances, Steelkilt systematically built the plan of his revenge.

"During the night, Radney had an unseamanlike way of sitting on the bulwarks of the quarter-deck, and leaning his arm upon the gunwale of the boat which was hoisted up there, a little above the ship's side. In this attitude, it was well known, he sometimes dozed. There was a considerable vacancy between the boat and the ship, and down between this was the sea. Steelkilt calculated his time, and found that his next trick at the helm would come round at two o'clock, in the morning of the third day from that in which he had been betrayed. At his leisure, he employed the interval in braiding something very carefully in his watches below.

"'What are you making there?' said a shipmate.

"'What do you think? what does it look like?'

"'Like a lanyard for your bag; but it's an odd one, seems to me.'

'Yes, rather oddish,' said the Lakeman, holding it at arm's length before him; 'but I think it will answer. Shipmate, I haven't enough twine,—have you any?'

"But there was none in the forecastle.

"'Then I must get some from old Rad;' and he rose to go aft.

"'You don't mean to go a begging to *him!*' said a sailor.

"'Why not? Do you think he won't do me a turn, when it's to help himself in the end, shipmate?' and going to the mate, he looked at him quietly, and asked him for some twine to mend his hammock. It was given him—neither twine nor lanyard were seen again; but the next night an iron ball, closely netted, partly rolled from the pocket of the Lakeman's monkey jacket, as he was tucking the coat into his hammock for a pillow. Twenty-four hours after, his trick at the silent helm—nigh to the man who was apt to doze over the grave always ready dug to the seaman's hand—that fatal hour was then to come; and in the fore-ordaining soul of Steelkilt, the mate was already stark and stretched as a corpse, with his forehead crushed in.

"But, gentlemen, a fool saved the would-be murderer from the bloody deed he had planned. Yet complete revenge he had, and without being the avenger. For by a mysterious fatality, Heaven itself seemed to step in to take out of his hands into its own the damning thing he would have done.

"It was just between daybreak and sunrise of the morning of the second day, when they were washing down the decks, that a stupid Teneriffe man, drawing water in the main-chains, all at once shouted out, 'There she rolls! there she rolls! Jesu, what a whale!' It was Moby Dick."

"'Moby Dick!' cried Don Sebastian; 'St. Dominic! Sir sailor, but do whales have christenings? Whom call you Moby Dick?"

"A very white, and famous, and most deadly immortal monster, Don;—but that would be too long a story."

"How? how?" cried all the young Spaniards, crowding.

"Nay, Dons, Dons—nay, nay! I cannot rehearse that now. Let me get more into the air, Sirs."

"The chicha! the chicha!" cried Don Pedro; "our vigorous friend looks faint;—fill up his empty glass!"

"No need, gentlemen; one moment, and I proceed.—Now, gentlemen, so suddenly perceiving the snowy whale within fifty yards of the ship—forgetful of the compact among the crew—in the excitement of the moment, the Teneriffe man had instinctively and involuntarily lifted his voice for the monster, though for some little time past it had been plainly beheld from the three sullen mast-heads. All was now a phrensy. 'The White Whale—the White Whale!' was the cry from captain, mates, and harpooneers, who, undeterred by fearful rumors, were all anxious to capture so famous and precious a fish; while the dogged crew eyed askance, and with curses, the appalling beauty of the vast milky mass, that lit up by a horizontal spangling sun, shifted and glistened like a living opal in the blue morning sea. Gentlemen, a strange fatality pervades the whole career of these events, as if verily mapped out before the world itself was charted. The mutineer was the bowsman of the mate, and when fast to a fish, it was his duty to sit next him, while Radney stood up with his lance in the prow, and haul in or slacken the line, at the word of command. Moreover, when the four boats were lowered, the mate's got the start; and none howled more fiercely with delight than did Steelkilt, as he strained at his oar. After a stiff pull, their harpooneer got fast, and, spear in hand, Radney sprang to the bow. He was always a furious man, it seems, in a boat. And now his bandaged cry was, to beach him on the whale's topmost back. Nothing loath, his bowsman hauled him up and up, through a blinding foam that blent two whitenesses together; till of a sudden the boat struck as against a sunken ledge, and keeling over, spilled out the standing mate. That instant, as he fell on the whale's slippery back, the boat righted, and was dashed aside by the swell, while Radney was tossed over into the sea, on the other flank of the whale. He struck out through the spray, and, for an instant, was dimly seen through that veil, wildly seeking to remove himself from the eye of Moby Dick. But the whale rushed round in a sudden maelstrom; seized the swimmer between his jaws; and rearing high up with him, plunged headlong again, and went down.

"Meantime, at the first tap of the boat's bottom, the Lakeman had slackened the line, so as to drop astern from the whirlpool; calmly looking on, he thought his own thoughts. But a sudden, terrific, downward jerking of the boat, quickly brought his knife to the line. He cut it; and the whale was free. But, at some distance, Moby Dick rose again, with some tatters of Radney's red woollen shirt, caught in the teeth that had destroyed him. All four boats gave chase again; but the whale eluded them, and finally wholly disappeared.

"In good time, the Town-Ho reached her port—a savage, solitary place— where no civilized creature resided. There, headed by the Lakeman, all but five or six of the foremastmen deliberately deserted among the palms; eventually, as it turned out, seizing a large double war-canoe of the savages, and setting sail for some other harbor.

"The ship's company being reduced to but a handful, the captain called upon the Islanders to assist him in the laborious business of heaving down the ship to stop the leak. But to such unresting vigilance over their dangerous allies was this small band of whites necessitated, both by night and by day, and so extreme was the hard work they underwent, that upon the vessel being ready again for sea, they were in such a weakened condition that the captain durst not put off with them in so heavy a vessel. After taking counsel with his officers, he anchored the ship as far off shore as possible; loaded and ran out his two cannon from the bows; stacked his muskets on the poop; and warning the Islanders not to approach the ship at their peril, took one man with him, and setting the sail of his best whale-boat, steered straight before the wind for Tahiti, five hundred miles distant, to procure a reinforcement to his crew.

"On the fourth day of the sail, a large canoe was descried, which seemed to have touched at a low isle of corals. He steered away from it; but the savage craft bore down on him; and soon the voice of Steelkilt hailed him to heave to, or he would run him under water. The captain presented a pistol. With one foot on each prow of the yoked war-canoes, the Lakeman laughed him to scorn; assuring him that if the pistol so much as clicked in the lock, he would bury him in bubbles and foam.

"'What do you want of me?' cried the captain.

"'Where are you bound? and for what are you bound?' demanded Steelkilt; 'no lies.'

"'I am bound to Tahiti for more men.'

"'Very good. Let me board you a moment—I come in peace.' With that he leaped from the canoe, swam to the boat; and climbing the gunwale, stood face to face with the captain.

"'Cross your arms, sir; throw back your head. Now, repeat after me. "As soon as Steelkilt leaves me, I swear to beach this boat on yonder island, and remain there six days. If I do not, may lightning strike me!"'

"'A pretty scholar,' laughed the Lakeman. 'Adios, Senor!' and leaping into the sea, he swam back to his comrades.

"Watching the boat till it was fairly beached, and drawn up to the roots of the cocoa-nut trees, Steelkilt made sail again, and in due time arrived at Tahiti, his own place of destination. There, luck befriended him; two ships were about to sail for France, and were providentially in want of precisely that number of men which the sailor headed. They embarked; and so for ever got the start of their former captain, had he been at all minded to work them legal retribution.

"Some ten days after the French ships sailed, the whale-boat arrived, and the captain was forced to enlist some of the more civilized Tahitians, who had been somewhat used to the sea. Chartering a small native schooner, he returned with them to his vessel; and finding all right there, again resumed his cruisings.

"Where Steelkilt now is, gentlemen, none know; but upon the island of Nantucket, the widow of Radney still turns to the sea which refuses to give up its dead; still in dreams sees the awful white whale that destroyed him."   *   *   *   *   *

"Are you through?" said Don Sebastian, quietly.

"I am, Don."

"Then I entreat you, tell me if to the best of your own convictions, this your story is in substance really true? It is so passing wonderful! Did you get it from an unquestionable source? Bear with me if I seem to press."

"Also bear with all of us, sir sailor; for we all join in Don Sebastian's suit," cried the company, with exceeding interest.

"Is there a copy of the Holy Evangelists in the Golden Inn, gentlemen?"

"Nay," said Don Sebastian; "but I know a worthy priest near by, who will quickly procure one for me. I go for it; but are you well advised? this may grow too serious."

"Will you be so good as to bring the priest also, Don?"

"Though there are no Auto-da-Fés in Lima now," said one of the company to another; "I fear our sailor friend runs risk of the archiepiscopacy. Let us withdraw more out of the moonlight. I see no need of this."

"Excuse me for running after you, Don Sebastian; but may I also beg that you will be particular in procuring the largest sized Evangelists you can."

*   *   *   *   *

"This is the priest, he brings you the Evangelists," said Don Sebastian, gravely, returning with a tall and solemn figure.

"Let me remove my hat. Now, venerable priest, further into the light, and hold the Holy Book before me that I may touch it.

"So help me Heaven, and on my honor the story I have told ye, gentlemen, is in substance and its great items, true. I know it to be true; it happened on this ball; I trod the ship; I knew the crew; I have seen and talked with Steelkilt since the death of Radney."

CHAPTER 55

Of the Monstrous Pictures of Whales

I shall ere long paint to you as well as one can without canvas, something like the true form of the whale as he actually appears to the eye of the whaleman when in his own absolute body the whale is moored alongside the whale-ship so that he can be fairly stepped upon there. It may be worth while, therefore, previously to advert to those curious imaginary portraits of him which even down to the present day confidently challenge the faith of the landsman. It is time to set the world right in this matter, by proving such pictures of the whale all wrong.

It may be that the primal source of all those pictorial delusions will be found among the oldest Hindoo, Egyptian, and Grecian sculptures. For ever since those inventive but unscrupulous times when on the marble panellings of temples, the pedestals of statues, and on shields, medallions, cups, and coins, the dolphin was drawn in scales of chain-armor like Saladin's, and a helmeted head like St. George's; ever since then has something of the same sort of license prevailed, not only in most popular pictures of the whale, but in many scientific presentations of him.

Now, by all odds, the most ancient extant portrait anyways purporting to be the whale's, is to be found in the famous cavern-pagoda of Elephanta, in India. The Brahmins maintain that in the almost endless sculptures of that immemorial pagoda, all the trades and pursuits, every conceivable avocation of man, were prefigured ages before any of them actually came into being. No wonder then, that in some sort our noble profession of whaling should have been there shadowed forth. The Hindoo whale referred to, occurs in a separate department of the wall, depicting the incarnation of Vishnu in the form of leviathan, learnedly known as the Matse Avatar. But though this sculpture is half man and half whale, so as only to give the tail of the latter, yet that small section of him is all wrong. It looks more like the tapering tail of an anaconda, than the broad palms of the true whale's majestic flukes.

But go to the old Galleries, and look now at a great Christian painter's portrait of this fish; for he succeeds no better than the antediluvian Hindoo. It is Guido's picture of Perseus rescuing Andromeda from the sea-monster or whale. Where did Guido get the model of such a strange creature as that? Nor does Hogarth, in painting the same scene in his own "Perseus Descending," make out one whit better. The huge corpulence of that Hogarthian monster undulates on the surface, scarcely drawing one inch of water. It has a sort of howdah on its back, and its distended tusked mouth into which the billows are rolling, might be taken for the Traitors' Gate leading from the Thames by water into the Tower. Then, there are the Prodromus whales of old Scotch Sibbald, and Jonah's whale, as depicted in the prints of old Bibles and the cuts of old primers. What shall be said of these? As for the book-binder's whale winding like a vine-stalk round the stock of a descending anchor—as stamped and gilded on the backs and title-pages of many books both old and new—that is a very picturesque but purely fabulous creature, imitated, I take it, from the like figures on antique vases. Though universally denominated a dolphin, I nevertheless call this book-binder's fish an attempt at a whale; because it was so intended when the device was first introduced. It was introduced by an old Italian publisher somewhere about the 15th century, during the Revival of Learning; and in those days, and even down to a comparatively late period, dolphins were popularly supposed to be a species of the Leviathan.

In the vignettes and other embellishments of some ancient books you will at times meet with very curious touches at the whale, where all manner of spouts, jets d'eau, hot springs and cold, Saratoga and Baden-Baden, come bubbling up from his unexhausted brain. In the title-page of the original edition of the "Advancement of Learning" you will find some curious whales.

But quitting all these unprofessional attempts, let us glance at those pictures of leviathan purporting to be sober, scientific delineations, by those who know. In old Harris's collection of voyages there are some plates of whales extracted from a Dutch book of voyages, A.D. 1671, entitled "A Whaling Voyage to Spitzbergen in the ship Jonas in the Whale, Peter Peterson of Friesland, master." In one of those plates the whales, like great rafts of logs, are represented lying among ice-isles, with white bears running over their living backs. In another plate, the prodigious blunder is made of representing the whale with perpendicular flukes.

Then again, there is an imposing quarto, written by one Captain Colnett, a Post Captain in the English navy, entitled "A Voyage round Cape Horn into the South Seas, for the purpose of extending the Spermaceti Whale Fisheries." In this book is an outline purporting to be a "Picture of a Physeter or Spermaceti whale, drawn by scale from one killed on the coast of Mexico, August, 1793, and hoisted on deck." I doubt not the captain had this veracious picture taken for the benefit of his marines. To mention but one thing about it, let me say that it has an eye which applied, according to the accompanying scale, to a full grown sperm whale, would make the eye of that whale a bow-window some five feet long. Ah, my gallant captain, why did ye not give us Jonah looking out of that eye!

Nor are the most conscientious compilations of Natural History for the benefit of the young and tender, free from the same heinousness of mistake. Look at that popular work "Goldsmith's Animated Nature." In the abridged London edition of 1807, there are plates of an alleged "whale" and a "narwhale." I do not wish to seem inelegant, but this unsightly whale looks much like an amputated sow; and, as for the narwhale, one glimpse at it is enough to amaze one, that in this nineteenth century such a hippogriff could be palmed for genuine upon any intelligent public of schoolboys.

Then, again, in 1825, Bernard Germain, Count de Lacépède, a great naturalist, published a scientific systemized whale book, wherein are several pictures of the different species of the Leviathan. All these are not only incorrect, but the picture of the Mysticetus or Greenland whale (that is to say, the Right whale), even Scoresby, a long experienced man as touching that species, declares not to have its counterpart in nature.

But the placing of the cap-sheaf to all this blundering business was reserved for the scientific Frederick Cuvier, brother to the famous Baron. In 1836, he published a Natural History of Whales, in which he gives what he calls a picture of the Sperm Whale. Before showing that picture to any Nantucketer, you had best provide for your summary retreat from Nantucket. In a word, Frederick Cuvier's Sperm Whale is not a Sperm Whale, but a squash. Of course, he never had the benefit of a whaling voyage (such men seldom have), but whence he derived that picture, who can tell? Perhaps he got it as his scientific predecessor in the same field, Desmarest, got one of his authentic abortions; that is, from a Chinese drawing. And what sort of lively lads with the pencil those Chinese are, many queer cups and saucers inform us.

As for the sign-painters' whales seen in the streets hanging over the shops of oil-dealers, what shall be said of them? They are generally Richard III. whales, with dromedary humps, and very savage; breakfasting on three or four sailor tarts, that is whaleboats full of mariners: their deformities floundering in seas of blood and blue paint.

But these manifold mistakes in depicting the whale are not so very surprising after all. Consider! Most of the scientific drawings have been taken from the stranded fish; and these are about as correct as a drawing of a wrecked ship, with broken back, would correctly represent the noble animal itself in all its undashed pride of hull and spars. Though elephants have stood for their full-lengths, the living Leviathan has never yet fairly floated himself for his portrait. The living whale, in his full majesty and significance, is only to be seen at sea in unfathomable waters; and afloat the vast bulk of him is out of sight, like a launched line-of-battle ship; and out of that element it is a thing eternally impossible for mortal man to hoist him bodily into the air, so as to preserve all his mighty swells and undulations. And, not to speak of the highly presumable difference of contour between a young sucking whale and a full-grown Platonian Leviathan; yet, even in the case of one of those young sucking whales hoisted to a ship's deck, such is then the outlandish, eel-like, limbered, varying shape of him, that his precise expression the devil himself could not catch.

But it may be fancied, that from the naked skeleton of the stranded whale, accurate hints may be derived touching his true form. Not at all. For it is one of the more curious things about this Leviathan, that his skeleton gives very little idea of his general shape. Though Jeremy Bentham's skeleton, which hangs for candelabra in the library of one of his executors, correctly conveys the idea of a burly-browed utilitarian old gentleman, with all Jeremy's other leading personal characteristics; yet nothing of this kind could be inferred from any leviathan's articulated bones. In fact, as the great Hunter says, the mere skeleton of the whale bears the same relation to the fully invested and padded animal as the insect does to the chrysalis that so roundingly envelopes it. This peculiarity is strikingly evinced in the head, as in some part of this book will be incidentally shown. It is also very curiously displayed in the side fin, the bones of which almost exactly answer to the bones of the human hand, minus only the thumb. This fin has four regular bone-fingers, the index, middle, ring, and little finger. But all these are permanently lodged in their fleshy covering, as the human fingers in an artificial covering. "However recklessly the whale may sometimes serve us," said humorous Stubb one day, "he can never be truly said to handle us without mittens."

For all these reasons, then, any way you may look at it, you must needs conclude that the great Leviathan is that one creature in the world which must remain unpainted to the last. True, one portrait may hit the mark much nearer than another, but none can hit it with any very considerable degree of exactness. So there is no earthly way of finding out precisely what the whale really looks like. And the only mode in which you can derive even a tolerable idea of his living contour, is by going a whaling yourself; but by so doing, you run no small risk of being eternally stove and sunk by him. Wherefore, it seems to me you had best not be too fastidious in your curiosity touching this Leviathan.

CHAPTER 56

Of the Less Erroneous Pictures of Whales,
and the True Pictures of Whaling Scenes

In connexion with the monstrous pictures of whales, I am strongly tempted here to enter upon those still more monstrous stories of them which are to be found in certain books, both ancient and modern, especially in Pliny, Purchas, Hackluyt, Harris, Cuvier, &c. But I pass that matter by.

I know of only four published outlines of the great Sperm Whale; Colnett's, Huggins's, Frederick Cuvier's, and Beale's. In the previous chapter Colnett and Cuvier have been referred to. Huggins's is far better than theirs; but, by great odds, Beale's is the best. All Beale's drawings of this whale are good, excepting the middle figure in the picture of three whales in various attitudes, capping his second chapter. His frontispiece, boats attacking Sperm Whales, though no doubt calculated to excite the civil scepticism of some parlor men, is admirably correct and life-like in its general effect. Some of the Sperm Whale drawings in J. Ross Browne are pretty correct in contour; but they are wretchedly engraved. That is not his fault though.

Of the Right Whale, the best outline pictures are in Scoresby; but they are drawn on too small a scale to convey a desirable impression. He has but one picture of whaling scenes, and this is a sad deficiency, because it is by such pictures only, when at all well done, that you can derive anything like a truthful idea of the living whale as seen by his living hunters.

But, taken for all in all, by far the finest, though in some details not the most correct, presentations of whales and whaling scenes to be anywhere found, are two large French engravings, well executed, and taken from paintings by one Garnery. Respectively, they represent attacks on the Sperm and Right Whale. In the first engraving a noble Sperm Whale is depicted in full majesty of might, just risen beneath the boat from the profundities of the ocean, and bearing high in the air upon his back the terrific wreck of the stoven planks. The prow of the boat is partially unbroken, and is drawn just balancing upon the monster's spine; and standing in that prow, for that one single incomputable flash of time, you behold an oarsman, half shrouded by the incensed boiling spout of the whale, and in the act of leaping, as if from a precipice. The action of the whole thing is wonderfully good and true. The half-emptied line-tub floats on the whitened sea; the wooden poles of the spilled harpoons obliquely bob in it; the heads of the swimming crew are scattered about the whale in contrasting expressions of affright; while in the black stormy distance the ship is bearing down upon the scene. Serious fault might be found with the anatomical details of this whale, but let that pass; since, for the life of me, I could not draw so good a one.

In the second engraving, the boat is in the act of drawing alongside the barnacled flank of a large running Right Whale, that rolls his black weedy bulk in the sea like some mossy rock-slide from the Patagonian cliffs. His jets are erect, full, and black like soot; so that from so abounding a smoke in the chimney, you would think there must be a brave supper cooking in the great bowels below. Sea fowls are pecking at the small crabs, shell-fish, and other sea candies and maccaroni, which the Right Whale sometimes carries on his pestilent back. And all the while the thick-lipped leviathan is rushing through the deep, leaving tons of tumultuous white curds in his wake, and causing the slight boat to rock in the swells like a skiff caught nigh the paddle-wheels of an ocean steamer. Thus, the foreground is all raging commotion; but behind, in admirable artistic contrast, is the glassy level of a sea becalmed, the drooping unstarched sails of the powerless ship, and the inert mass of a dead whale, a conquered fortress, with the flag of capture lazily hanging from the whale-pole inserted into his spout-hole.

Who Garnery the painter is, or was, I know not. But my life for it he was either practically conversant with his subject, or else marvellously tutored by some experienced whaleman. The French are the lads for painting action. Go and gaze upon all the paintings of Europe, and where will you find such a gallery of living and breathing commotion on canvas, as in that triumphal hall at Versailles; where the beholder fights his way, pell-mell, through the consecutive great battles of France; where every sword seems a flash of the Northern Lights, and the successive armed kings and Emperors dash by, like a charge of crowned centaurs? Not wholly unworthy of a place in that gallery, are these sea battle-pieces of Garnery.

The natural aptitude of the French for seizing the picturesqueness of things seems to be peculiarly evinced in what paintings and engravings they have of their whaling scenes. With not one tenth of England's experience in the fishery, and not the thousandth part of that of the Americans, they have nevertheless furnished both nations with the only finished sketches at all capable of conveying the real spirit of the whale hunt. For the most part, the English and American whale draughtsmen seem entirely content with presenting the mechanical outline of things, such as the vacant profile of the whale; which, so far as picturesqueness of effect is concerned, is about tantamount to sketching the profile of a pyramid. Even Scoresby, the justly renowned Right whaleman, after giving us a stiff full length of the Greenland whale, and three or four delicate miniatures of narwhales and porpoises, treats us to a series of classical engravings of boat hooks, chopping knives, and grapnels; and with the microscopic diligence of a Leuwenhoeck submits to the inspection of a shivering world ninety-six fac-similes of magnified Arctic snow crystals. I mean no disparagement to the excellent voyager (I honor him for a veteran), but in so important a matter it was certainly an oversight not to have procured for every crystal a sworn affidavit taken before a Greenland Justice of the Peace.

In addition to those fine engravings from Garnery, there are two other French engravings worthy of note, by some one who subscribes himself "H. Durand." One of them, though not precisely adapted to our present purpose, nevertheless deserves mention on other accounts. It is a quiet noon-scene among the isles of the Pacific; a French whaler anchored, inshore, in a calm, and lazily taking water on board; the loosened sails of the ship, and the long leaves of the palms in the background, both drooping together in the breezeless air. The effect is very fine, when considered with reference to its presenting the hardy fishermen under one of their few aspects of oriental repose. The other engraving is quite a different affair: the ship hove-to upon the open sea, and in the very heart of the Leviathanic life, with a Right Whale alongside; the vessel (in the act of cutting-in) hove over to the monster as if to a quay; and a boat, hurriedly pushing off from this scene of activity, is about giving chase to whales in the distance. The harpoons and lances lie levelled for use; three oarsmen are just setting the mast in its hole; while from a sudden roll of the sea, the little craft stands half-erect out of the water, like a rearing horse. From the ship, the smoke of the torments of the boiling whale is going up like the smoke over a village of smithies; and to windward, a black cloud, rising up with earnest of squalls and rains, seems to quicken the activity of the excited seamen.

Chapter 57

Of Whales in Paint; in Teeth;
in Wood; in Sheet-Iron; in Stone;
in Mountains; in Stars

On Tower-hill, as you go down to the London docks, you may have seen a crippled beggar (or *kedger*, as the sailors say) holding a painted board before him, representing the tragic scene in which he lost his leg. There are three whales and three boats; and one of the boats (presumed to contain the missing leg in all its original integrity) is being crunched by the jaws of the foremost whale. Any time these ten years, they tell me, has that man held up that picture, and exhibited that stump to an incredulous world. But the time of his justification has now come. His three whales are as good whales as were ever published in Wapping, at any rate; and his stump as unquestionable a stump as any you will find in the western clearings. But, though for ever mounted on that stump, never a stump-speech does the poor whale-man make; but, with downcast eyes, stands ruefully contemplating his own amputation.

Throughout the Pacific, and also in Nantucket, and New Bedford, and Sag Harbor, you will come across lively sketches of whales and whaling-scenes, graven by the fishermen themselves on Sperm Whale-teeth, or ladies' busks wrought out of the Right Whale-bone, and other like skrimshander articles, as the whalemen call the numerous little ingenious contrivances they elaborately carve out of the rough material, in their hours of ocean leisure. Some of them have little boxes of dentistical-looking implements, specially intended for the skrimshandering business. But, in general, they toil with their jack-knives alone; and, with that almost omnipotent tool of the sailor, they will turn you out anything you please, in the way of a mariner's fancy.

Long exile from Christendom and civilization inevitably restores a man to that condition in which God placed him, *i.e.* what is called savagery. Your true whale-hunter is as much a savage as an Iroquois. I myself am a savage, owning no allegiance but to the King of the Cannibals; and ready at any moment to rebel against him.

Now, one of the peculiar characteristics of the savage in his domestic hours, is his wonderful patience of industry. An ancient Hawaiian war-club or spear-paddle, in its full multiplicity and elaboration of carving, is as great a trophy of human perseverance as a Latin lexicon. For, with but a bit of broken sea-shell or a shark's tooth, that miraculous intricacy of wooden net-work has been achieved; and it has cost steady years of steady application.

As with the Hawaiian savage, so with the white sailor-savage. With the same marvellous patience, and with the same single shark's tooth, of his one poor jack-knife, he will carve you a bit of bone sculpture, not quite as workmanlike, but as close packed in its maziness of design, as the Greek savage, Achilles's shield; and full of barbaric spirit and suggestiveness, as the prints of that fine old Dutch savage, Albert Durer.

Wooden whales, or whales cut in profile out of the small dark slabs of the noble South Sea war-wood, are frequently met with in the forecastles of American whalers. Some of them are done with much accuracy.

At some old gable-roofed country houses you will see brass whales hung by the tail for knockers to the road-side door. When the porter is sleepy, the anvil-headed whale would be best. But these knocking whales are seldom remarkable as faithful essays. On the spires of some old-fashioned churches you will see sheet-iron whales placed there for weather-cocks; but they are so elevated, and besides that are to all intents and purposes so labelled with "*Hands off!*" you cannot examine them closely enough to decide upon their merit.

In bony, ribby regions of the earth, where at the base of high broken cliffs masses of rock lie strewn in fantastic groupings upon the plain, you will often discover images as of the petrified forms of the Leviathan partly merged in grass, which of a windy day breaks against them in a surf of green surges.

Then, again, in mountainous countries where the traveller is continually girdled by amphitheatrical heights; here and there from some lucky point of view you will catch passing glimpses of the profiles of whales defined along the undulating ridges. But you must be a thorough whaleman, to see these sights; and not only that, but if you wish to return to such a sight again, you must be sure and take the exact intersecting latitude and longitude of your first stand-point, else so chance-like are such observations of the hills, that your precise, previous stand-point would require a laborious re-discovery; like the Soloma Islands, which still remain incognita, though once high-ruffed Mendanna trod them and old Figuera chronicled them.

Nor when expandingly lifted by your subject, can you fail to trace out great whales in the starry heavens, and boats in pursuit of them; as when long filled with thoughts of war the Eastern nations saw armies locked in battle among the clouds. Thus at the North have I chased Leviathan round and round the Pole with the revolutions of the bright points that first defined him to me. And beneath the effulgent Antarctic skies I have boarded the Argo-Navis, and joined the chase against the starry Cetus far beyond the utmost stretch of Hydrus and the Flying Fish.

With a frigate's anchors for my bridle-bitts and fasces of harpoons for spurs, would I could mount that whale and leap the topmost skies, to see whether the fabled heavens with all their countless tents really lie encamped beyond my mortal sight!

CHAPTER 58

Brit

*

Indeed, in other respects, you can hardly regard any creatures of the deep with the same feelings that you do those of the shore. For though some old naturalists have maintained that all creatures of the land are of their kind in the sea; and though taking a broad general view of the thing, this may very well be; yet coming to specialties, where, for example, does the ocean furnish any fish that in disposition answers to the sagacious kindness of the dog? The accursed shark alone can in any generic respect be said to bear comparative analogy to him.

------

* That part of the sea known among whalemen as the "Brazil Banks" does not bear that name as the Banks of Newfoundland do, because of there being shallows and soundings there, but because of this remarkable meadow-like appearance, caused by the vast drifts of brit continually floating in those latitudes, where the Right Whale is often chased.

But though, to landsmen in general, the native inhabitants of the seas have ever been regarded with emotions unspeakably unsocial and repelling; though we know the sea to be an everlasting terra incognita, so that Columbus sailed over numberless unknown worlds to discover his one superficial western one; though, by vast odds, the most terrific of all mortal disasters have immemorially and indiscriminately befallen tens and hundreds of thousands of those who have gone upon the waters; though but a moment's consideration will teach, that however baby man may brag of his science and skill, and however much, in a flattering future, that science and skill may augment; yet for ever and for ever, to the crack of doom, the sea will insult and murder him, and pulverize the stateliest, stiffest frigate he can make; nevertheless, by the continual repetition of these very impressions, man has lost that sense of the full awfulness of the sea which aboriginally belongs to it.

The first boat we read of, floated on an ocean, that with Portuguese vengeance had whelmed a whole world without leaving so much as a widow. That same ocean rolls now; that same ocean destroyed the wrecked ships of last year. Yea, foolish mortals, Noah's flood is not yet subsided; two thirds of the fair world it yet covers.

Wherein differ the sea and the land, that a miracle upon one is not a miracle upon the other? Preternatural terrors rested upon the Hebrews, when under the feet of Korah and his company the live ground opened and swallowed them up for ever; yet not a modern sun ever sets, but in precisely the same manner the live sea swallows up ships and crews.

But not only is the sea such a foe to man who is an alien to it, but it is also a fiend to its own off-spring; worse than the Persian host who murdered his own guests; sparing not the creatures which itself hath spawned. Like a savage tigress that tossing in the jungle overlays her own cubs, so the sea dashes even the mightiest whales against the rocks, and leaves them there side by side with the split wrecks of ships. No mercy, no power but its own controls it. Panting and snorting like a mad battle steed that has lost its rider, the masterless ocean overruns the globe.

Consider the subtleness of the sea; how its most dreaded creatures glide under water, unapparent for the most part, and treacherously hidden beneath the loveliest tints of azure. Consider also the devilish brilliance and beauty of many of its most remorseless tribes, as the dainty embellished shape of many species of sharks. Consider, once more, the universal cannibalism of the sea; all whose creatures prey upon each other, carrying on eternal war since the world began.

Consider all this; and then turn to this green, gentle, and most docile earth; consider them both, the sea and the land; and do you not find a strange analogy to something in yourself? For as this appalling ocean surrounds the verdant land, so in the soul of man there lies one insular Tahiti, full of peace and joy, but encompassed by all the horrors of the half known life. God keep thee! Push not off from that isle, thou canst never return!

CHAPTER 59

Squid

in the surrounding serenity her

, however unattended with any stagnant calm

Whether the flitting attendance of the one still and solitary jet had gradually worked upon Ahab, so that he was now prepared to connect the ideas of mildness and repose with the first sight of the particular whale he pursued; however this was, or whether his eagerness betrayed him; whichever way it might have been,

There seems some ground to imagine that the great Kraken of Bishop Pontoppodan may ultimately resolve itself into Squid. The manner in which the Bishop describes it, as alternately rising and sinking, with some other particulars he narrates, in all this the two correspond. But much abatement is necessary with respect to the incredible bulk he assigns it.

By some naturalists who have vaguely heard rumors of the mysterious creature, here spoken of, it is included among the class of cuttle-fish, to which, indeed, in certain external respects it would seem to belong, but only as the Anak of the tribe.

CHAPTER 60

The Line

most

, not like the worm-pipe of a still though, but

In the English boats two tubs are used instead of one; the same line being continuously coiled in both tubs. There is some advantage in this; because these twin-tubs being so small they fit more readily into the boat, and do not strain it so much; whereas,   American   American

,

Again: as the profound calm which only apparently precedes and prophesies of the storm, is perhaps more awful than the storm itself; for, indeed, the calm is but the wrapper and envelope of the storm; and contains it in itself, as the seemingly harmless rifle holds the fatal powder, and the ball, and the explosion; so the graceful repose of the line, as it silently serpentines about the oarsmen before being brought into actual play—this is a thing which carries more of true terror than any other aspect of this dangerous affair. But why say more? All men live enveloped in whale-lines. All are born with halters round their necks; but it is only when caught in the swift, sudden turn of death, that mortals realize the silent, subtle, ever-present perils of life. And if you be a philosopher, though seated in the whale-boat, you would not at heart feel one whit more of terror, than though seated before your evening fire with a poker, and not a harpoon, by your side.

CHAPTER 61

Stubb Kills a Whale

slowly and regularly

; that part obliquely projecting from the mad yeast which he brewed *

**

, for a moment,

---

* It will be seen in some other place of what a very light substance the entire interior of the sperm whale's enormous head consists. Though apparently the most massive, it is by far the most buoyant part about him. So that with ease he elevates it in the air, and invariably does so when going at his utmost speed. Besides, such is the breadth of the upper part of the front of his head, and such the tapering cut-water formation of the lower part, that by obliquely elevating his head, he thereby may be said to transform himself from a bluff-bowed sluggish galliot into a sharppointed New York pilot-boat.

** Partly to show the indispensableness of this act, it may here be stated, that, in the old Dutch fishery, a mop was used to dash the running line with water; in many other ships, a wooden piggin, or bailer, is set apart for that purpose. Your hat, however, is the most convenient.

CHAPTER 62

The Dart

hapless

CHAPTER 63

The Crotch

Out of the trunk, the branches grow; out of them, the twigs. So, in productive subjects, grow the chapters.

(mentioned in a preceding chapter)

CHAPTER 64

Stubb's Supper

*

small,   ,

---

*   A little item may as well be related here. The strongest and most reliable hold which the ship has upon the whale when moored alongside, is by the flukes or tail; and as from its greater density that part is relatively heavier than any other (excepting the side-fins), its flexibility even in death, causes it to sink low beneath the surface; so that with the hand you cannot get at it from the boat, in order to put the chain round it. But this difficulty is ingeniously overcome: a small, strong line is prepared with a wooden float at its outer end, and a weight in its middle, while the other end is secured to the ship. By adroit management the wooden float is made to rise on the other side of the mass, so that now having girdled the whale, the chain is readily made to follow suit; and being slipped along the body, is at last locked fast round the smallest part of the tail, at the point of junction with its broad flukes or lobes.

(as before you heard them)   This particular feat of the shark seems all but miraculous. How at such an apparently unassailable surface, they contrive to gouge out such symmetrical mouthfuls, remains a part of the universal problem of all things. The mark they thus leave on the whale, may best be likened to the hollow made by a carpenter in countersinking for a screw.

a parcel is to be carried anywhere, or   and though one or two other like instances might be set down, touching the set terms, places, and occasions, when sharks do most socially congregate, and most hilariously feast;   at sea

But, as yet, Stubb heeded not the mumblings of the banquet that was going on so nigh him, no more than the sharks heeded the smacking of his own epicurean lips.

"Cook, cook!—where's that old Fleece?" he cried at length, widening his legs still further, as if to form a more secure base for his supper; and, at the same time darting his fork into the dish, as if stabbing with his lance; "cook, you cook!—sail this way, cook!"

The old black, not in any very high glee at having been previously roused from his warm hammock at a most unseasonable hour, came shambling along from his galley, for, like many old blacks, there was something the matter with his knee-pans, which he did not keep well scoured like his other pans; this old Fleece, as they called him, came shuffling and limping along, assisting his step with his tongs, which, after a clumsy fashion, were made of straightened iron hoops; this old Ebony floundered along, and in obedience to the word of command, came to a dead stop on the opposite side of Stubb's sideboard; when, with both hands folded before him, and resting on his two-legged cane, he bowed his arched back still further over, at the same time sideways inclining his head, so as to bring his best ear into play.

"Cook," said Stubb, rapidly lifting a rather reddish morsel to his mouth, "don't you think this steak is rather overdone? You've been beating this steak too much, cook; it's too tender. Don't I always say that to be good, a whale-steak must be tough? There are those sharks now over the side, don't you see they prefer it tough and rare? What a shindy they are kicking up! Cook, go and talk to 'em; tell 'em they are welcome to help themselves civilly, and in moderation, but they must keep quiet. Blast me, if I can hear my own voice. Away, cook, and deliver my message. Here, take this lantern," snatching one from his sideboard; "now then, go and preach to 'em!"

Sullenly taking the offered lantern, old Fleece limped across the deck to the bulwarks; and then, with one hand dropping his light low over the sea, so as to get a good view of his congregation, with the other hand he solemnly flourished his tongs, and leaning far over the side in a mumbling voice began addressing the sharks, while Stubb, softly crawling behind, overheard all that was said.

"Fellow-critters: I'se ordered here to say dat you must stop dat dam noise dare. You hear? Stop dat dam smackin' ob de lip! Massa Stubb say dat you can fill your dam bellies up to de hatchings, but by Gor! you must stop dat dam racket!"

"Cook," here interposed Stubb, accompanying the word with a sudden slap on the shoulder,—"Cook! why, damn your eyes, you mustn't swear that way when you're preaching. That's no way to convert sinners, cook!"

"Who dat? Den preach to him yourself," sullenly turning to go.

"No, cook; go on, go on."

"Well, den, Belubed fellow-critters:"—

"Right!" exclaimed Stubb, approvingly, "coax 'em to it; try that," and Fleece continued.

"Dough you is all sharks, and by natur wery woracious, yet I zay to you, fellow-critters, dat dat woraciousness—'top dat dam slappin' ob de tail! How you tink to hear, 'spose you keep up such a dam slappin' and bitin' dare?"

"Cook," cried Stubb, collaring him, "I won't have that swearing. Talk to 'em gentlemanly."

Once more the sermon proceeded.

"Your woraciousness, fellow-critters, I don't blame ye so much for; dat is natur, and can't be helped; but to gobern dat wicked natur, dat is de pint. You is sharks, sartin; but if you gobern de shark in you, why den you be angel; for all angel is not'ing more dan de shark well goberned. Now, look here, bred'ren, just try wonst to be cibil, a helping yourselbs from dat whale. Don't be tearin' de blubber out your neighbor's mout, I say. Is not one shark good right as toder to dat whale? And, by Gor, none on you has de right to dat whale; dat whale belong to some one else. I know some o' you has berry brig mout, brigger dan oders; but den de brig mouts sometimes has de small bellies; so dat de brigness of de mout is not to swaller wid, but to bit off de blubber for de small fry ob sharks, dat can't get into de scrouge to help demselves."

"Well done, old Fleece!" cried Stubb, "that's Christianity; go on."

"No use goin' on; de dam willains will keep a scougin' and slappin' each oder, Massa Stubb; dey don't hear one word; no use a-preachin' to such dam g'uttons as you call 'em, till dare bellies is full, and dare bellies is bottomless; and when dey do get em full, dey wont hear you den; for den dey sink in the sea, go fast to sleep on de coral, and can't hear not'ing at all, no more, for eber and eber."

"Upon my soul, I am about of the same opinion; so give the benediction, Fleece, and I'll away to my supper."

Upon this, Fleece, holding both hands over the fishy mob, raised his shrill voice, and cried—

"Cussed fellow-critters! Kick up de damndest row as ever you can; fill your dam' bellies 'till dey bust—and den die."

"Now, cook," said Stubb, resuming his supper at the capstan; "stand just where you stood before, there, over against me, and pay particular attention."

"All dention," said Fleece, again stooping over upon his tongs in the desired position.

"Well," said Stubb, helping himself freely meanwhile; "I shall now go back to the subject of this steak. In the first place, how old are you, cook?"

"What dat do wid de 'teak," said the old black, testily.

"Silence! How old are you, cook?"

"'Bout ninety, dey say," he gloomily muttered.

"And you have lived in this world hard upon one hundred years, cook, and don't know yet how to cook a whale-steak?" rapidly bolting another mouthful at the last word, so that morsel seemed a continuation of the question. "Where were you born, cook?"

"'Hind de hatchway, in ferry-boat, goin' ober de Roanoke."

"Born in a ferry-boat! That's queer, too. But I want to know what country you were born in, cook!"

"Didn't I say de Roanoke country?" he cried sharply.

"No, you didn't, cook; but I'll tell you what I'm coming to, cook. You must go home and be born over again; you don't know how to cook a whale-steak yet."

"Bress my soul, if I cook noder one," he growled, angrily, turning round to depart.

"Come back here, cook;—here, hand me those tongs;—now take that bit of steak there, and tell me if you think that steak cooked as it should be? Take it, I say"—holding the tongs towards him—"take it, and taste it."

Faintly smacking his withered lips over it for a moment, the old negro muttered, "Best cooked 'teak I eber taste; joosy, berry joosy."

"Cook," said Stubb, squaring himself once more; "do you belong to the church?"

"Passed one once in Cape-Down," said the old man sullenly.

"And you have once in your life passed a holy church in Cape-Town, where you doubtless overheard a holy parson addressing his hearers as his beloved fellow-creatures, have you, cook! And yet you come here, and tell me such a dreadful lie as you did just now, eh?" said Stubb. "Where do you expect to go to, cook?"

"Go to bed berry soon," he mumbled, half-turning as he spoke.

"Avast! heave to! I mean when you die, cook. It's an awful question. Now what's your answer?"

"When dis old brack man dies," said the negro slowly, changing his whole air and demeanor, "he hisself won't go nowhere; but some bressed angel will come and fetch him."

"Fetch him? How? In a coach and four, as they fetched Elijah? And fetch him where?"

"Up dere," said Fleece, holding his tongs straight over his head, and keeping it there very solemnly.

"So, then, you expect to go up into our main-top, do you, cook, when you are dead? But don't you know the higher you climb, the colder it gets? Main-top, eh?"

"Didn't say dat t'all," said Fleece, again in the sulks.

"You said up there, didn't you? and now look yourself, and see where your tongs are pointing. But, perhaps you expect to get into heaven by crawling through the lubber's hole, cook; but, no, no, cook, you don't get there, except you go the regular way, round by the rigging. It's a ticklish business, but must be done, or else it's no go. But none of us are in heaven yet. Drop your tongs, cook, and hear my orders. Do ye hear? Hold your hat in one hand, and clap t'other a'top of your heart, when I'm giving my orders, cook. What! that your heart, there?—that's your gizzard! Aloft! aloft!—that's it—now you have it. Hold it there now, and pay attention."

"All 'dention," said the old black, with both hands placed as desired, vainly wriggling his grizzled head, as if to get both ears in front at one and the same time.

"Well then, cook, you see this whale-steak of yours was so very bad, that I have put it out of sight as soon as possible; you see that, don't you? Well, for the future, when you cook another whale-steak for my private table here, the capstan, I'll tell you what to do so as not to spoil it by overdoing. Hold the steak in one hand, and show a live coal to it with the other; that done, dish it; d'ye hear? And now to-morrow, cook, when we are cutting in the fish, be sure you stand by to get the tips of his fins; have them put in pickle. As for the ends of the flukes, have them soused, cook. There, now ye may go."

But Fleece had hardly got three paces off, when he was recalled.

"Cook, give me cutlets for supper to-morrow night in the mid-watch. D'ye hear? away you sail, then.—Halloa! stop! make a bow before you go.—Avast heaving again! Whale-balls for breakfast—don't forget."

"Wish, by gor! whale eat him, 'stead of him eat whale. I'm bressed if he ain't more of shark dan Massa Shark hisself," muttered the old man, limping away; with which sage ejaculation he went to his hammock.

CHAPTER 65

The Whale as a Dish

this   so   a thing that one must needs go a little into the history and phi-losophy of it

It is upon record, that three centuries ago the tongue of the Right Whale was esteemed a great delicacy in France, and commanded large prices there. Also, that in Henry VIIIth's time, a certain cook of the court obtained a handsome reward for inventing an admirable sauce to be eaten with barbacued por-poises, which, you remember, are a species of whale. Porpoises, indeed, are to this day considered fine eating. The meat is made into balls about the size of billiard balls, and being well seasoned and spiced might be taken for turtle-balls or veal balls. The old monks of Dunfermline were very fond of them. They had a great porpoise grant from the crown.

,

,

It is not, perhaps, entirely because the whale is so excessively unctuous that landsmen seem to regard the eating of him with abhorrence; that appears to result, in some way, from the consideration before mentioned: i.e. that a man should eat a newly murdered thing of the sea, and eat it too by its own light. But no doubt the first man that ever murdered an ox was regarded as a murderer; perhaps he was hung; and if he had been put on his trial by oxen, he certainly would have been; and he certainly deserved it if any murderer does. Go to the meat-market of a Saturday night and see the crowds of live bipeds staring up at the long rows of dead quadrupeds. Does not that sight take a tooth out of the cannibal's jaw? Cannibals? who is not a cannibal? I tell you it will be more tolerable for the Fejee that salted down a lean missionary in his cellar against a coming famine; it will be more tolerable for that provident Fejee, I say, in the day of judgment, than for thee, civilized and enlightened gourmand, who nailest geese to the ground and feastest on their bloated livers in thy pate-de-foie-gras.

But Stubb, he eats the whale by its own light, does he? and that is adding insult to injury, is it? Look at your knife-handle, there, my civilized and enlightened gourmand dining off that roast beef, what is that handle made of?—what but the bones of the brother of the very ox you are eating? And what do you pick your teeth with, after devouring that fat goose? With a feather of the same fowl. And with what quill did the Secretary of the Society for the Suppression of Cruelty to Ganders formally indite his circulars? It is only within the last month or two that that society passed a resolution to patronize nothing but steel pens.

CHAPTER 66

The Shark Massacre

, to be sure,

*

Nor was this all. It was unsafe to meddle with the corpses and ghosts of these creatures. A sort of generic or Pantheistic vitality seemed to lurk in their very joints and bones, after what might be called the individual life had departed. Killed and hoisted on deck for the sake of his skin, one of these sharks almost took poor Queequeg's hand off, when he tried to shut down the dead lid of his murderous jaw.

"Queequeg no care what god made him shark," said the savage, agonizingly lifting his hand up and down; "wedder Fejee god or Nantucket god; but de god wat made shark must be one dam Ingin."

CHAPTER 67

Cutting In

CHAPTER 68

The Blanket

I have had controversies about it with experienced whalemen afloat, and learned naturalists ashore. My original opinion remains unchanged; but it is only an opinion.

I have several such dried bits, which I use for marks in my whale-books. It is transparent, as I said before; and being laid upon the printed page, I have

---

*

sometimes pleased myself with fancying it exerted a magnifying influence. At any rate, it is pleasant to read about whales through their own spectacles, as you may say. But   But no more of this.

In life, the visible surface of the Sperm Whale is   Almost invariably it is all over obliquely crossed and re-crossed with numberless straight marks in thick array, something like those in the finest Italian line engravings. But these marks do not seem to be impressed upon the isinglass substance above mentioned, but seem to be seen through it, as if they were engraved upon the body itself. Nor is this all. In some instances, to the quick, observant eye, those linear marks, as in a veritable engraving, but afford the ground for far other delineations. These are hieroglyphical; that is, if you call those mysterious cyphers on the walls of pyramids hieroglyphics, then that is the proper word to use in the present connexion. By my retentive memory of the hieroglyphics upon one Sperm Whale in particular, I was much struck with a plate representing the old Indian characters chiselled on the famous hieroglyphic palisades on the banks of the Upper Mississippi. Like those mystic rocks, too, the mystic-marked whale remains undecipherable. This allusion to the Indian rocks reminds me of another thing. Besides all the other phenomena which the exterior of the Sperm Whale presents, he not seldom displays the back, and more especially his flanks, effaced in great part of the regular linear appearance, by reason of numerous rude scratches, altogether of an irregular, random aspect. I should say that those New England rocks on the sea-coast, which Agassiz imagines to bear the marks of violent scraping contact with vast floating icebergs—I should say, that those rocks must not a little resemble the Sperm Whale in this particular. It also seems to me that such scratches in the whale are probably made by hostile contact with other whales; for I have most remarked them in the large, full-grown bulls of the species.

A word or two more concerning this matter of the skin or blubber of the whale. It has already been said, that it is stript from him in long pieces, called blanket-pieces. Like most sea-terms, this one is very happy and significant.

For the whale is indeed wrapt up in his blubber as in a real blanket or counterpane; or, still better, an Indian poncho slipt over his head, and skirting his extremity. It is by reason of this cosy blanketing of his body, that the whale is enabled to keep himself comfortable in all weathers, in all seas, times, and tides. What would become of a Greenland whale, say, in those shuddering, icy seas of the North, if unsupplied with his cosy surtout? True, other fish are found exceedingly brisk in those Hyperborean waters; but these, be it observed, are your cold-blooded, lungless fish, whose very bellies are refrigerators; creatures, that warm themselves under the lee of an iceberg, as a traveller in winter would bask before an inn fire; whereas, like man, the whale has lungs and warm blood. Freeze his blood, and he dies. How wonderful is it then—except after explanation—that this great monster, to whom corporeal warmth is as indispensable as it is to man; how wonderful that he should be found at home, immersed to his lips for life in those Arctic waters! where, when seamen fall overboard, they are sometimes found, months afterwards, perpendicularly frozen into the hearts of fields of ice, as a fly is found glued in amber. But more surprising is it to know, as has been proved by experiment, that the blood of a Polar whale is warmer than that of a Borneo negro in summer.

It does seem to me, that herein we see the rare virtue of a strong individual vitality, and the rare virtue of thick walls, and the rare virtue of interior spaciousness. Oh, man! admire and model thyself after the whale! Do thou, too, remain warm among ice. Do thou, too, live in this world without being of it. Be cool at the equator; keep thy blood fluid at the Pole. Like the great dome of St. Peter's, and like the great whale, retain, O man! in all seasons a temperature of thine own.

But how easy and how hopeless to teach these fine things! Of erections, how few are domed like St. Peter's! of creatures, how few vast as the whale!

CHAPTER 69

The Funeral

,

The sea-vultures all in pious mourning, the air-sharks all punctiliously in black or speckled. In life but few of them would have helped the whale, I ween, if peradventure he had needed it; but upon the banquet of his funeral they most piously do pounce. Oh, horrible vultureism of earth! from which not the mightiest whale is free.

Nor is this the end. Desecrated as the body is, a vengeful ghost survives and hovers over it to scare. Espied by some timid man-of-war or blundering discovery-vessel from afar, when the distance obscuring the swarming fowls, nevertheless still shows the white mass floating in the sun, and the white spray heaving high against it; straightway the whale's unharming corpse, with trembling fingers is set down in the log—*shoals, rocks, and breakers hereabouts: beware!* And for years afterwards, perhaps, ships shun the place; leaping over it as silly sheep leap over a vacuum, because their leader originally leaped there when a stick was held. There's your law of precedents; there's your utility of traditions; there's the story of your obstinate survival of old beliefs never bottomed on the earth, and now not even hovering in the air! There's orthodoxy!

Thus, while in life the great whale's body may have been a real terror to his foes, in his death his ghost becomes a powerless panic to a world.

Are you a believer in ghosts, my friend? There are other ghosts than the Cock-Lane one, and far deeper men than Doctor Johnson who believe in them.

CHAPTER 70

The Sphynx

, even by the immense tackles of a whaler, this

"which, though ungarnished with a beard, yet here and there lookest hoary with mosses; Thou hast been where bell or diver never went; hast slept by many a sailor's side, where sleepless mothers would give their lives to lay them down. Thou saw'st the locked lovers when leaping from their flaming ship; heart to heart they sank beneath the exulting wave; true to each other, when heaven seemed false to them. Thou saw'st the murdered mate when tossed by pirates from the midnight deck; for hours he fell into the deeper midnight of the insatiate maw; and his murderers still sailed on unharmed—while swift lightnings shivered the neighboring ship that would have borne a righteous husband to outstretched, longing arms."

"Sail ho!" cried a triumphant voice from the main-mast-head.

"Aye? Well, now, that's cheering," cried Ahab, suddenly erecting himself, while whole thunder-clouds swept aside from his brow. "That lively cry upon this deadly calm might almost convert a better man.—Where away?"

"Three points on the starboard bow, sir, and bringing down her breeze to us!"

"Better and better, man. Would now St. Paul would come along that way, and to my breezelessness bring his breeze! O Nature, and O soul of man! how far beyond all utterance are your linked analogies! not the smallest atom stirs or lives on matter, but has its cunning duplicate in mind."

CHAPTER 71

The Jeroboam's Story

Hand in hand, ship and breeze blew on; but the breeze came faster than the ship, and soon the Pequod began to rock.

By and by, through the glass the stranger's boats and manned mast-heads proved her a whale-ship. But as she was so far to windward, and shooting by, apparently making a passage to some other ground, the Pequod could not hope to reach her. So the signal was set to see what response would be made.

Here be it said, that like the vessels of military marines, the ships of the American Whale Fleet have each a private signal; all which signals being collected in a book with the names of the respective vessels attached, every captain is provided with it. Thereby, the whale commanders are enabled to recognize each other upon the ocean, even at considerable distances and with no small facility.

The Pequod's signal was at last responded to by the stranger's setting her own; which proved the ship to be the Jeroboam of Nantucket. Squaring her yards, she bore down, ranged abeam under the Pequod's lee, and lowered a boat; it soon drew nigh; but, as the side-ladder was being rigged by Starbuck's order to accommodate the visiting captain, the stranger in question waved his hand from his boat's stern in token of that proceeding being entirely unnecessary. It turned out that the Jeroboam had a malignant epidemic on board, and that Mayhew, her captain, was fearful of infecting the Pequod's company. For, though himself and boat's crew remained untainted, and though his ship was half a rifle-shot off, and an incorruptible sea and air rolling and flowing between; yet conscientiously adhering to the timid quarantine of the land, he peremptorily refused to come into direct contact with the Pequod.

But this did by no means prevent all communications. Preserving an interval of some few yards between itself and the ship, the Jeroboam's boat by the occasional use of its oars contrived to keep parallel to the Pequod, as she heavily forged through the sea (for by this time it blew very fresh), with her main-topsail aback; though, indeed, at times by the sudden onset of a large rolling wave, the boat would be pushed some way ahead; but would be soon skilfully brought to her proper bearings again. Subject to this, and other the like interruptions now and then, a conversation was sustained between the two parties; but at intervals not without still another interruption of a very different sort.

Pulling an oar in the Jeroboam's boat, was a man of a singular appearance, even in that wild whaling life where individual notabilities make up all totalities. He was a small, short, youngish man, sprinkled all over his face with freckles, and wearing redundant yellow hair. A long-skirted, cabalistically-cut coat of a faded walnut tinge enveloped him; the overlapping sleeves of which were rolled up on his wrists. A deep, settled, fanatic delirium was in his eyes.

So soon as this figure had been first descried, Stubb had exclaimed—"That's he! that's he!—the long-togged scaramouch the Town-Ho's company told us of!" Stubb here alluded to a strange story told of the Jeroboam, and a certain man among her crew, some time previous when the Pequod spoke the Town-Ho. According to this account and what was subsequently learned, it seemed that the scaramouch in question had gained a wonderful ascendency over almost everybody in the Jeroboam. His story was this:

He had been originally nurtured among the crazy society of Neskyeuna Shakers, where he had been a great prophet; in their cracked, secret meetings having several times descended from heaven by the way of a trap-door, announcing the speedy opening of the seventh vial, which he carried in his vest-pocket; but, which, instead of containing gunpowder, was supposed to be charged with laudanum. A strange, apostolic whim having seized him, he had left Neskyeuna for Nantucket, where, with that cunning peculiar to craziness, he assumed a steady, common-sense exterior, and offered himself as a green-hand candidate for the Jeroboam's whaling voyage. They engaged him; but straightway upon the ship's getting out of sight of land, his insanity broke out in a freshet. He announced himself as the archangel Gabriel, and commanded the captain to jump overboard. He published his manifesto, whereby he set himself forth as the deliverer of the isles of the sea and vicar-general of all Oceanica. The unflinching earnestness with which he declared these things;—the dark, daring play of his sleepless, excited imagination, and all the preternatural terrors of real delirium, united to invest this Gabriel in the minds of the majority of the ignorant crew, with an atmosphere of sacredness. Moreover, they were afraid of him. As such a man, however, was not of much practical use in the ship, especially as he refused to work except when he pleased, the incredulous captain would fain have been rid of him; but apprised that that individual's intention was to land him in the first convenient port, the archangel forthwith opened all his seals and vials—devoting the ship and all hands to unconditional perdition, in case this intention was carried out. So strongly did he work upon his disciples among the crew, that at last in a body they went to the captain and told him if Gabriel was sent from the ship, not a man of them would remain. He was therefore forced to relinquish his plan. Nor would they permit Gabriel to be any way maltreated, say or do what he would; so that it came to pass that Gabriel had the complete freedom of the ship. The consequence of all this was, that the archangel cared little or nothing for the captain and mates; and since the epidemic had broken out, he carried a higher hand than ever; declaring that the plague, as he called it, was at his sole command; nor should it be stayed but according to his good pleasure. The sailors, mostly poor devils, cringed, and some of them fawned before him; in obedience to his instructions, sometimes rendering him personal homage, as to a god. Such things may seem incredible; but, however wondrous, they are true. Nor is the history of fanatics half so striking in respect to the measureless self-deception of the fanatic himself, as his measureless power of deceiving and bedevilling so many others. But it is time to return to the Pequod.

"I fear not thy epidemic, man," said Ahab from the bulwarks, to Captain Mayhew, who stood in the boat's stern; "come on board."

But now Gabriel started to his feet.

"Think, think of the fevers, yellow and bilious! Beware of the horrible plague!"

"Gabriel! Gabriel!" cried Captain Mayhew; "thou must either—" But that instant a headlong wave shot the boat far ahead, and its seethings drowned all speech.

"Hast thou seen the White Whale?" demanded Ahab, when the boat drifted back.

"Think, think of thy whale-boat, stoven and sunk! Beware of the horrible tail!"

"I tell thee again, Gabriel, that—" But again the boat tore ahead as if dragged by fiends. Nothing was said for some moments, while a succession of riotous waves rolled by, which by one of those occasional caprices of the seas were tumbling, not heaving it. Meantime, the hoisted sperm whale's head jogged about very violently, and Gabriel was seen eyeing it with rather more apprehensiveness than his archangel nature seemed to warrant.

When this interlude was over, Captain Mayhew began a dark story concerning Moby Dick; not, however, without frequent interruptions from Gabriel, whenever his name was mentioned, and the crazy sea that seemed leagued with him.

It seemed that the Jeroboam had not long left home, when upon speaking a whale-ship, her people were reliably apprised of the existence of Moby Dick, and the havoc he had made. Greedily sucking in this intelligence, Gabriel solemnly warned the captain against attacking the White Whale, in case the monster should be seen; in his gibbering insanity, pronouncing the White Whale to be no less a being than the Shaker God incarnated; the Shakers receiving the Bible. But when, some year or two afterwards, Moby Dick was fairly sighted from the mast-heads, Macey, the chief mate, burned with ardor to encounter him; and the captain himself being not unwilling to let him have the opportunity, despite all the archangel's denunciations and forewarnings, Macey succeeded in persuading five men to man his boat. With them he pushed off; and, after much weary pulling, and many perilous, unsuccessful onsets, he at last succeeded in getting one iron fast. Meantime, Gabriel, ascending to the main-royal mast-head, was tossing one arm in frantic gestures, and hurling forth prophecies of speedy doom to the sacrilegious assailants of his divinity. Now, while Macey, the mate, was standing up in his boat's bow, and with all the reckless energy of his tribe was venting his wild exclamations upon the whale, and essaying to get a fair chance for his poised lance, lo! a broad white shadow rose from the sea; by its quick, fanning motion, temporarily taking the breath out of the bodies of the oarsmen. Next instant, the luckless mate, so full of furious life, was smitten bodily into the air, and making a long arc in his descent, fell into the sea at the distance of about fifty yards. Not a chip of the boat was harmed, nor a hair of any oarsman's head; but the mate for ever sank.

It is well to parenthesize here, that of the fatal accidents in the Sperm-Whale Fishery, this kind is perhaps almost as frequent as any. Sometimes, nothing is injured but the man who is thus annihilated; oftener the boat's bow is knocked off, or the thigh-board, in which the headsman stands, is torn from its place and accompanies the body. But strangest of all is the circumstance, that in more instances than one, when the body has been recovered, not a single mark of violence is discernible; the man being stark dead.

The whole calamity, with the falling form of Macey, was plainly descried from the ship. Raising a piercing shriek—"The vial! the vial!" Gabriel called off the terror-stricken crew from the further hunting of the whale. This terrible event clothed the archangel with added influence; because his credulous disciples believed that he had specifically fore-announced it, instead of only making a general prophecy, which any one might have done, and so have chanced to hit one of many marks in the wide margin allowed. He became a nameless terror to the ship.

Mayhew having concluded his narration, Ahab put such questions to him, that the stranger captain could not forbear inquiring whether he intended to hunt the White Whale, if opportunity should offer. To which Ahab answered—"Aye." Straightway, then, Gabriel once more started to his feet, glaring upon the old man, and vehemently exclaimed, with downward pointed finger—"Think, think of the blasphemer—dead, and down there!—beware of the blasphemer's end!"

Ahab stolidly turned aside; then said to Mayhew, "Captain, I have just bethought me of my letter-bag; there is a letter for one of thy officers, if I mistake not. Starbuck, look over the bag."

Every whale-ship takes out a goodly number of letters for various ships, whose delivery to the persons to whom they may be addressed, depends upon the mere chance of encountering them in the four oceans. Thus, most letters never reach their mark; and many are only received after attaining an age of two or three years or more.

Soon Starbuck returned with a letter in his hand. It was sorely tumbled, damp, and covered with a dull, spotted, green mould, in consequence of being kept in a dark locker of the cabin. Of such a letter, Death himself might well have been the post-boy.

"Can'st not read it?" cried Ahab. "Give it me, man. Aye, aye, it's but a dim scrawl;—what's this?" As he was studying it out, Starbuck took a long cutting-spade pole, and with his knife slightly split the end, to insert the letter there, and in that way, hand it to the boat, without its coming any closer to the ship.

Meantime, Ahab holding the letter, muttered, "Mr. Har—yes, Mr. Harry—(a woman's pinny hand,—the man's wife, I'll wager)—Aye—Mr. Harry Macey, Ship Jeroboam;—why it's Macey, and he's dead!"

"Poor fellow! poor fellow! and from his wife," sighed Mayhew; "but let me have it."

"Nay, keep it thyself," cried Gabriel to Ahab; "thou art soon going that way."

"Curses throttle thee!" yelled Ahab. "Captain Mayhew, stand by now to receive it;" and taking the fatal missive from Starbuck's hands, he caught it in the slit of the pole, and reached it over towards the boat. But as he did so, the oarsmen expectantly desisted from rowing; the boat drifted a little towards the ship's stern; so that, as if by magic, the letter suddenly ranged along with Gabriel's eager hand. He clutched it in an instant, seized the boat-knife, and impaling the letter on it, sent it thus loaded back into the ship. It fell at Ahab's feet. Then Gabriel shrieked out to his comrades to give way with their oars, and in that manner the mutinous boat rapidly shot away from the Pequod.

As, after this interlude, the seamen resumed their work upon the jacket of the whale, many strange things were hinted in reference to this wild affair.

CHAPTER 72

The Monkey-rope

Therefore, I saw that here was a sort of interregnum in Providence; for its even-handed equity never could have so gross an injustice. And yet still further pondering—while   —still further pondering, I say, I saw that this situation of mine was the precise situation of every mortal that breathes; only, in most cases, he, one way or other, has this Siamese connexion with a plurality of other mortals. If your banker breaks, you snap; if your apothecary by mistake sends you poison in your pills, you die. True, you may say that, by exceeding caution, you may possibly escape these and the multitudinous other evil chances of life *

—what? Some hot Cognac? No! hands him, ye gods! hands him a cup of tepid ginger and water!

"Ginger? Do I smell ginger?" suspiciously asked Stubb, coming near. "Yes, this must be ginger," peering into the as yet untasted cup. Then standing as if incredulous for a while, he calmly walked towards the astonished steward slowly saying, "Ginger? ginger? and will you have the goodness to tell me, Mr. Dough-Boy, where lies the virtue of ginger? Ginger! is ginger the sort of fuel you use, Dough-boy, to kindle a fire in this shivering cannibal? Ginger!— what the devil is ginger?—sea-coal? firewood?—lucifer matches?—tinder?— gunpowder?—what the devil is ginger, I say, that you offer this cup to our poor Queequeg here."

"There is some sneaking Temperance Society movement about this business," he suddenly added, now approaching Starbuck, who had just come from forward. "Will you look at that kannakin, sir; smell of it, if you please." Then watching the mate's countenance, he added, "The steward, Mr. Starbuck, had the face to offer that calomel and jalap to Queequeg, there, this instant off the whale. Is the steward an apothecary, sir? and may I ask whether this is the sort of bitters by which he blows back the life into a half-drowned man?"

---

* The monkey-rope is found in all whalers; but it was only in the Pequod that the monkey and his holder were ever tied together. This improvement upon the original usage was introduced by no less a man than Stubb, in order to afford the imperilled harpooneer the strongest possible guarantee for the faithfulness and vigilance of his monkey-rope holder.

"I trust not," said Starbuck, "it is poor stuff enough."

"Aye, aye, steward," cried Stubb, "we'll teach you to drug it harpooneer; none of your apothecary's medicine here; you want to poison us, do ye? You have got out insurances on our lives and want to murder us all, and pocket the proceeds, do ye?"

"It was not me," cried Dough-Boy, "it was Aunt Charity that brought the ginger on board; and bade me never give the harpooneers any spirits, but only this ginger-jub—so she called it."

"Ginger-jub! you gingerly rascal! take that! and run along with ye to the lockers, and get something better. I hope I do no wrong, Mr. Starbuck. It is the captain's orders—grog for the harpooneer on a whale."

"Enough," replied Starbuck, "only don't hit him again, but—"

"Oh, I never hurt when I hit, except when I hit a whale or something of that sort; and this fellow's a weazel. What were you about saying, sir?"

"Only this: go down with him, and get what thou wantest thyself."

When Stubb reappeared, he came with   in one hand, and a sort of teacaddy in the other. The first contained   , and was handed to Queequeg; the second was Aunt Charity's gift, and that was freely given to the waves.

CHAPTER 73

*Stubb and Flask kill a Right Whale; and
Then Have a Talk over Him*

,

,

"at last. I don't half like that chap, Stubb."

"the toes of"

"Pooh!"

"Why, they say as how he went a sauntering into the old flag-ship once, switching his tail about devilish easy and gentlemanlike, and inquiring if the old governor was at home. Well, he was at home, and asked the devil what he wanted. The devil, switching his hoofs, up and says, 'I want John.' 'What for?' says the old governor. 'What business is that of yours,' says the devil, getting mad,—'I want to use him.' 'Take him,' says the governor—and by the Lord, Flask, if the devil didn't give John the Asiatic cholera before he got through with him, I'll eat this whale in one mouthful."

"I think I remember some   story as   ,"   "but I can't remember where."

"Three Spaniards? Adventures of those three bloody-minded soldadoes? Did ye read it there, Flask? I guess ye did?"

"No: never saw such a book; heard of it, though. But now, tell me, Stubb, do you suppose that that devil you was speaking of just now, was the same you say is now on board the Pequod?"

"Am I the same man that helped kill this whale? Doesn't the devil live for ever; who ever heard that the devil was dead? Did you ever see any parson a wearing mourning for the devil? And if the devil has a latch-key to get into the admiral's cabin, don't you suppose he can crawl into a porthole? Tell me that, Mr. Flask?"

"How old do you suppose Fedallah is, Stubb?"

"Do you see that mainmast there?" pointing to the ship; "well, that's the figure one; now take all the hoops in the Pequod's hold, and string along in a row with that mast, for oughts, do you see; well, that wouldn't begin to be Fedallah's age. Nor all the coopers in creation couldn't show hoops enough to make oughts enough."

"But see here, Stubb, I thought you a little boasted just now,   he's so old as all those hoops of yours come to, and if"

"in the admiral's cabin   let alone down in the orlop there, where he lives, and   on the upper decks"

passing

CHAPTER 74

The Sperm Whale's Head—
Contrasted View

:

A curious and most puzzling question might be started concerning this visual matter as touching the Leviathan. But I must be content with a hint. So long as a man's eyes are open in the light, the act of seeing is involuntary; that is, he cannot then help mechanically seeing whatever objects are before him. Nevertheless, any one's experience will teach him, that though he can take in an undiscriminating sweep of things at one glance, it is quite impossible for him, attentively, and completely, to examine any two things—however large or however small—at one and the same instant of time; never mind if they lie side by side and touch each other. But if you now come to separate these two objects, and surround each by a circle of profound darkness; then, in order to see one of them, in such a manner as to bring your mind to bear on it, the other will be utterly excluded from your contemporary consciousness. How is it, then, with the whale? True, both his eyes, in themselves, must simultaneously act; but is his brain so much more comprehensive, combining, and subtle than man's, that he can at the same moment of time attentively examine two distinct prospects, one on one side of him, and the other in an exactly opposite direction? If he can, then is it as marvellous a thing in him, as if a man were able simultaneously to go through the demonstrations of two distinct problems in Euclid. Nor, strictly investigated, is there any incongruity in this comparison.

It may be but an idle whim, but it has always seemed to me, that the extraordinary vacillations of movement displayed by some whales when beset by three or four boats; the timidity and liability to queer frights, so common to such whales; I think that all this indirectly proceeds from the helpless perplexity of volition, in which their divided and diametrically opposite powers of vision must involve them.

—

,

CHAPTER 75

The Right Whale's Head—
Contrasted View

(especially in front, where it is so broadly rounded)

Probably the mother during an important interval was sailing down the Peruvian coast, when earthquakes caused the beach to gape.   those   which have elsewhere been cursorily mentioned   Though the certainty of this criterion is far from demonstrable, yet it has the savor of analogical probability. At any rate, if we yield to it, we must grant a far greater age to the Right Whale than at first glance will seem reasonable.

*

To sum up, then: in the Right Whale's there is no great well of sperm; no ivory teeth at all; no long, slender mandible of a lower jaw, like the Sperm Whale's. Nor in the Sperm Whale are there any of those blinds of bone; no huge lower lip; and scarcely anything of a tongue. Again, the Right Whale has two external spout-holes, the Sperm Whale only one.

CHAPTER 76

The Battering-Ram

, much in the same way, indeed, as though your own mouth were entirely under your chin   ,

For unless you own the whale, you are but a provincial and sentimentalist in Truth. But clear Truth is a thing for salamander giants only to encounter; how small the chances for the provincials then? What befell the weakling youth lifting the dread goddess's veil at Lais?

---

* This reminds us that the Right Whale really has a sort of whisker, or rather a moustache, consisting of a few scattered white hairs on the upper part of the outer end of the lower jaw. Sometimes these tufts impart a rather brigandish expression to his otherwise solemn countenance.

CHAPTER 77

The Great Heidelburgh Tun

*

Sperm Whale's

CHAPTER 78

Cistern and Buckets

, from his now quiet, swinging perch overhead

—

, too,

I know that this queer adventure of the Gay-Header's will be sure to seem incredible to some landsmen, though they themselves may have either seen or heard of some one's falling into a cistern ashore; an accident which not seldom happens, and with much less reason too than the Indian's, considering the exceeding slipperiness of the curb of the Sperm Whale's well.

But, peradventure, it may be sagaciously urged, how is this? We thought the tissued, infiltrated head of the Sperm Whale, was the lightest and most corky part about him; and yet thou makest it sink in an element of a far greater specific gravity than itself. We have thee there. Not at all, but I have ye; for at the

---

*   Quoin is not a Euclidean term. It belongs to the pure nautical mathematics. I know not that it has been defined before. A quoin is a solid which differs from a wedge in having its sharp end formed by the steep inclination of one side, instead of the mutual tapering of both sides.

time poor Tash fell in, the case had been nearly emptied of its lighter contents, leaving little but the dense tendinous wall of the well—a double welded, hammered substance, as I have before said, much heavier than the sea water, and a lump of which sinks in it like lead almost. But the tendency to rapid sinking in this substance was in the present instance materially counteracted by the other parts of the head remaining undetached from it, so that it sank very slowly and deliberately indeed, affording Queequeg a fair chance for performing his agile obstetrics on the run, as you may say. Yes, it was a running delivery, so it was.

Now, had Tashtego perished in that head, it had been a very precious perishing; smothered in the very whitest and daintiest of fragrant spermaceti; coffined, hearsed, and tombed in the secret inner chamber and sanctum sanctorum of the whale. Only one sweeter end can readily be recalled—the delicious death of an Ohio honey-hunter, who seeking honey in the crotch of a hollow tree, found such exceeding store of it, that leaning too far over, it sucked him in, so that he died embalmed. How many, think ye, have likewise fallen into Plato's honey head, and sweetly perished there?

CHAPTER 79

The Prairie

And since the nose is the central and most conspicuous of the features; and since it perhaps most modifies and finally controls their combined expres- sion; hence it would seem that its entire absence, as an external appendage, must very largely affect the countenance of the whale. For as in landscape gardening, a spire, cupola, monument, or tower of some sort, is deemed almost indispensable to the completion of the scene; so no face can be physiognomically in keeping without the elevated open-work belfry of the nose. Dash the nose from Phidias's marble Jove, and what a sorry remainder!   same   which in the sculptured Jove were hideous, in him   A nose to the whale would have been impertinent.   in your jolly-boat

Few are the foreheads which like Shakespeare's or Melancthon's rise so high, and descend so low, that the eyes themselves seem clear, eternal, tideless mountain lakes; and all above them in the forehead's wrinkles, you seem to track the antlered thoughts descending there to drink, as the Highland hunters track the snow prints of the deer.

And this reminds me that had the great Sperm Whale been known to the young Orient World, he would have been deified by their child-magian thoughts. They deified the crocodile of the Nile, because the crocodile is tongueless; and the Sperm Whale has no tongue, or at least it is so exceedingly small, as to be incapable of protrusion. If hereafter any highly cultured, poetical nation shall lure back to their birth-right, the merry May-day gods of old; and livingly enthrone them again in the now egotistical sky; in the now unhaunted hill; then be sure, exalted to Jove's high seat, the great Sperm Whale shall lord it.

CHAPTER 80

The Nut

So like a choice casket is it secreted in him, that I have known some whalemen who peremptorily deny that the Sperm Whale has any other brain than that palpable semblance of one formed by the cubic-yards of his sperm magazine. Lying in strange folds, courses, and convolutions, to their apprehensions, it seems more in keeping with the idea of his general might to regard that mystic part of him as the seat of his intelligence.

It is plain, then, that phrenologically the head of this Leviathan, in the creature's living intact state, is an entire delusion. As for his true brain, you can then see no indications of it, nor feel any. The whale, like all things that are mighty, wears a false brow to the common world.

If you unload his skull of its spermy heaps and then take a rear view of its rear end, which is the high end, you will be struck by its resemblance to the human skull, beheld in the same situation, and from the same point of view. Indeed, place this reversed skull (scaled down to the human magnitude) among a plate of men's skulls, and you would involuntarily confound it with them; and remarking the depressions on one part of its summit, in phrenological phrase you would say—This man had no self-esteem, and no veneration. And by those negations, considered along with the affirmative fact of his prodigious bulk and power, you can best form to yourself the truest, though not the most exhilarating conception of what the most exalted potency is.

But if from the comparative dimensions of the whale's proper brain, you deem it incapable of being adequately charted, then I have another idea for you. If you attentively regard almost any quadruped's spine, you will be struck with the resemblance of its vertebrae to a strung necklace of dwarfed skulls, all bearing rudimental resemblance to the skull proper. It is a German conceit, that the vertebrae are absolutely undeveloped skulls. But the curious external resemblance, I take it the Germans were not the first men to perceive. A foreign friend once pointed it out to me, in the skeleton of a foe he had slain, and with the vertebrae of which he was inlaying, in a sort of basso-relievo, the beaked prow of his canoe. Now, I consider that the phrenologists have omitted an important thing in not pushing their investigations from the cerebellum through the spinal canal. For I believe that much of a man's character will be found betokened in his backbone. I would rather feel your spine than your skull, whoever you are. A thin joist of a spine never yet upheld a full and noble soul. I rejoice in my spine, as in the firm audacious staff of that flag which I fling half out to the world.

Apply this spinal branch of phrenology to the Sperm Whale. His cranial cavity is continuous with the first neck-vertebra; and in that vertebra the bottom of the spinal canal will measure ten inches across, being eight in height, and of a triangular figure with the base downwards. As it passes through the remaining vertebrae the canal tapers in size, but for a considerable distance remains of large capacity. Now, of course, this canal is filled with much the same strangely fibrous substance—the spinal cord—as the brain; and directly communicates with the brain. And what is still more, for many feet after emerging from the brain's cavity, the spinal cord remains of an undecreasing girth, almost equal to that of the brain. Under all these circumstances, would it be unreasonable to survey and map out the whale's spine phrenologically? For, viewed in this light, the wonderful comparative smallness of his brain proper is more than compensated by the wonderful comparative magnitude of his spinal cord.

But leaving this hint to operate as it may with the phrenologists, I would merely assume the spinal theory for a moment, in reference to the Sperm Whale's hump. This august hump, if I mistake not, rises over one of the larger vertebrae, and is, therefore, in some sort, the outer convex mould of it. From its relative situation then, I should call this high hump the organ of firmness or indomitableness in the Sperm Whale. And that the great monster is indomitable, you will yet have reason to know.

CHAPTER 81

The Pequod meets the Virgin

at very wide intervals of latitude and longitude,

profound

,   , rubbing their flanks as closely as so many spans of horses in harness.

, humped   by his comparatively slow progress, as well as   in advance,   , because the white-bone or swell at his broad muzzle was a dashed one, like the swell formed when two hostile currents meet.

cumbrous

, and the other whales were going with such great velocity, moreover, as almost to defy pursuit for the time   from the great start he had had,   completely   and pass

;

So have I seen a bird with clipped wing making affrighted broken circles in the air, vainly striving to escape the piratical hawks. But the bird has a voice, and with plaintive cries will make known her fear; but the fear of this vast dumb brute of the sea, was chained up and enchanted in him; he had no voice, save that choking respiration through his spiracle, and

"This puts me in mind of fastening to an elephant in a tilbury on a plain— makes the wheel-spokes fly, boys, when you fasten to him that way; and there's danger of being pitched out too, when you strike a hill.   Hurrah! this whale carries the everlasting mail!"

We all know what an astonishing atmospheric weight we ourselves stand up under; even here, above-ground, in the air; how vast, then, the burden of a whale, bearing on his back a column of two hundred fathoms of ocean! It must at least equal the weight of fifty atmospheres.

like the big weight to an eight day clock   Is this the creature of whom it was once so triumphantly said—"Canst thou fill his skin with barbed irons? or his head with fish-spears? The sword of him that layeth at him cannot hold, the spear, the dart, nor the habergeon: he esteemeth iron as straw; the arrow cannot make him flee; darts are counted as stubble; he laugheth at the shaking of a spear!" This the creature? this he? Oh! that unfulfilments should follow the prophets. For with the strength of a thousand thighs in his tail, Leviathan had run his head under the mountains of the sea, to hide him from the Pequod's fish-spears!

In that sloping afternoon sunlight, the shadows that the three boats sent down beneath the surface, must have been long enough and broad enough to shade half Xerxes' army. Who can tell how appalling to the wounded whale must have been such huge phantoms flitting over his head!

, distinctly conducting upwards to them, as by magnetic wires, the life and death throbs of the whale, so that every oarsman felt them in his seat   relieved in great part from the downward strain at the bows,

His motions plainly denoted his extreme exhaustion.   at least   and bleeding ; even as in a drought a river will flow, whose source is in the well-springs of far-off and undiscernible hills.   , however rapid,

As strange misgrown masses gather in the knot-holes of the noblest oaks when prostrate, so

glorying   showers of   , by this time,   It was most piteous, that last expiring spout. As when by unseen hands the water is gradually drawn off from some mighty fountain, and with half-stifled melancholy gurglings the spray-column lowers and lowers to the ground—so the last long dying spout of the whale.

very

Be it said, however, that the Sperm Whale is far less liable to this accident than any other species. Where one of that sort go down, twenty Right Whales do. This difference in the species is no doubt imputable in no small degree to the greater quantity of bone in the Right Whale; his Venetian blinds alone sometimes weighing more than a ton; from this incumbrance the Sperm Whale is wholly free. But there are instances where, after the lapse of many hours or several days, the sunken whale again rises, more buoyant than in life. But the reason of this is obvious. Gases are generated in him; he swells to a prodigious magnitude; becomes a sort of animal balloon. A line-of-battle ship could hardly keep him under then. In the Shore Whaling, on soundings, among the Bays of New Zealand, when a Right Whale gives token of sinking, they fasten buoys to him, with plenty of rope; so that when the body has gone down, they know where to look for it when it shall have ascended again.

Oh! many are the Fin-Backs, and many are the Dericks, my friend.

CHAPTER 82

The Honor and Glory of Whaling

There are some enterprises in which a careful disorderliness is the true method.

The more I dive into this matter of whaling, and push my researches up to the very spring-head of it so much the more am I impressed with its great honor-ableness and antiquity; and especially when I find so many great demi-gods and heroes, prophets of all sorts, who one way or other have shed distinction upon it, I am transported with the reflection that I myself belong, though but subordinately, to so emblazoned a fraternity.

The gallant Perseus, a son of Jupiter, was the first whaleman; and to the eternal honor of our calling be it said, that the first whale attacked by our brotherhood was not killed with any sordid intent. Those were the knightly days of our profession, when we only bore arms to succor the distressed, and not to fill men's lamp-feeders. Every one knows the fine story of Perseus and Andromeda; how the lovely Andromeda, the daughter of a king, was tied to a rock on the sea-coast, and as Leviathan was in the very act of carrying her off, Perseus, the prince of whalemen, intrepidly advancing, harpooned the monster, and delivered and married the maid. It was an admirable artistic exploit, rarely achieved by the best harpooneers of the present day; inasmuch as this Leviathan was slain at the very first dart. And let no man doubt this Arkite story; for in the ancient Joppa, now Jaffa, on the Syrian coast, in one of the Pagan temples, there stood for many ages the vast skeleton of a whale, which the city's legends and all the inhabitants asserted to be the identical bones of the monster that Perseus slew. When the Romans took Joppa, the same skeleton was carried to Italy in triumph. What seems most singular and suggestively important in this story, is this: it was from Joppa that Jonah set sail.

Akin to the adventure of Perseus and Andromeda—indeed, by some supposed to be indirectly derived from it—is that famous story of St. George and the Dragon; which dragon I maintain to have been a whale; for in many old chronicles whales and dragons are strangely jumbled together, and often stand for each other. "Thou art as a lion of the waters, and as a dragon of the sea," saith Ezekiel; hereby, plainly meaning a whale; in truth, some versions of the Bible use that word itself. Besides, it would much subtract from the glory of the exploit had St. George but encountered a crawling reptile of the land, instead of doing battle with the great monster of the deep. Any man may kill a snake, but only a Perseus, a St. George, a Coffin, have the heart in them to march boldly up to a whale.

Let not the modern paintings of this scene mislead us; for though the creature encountered by that valiant whaleman of old is vaguely represented of a griffin-like shape, and though the battle is depicted on land and the saint on horseback, yet considering the great ignorance of those times, when the true form of the whale was unknown to artists; and considering that as in Perseus' case, St. George's whale might have crawled up out of the sea on the beach; and considering that the animal ridden by St. George might have been only a large seal, or sea-horse; bearing all this in mind, it will not appear altogether incompatible with the sacred legend and the ancientest draughts of the scene, to hold this so-called dragon no other than the great Leviathan himself. In fact, placed before the strict and piercing truth, this whole story will fare like that fish, flesh, and fowl idol of the Philistines, Dagon by name; who being planted before the ark of Israel, his horse's head and both the palms of his hands fell off from him, and only the stump or fishy part of him remained. Thus, then, one of our own noble stamp, even a whaleman, is the tutelary guardian of England; and by good rights, we harpooneers of Nantucket should be enrolled in the most noble order of St. George. And therefore, let not the knights of that honorable company (none of whom, I venture to say, have ever had to do with a whale like their great patron), let them never eye a Nantucketer with disdain, since even in our woollen frocks and tarred trowsers we are much better entitled to St. George's decoration than they.

Whether to admit Hercules among us or not, concerning this I long remained dubious: for though according to the Greek mythologies, that antique Crockett and Kit Carson—that brawny doer of rejoicing good deeds, was swallowed down and thrown up by a whale; still, whether that strictly makes a whaleman of him, that might be mooted. It nowhere appears that he ever actually harpooned his fish, unless, indeed, from the inside. Nevertheless, he may be deemed a sort of involuntary whaleman; at any rate the whale caught him, if he did not the whale. I claim him for one of our clan.

But, by the best contradictory authorities, this Grecian story of Hercules and the whale is considered to be derived from the still more ancient Hebrew story of Jonah and the whale; and vice versa; certainly they are very similar. If I claim the demigod then, why not the prophet?

Nor do heroes, saints, demigods, and prophets alone comprise the whole roll of our order. Our grand master is still to be named; for like royal kings of old times, we find the head waters of our fraternity in nothing short of the great gods themselves. That wondrous oriental story is now to be rehearsed from the Shaster, which gives us the dread Vishnoo, one of the three persons in the godhead of the Hindoos; gives us this divine Vishnoo himself for our Lord;—Vishnoo, who, by the first of his ten earthly incarnations, has for ever set apart and sanctified the whale. When Brahma, or the God of Gods, saith the Shaster, resolved to recreate the world after one of its periodical disso-lutions, he gave birth to Vishnoo, to preside over the work; but the Vedas, or mystical books, whose perusal would seem to have been indispensable to Vishnoo before beginning the creation, and which therefore must have con-tained something in the shape of practical hints to young architects, these Vedas were lying at the bottom of the waters; so Vishnoo became incarnate in a whale, and sounding down in him to the uttermost depths, rescued the sacred volumes. Was not this Vishnoo a whaleman, then? even as a man who rides a horse is called a horseman?

Perseus, St. George, Hercules, Jonah, and Vishnoo! there's a member-roll for you! What club but the whaleman's can head off like that?

CHAPTER 83

Jonah Historically Regarded

Reference was made to the historical story of Jonah and the whale in the pre-ceding chapter. Now some Nantucketers rather distrust this historical story of Jonah and the whale. But then there were some sceptical Greeks and Ro-mans, who, standing out from the orthodox pagans of their times, equally doubted the story of Hercules and the whale, and Arion and the dolphin; and yet their doubting those traditions did not make those traditions one whit the less facts, for all that.

One old Sag-Harbor whaleman's chief reason for questioning the Hebrew story was this:—He had one of those quaint old-fashioned Bibles, embel-lished with curious, unscientific plates; one of which represented Jonah's whale with two spouts in his head—a peculiarity only true with respect to a species of the Leviathan (the Right Whale, and the varieties of that or-der), concerning which the fishermen have this saying, "A penny roll would choke him;" his swallow is so very small. But, to this, Bishop Jebb's anticipative answer is ready. It is not necessary, hints the Bishop, that we consider Jonah as tombed in the whale's belly, but as temporarily lodged in some part of his mouth. And this seems reasonable enough in the good Bishop. For truly, the Right Whale's mouth would accommodate a couple of whist-tables, and comfortably seat all the players. Possibly, too, Jonah might have ensconced himself in a hollow tooth; but, on second thoughts, the Right Whale is toothless.

Another reason which Sag-Harbor (he went by that name) urged for his want of faith in this matter of the prophet, was something obscurely in reference to his incarcerated body and the whale's gastric juices. But this objection like-wise falls to the ground, because a German exegetist supposes that Jonah must have taken refuge in the floating body of a *dead* whale—even as the French soldiers in the Russian campaign turned their dead horses into tents, and crawled into them. Besides, it has been divined by other continental com-mentators, that when Jonah was thrown overboard from the Joppa ship, he straightway effected his escape to another vessel near by, some vessel with a whale for a figure-head; and, I would add, possibly called "The Whale," as some craft are nowadays christened the "Shark," the "Gull," the "Eagle." Nor have there been wanting learned exegetists who have opined that the whale mentioned in the book of Jonah merely meant a life-preserver—an inflated bag of wind—which the endangered prophet swam to, and so was saved from a watery doom. Poor Sag-Harbor, therefore, seems worsted all round. But he had still another reason for his want of faith. It was this, if I remember right: Jonah was swallowed by the whale in the Mediterranean Sea, and after three days he was vomited up somewhere within three days' journey of Nineveh, a city on the Tigris, very much more than three days' journey across from the nearest point of the Mediterranean coast. How is that?

But was there no other way for the whale to land the prophet within that short distance of Nineveh? Yes. He might have carried him round by the way of the Cape of Good Hope. But not to speak of the passage through the whole length of the Mediterranean, and another passage up the Persian Gulf and Red Sea, such a supposition would involve the complete circumnavigation of all Africa in three days, not to speak of the Tigris waters, near the site of Nineveh, being too shallow for any whale to swim in. Besides, this idea of Jonah's weathering the Cape of Good Hope at so early a day would wrest the honor of the discovery of that great headland from Bartholomew Diaz, its reputed discoverer, and so make modern history a liar.

But all these foolish arguments of old Sag-Harbor only evinced his foolish pride of reason—a thing still more reprehensible in him, seeing that he had but little learning except what he had picked up from the sun and the sea. I say it only shows his foolish, impious pride, and abominable, devilish rebellion against the reverend clergy. For by a Portuguese Catholic priest, this very idea of Jonah's going to Nineveh via the Cape of Good Hope was advanced as a signal magnification of the general miracle. And so it was. Besides, to this day, the highly enlightened Turks devoutly believe in the historical story of Jonah. And some three centuries ago, an English traveller in old Harris's Voyages, speaks of a Turkish Mosque built in honor of Jonah, in which Mosque was a miraculous lamp that burnt without any oil.

CHAPTER 84

Pitchpoling

not long after the German ship Jungfrau disappeared,

with swift precipitancy

of considerable length,

, which in effect become serious drawbacks

He minds you somewhat of a juggler, balancing a long staff on his chin.
with a rapid, nameless impulse

CHAPTER 85

The Fountain

That for six thousand years—and no one knows how many millions of ages before—the great whales should have been spouting all over the sea, and sprinkling and mistifying the gardens of the deep, as with so many sprinkling or mistifying pots; and that for some centuries back, thousands of hunters should have been close by the fountain of the whale, watching these sprinklings and spoutings—that all this should be, and yet, that down to this blessed minute (fifteen and a quarter minutes past one o'clock P.M. of this sixteenth day of December, A.D. 1850), it should still remain a problem, whether these spoutings are, after all, really water, or nothing but vapor—this is surely a noteworthy thing.

Let us, then, look at this matter, along with some interesting items contingent. Every one knows that by the peculiar cunning of their gills, the finny tribes in general breathe the air which at all times is combined with the element in which they swim; hence, a herring or a cod might live a century, and never once raise its head above the surface. But owing to his marked internal structure which gives him regular lungs, like a human being's, the whale can only live by inhaling the disengaged air in the open atmosphere. Wherefore the necessity for his periodical visits to the upper world. But he cannot in any degree breathe through his mouth, for, in his ordinary attitude, the Sperm Whale's mouth is buried at least eight feet beneath the surface; and what is still more, his windpipe has no connexion with his mouth. No, he breathes through his spiracle alone; and this is on the top of his head.

If I say, that in any creature breathing is only a function indispensable to vitality, inasmuch as it withdraws from the air a certain element, which being subsequently brought into contact with the blood imparts to the blood its vivifying principle, I do not think I shall err; though I may possibly use some superfluous scientific words. Assume it, and it follows that if all the blood in a man could be aerated with one breath, he might then seal up his nostrils and not fetch another for a considerable time. That is to say, he would then live without breathing. Anomalous as it may seem, this is precisely the case with the whale, who systematically lives, by intervals, his full hour and more (when at the bottom) without drawing a single breath, or so much as in any way inhaling a particle of air; for, remember, he has no gills. How is this? Between his ribs and on each side of his spine he is supplied with a remarkable involved Cretan labyrinth of vermicelli-like vessels, which vessels, when he quits the surface, are completely distended with oxygenated blood. So that for an hour or more, a thousand fathoms in the sea, he carries a surplus stock of vitality in him, just as the camel crossing the waterless desert carries a surplus supply of drink for future use in its four supplementary stomachs. The anatomical fact of this labyrinth is indisputable; and that the supposition founded upon it is reasonable and true, seems the more cogent to me, when I consider the otherwise inexplicable obstinacy of that leviathan in *having his spoutings out*, as the fishermen phrase it. This is what I mean. If unmolested, upon rising to the surface, the Sperm Whale will continue there for a period of time exactly uniform with all his other unmolested risings. Say he stays eleven minutes, and jets seventy times, that is, respires seventy breaths; then whenever he rises again, he will be sure to have his seventy breaths over again, to a minute. Now, if after he fetches a few breaths you alarm him, so that he sounds, he will be always dodging up again to make good his regular allowance of air. And not till those seventy breaths are told, will he finally go down to stay out his full term below. Remark, however, that in different individuals these rates are different; but in any one they are alike. Now, why should the whale thus insist upon having his spoutings out, unless it be to replenish his reservoir of air, ere descending for good? How obvious is it, too, that this necessity for the whale's rising exposes him to all the fatal hazards of the chase. For not by hook or by net could this vast leviathan be caught, when sailing a thousand fathoms beneath the sunlight. Not so much thy skill, then, O hunter, as the great necessities that strike the victory to thee!

In man, breathing is incessantly going on—one breath only serving for two or three pulsations; so that whatever other business he has to attend to, waking or sleeping, breathe he must, or die he will. But the Sperm Whale only breathes about one seventh or Sunday of his time.

It has been said that the whale only breathes through his spout-hole; if it could truthfully be added that his spouts are mixed with water, then I opine we should be furnished with the reason why his sense of smell seems obliterated in him; for the only thing about him that at all answers to his nose is that identical spout-hole; and being so clogged with two elements, it could not be expected to have the power of smelling. But owing to the mystery of the spout—whether it be water or whether it be vapor—no absolute certainty can as yet be arrived at on this head. Sure it is, nevertheless, that the Sperm Whale has no proper olfactories. But what does he want of them? No roses, no violets, no Cologne-water in the sea.

Furthermore, as his windpipe solely opens into the tube of his spouting canal, and as that long canal—like the grand Erie Canal—is furnished with a sort of locks (that open and shut) for the downward retention of air or the upward exclusion of water, therefore the whale has no voice; unless you insult him by saying, that when he so strangely rumbles, he talks through his nose. But then again, what has the whale to say? Seldom have I known any profound being that had anything to say to this world, unless forced to stammer out something by way of getting a living. Oh! happy that the world is such an excellent listener!

Now, the spouting canal of the Sperm Whale, chiefly intended as it is for the conveyance of air, and for several feet laid along, horizontally, just beneath the upper surface of his head, and a little to one side; this curious canal is very much like a gas-pipe laid down in a city on one side of a street. But the question returns whether this gas-pipe is also a water-pipe; in other words, whether the spout of the Sperm Whale is the mere vapor of the exhaled breath, or whether that exhaled breath is mixed with water taken in at the mouth, and discharged through the spiracle. It is certain that the mouth indirectly communicates with the spouting canal; but it cannot be proved that this is for the purpose of discharging water through the spiracle. Because the greatest necessity for so doing would seem to be, when in feeding he accidentally takes in water. But the Sperm Whale's food is far beneath the surface, and there he cannot spout even if he would. Besides, if you regard him very closely, and time him with your watch, you will find that when unmolested, there is an undeviating rhyme between the periods of his jets and the ordinary periods of respiration.

But why pester one with all this reasoning on the subject? Speak out! You have seen him spout; then declare what the spout is; can you not tell water from air? My dear sir, in this world it is not so easy to settle these plain things. I have ever found your plain things the knottiest of all. And as for this whale spout, you might almost stand in it, and yet be undecided as to what it is precisely.

The central body of it is hidden in the snowy sparkling mist enveloping it; and how can you certainly tell whether any water falls from it, when, always, when you are close enough to a whale to get a close view of his spout, he is in a prodigious commotion, the water cascading all around him. And if at such times you should think that you really perceived drops of moisture in the spout, how do you know that they are not merely condensed from its vapor; or how do you know that they are not those identical drops superficially lodged in the spout-hole fissure, which is countersunk into the summit of the whale's head?

For even when tranquilly swimming through the mid-day sea in a calm, with his elevated hump sun-dried as a dromedary's in the desert; even then, the whale always carries a small basin of water on his head, as under a blazing sun you will sometimes see a cavity in a rock filled up with rain.

Nor is it at all prudent for the hunter to be over curious touching the precise nature of the whale spout. It will not do for him to be peering into it, and putting his face in it. You cannot go with your pitcher to this fountain and fill it, and bring it away. For even when coming into slight contact with the outer, vapory shreds of the jet, which will often happen, your skin will feverishly smart, from the acridness of the thing so touching it. And I know one, who coming into still closer contact with the spout, whether with some scientific object in view, or otherwise, I cannot say, the skin peeled off from his cheek and arm. Wherefore, among whalemen, the spout is deemed poisonous; they try to evade it. Another thing; I have heard it said, and I do not much doubt it, that if the jet is fairly spouted into your eyes, it will blind you. The wisest thing the investigator can do then, it seems to me, is to let this deadly spout alone.

Still, we can hypothesize, even if we cannot prove and establish. My hypothesis is this: that the spout is nothing but mist. And besides other reasons, to this conclusion I am impelled, by considerations touching the great inherent dignity and sublimity of the Sperm Whale; I account him no common, shallow being, inasmuch as it is an undisputed fact that he is never found on soundings, or near shores; all other whales sometimes are. He is both ponderous and profound. And I am convinced that from the heads of all ponderous profound beings, such as Plato, Pyrrho, the Devil, Jupiter, Dante, and so on, there always goes up a certain semi-visible steam, while in the act of thinking deep thoughts. While composing a little treatise on Eternity, I had the curiosity to place a mirror before me; and ere long saw reflected there, a curious involved worming and undulation in the atmosphere over my head. The invariable moisture of my hair, while plunged in deep thought, after six cups of hot tea in my thin shingled attic, of an August noon; this seems an additional argument for the above supposition.

And how nobly it raises our conceit of the mighty, misty monster, to behold him solemnly sailing through a calm tropical sea; his vast, mild head over-hung by a canopy of vapor, engendered by his incommunicable contempla-tions, and that vapor—as you will sometimes see it—glorified by a rainbow, as if Heaven itself had put its seal upon his thoughts. For, d'ye see, rainbows do not visit the clear air; they only irradiate vapor. And so, through all the thick mists of the dim doubts in my mind, divine intuitions now and then shoot, enkindling my fog with a heavenly ray. And for this I thank God; for all have doubts; many deny; but doubts or denials, few along with them, have intu-itions. Doubts of all things earthly, and intuitions of some things heavenly; this combination makes neither believer nor infidel, but makes a man who regards them both with equal eye.

CHAPTER 86

The Tail

,   To the student of old Roman walls, the middle layer will furnish a curious parallel to the thin course of tiles always alternating with the stone in those wonderful relics of the antique, and which undoubtedly contribute so much to the great strength of the masonry.

Nor does this—its amazing strength, at all tend to cripple the graceful flexion of its motions; where infantileness of ease undulates through a Titanism of power. On the contrary, those motions derive their most appalling beauty from it. Real strength never impairs beauty or harmony, but it often bestows it; and in everything imposingly beautiful, strength has much to do with the magic. Take away the tied tendons that all over seem bursting from the marble in the carved Hercules, and its charm would be gone. As devout Eckerman lifted the linen sheet from the naked corpse of Goethe, he was overwhelmed with the massive chest of the man, that seemed as a Roman triumphal arch. When Angelo paints even God the Father in human form, mark what robustness is there. And whatever they may reveal of the divine love in the Son, the soft, curled, hermaphroditical Italian pictures, in which his idea has been most successfully embodied; these pictures, so destitute as they are of all brawniness, hint nothing of any power, but the mere negative, feminine one of submission and endurance, which on all hands it is conceded, form the peculiar practical virtues of his teachings.

in maidenly gentleness   Had this tail any prehensile power, I should straightway bethink me of Darmonodes' elephant that so frequented the flower-market, and with low salutations presented nosegays to damsels, and then caressed their zones. On more accounts than one, a pity it is that the whale does not possess this prehensile virtue in his tail; for I have heard of yet another elephant, that when wounded in the fight, curved round his trunk and extracted the dart.

So in dreams, have I seen majestic Satan thrusting forth his tormented colossal claw from the flame Baltic of Hell. But in gazing at such scenes, it is all in all what mood you are in; if in the Dantean, the devils will occur to you; if in that of Isaiah, the archangels.   African

so far as some aspects of the tail of the one and the trunk of the other are concerned,   opposite organs   , much less the creatures to which they respectively belong.   *

---

* Though all comparison in the way of general bulk between the whale and the elephant is preposterous, inasmuch as in that particular the elephant stands in much the same respect to the whale that a dog does to the elephant; nevertheless, there are not wanting some points of curious similitude; among these is the spout. It is well known that the elephant will often draw up water or dust in his trunk, and then elevating it, jet it forth in a stream.

The more I consider this mighty tail, the more do I deplore my inability to express it. At times there are gestures in it, which, though they would well grace the hand of man, remain wholly inexplicable. In an extensive herd, so remarkable, occasionally, are these mystic gestures, that I have heard hunters who have declared them akin to Free-Mason signs and symbols; that the whale, indeed, by these methods intelligently conversed with the world. Nor are there wanting other motions of the whale in his general body, full of strangeness, and unaccountable to his most experienced assailant. Dissect him how I may, then, I but go skin deep; I know him not, and never will. But if I know not even the tail of this whale, how understand his head? much more, how comprehend his face, when face he has none? Thou shalt see my back parts, my tail, he seems to say, but my face shall not be seen. But I cannot completely make out his back parts; and hint what he will about his face, I say again he has no face.

CHAPTER 87

The Grand Armada

Those narrow straits of Sunda divide Sumatra from Java; and standing midway in that vast rampart of islands, buttressed by that bold green promontory, known to seamen as Java Head; they not a little correspond to the central gateway opening into some vast walled empire: and considering the inexhaustible wealth of spices, and silks, and jewels, and gold, and ivory, with which the thousand islands of that oriental sea are enriched, it seems a significant provision of nature, that such treasures, by the very formation of the land, should at least bear the appearance, however ineffectual, of being guarded from the all-grasping western world. The shores of the Straits of Sunda are unsupplied with those domineering fortresses which guard the entrances to the Mediterranean, the Baltic, and the Propontis. Unlike the Danes, these Orientals do not demand the obsequious homage of lowered top-sails from the endless procession of ships before the wind, which for centuries past, by night and by day, have passed between the islands of Sumatra and Java, freighted with the costliest cargoes of the east. But while they freely waive a ceremonial like this, they do by no means renounce their claim to more solid tribute.

. By these means, the circumnavigating Pequod would sweep almost all the known Sperm Whale cruising grounds of the world, previous to descending upon the Line in the Pacific;   , though everywhere else foiled in his pursuit,

For a long time, now, the circus-running sun has raced within his fiery ring, and needs no sustenance but what's in himself. So Ahab. Mark this, too, in the whaler.   She has a whole lake's contents bottled in her ample hold. She is ballasted with utilities; not altogether with unusable pig-lead and kentledge.
　　　So that did you carry them the news that another flood had come; they would only answer—"Well, boys, here's the ark!"

Almost renouncing all thought of falling in with any game hereabouts,

, sometimes embracing so great a multitude, that it would almost seem as if numerous nations of them had sworn solemn league and covenant for mutual assistance and protection   , ,   suddenly

Unlike the straight perpendicular twin-jets of the Right Whale, which, dividing at top, fall over in two branches, like the cleft drooping boughs of a willow, the single forward-slanting spout of the Sperm Whale presents a thick curled bush of white mist, continually rising and falling away to leeward.

, descried of a balmy autumnal morning, by some horseman on a height

,   all eagerness to place that perilous passage in their rear, and once more expand in comparative security upon the plain;

If the wind only held, little doubt had they, that chased through these Straits of Sunda, the vast host would only deploy into the Oriental seas to witness the capture of not a few of their number. And who could tell whether, in that congregated caravan, Moby Dick himself might not temporarily be swimming, like the worshipped white-elephant in the coronation procession of the Siamese!

As if too long lurking behind the headlands, till the Pequod should fairly have entered the straits, these rascally Asiatics were now in hot pursuit, to make up for their over-cautious delay. But when the swift Pequod, with a fresh leading wind, was herself in hot chase; how very kind of these tawny philanthropists to assist in speeding her on to her own chosen pursuit,—mere riding-whips and rowels to her, that they were. As   ; some such fancy as the above seemed his.

, by some presumed wonderful instinct of the Sperm Whale,   —   —   so that their spouts all looked like flashing lines of stacked bayonets,

˙   rapidly and steadily ,   Had these Leviathans been but a flock of simple sheep, pursued over the pasture by three fierce wolves, they could not possibly have evinced such excessive dismay. But this occasional timidity is characteristic of almost all herding creatures. Though banding together in tens of

---

* To *gally*, or *gallow*, is to frighten excessively,—to confound with fright. It is an old Saxon word. It occurs once in Shakspere:—

> "The wrathful skies
> *Gallow* the very wanderers of the dark,
> And make them keep their caves
>
> *Lear*, Act III. sc.ii.

To common land usages, the word is now completely obsolete. When the polite landsman first hears it from the gaunt Nantucketer, he is apt to set it down as one of the whaleman's self-derived savageries. Much the same is it with many other sinewy Saxonisms of this sort, which emigrated to the New-England rocks with the noble brawn of the old English emigrants in the time of the Commonwealth. Thus, some of the best and furthest-descended English words—the etymological Howards and Percys—are now democratised, nay, plebeianised—so to speak—in the New World.

thousands, the lion-maned buffaloes of the West have fled before a solitary horseman. Witness, too, all human beings, how when herded together in the sheepfold of a theatre's pit, they will, at the slightest alarm of fire, rush helter-skelter for the outlets, crowding, trampling, jamming, and remorselessly dashing each other to death. Best, therefore, withhold any amazement at the strangely gallied whales before us, for there is no folly of the beasts of the earth which is not infinitely outdone by the madness of men.

, as has been said,   it is to be observed that   Though   struck under such circumstances,   and indeed is almost always more or less anticipated;

As, blind and deaf, the whale plunged forward, as if by sheer power of speed to rid himself of the iron leech that had fastened to him; as we thus tore a white gash in the sea, on all sides menaced as we flew, by the crazed creatures to and fro rushing about us; our beset boat was like a ship mobbed by ice-isles in a tempest, and striving to steer through their complicated channels and straits, knowing not at what moment it may be locked in and crushed.

Nor were the oarsmen quite idle, though their wonted duty was now altogether dispensed with. They chiefly attended to the shouting part of the business. "Out of the way, Commodore!" cried one, to a great dromedary that of a sudden rose bodily to the surface, and for an instant threatened to swamp us. "Hard down with your tail, there!" cried a second to another, which, close to our gunwale, seemed calmly cooling himself with his own fan-like extremity.

,

,

Now, inclusive of the occasional wide intervals between the revolving outer circles, and inclusive of the spaces between the various pods in any one of those circles, the entire area at this juncture, embraced by the whole multitude, must have contained at least two or three square miles. At any rate—

though indeed such a test at such a time might be deceptive—spoutings might be discovered from our low boat that seemed playing up almost from the rim of the horizon. I mention this circumstance, because, as if the cows and calves had been purposely locked up in this innermost fold; and as if the wide extent of the herd had hitherto prevented them from learning the precise cause of its stopping; or, possibly, being so young, unsophisticated, and every way innocent and inexperienced; however it may have been, these smaller whales—now and then visiting our becalmed boat from the margin of the lake—evinced a wondrous fearlessness and confidence, or else a still becharmed panic which it was impossible not to marvel at.　　round us,　　for the time

— ; where, tail to head, and all ready for the final spring, the unborn whale lies bent like a Tartar's bow.

*

'

and an appalling spectacle enough, any way;　,　,　flailing with his flexible tail, and

Yes, the long calm was departing.

seizing the helm—　　"—"

---

*　The sperm whale, as with all other species of the Leviathan, but unlike most other fish, breeds indifferently at all seasons; after a gestation which may probably be set down at nine months, producing but one at a time; though in some few known instances giving birth to an Esau and Jacob:—a contingency provided for in suckling by two teats, curiously situated, one on each side of the anus; but the breasts themselves extend upwards from that. When by chance these precious parts in a nursing whale are cut by the hunter's lance, the mother's pouring milk and blood rivallingly discolor the sea for rods. The milk is very sweet and rich; it has been tasted by man; it might do well with strawberries. When overflowing with mutual esteem, the whales salute *more hominum*.

CHAPTER 88

Schools and Schoolmasters

The previous chapter gave account of an immense body or herd of Sperm Whales, and there was also then given the probable cause inducing those vast aggregations.

Now, though such great bodies are at times encountered, yet, as must have been seen, even at the present day, small detached bands are occasionally observed, embracing from twenty to fifty individuals each. Such bands are known as schools. They generally are of two sorts; those composed almost entirely of females, and those mustering none but young vigorous males, or bulls, as they are familiarly designated.

In cavalier attendance upon the school of females, you invariably see a male of full grown magnitude, but not old; who, upon any alarm, evinces his gallantry by falling in the rear and covering the flight of his ladies. In truth, this gentleman is a luxurious Ottoman, swimming about over the watery world, surroundingly accompanied by all the solaces and endearments of the harem. The contrast between this Ottoman and his concubines is striking; because, while he is always of the largest leviathanic proportions, the ladies, even at full growth, are not more than one-third of the bulk of an average-sized male. They are comparatively delicate, indeed; I dare say, not to exceed half a dozen yards round the waist. Nevertheless, it cannot be denied, that upon the whole they are hereditarily entitled to *en bon point*.

It is very curious to watch this harem and its lord in their indolent ramblings. Like fashionables, they are for ever on the move in leisurely search of variety. You meet them on the Line in time for the full flower of the Equatorial feeding season, having just returned, perhaps, from spending the summer in the Northern seas, and so cheating summer of all unpleasant weariness and warmth. By the time they have lounged up and down the promenade of the

Equator awhile, they start for the Oriental waters in anticipation of the cool season there, and so evade the other excessive temperature of the year.

When serenely advancing on one of these journeys, if any strange suspicious sights are seen, my lord whale keeps a wary eye on his interesting family. Should any unwarrantably pert young Leviathan coming that way, presume to draw confidentially close to one of the ladies, with what prodigious fury the Bashaw assails him, and chases him away! High times, indeed, if unprincipled young rakes like him are to be permitted to invade the sanctity of domestic bliss; though do what the Bashaw will, he cannot keep the most notorious Lothario out of his bed; for, alas! all fish bed in common. As ashore, the ladies often cause the most terrible duels among their rival admirers; just so with the whales, who sometimes come to deadly battle, and all for love. They fence with their long lower jaws, sometimes locking them together, and so striving for the supremacy like elks that warringly interweave their antlers. Not a few are captured having the deep scars of these encounters,—furrowed heads, broken teeth, scolloped fins; and in some instances, wrenched and dislocated mouths.

But supposing the invader of domestic bliss to betake himself away at the first rush of the harem's lord, then is it very diverting to watch that lord. Gently he insinuates his vast bulk among them again and revels there awhile, still in tantalizing vicinity to young Lothario, like pious Solomon devoutly worshipping among his thousand concubines. Granting other whales to be in sight, the fishermen will seldom give chase to one of these Grand Turks; for these Grand Turks are too lavish of their strength, and hence their unctuousness is small. As for the sons and the daughters they beget, why, those sons and daughters must take care of themselves; at least, with only the maternal help. For like certain other omnivorous roving lovers that might be named, my Lord Whale has no taste for the nursery, however much for the bower; and so, being a great traveller, he leaves his anonymous babies all over the world; every baby an exotic. In good time, nevertheless, as the ardor of youth declines; as years and dumps increase; as reflection lends her solemn pauses; in short, as a general lassitude overtakes the sated Turk; then a love of ease and virtue supplants the love for maidens; our Ottoman enters upon the impotent, repentant, admonitory stage of life, forswears, disbands the harem, and grown to an exemplary, sulky old soul, goes about all alone among the meridians and parallels saying his prayers, and warning each young Leviathan from his amorous errors.

Now, as the harem of whales is called by the fishermen a school, so is the lord and master of that school technically known as the schoolmaster. It is therefore not in strict character, however admirably satirical, that after going to school himself, he should then go abroad inculcating not what he learned there, but the folly of it. His title, schoolmaster, would very naturally seem derived from the name bestowed upon the harem itself, but some have surmised that the man who first thus entitled this sort of Ottoman whale, must have read the memoirs of Vidocq, and informed himself what sort of a country-schoolmaster that famous Frenchman was in his younger days, and what was the nature of those occult lessons he inculcated into some of his pupils.

The same secludedness and isolation to which the schoolmaster whale betakes himself in his advancing years, is true of all aged Sperm Whales. Almost universally, a lone whale—as a solitary Leviathan is called—proves an ancient one. Like venerable moss-bearded Daniel Boone, he will have no one near him but Nature herself; and her he takes to wife in the wilderness of waters, and the best of wives she is, though she keeps so many moody secrets.

The schools composing none but young and vigorous males, previously mentioned, offer a strong contrast to the harem schools. For while those female whales are characteristically timid, the young males, or forty-barrel-bulls, as they call them, are by far the most pugnacious of all Leviathans, and proverbially the most dangerous to encounter; excepting those wondrous grey-headed, grizzled whales, sometimes met, and these will fight you like grim fiends exasperated by a penal gout.

The Forty-barrel-bull schools are larger than the harem schools. Like a mob of young collegians, they are full of fight, fun, and wickedness, tumbling round the world at such a reckless, rollicking rate, that no prudent underwriter would insure them any more than he would a riotous lad at Yale or Harvard. They soon relinquish this turbulence though, and when about three-fourths grown, break up, and separately go about in quest of settlements, that is, harems.

Another point of difference between the male and female schools is still more characteristic of the sexes. Say you strike a Forty-barrel-bull—poor devil! all his comrades quit him. But strike a member of the harem school, and her companions swim around her with every token of concern, sometimes lingering so near her and so long, as themselves to fall a prey.

CHAPTER 89

Fast-Fish and Loose-Fish

in the last chapter but one,

,—a mast, an oar, a nine-inch cable, a telegraph wire, or a strand of cobweb, it is all the same

—the Coke-upon-Littleton of the fist

Now in the present case Erskine contended that the examples of the whale and the lady were reciprocally illustrative of each other.

(the fish)

,

poor

CHAPTER 90

Heads or Tails

"*De balena vero sufficit, si rex habeat caput, et regina caudam.*"
—Bracton, l. 3, c. 3.

Latin from the books of the Laws of England, which taken along with the context, means, that of all whales captured by anybody on the coast of that land,
the King, as Honorary Grand Harpooneer, must have the head, and the Queen
be respectfully presented with the tail. A division which, in the whale, is much
like halving an apple; there is no intermediate remainder. Now as this law, under a modified form, is to this day in force in England; and as it offers in various
respects a strange anomaly touching the general law of Fast and Loose-Fish,
it is here treated of in a separate chapter, on the same courteous principle that
prompts the English railways to be at the expense of a separate car, specially
reserved for the accommodation of royalty. In the first place, in curious proof
of the fact that the above-mentioned law is still in force, I proceed to lay before
you a circumstance that happened within the last two years.

It seems that some honest mariners of Dover, or Sandwich, or some one of
the Cinque Ports, had after a hard chase succeeded in killing and beaching a
fine whale which they had originally descried afar off from the shore. Now
the Cinque Ports are partially or somehow under the jurisdiction of a sort of
policeman or beadle, called a Lord Warden. Holding the office directly from
the crown, I believe, all the royal emoluments incident to the Cinque Port
territories become by assignment his. By some writers this office is called a
sinecure. But not so. Because the Lord Warden is busily employed at times in
fobbing his perquisites; which are his chiefly by virtue of that same fobbing
of them.

Now when these poor sun-burnt mariners, bare-footed, and with their trowsers rolled high up on their eely legs, had wearily hauled their fat fish high

and dry, promising themselves a good £150 from the precious oil and bone; and in fantasy sipping rare tea with their wives, and good ale with their cronies, upon the strength of their respective shares; up steps a very learned and most Christian and charitable gentleman, with a copy of Blackstone under his arm; and laying it upon the whale's head, he says—"Hands off! this fish, my masters, is a Fast-Fish. I seize it as the Lord Warden's." Upon this the poor mariners in their respectful consternation—so truly English—knowing not what to say, fall to vigorously scratching their heads all round; meanwhile ruefully glancing from the whale to the stranger. But that did in nowise mend the matter, or at all soften the hard heart of the learned gentleman with the copy of Blackstone. At length one of them, after long scratching about for his ideas, made bold to speak,

"Please, sir, who is the Lord Warden?"

"The Duke."

"But the duke had nothing to do with taking this fish?"

"It is his."

"We have been at great trouble, and peril, and some expense, and is all that to go to the Duke's benefit; we getting nothing at all for our pains but our blisters?"

"It is his."

"Is the Duke so very poor as to be forced to this desperate mode of getting a livelihood?"

"It is his."

"I thought to relieve my old bed-ridden mother by part of my share of this whale."

"It is his."

"Won't the Duke be content with a quarter or a half?"

"It is his."

In a word, the whale was seized and sold, and his Grace the Duke of Wellington received the money. Thinking that viewed in some particular lights, the case might by a bare possibility in some small degree be deemed, under the circumstances, a rather hard one, an honest clergyman of the town respectfully addressed a note to his Grace, begging him to take the case of those unfortunate mariners into full consideration. To which my Lord Duke in substance replied (both letters were published) that he had already done so, and received the money, and would be obliged to the reverend gentleman if for the future he (the reverend gentleman) would decline meddling with other people's business. Is this the still militant old man, standing at the corners of the three kingdoms, on all hands coercing alms of beggars?

It will readily be seen that in this case the alleged right of the Duke to the whale was a delegated one from the Sovereign. We must needs inquire then on what principle the Sovereign is originally invested with that right. The law itself has already been set forth. But Plowdon gives us the reason for it. Says Plowdon, the whale so caught belongs to the King and Queen, "because of its superior excellence." And by the soundest commentators this has ever been held a cogent argument in such matters.

But why should the King have the head, and the Queen the tail? A reason for that, ye lawyers!

In his treatise on "Queen-Gold," or Queen-pinmoney, an old King's Bench author, one William Prynne, thus discourseth: "Y^e tail is ye Queen's, that ye Queen's wardrobe may be supplied with ye whalebone." Now this was written at a time when the black limber bone of the Greenland or Right whale was largely used in ladies' bodices. But this same bone is not in the tail; it is in the head, which is a sad mistake for a sagacious lawyer like Prynne. But is the Queen a mermaid, to be presented with a tail? An allegorical meaning may lurk here.

There are two royal fish so styled by the English law writers—the whale and the sturgeon; both royal property under certain limitations, and nominally supplying the tenth branch of the crown's ordinary revenue. I know not that any other author has hinted of the matter; but by inference it seems to me that the sturgeon must be divided in the same way as the whale, the King receiving the highly dense and elastic head peculiar to that fish, which, symbolically regarded, may possibly be humorously grounded upon some presumed con-geniality. And thus there seems a reason in all things, even in law.

CHAPTER 91

The Pequod meets the Rose-bud

"*In vain it was to rake for Ambergriese in the paunch of this Leviathan,
insufferable fetor denying not inquiry.*"   —Sir T. Browne, V.E.

the many noses on the Pequod's deck proved more vigilant discoverers than the three pairs of eyes aloft.

with the expiring breeze

of these   s

>

"my Bouton-de-Rose-bud,"

, who did not seem to relish the job he was at very much

", d'ye see,   here"

All their noses upwardly projected from their faces like so many jib-booms.
   drop their work, and

Sounding him carefully,   at all   little

"He wants you to take a glass of wine with him," said the interpreter.

"to drink"

>

and yelling,   especially as the horrible nosegay increased,

CHAPTER 92

Ambergris

Now this ambergris is a very curious substance, and so important as an article of commerce, that in 1791 a certain Nantucket-born Captain Coffin was
examined at the bar of the English House of Commons on that subject. For
at that time, and indeed until a comparatively late day, the precise origin of
ambergris remained, like amber itself, a problem to the learned. Though the
word ambergris is but the French compound for grey amber, yet the two substances are quite distinct. For amber, though at times found on the sea-coast,

is also dug up in some far inland soils, whereas ambergris is never found except upon the sea. Besides, amber is a hard, transparent, brittle, odorless substance, used for mouth-pieces to pipes, for beads and ornaments; but ambergris is soft, waxy, and so highly fragrant and spicy, that it is largely used in perfumery, in pastiles, precious candles, hair-powders, and pomatum. The Turks use it in cooking, and also carry it to Mecca, for the same purpose that frankincense is carried to St. Peter's in Rome. Some wine merchants drop a few grains into claret, to flavor it.

Who would think, then, that such fine ladies and gentlemen should regale themselves with an essence found in the inglorious bowels of a sick whale! Yet so it is. By some, ambergris is supposed to be the cause, and by others the effect, of the dyspepsia in the whale. How to cure such a dyspepsia it were hard to say, unless by administering three or four boat loads of Brandreth's pills, and then running out of harm's way, as laborers do in blasting rocks.

I have forgotten to say that there were found in this ambergris, certain hard, round, bony plates, which at first Stubb thought might be sailors' trowsers buttons; but it afterwards turned out that they were nothing more than pieces of small squid bones embalmed in that manner.

Now that the incorruption of this most fragrant ambergris should be found in the heart of such decay; is this nothing? Bethink thee of that saying of St. Paul in Corinthians, about corruption and incorruption; how that we are sown in dishonor, but raised in glory. And likewise call to mind that saying of Paracelsus about what it is that maketh the best musk. Also forget not the strange fact that of all things of ill-savor, Cologne-water, in its rudimental manufacturing stages, is the worst.

I should like to conclude the chapter with the above appeal, but cannot, owing to my anxiety to repel a charge often made against whalemen, and which, in the estimation of some already biased minds, might be considered as indirectly substantiated by what has been said of the Frenchman's two whales.

Elsewhere in this volume the slanderous aspersion has been disproved, that the vocation of whaling is throughout a slatternly, untidy business. But there is another thing to rebut. They hint that all whales always smell bad. Now how did this odious stigma originate?

I opine, that it is plainly traceable to the first arrival of the Greenland whaling ships in London, more than two centuries ago. Because those whalemen did not then, and do not now, try out their oil at sea as the Southern ships have always done; but cutting up the fresh blubber in small bits, thrust it through the bung holes of large casks, and carry it home in that manner; the shortness of the season in those Icy Seas, and the sudden and violent storms to which they are exposed, forbidding any other course. The consequence is, that upon breaking into the hold, and unloading one of these whale cemeteries, in the Greenland dock, a savor is given forth somewhat similar to that arising from excavating an old city grave-yard, for the foundations of a Lying-in Hospital.

I partly surmise also, that this wicked charge against whalers may be likewise imputed to the existence on the coast of Greenland, in former times, of a Dutch village called Schmerenburgh or Smeerenberg, which latter name is the one used by the learned Fogo Von Slack, in his great work on Smells, a text-book on that subject. As its name imports (smeer, fat; berg, to put up), this village was founded in order to afford a place for the blubber of the Dutch whale fleet to be tried out, without being taken home to Holland for that purpose. It was a collection of furnaces, fat-kettles, and oil sheds; and when the works were in full operation certainly gave forth no very pleasant savor. But all this is quite different with a South Sea Sperm Whaler; which in a voyage of four years perhaps, after completely filling her hold with oil, does not, perhaps, consume fifty days in the business of boiling out; and in the state that it is casked, the oil is nearly scentless. The truth is, that living or dead, if but decently treated, whales as a species are by no means creatures of ill odor; nor can whalemen be recognized, as the people of the middle ages affected to detect a Jew in the company, by the nose. Nor indeed can the whale possibly be otherwise than fragrant, when, as a general thing, he enjoys such high health; taking abundance of exercise; always out of doors; though, it is true, seldom in the open air. I say, that the motion of a Sperm Whale's flukes above water dispenses a perfume, as when a musk-scented lady rustles her dress in a warm parlor. What then shall I liken the Sperm Whale to for fragrance, considering his magnitude? Must it not be to that famous elephant, with jewelled tusks, and redolent with myrrh, which was led out of an Indian town to do honor to Alexander the Great?

CHAPTER 93

The Castaway

Poor Pip! ye have heard of him before; ye must remember his tambourine on that dramatic midnight, so gloomy-jolly.

In outer aspect, Pip and Dough-Boy made a match, like a black pony and a white one, of equal developments, though of dissimilar color, driven in one eccentric span. But while hapless Dough-Boy was by nature dull and torpid in his intellects,   unaccountably   ; though, as ere long will be seen, what was thus temporarily subdued in him, in the end was destined to be luridly illumined by strange wild fires, that fictitiously showed him off to ten times the natural lustre with which in his native Tolland County in Connecticut, he had once enlivened many a fiddler's frolic on the green; and at melodious even-tide, with his gay ha-ha! had turned the round horizon into one star-belled tambourine. So, though in the clear air of day, suspended against a blue-veined neck, the pure-watered diamond drop will healthful glow; yet, when the cunning jeweller would show you the diamond in its most impressive lustre, he lays it against a gloomy ground, and then lights it up, not by the sun, but by some unnatural gases. Then come out those fiery effulgences, infernally superb; then the evil-blazing diamond, once the divinest symbol of the crystal skies, looks like some crown-jewel stolen from the King of Hell.

But let us to the story

, as for a time to become quite maimed

He hated Pip for a poltroon.

calm and cool, and   , all round,

Mark, how when sailors in a dead calm bathe in the open sea—mark how closely they hug their ship and only coast along her sides.

; though, indeed, such considerations towards oarsmen jeopardized through their own timidity, is not always manifested by the hunters in all similar instances; and such instances not unfrequently occur; almost invariably in the fishery, a coward, so called, is marked with the same ruthless detestation peculiar to military navies and armies

CHAPTER 94

A Squeeze of the Hand

,

such a delicious molifier!   , and began, as it were, to serpentine and spiralize

after the bitter exertion at the windlass;   as they richly broke to my fingers, and discharged all their opulence, like fully ripe grapes their wine; ,   I forgot all about our horrible oath; in that inexpressible sperm, I washed my hands and my heart of it; I almost began to credit the old Paracelsan superstition that sperm is of rare virtue in allaying the heat of anger;

Squeeze! squeeze! squeeze! all the morning long; I squeezed that sperm till I myself almost melted into it; I squeezed that sperm till a strange sort of insanity came over me; and I found myself unwittingly squeezing my co-laborers' hands in it, mistaking their hands for the gentle globules. Such an abounding, affectionate, friendly, loving feeling did this avocation beget; that at last I was continually squeezing their hands, and looking up into their eyes sentimentally; as much as to say,—Oh! my dear fellow beings, why should we longer cherish any social acerbities, or know the slightest ill-humor or envy! Come; let us squeeze hands all round; nay, let us all squeeze ourselves into each other; let us squeeze ourselves universally into the very milk and sperm of kindness.

For now, since by many prolonged, repeated experiences, I have perceived that in all cases man must eventually lower, or at least shift, his conceit of attainable felicity; not placing it anywhere in the intellect or the fancy; but in the wife, the heart, the bed, the table, the saddle, the fireside, the country; now that I have perceived all this, I am ready to squeeze case eternally. In thoughts of the visions of the night, I saw long rows of angels in paradise, each with his hands in a jar of spermaceti.

*   *   *   *   *

They look much like blocks of Berkshire marble.

There is another substance, and a very singular one, which turns up in the course of this business, but which I feel it to be very puzzling adequately to describe. It is called slobgollion; an appellation original with the whalemen, and even so is the nature of the substance. It is an ineffably oozy, stringy affair, most frequently found in the tubs of sperm, after a prolonged squeezing, and subsequent decanting. I hold it to be the wondrously thin, ruptured membranes of the case, coalescing.

Gurry, so called, is a term properly belonging to right whalemen, but some-times incidentally used by the sperm fishermen. It designates the dark, gluti-nous substance which is scraped off the back of the Greenland or right whale, and much of which covers the decks of those inferior souls who hunt that ignoble Leviathan.

Nippers. Strictly this word is not indigenous to the whale's vocabulary. But as applied by whalemen, it becomes so. A whaleman's nipper is a short firm strip of tendinous stuff cut from the tapering part of Leviathan's tail: it aver-ages an inch in thickness, and for the rest, is about the size of the iron part of a hoe. Edgewise moved along the oily deck, it operates like a leathern squilgee; and by nameless blandishments, as of magic, allures along with it all impurities.

to learn all about these recondite matters, your best way is at once   have a long talk with   This place has previously been mentioned as the receptacle for the blanket-pieces, when stript and hoisted from the whale.   ,   and lurches

CHAPTER 95

The Cassock

, lying along lengthwise in the lee scuppers   ,

as if he were a grenadier carrying a dead comrade from the field

*

---

*

CHAPTER 96

The Try-Works

So the pitch and sulphur-freighted brigs of the bold Hydriote, Canaris, issuing from their midnight harbors, with broad sheets of flame for sails, bore down upon the Turkish frigates, and folded them in conflagrations.

Wrapped, for that interval, in darkness myself, I but the better saw the redness, the madness, the ghastliness of others. The continual sight of the fiend shapes before me, capering half in smoke and half in fire, these at last begat kindred visions in my soul, so soon as I began to yield to that unaccountable drowsiness which ever would come over me at a midnight helm.

But that night, in particular, a strange (and ever since inexplicable) thing occurred to me. Starting from a brief standing sleep, I was horribly conscious of something fatally wrong. The jaw-bone tiller smote my side, which leaned against it; in my ears was the low hum of sails, just beginning to shake in the wind; I thought my eyes were open; I was half conscious of putting my fingers to the lids and mechanically stretching them still further apart. But, spite of all this, I could see no compass before me to steer by; though it seemed but a minute since I had been watching the card, by the steady binnacle lamp illuminating it. Nothing seemed before me but a jet gloom, now and then made ghastly by flashes of redness. Uppermost was the impression, that whatever swift, rushing thing I stood on was not so much bound to any haven ahead as rushing from all havens astern. A stark, bewildered feeling, as of death, came over me. Convulsively my hands grasped the tiller, but with the crazy conceit that the tiller was, somehow, in some enchanted way, inverted. My God! what is the matter with me? thought I. Lo! in my brief sleep I had turned myself about, and was fronting the ship's stern, with my back to her prow and the compass. In an instant I faced back, just in time to prevent the vessel from flying up into the wind, and very probably capsizing her. How glad and how grateful the relief from this unnatural hallucination of the night, and the fatal contingency of being brought by the lee!

Look not too long in the face of the fire, O man! Never dream with thy hand on the helm! Turn not thy back to the compass; accept the first hint of the hitching tiller; believe not the artificial fire, when its redness makes all things look ghastly. To-morrow, in the natural sun, the skies will be bright; those who glared like devils in the forking flames, the morn will show in far other, at least gentler, relief; the glorious, golden, glad sun, the only true lamp—all others but liars!

Nevertheless the sun hides not Virginia's Dismal Swamp, nor Rome's accursed Campagna, nor wide Sahara, nor all the millions of miles of deserts and of griefs beneath the moon. The sun hides not the ocean, which is the dark side of this earth, and which is two thirds of this earth. So, therefore, that mortal man who hath more of joy than sorrow in him, that mortal man cannot be true—not true, or undeveloped. With books the same. The truest of all men was the Man of Sorrows, and the truest of all books is Solomon's, and Ecclesiastes is the fine hammered steel of woe. "All is vanity." ALL. This wilful world hath not got hold of unchristian Solomon's wisdom yet. But he who dodges hospitals and jails, and walks fast crossing graveyards, and would rather talk of operas than hell; calls Cowper, Young, Pascal, Rousseau, poor devils all of sick men; and throughout a care-free lifetime swears by Rabelais as passing wise, and therefore jolly;—not that man is fitted to sit down on tomb-stones, and break the green damp mould with unfathomably wondrous Solomon.

But even Solomon, he says, "the man that wandereth out of the way of understanding shall remain" (*i.e.* even while living) "in the congregation of the dead." Give not thyself up, then, to fire, lest it invert thee, deaden thee; as for the time it did me. There is a wisdom that is woe; but there is a woe that is madness. And there is a Catskill eagle in some souls that can alike dive down into the blackest gorges, and soar out of them again and become invisible in the sunny spaces. And even if he for ever flies within the gorge, that gorge is in the mountains; so that even in his lowest swoop the mountain eagle is still higher than other birds upon the plain, even though they soar.

CHAPTER 97

The Lamp

Had you descended from the Pequod's try-works to the Pequod's forecastle, where the off duty watch were sleeping, for one single moment you would have almost thought you were standing in some illuminated shrine of canonized kings and counsellors. There they lay in their triangular oaken vaults, each mariner a chiselled muteness; a score of lamps flashing upon his hooded eyes.

In merchantmen, oil for the sailor is more scarce than the milk of queens. To dress in the dark, and eat in the dark, and stumble in darkness to his pallet, this is his usual lot. But the whaleman, as he seeks the food of light, so he lives in light. He makes his berth an Aladdin's lamp, and lays him down in it; so that in the pitchiest night the ship's black hull still houses an illumination.

See with what entire freedom the whaleman takes his handful of lamps—often but old bottles and vials, though—to the copper cooler at the try-works, and replenishes them there, as mugs of ale at a vat. He burns, too, the purest of oil, in its unmanufactured, and, therefore, unvitiated state; a fluid unknown to solar, lunar, or astral contrivances ashore. It is sweet as early grass butter in April. He goes and hunts for his oil, so as to be sure of its freshness and genuineness, even as the traveller on the prairie hunts up his own supper of game.

CHAPTER 98

Stowing Down and Clearing Up

—

— , and go through the whole weary thing again   by long toilings extracted from this world's vast bulk its small but valuable sperm; and then, with weary patience,   from its defilements,

CHAPTER 99

The Doubloon

Ere now it has been related how Ahab was wont to pace his quarter-deck, taking regular turns at either limit, the binnacle and mainmast; but in the multiplicity of other things requiring narration it has not been added how that sometimes in these walks, when most plunged in his mood, he was wont to pause in turn at each spot, and stand there strangely eyeing the particular object before him. When he halted before the binnacle, with his glance fastened on the pointed needle in the compass, that glance shot like a javelin with the pointed intensity of his purpose; and when resuming his walk he again paused before the mainmast, then, as the same riveted glance fastened upon the riveted gold coin there, he still wore the same aspect of nailed firmness, only dashed with a certain wild longing, if not hopefulness.

But one morning, turning to pass the doubloon, he seemed to be newly attracted by the strange figures and inscriptions stamped on it, as though now for the first time beginning to interpret for himself in some monomaniac way whatever significance might lurk in them. And some certain significance lurks in all things, else all things are little worth, and the round world itself but an empty cipher, except to sell by the cartload, as they do hills about Boston, to fill up some morass in the Milky Way.

Now this doubloon was of purest, virgin gold, raked somewhere out of the heart of gorgeous hills, whence, east and west, over golden sands, the head-waters of many a Pactolus flows. And though now nailed amidst all the rusti-ness of iron bolts and the verdigris of copper spikes, yet, untouchable and immaculate to any foulness, it still preserved its Quito glow. Nor, though placed amongst a ruthless crew and every hour passed by ruthless hands, and through the livelong nights shrouded with thick darkness which might cover any pilfering approach, nevertheless every sunrise found the doubloon where the sunset left it last. For it was set apart and sanctified to one awe-striking end; and however wanton in their sailor ways, one and all, the mariners re-vered it as the white whale's talisman. Sometimes they talked it over in the weary watch by night, wondering whose it was to be at last, and whether he would ever live to spend it.

Now those noble golden coins of South America are as medals of the sun and tropic token-pieces. Here palms, alpacas, and volcanoes; sun's disks and stars; ecliptics, horns-of-plenty, and rich banners waving, are in luxuriant profusion stamped; so that the precious gold seems almost to derive an added precious-ness and enhancing glories, by passing through those fancy mints, so Span-ishly poetic.

It so chanced that the doubloon of the Pequod was a most wealthy example of these things. On its round border it bore the letters, REPUBLICA DEL ECUADOR: QUITO. So this bright coin came from a country planted in the middle of the world, and beneath the great equator, and named after it; and it had been cast midway up the Andes, in the unwaning clime that knows no autumn. Zoned by those letters you saw the likeness of three Andes' summits; from one a flame; a tower on another; on the third a crowing cock; while arch-ing over all was a segment of the partitioned zodiac, the signs all marked with their usual cabalistics, and the keystone sun entering the equinoctial point at Libra.

Before this equatorial coin, Ahab, not unobserved by others, was now pausing.

"There's something ever egotistical in mountain-tops and towers, and all other grand and lofty things; look here,—three peaks as proud as Lucifer. The firm tower, that is Ahab; the volcano, that is Ahab; the courageous, the undaunted, and victorious fowl, that, too, is Ahab; all are Ahab; and this round gold is but the image of the rounder globe, which, like a magician's glass, to each and every man in turn but mirrors back his own mysterious self. Great pains, small gains for those who ask the world to solve them; it cannot solve itself. Methinks now this coined sun wears a ruddy face; but see! aye, he enters the sign of storms, the equinox! and but six months before he wheeled out of a former equinox at Aries! From storm to storm! So be it, then. Born in throes, 't is fit that man should live in pains and die in pangs! So be it, then! Here's stout stuff for woe to work on. So be it, then."

"No fairy fingers can have pressed the gold, but devil's claws must have left their mouldings there since yesterday," murmured Starbuck to himself, leaning against the bulwarks. "The old man seems to read Belshazzar's awful writing. I have never marked the coin inspectingly. He goes below; let me read. A dark valley between three mighty, heaven-abiding peaks, that almost seem the Trinity, in some faint earthly symbol. So in this vale of Death, God girds us round; and over all our gloom, the sun of Righteousness still shines a beacon and a hope. If we bend down our eyes, the dark vale shows her mouldy soil; but if we lift them, the bright sun meets our glance half way, to cheer. Yet, oh, the great sun is no fixture; and if, at midnight, we would fain snatch some sweet solace from him, we gaze for him in vain! This coin speaks wisely, mildly, truly, but still sadly to me. I will quit it, lest Truth shake me falsely."

"There now's the old Mogul," soliloquized Stubb by the try-works, "he's been twigging it; and there goes Starbuck from the same, and both with faces which I should say might be somewhere within nine fathoms long. And all from looking at a piece of gold, which did I have it now on Negro Hill or in Corlaer's Hook, I'd not look at it very long ere spending it. Humph! in my poor, insignificant opinion, I regard this as queer. I have seen doubloons before now in my voyagings; your doubloons of old Spain, your doubloons of Peru, your doubloons of Chili, your doubloons of Bolivia, your doubloons of Popayan; with plenty of gold moidores and pistoles, and joes, and half joes, and quarter joes. What then should there be in this doubloon of the Equator that is so killing wonderful? By Golconda! let me read it once. Halloa! here's signs and wonders truly! That, now, is what old Bowditch in his Epitome calls the zodiac, and what my almanac below calls ditto. I'll get the almanac and as I have heard devils can be raised with Daboll's arithmetic, I'll try my hand at raising a meaning out of these queer curvicues here with the Massachusetts calendar. Here's the book. Let's see now. Signs and wonders; and the sun, he's always among 'em. Hem, hem, hem; here they are—here they go—all alive:—Aries, or the Ram; Taurus, or the Bull and Jimimi! here's Gemini himself, or the Twins. Well; the sun he wheels among 'em. Aye, here on the coin he's just crossing the threshold between two of twelve sitting-rooms all in a ring. Book! you lie there; the fact is, you books must know your places. You'll do to give us the bare words and facts, but we come in to supply the thoughts. That's my small experience, so far as the Massachusetts calendar, and Bowditch's navigator, and Daboll's arithmetic go. Signs and wonders, eh? Pity if there is nothing wonderful in signs, and significant in wonders! There's a clue somewhere; wait a bit; hist—hark! By Jove, I have it! Look you, Doubloon, your zodiac here is the life of man in one round chapter; and now I'll read it off, straight out of the book. Come, Almanack! To begin: there's Aries, or the Ram—lecherous dog, he begets us; then, Taurus, or the Bull—he bumps us the first thing; then Gemini, or the Twins—that is, Virtue and Vice; we try to reach Virtue, when lo! comes Cancer the Crab, and drags us back; and here, going from Virtue, Leo, a roaring Lion, lies in the path—he gives a few fierce bites and surly dabs with his paw; we escape, and hail Virgo, the Virgin! that's our first love; we marry and think to be happy for aye, when pop comes Libra, or the Scales—happiness weighed and found wanting; and while we are very sad about that, Lord! how we suddenly jump, as Scorpio, or the Scorpion, stings us in the rear; we are curing the wound, when whang come the arrows all round; Sagittarius, or the Archer, is amusing himself. As we pluck out the shafts, stand aside! here's the battering-ram, Capricornus, or the Goat; full tilt, he comes rushing, and headlong we are tossed; when Aquarius, or the Water-bearer, pours out his whole deluge and drowns us; and to wind up with Pisces, or the Fishes, we sleep. There's a sermon now, writ in high heaven, and the sun goes through it every year, and yet comes out of it all alive and hearty. Jollily he, aloft there, wheels through toil and trouble; and so, alow here, does jolly Stubb. Oh, jolly's the word for aye! Adieu, Doubloon! But stop; here comes little King-Post; dodge round the try-works, now, and let's hear what he'll have to say. There; he's before it; he'll out with something presently. So, so; he's beginning."

"I see nothing here, but a round thing made of gold, and whoever raises a certain whale, this round thing belongs to him. So, what's all this staring been about? It is worth sixteen dollars, that's true; and at two cents the cigar, that's nine hundred and sixty cigars. I won't smoke dirty pipes like Stubb, but I like cigars, and here's nine hundred and sixty of them; so here goes Flask aloft to spy 'em out."

"Shall I call that wise or foolish, now; if it be really wise it has a foolish look to it; yet, if it be really foolish, then has it a sort of wiseish look to it. But, avast; here comes our old Manxman—the old hearse-driver, he must have been, that is, before he took to the sea. He luffs up before the doubloon; halloa, and goes round on the other side of the mast; why, there's a horse-shoe nailed on that side; and now he's back again; what does that mean? Hark! he's muttering— voice like an old worn-out coffee-mill. Prick ears, and listen!"

"If the White Whale be raised, it must be in a month and a day, when the sun stands in some one of these signs. I've studied signs, and know their marks; they were taught me two score years ago, by the old witch in Copenhagen. Now, in what sign will the sun then be? The horse-shoe sign; for there it is, right opposite the gold. And what's the horse-shoe sign? The lion is the horse-shoe sign—the roaring and devouring lion. Ship, old ship! my old head shakes to think of thee."

"There's another rendering now; but still one text. All sorts of men in one kind of world, you see. Dodge again! here comes Queequeg—all tattooing—looks like the signs of the Zodiac himself. What says the Cannibal? As I live he's comparing notes; looking at his thigh bone; thinks the sun is in the thigh, or in the calf, or in the bowels, I suppose, as the old women talk Surgeon's Astronomy in the back country. And by Jove, he's found something there in the vicinity of his thigh—I guess it's Sagittarius, or the Archer. No: he don't know what to make of the doubloon; he takes it for an old button off some king's trowsers. But, aside again! here comes that ghost-devil, Fedallah; tail coiled out of sight as usual, oakum in the toes of his pumps as usual. What does he say, with that look of his? Ah, only makes a sign to the sign and bows himself; there is a sun on the coin—fire worshipper, depend upon it. Ho! more and more. This way comes Pip—poor boy! would he had died, or I; he's half horrible to me. He too has been watching all of these interpreters—myself included—and look now, he comes to read, with that unearthly idiot face. Stand away again and hear him. Hark!"

"I look, you look, he looks; we look, ye look, they look."

"Upon my soul, he's been studying Murray's Grammar! Improving his mind, poor fellow! But what's that he says now—hist!"

"I look, you look, he looks; we look, ye look, they look."

"Why, he's getting it by heart—hist! again."

"I look, you look, he looks; we look, ye look, they look."

"Well, that's funny."

"And I, you, and he; and we, ye, and they, are all bats; and I'm a crow, especially when I stand a'top of this pine tree here. Caw! caw! caw! caw! caw! caw! Ain't I a crow? And where's the scare-crow? There he stands; two bones stuck into a pair of old trowsers, and two more poked into the sleeves of an old jacket."

"Wonder if he means me?—complimentary!—poor lad!—I could go hang myself. Any way, for the present, I'll quit Pip's vicinity. I can stand the rest, for they have plain wits; but he's too crazy-witty for my sanity. So, so, I leave him muttering."

"Here's the ship's navel, this doubloon here, and they are all on fire to unscrew it. But, unscrew your navel, and what's the consequence? Then again, if it stays here, that is ugly, too, for when aught's nailed to the mast it's a sign that things grow desperate. Ha, ha! old Ahab! the White Whale; he'll nail ye! This is a pine tree. My father, in old Tolland county, cut down a pine tree once, and found a silver ring grown over in it; some old darkey's wedding ring. How did it get there? And so they'll say in the resurrection, when they come to fish up this old mast, and find a doubloon lodged in it, with bedded oysters for the shaggy bark. Oh, the gold! the precious, precious, gold! the green miser'll hoard ye soon! Hish! hish! God goes 'mong the worlds blackberrying. Cook! ho, cook! and cook us! Jenny! hey, hey, hey, hey, hey, Jenny, Jenny! and get your hoe-cake done!"

Chapter 100

Leg and Arm • *The Pequod, of Nantucket,*
meets the Samuel Enderby, of London

like the broidered arm of a hussar's surcoat

without quitting his little craft,   here a curious difficulty presented itself.
   ; hopelessly eyeing the uncertain changeful height he could hardly hope
to attain

tastefully-   , observing at a glance how affairs stood,

comprehending it all,   (it was like sitting in the fluke of an anchor, or the
crotch of an apple tree), and then giving the word, held himself fast,   "—how
long ago?"

, and taking a rueful sight along it, as if it had been a telescope

"I was ignorant of the White Whale at that time.   regular"

, suddenly letting out his suspended breath

";   (for I have a devil of a boat's crew for a pull on a whale-line)   (by
the way, Captain—Mounttop; Mounttop—the captain);   as I was saying, I
jumped into Mounttop's boat,   —hearts and souls alive man—   in a jiff,
      like a sucking fish   , taking one good dart forwards,   ;—and that
gentleman there will tell you the rest (by the way, captain—Dr. Bunger, ship's
surgeon: Bunger, my lad,—the captain)   Now, Bunger boy, spin your part of
the yarn."

The professional gentleman thus familiarly pointed out, had been all the time
standing near them, with nothing specific visible, to denote his gentlemanly

rank on board. His face was an exceedingly round but sober one; he was dressed in a faded blue woollen frock or shirt, and patched trowsers; and had thus far been dividing his attention between a marlingspike he held in one hand, and a pill-box held in the other, occasionally casting a critical glance at the ivory limbs of the two crippled captains. But, at his superior's introduction of him to Ahab, he politely bowed, and straightway went on to do his captain's bidding.

"It was a shocking bad wound," began the whale-surgeon; "and, taking my advice, Captain Boomer here, stood our old Sammy—"

"Samuel Enderby is the name of my ship," interrupted the one-armed captain, addressing Ahab; "go on, boy."

"Stood our old Sammy off to the northward, to get out of the blazing hot weather there on the Line. But it was no use—I did all I could; sat up with him nights; was very severe with him in the matter of diet—"

"Oh, very severe!" chimed in the patient himself; then suddenly altering his voice, "Drinking hot rum toddies with me every night, till he couldn't see to put on the bandages; and sending me to bed, half seas over, about three o'clock in the morning. Oh, ye stars! he sat up with me indeed, and was very severe in my diet. Oh! a great watcher, and very dietetically severe, is Dr. Bunger. (Bunger, you dog, laugh out! why don't ye? You know you're a precious jolly rascal.) But, heave ahead, boy, I'd rather be killed by you than kept alive by any other man."

"My captain, you must have ere this perceived, respected sir"—said the imperturbable godly-looking Bunger, slightly bowing to Ahab—"is apt to be facetious at times; he spins us many clever things of that sort. But I may as well say—en passant, as the French remark—that I myself—that is to say, Jack Bunger, late of the reverend clergy—am a strict total abstinence man; I never drink—"

"Water!" cried the captain; "he never drinks it; it's a sort of fits to him; fresh water throws him into the hydrophobia; but go on—go on with the arm story."

"Yes, I may as well," said the surgeon, coolly. "I was about observing, sir, before Captain Boomer's facetious interruption, that spite of my best and severest endeavors, the wound kept getting worse and worse; the truth was, sir, it was as ugly gaping wound as surgeon ever saw; more than two feet and several inches long. I measured it with the lead line. In short, it grew black; I knew what was threatened, and off it came. But I had no hand in shipping that ivory arm there; that thing is against all rule"—pointing at it with the marlingspike—"that is the captain's work, not mine; he ordered the carpenter to make it; he had that club-hammer there put to the end, to knock some one's brains out with, I suppose, as he tried mine once. He flies into diabolical passions sometimes. Do ye see this dent, sir"—removing his hat, and brushing aside his hair, and exposing a bowl-like cavity in his skull, but which bore not the slightest scarry trace, or any token of ever having been a wound—"Well, the captain there will tell you how that came here; he knows."

"No, I don't," said the captain, "but his mother did; he was born with it. Oh, you solemn rogue, you—you Bunger! was there ever such another Bunger in the watery world? Bunger, when you die, you ought to die in pickle, you dog; you should be preserved to future ages, you rascal."

to this by-play between the two Englishmen

"What should I do without this other arm?"

"Well, then," interrupted Bunger, "give him your left arm for bait to get the right. Do you know, gentlemen"—very gravely and mathematically bowing to each Captain in succession—"Do you know, gentlemen, that the digestive organs of the whale are so inscrutably constructed by Divine Providence, that it is quite impossible for him to completely digest even a man's arm? And he knows it too. So that what you take for the White Whale's malice is only his awkwardness. For he never means to swallow a single limb; he only thinks to terrify by feints. But sometimes he is like the old juggling fellow, formerly a patient of mine in Ceylon, that making believe swallow jack-knives, once upon a time let one drop into him in good earnest, and there it stayed for a twelvemonth or more; when I gave him an emetic, and he heaved it up in small tacks, d'ye see. No possible way for him to digest that jack-knife, and fully incorporate it into his general bodily system. Yes, Captain Boomer, if you are quick enough about it, and have a mind to pawn one arm for the sake of the privilege of giving decent burial to the other, why in that case the arm is yours; only let the whale have another chance at you shortly, that's all."

"No, thank ye, Bunger," said the English Captain, "he's welcome to the arm he has, since I can't help it, and didn't know him then; but not to another one.   ; I've lowered for him once, and that has satisfied me"

," cried Bunger, stoopingly walking round Ahab, and like a dog, strangely snuff-ing; "   —bring the thermometer!   —his pulse makes these planks beat!—sir!"—taking a lancet from his pocket, and drawing near to Ahab's arm.

"Avast!" roared Ahab, dashing him against the bulwarks—"Man the boat! Which way heading?"

"Good God!" cried the English Captain, to whom the question was put. "What's the matter?   —Is your Captain crazy?" whispering Fedallah.

But   , putting a finger on his lip,

CHAPTER 101

The Decanter

Ere the English ship fades from sight, be it set down here, that she hailed from London, and was named after the late Samuel Enderby, merchant of that city, the original of the famous whaling house of Enderby & Sons; a house which in my poor whaleman's opinion, comes not far behind the united royal houses of the Tudors and Bourbons, in point of real historical interest. How long, prior to the year of our Lord 1775, this great whaling house was in existence, my numerous fish-documents do not make plain; but in that year (1775) it fitted out the first English ships that ever regularly hunted the Sperm Whale; though for some score of years previous (ever since 1726) our valiant Coffins and Maceys of Nantucket and the Vineyard had in large fleets pursued that Leviathan, but only in the North and South Atlantic: not elsewhere. Be it distinctly recorded here, that the Nantucketers were the first among mankind to harpoon with civilized steel the great Sperm Whale; and that for half a century they were the only people of the whole globe who so harpooned him.

In 1778, a fine ship, the Amelia, fitted out for the express purpose, and at the sole charge of the vigorous Enderbys, boldly rounded Cape Horn, and was the first among the nations to lower a whale-boat of any sort in the great South Sea. The voyage was a skilful and lucky one; and returning to her berth with her hold full of the precious sperm, the Amelia's example was soon followed by other ships, English and American, and thus the vast Sperm Whale grounds of the Pacific were thrown open. But not content with this good deed, the indefatigable house again bestirred itself: Samuel and all his Sons—how many, their mother only knows—and under their immediate auspices, and partly, I think, at their expense, the British government was induced to send the sloop-of-war Rattler on a whaling voyage of discovery into the South Sea. Commanded by a naval Post-Captain, the Rattler made a rattling voyage of it, and did some service; how much does not appear. But this is not all. In 1819, the same house fitted out a discovery whale ship of their own, to go on a tasting cruise to the remote waters of Japan. That ship—well called the "Syren"—made a noble experimental cruise; and it was thus that the great Japanese Whaling Ground first became generally known. The Syren in this famous voyage was commanded by a Captain Coffin, a Nantucketer.

All honor to the Enderbies, therefore, whose house, I think, exists to the present day; though doubtless the original Samuel must long ago have slipped his
cable for the great South Sea of the other world.

The ship named after him was worthy of the honor, being a very fast sailer
and a noble craft every way. I boarded her once at midnight somewhere off
the Patagonian coast, and drank good flip down in the forecastle. It was a
fine gam we had, and they were all trumps—every soul on board. A short
life to them, and a jolly death. And that fine gam I had—long, very long after
old Ahab touched her planks with his ivory heel—it minds me of the noble,
solid, Saxon hospitality of that ship; and may my parson forget me, and the
devil remember me, if I ever lose sight of it. Flip? Did I say we had flip? Yes,
and we flipped it at the rate of ten gallons the hour; and when the squall came
(for it's squally off there by Patagonia), and all hands—visitors and all—were
called to reef topsails, we were so top-heavy that we had to swing each other
aloft in bowlines; and we ignorantly furled the skirts of our jackets into the
sails, so that we hung there, reefed fast in the howling gale, a warning example
to all drunken tars. However, the masts did not go overboard; and by and by
we scrambled down, so sober, that we had to pass the flip again, though the
savage salt spray bursting down the forecastle scuttle, rather too much diluted
and pickled it to my taste.

The beef was fine—tough, but with body in it. They said it was bull-beef; others, that it was dromedary beef; but I do not know, for certain, how that was.
They had dumplings too; small, but substantial, symmetrically globular, and
indestructible dumplings. I fancied that you could feel them, and roll them
about in you after they were swallowed. If you stooped over too far forward,
you risked their pitching out of you like billiard-balls. The bread—but that
couldn't be helped; besides, it was an anti-scorbutic; in short, the bread contained the only fresh fare they had. But the forecastle was not very light, and
it was very easy to step over into a dark corner when you ate it. But all in all,
taking her from truck to helm, considering the dimensions of the cook's boil-

ers, including his own live parchment boilers; fore and aft, I say, the Samuel Enderby was a jolly ship; of good fare and plenty; fine flip and strong; crack fellows all, and capital from boot heels to hat-band.

But why was it, think ye, that the Samuel Enderby, and some other English whalers I know of—not all though—were such famous, hospitable ships; that passed round the beef, and the bread, and the can, and the joke; and were not soon weary of eating, and drinking, and laughing? I will tell you. The abounding good cheer of these English whalers is matter for historical research. Nor have I been at all sparing of historical whale research, when it has seemed needed.

The English were preceded in the whale fishery by the Hollanders, Zealanders, and Danes; from whom they derived many terms still extant in the fishery; and what is yet more, their fat old fashions, touching plenty to eat and drink. For, as a general thing, the English merchant-ship scrimps her crew; but not so the English whaler. Hence, in the English, this thing of whaling good cheer is not normal and natural, but incidental and particular; and, therefore, must have some special origin, which is here pointed out, and will be still further elucidated.

During my researches in the Leviathanic histories, I stumbled upon an ancient Dutch volume, which, by the musty whaling smell of it, I knew must be about whalers. The title was, "Dan Coopman," wherefore I concluded that this must be the invaluable memoirs of some Amsterdam cooper in the fishery, as every whale ship must carry its cooper. I was reinforced in this opinion by seeing that it was the production of one "Fitz Swackhammer." But my friend Dr. Snodhead, a very learned man, professor of Low Dutch and High German in the college of Santa Claus and St. Pott's, to whom I handed the work for translation, giving him a box of sperm candles for his trouble—this same Dr. Snodhead, so soon as he spied the book, assured me that "Dan Coopman" did not mean "The Cooper," but "The Merchant." In short, this ancient and learned Low Dutch book treated of the commerce of Holland; and, among other subjects, contained a very interesting account of its whale fishery. And in this chapter it was, headed, "Smeer," or "Fat," that I found a long detailed list of the outfits for the larders and cellars of 180 sail of Dutch whalemen; from which list, as translated by Dr. Snodhead, I transcribe the following:

400,000	lbs. of beef.
60,000	lbs. Friesland pork.
150,000	lbs. of stock fish.
550,000	lbs. of biscuit.
72,000	lbs. of soft bread.
2,800	firkins of butter.
20,000	lbs. Texel & Leyden cheese.
144,000	lbs. cheese (probably an inferior article).
550	ankers of Geneva.
10,800	barrels of beer.

Most statistical tables are parchingly dry in the reading; not so in the present case, however, where the reader is flooded with whole pipes, barrels, quarts, and gills of good gin and good cheer.

At the time, I devoted three days to the studious digesting of all this beer, beef, and bread, during which many profound thoughts were incidentally suggested to me, capable of a transcendental and Platonic application; and, furthermore, I compiled supplementary tables of my own, touching the probable quantity of stock-fish, etc., consumed by every Low Dutch harpooneer in that ancient Greenland and Spitzbergen whale fishery. In the first place, the amount of butter, and Texel and Leyden cheese consumed, seems amazing. I impute it, though, to their naturally unctuous natures, being rendered still more unctuous by the nature of their vocation, and especially by their pursuing their game in those frigid Polar Seas, on the very coasts of that Esquimaux country where the convivial natives pledge each other in bumpers of train oil.

The quantity of beer, too, is very large, 10,800 barrels. Now, as those polar fisheries could only be prosecuted in the short summer of that climate, so that the whole cruise of one of these Dutch whalemen, including the short voyage to and from the Spitzbergen sea, did not much exceed three months, say, and reckoning 30 men to each of their fleet of 180 sail, we have 5,400 Low Dutch seamen in all; therefore, I say, we have precisely two barrels of beer per man, for a twelve weeks' allowance, exclusive of his fair proportion of that 550 ankers of gin. Now, whether these gin and beer harpooneers, so fuddled as one might fancy them to have been, were the right sort of men to stand up in a boat's head, and take good aim at flying whales; this would seem somewhat improbable. Yet they did aim at them, and hit them too. But this was very far North, be it remembered, where beer agrees well with the constitution; upon the Equator, in our southern fishery, beer would be apt to make the harpooneer sleepy at the mast-head and boozy in his boat; and grievous loss might ensue to Nantucket and New Bedford.

But no more; enough has been said to show that the old Dutch whalers of two or three centuries ago were high livers; and that the English whalers have not neglected so excellent an example. For, say they, when cruising in an empty ship, if you can get nothing better out of the world, get a good dinner out of it, at least. And this empties the decanter.

CHAPTER 102

A Bower in the Arsacides

Hitherto, in descriptively treating of the Sperm Whale, I have chiefly dwelt upon the marvels of his outer aspect; or separately and in detail upon some few interior structural features. But to a large and thorough sweeping comprehension of him, it behooves me now to unbutton him still further, and untagging the points of his hose, unbuckling his garters, and casting loose the hooks and the eyes of the joints of his innermost bones, set him before you in his ultimatum; that is to say, in his unconditional skeleton.

But how now, Ishmael? How is it, that you, a mere oarsman in the fishery, pretend to know aught about the subterranean parts of the whale? Did erudite Stubb, mounted upon your capstan, deliver lectures on the anatomy of the Cetacea; and by help of the windlass, hold up a specimen rib for exhibition? Explain thyself, Ishmael. Can you land a full-grown whale on your deck for examination, as a cook dishes a roast-pig? Surely not. A veritable witness have you hitherto been, Ishmael; but have a care how you seize the privilege of Jonah alone; the privilege of discoursing upon the joists and beams; the rafters, ridge-pole, sleepers, and under-pinnings, making up the frame-work of leviathan; and belike of the tallow-vats, dairy-rooms, butteries, and cheeseries in his bowels.

I confess, that since Jonah, few whalemen have penetrated very far beneath the skin of the adult whale; nevertheless, I have been blessed with an opportunity to dissect him in miniature. In a ship I belonged to, a small cub Sperm Whale was once bodily hoisted to the deck for his poke or bag, to make sheaths for the barbs of the harpoons, and for the heads of the lances. Think you I let that chance go, without using my boat-hatchet and jack-knife, and breaking the seal and reading all the contents of that young cub?

And as for my exact knowledge of the bones of the leviathan in their gigantic, full grown development, for that rare knowledge I am indebted to my late royal friend Tranquo, king of Tranque, one of the Arsacides. For being at Tranque, years ago, when attached to the trading-ship Dey of Algiers, I was invited to spend part of the Arsacidean holidays with the lord of Tranque, at his retired palm villa at Pupella; a sea-side glen not very far distant from what our sailors called Bamboo-Town, his capital.

Among many other fine qualities, my royal friend Tranquo, being gifted with a devout love for all matters of barbaric vertu, had brought together in Pupella whatever rare things the more ingenious of his people could invent; chiefly carved woods of wonderful devices, chiselled shells, inlaid spears, costly paddles, aromatic canoes; and all these distributed among whatever natural wonders, the wonder-freighted, tribute-rendering waves had cast upon his shores.

Chief among these latter was a great Sperm Whale, which, after an unusually long raging gale, had been found dead and stranded, with his head against a cocoanut tree, whose plumage-like, tufted droopings seemed his verdant jet. When the vast body had at last been stripped of its fathom-deep enfoldings, and the bones become dust dry in the sun, then the skeleton was carefully transported up the Pupella glen, where a grand temple of lordly palms now sheltered it.

The ribs were hung with trophies; the vertebrae were carved with Arsacidean annals, in strange hieroglyphics; in the skull, the priests kept up an unextinguished aromatic flame, so that the mystic head again sent forth its vapory spout; while, suspended from a bough, the terrific lower jaw vibrated over all the devotees, like the hair-hung sword that so affrighted Damocles.

It was a wondrous sight. The wood was green as mosses of the Icy Glen; the trees stood high and haughty, feeling their living sap; the industrious earth beneath was as a weaver's loom, with a gorgeous carpet on it, whereof the ground-vine tendrils formed the warp and woof, and the living flowers the figures. All the trees, with all their laden branches; all the shrubs, and ferns, and grasses; the message-carrying air; all these unceasingly were active. Through the lacings of the leaves, the great sun seemed a flying shuttle weaving the unwearied verdure. Oh, busy weaver! unseen weaver!—pause!—one word!—whither flows the fabric? what palace may it deck? wherefore all these ceaseless toilings? Speak, weaver!—stay thy hand!—but one single word with thee! Nay—the shuttle flies—the figures float from forth the loom; the freshet-rushing carpet for ever slides away. The weaver-god, he weaves; and by that weaving is he deafened, that he hears no mortal voice; and by that humming, we, too, who look on the loom are deafened; and only when we escape it shall we hear the thousand voices that speak through it. For even so it is in all material factories. The spoken words that are inaudible among the flying spindles; those same words are plainly heard without the walls, bursting from the opened casements. Thereby have villainies been detected. Ah, mortal! then, be heedful; for so, in all this din of the great world's loom, thy subtlest thinkings may be overheard afar.

Now, amid the green, life-restless loom of that Arsacidean wood, the great, white, worshipped skeleton lay lounging—a gigantic idler! Yet, as the ever-woven verdant warp and woof intermixed and hummed around him, the mighty idler seemed the cunning weaver; himself all woven over with the vines; every month assuming greener, fresher verdure; but himself a skeleton. Life folded Death; Death trellised Life; the grim god wived with youthful Life, and begat him curly-headed glories.

Now, when with royal Tranquo I visited this wondrous whale, and saw the skull an altar, and the artificial smoke ascending from where the real jet had issued, I marvelled that the king should regard a chapel as an object of vertu. He laughed. But more I marvelled that the priests should swear that smoky jet of his was genuine. To and fro I paced before this skeleton—brushed the vines aside—broke through the ribs—and with a ball of Arsacidean twine, wandered, eddied long amid its many winding, shaded colonnades and arbors. But soon my line was out; and following it back, I emerged from the opening where I entered. I saw no living thing within; naught was there but bones.

Cutting me a green measuring-rod, I once more dived within the skeleton. From their arrow-slit in the skull, the priests perceived me taking the altitude of the final rib, "How now!" they shouted; "Dar'st thou measure this our god! That's for us." "Aye, priests—well, how long do ye make him, then?" But hereupon a fierce contest rose among them, concerning feet and inches; they cracked each other's sconces with their yard-sticks—the great skull echoed— and seizing that lucky chance, I quickly concluded my own admeasurements.

These admeasurements I now propose to set before you. But first, be it recorded, that, in this matter, I am not free to utter any fancied measurement

I please. Because there are skeleton authorities you can refer to, to test my accuracy. There is a Leviathanic Museum, they tell me, in Hull, England, one of the whaling ports of that country, where they have some fine specimens of fin-backs and other whales. Likewise, I have heard that in the museum of Manchester, in New Hampshire, they have what the proprietors call "the only perfect specimen of a Greenland or River Whale in the United States." Moreover, at a place in Yorkshire, England, Burton Constable by name, a certain Sir Clifford Constable has in his possession the skeleton of a Sperm Whale, but of moderate size, by no means of the full-grown magnitude of my friend King Tranquo's.

In both cases, the stranded whales to which these two skeletons belonged, were originally claimed by their proprietors upon similar grounds. King Tranquo seizing his because he wanted it; and Sir Clifford, because he was lord of the seignories of those parts. Sir Clifford's whale has been articulated throughout; so that, like a great chest of drawers, you can open and shut him, in all his bony cavities—spread out his ribs like a gigantic fan—and swing all day upon his lower jaw. Locks are to be put upon some of his trap-doors and shutters; and a footman will show round future visitors with a bunch of keys at his side. Sir Clifford thinks of charging twopence for a peep at the whispering gallery in the spinal column; threepence to hear the echo in the hollow of his cerebellum; and sixpence for the unrivalled view from his forehead.

The skeleton dimensions I shall now proceed to set down are copied verbatim from my right arm, where I had them tattooed; as in my wild wanderings at that period, there was no other secure way of preserving such valuable statistics. But as I was crowded for space, and wished the other parts of my body to remain a blank page for a poem I was then composing—at least, what un-tattooed parts might remain—I did not trouble myself with the odd inches; nor, indeed, should inches at all enter into a congenial admeasurement of the whale.

CHAPTER 103

Measurement of the Whale's Skeleton

In the first place, I wish to lay before you a particular, plain statement, touching the living bulk of this leviathan, whose skeleton we are briefly to exhibit. Such a statement may prove useful here.

According to a careful calculation I have made, and which I partly base upon Captain Scoresby's estimate, of seventy tons for the largest sized Greenland whale of sixty feet in length; according to my careful calculation, I say, a Sperm Whale of the largest magnitude, between eighty-five and ninety feet in length, and something less than forty feet in its fullest circumference, such a whale will weigh at least ninety tons; so that, reckoning thirteen men to a ton, he would considerably outweigh the combined population of a whole village of one thousand one hundred inhabitants.

Think you not then that brains, like yoked cattle, should be put to this leviathan, to make him at all budge to any landsman's imagination?

Having already in various ways put before you his skull, spout-hole, jaw, teeth, tail, forehead, fins, and divers other parts, I shall now simply point out what is most interesting in the general bulk of his unobstructed bones. But as the colossal skull embraces so very large a proportion of the entire extent of the skeleton; as it is by far the most complicated part; and as nothing is to be repeated concerning it in this chapter, you must not fail to carry it in your mind, or under your arm, as we proceed, otherwise you will not gain a complete notion of the general structure we are about to view.

In length, the Sperm Whale's skeleton at Tranque measured seventy-two Feet; so that when fully invested and extended in life, he must have been ninety feet long; for in the whale, the skeleton loses about one fifth in length compared with the living body. Of this seventy-two feet, his skull and jaw comprised some twenty feet, leaving some fifty feet of plain back-bone. Attached to this back-bone, for something less than a third of its length, was the mighty circular basket of ribs which once enclosed his vitals.

To me this vast ivory-ribbed chest, with the long, unrelieved spine, extending far away from it in a straight line, not a little resembled the hull of a great ship new-laid upon the stocks, when only some twenty of her naked bow-ribs are inserted, and the keel is otherwise, for the time, but a long, disconnected timber.

The ribs were ten on a side. The first, to begin from the neck, was nearly six feet long; the second, third, and fourth were each successively longer, till you came to the climax of the fifth, or one of the middle ribs, which measured eight feet and some inches. From that part, the remaining ribs diminished, till the tenth and last only spanned five feet and some inches. In general thickness, they all bore a seemly correspondence to their length. The middle ribs were the most arched. In some of the Arsacides they are used for beams whereon to lay footpath bridges over small streams.

In considering these ribs, I could not but be struck anew with the circumstance, so variously repeated in this book, that the skeleton of the whale is by no means the mould of his invested form. The largest of the Tranque ribs, one of the middle ones, occupied that part of the fish which, in life, is greatest in depth. Now, the greatest depth of the invested body of this particular whale must have been at least sixteen feet; whereas, the corresponding rib measured but little more than eight feet. So that this rib only conveyed half of the true notion of the living magnitude of that part. Besides, for some way, where I now saw but a naked spine, all that had been once wrapped round with tons of added bulk in flesh, muscle, blood, and bowels. Still more, for the ample fins, I here saw but a few disordered joints; and in place of the weighty and majestic, but boneless flukes, an utter blank!

How vain and foolish, then, thought I, for timid untravelled man to try to comprehend aright this wondrous whale, by merely poring over his dead attenuated skeleton, stretched in this peaceful wood. No. Only in the heart of quickest perils; only when within the eddyings of his angry flukes; only on the profound unbounded sea, can the fully invested whale be truly and livingly found out.

But the spine. For that, the best way we can consider it is, with a crane, to pile its bones high up on end. No speedy enterprise. But now it's done, it looks much like Pompey's Pillar.

There are forty and odd vertebræ in all, which in the skeleton are not locked together. They mostly lie like the great knobbed blocks on a Gothic spire, forming solid courses of heavy masonry. The largest, a middle one, is in width something less than three feet, and in depth more than four. The smallest, where the spine tapers away into the tail, is only two inches in width, and looks something like a white billiard-ball. I was told that there were still smaller ones, but they had been lost by some little cannibal urchins, the priest's children, who had stolen them to play marbles with. Thus we see how that the spine of even the hugest of living things tapers off at last into simple child's play.

CHAPTER 104

The Fossil Whale

From his mighty bulk the whale affords a most congenial theme whereon to enlarge, amplify, and generally expatiate. Would you, you could not compress him. By good rights he should only be treated of in imperial folio. Not to tell over again his furlongs from spiracle to tail, and the yards he measures about the waist; only think of the gigantic involutions of his intestines, where they lie in him like great cables and hawsers coiled away in the subterranean orlop-deck of a line-of-battle-ship.

Since I have undertaken to manhandle this Leviathan, it behooves me to approve myself omnisciently exhaustive in the enterprise; not overlooking the minutest seminal germs of his blood, and spinning him out to the uttermost coil of his bowels. Having already described him in most of his present habitatory and anatomical peculiarities, it now remains to magnify him in an archaeological, fossiliferous, and antediluvian point of view. Applied to any other creature than the Leviathan—to an ant or a flea—such portly terms might justly be deemed unwarrantably grandiloquent. But when Leviathan is the text, the case is altered. Fain am I to stagger to this emprise under the weightiest words of the dictionary. And here be it said, that whenever it has been convenient to consult one in the course of these dissertations, I have invariably used a huge quarto edition of Johnson, expressly purchased for that purpose; because that famous lexicographer's uncommon personal bulk more fitted him to compile a lexicon to be used by a whale author like me.

One often hears of writers that rise and swell with their subject, though it may seem but an ordinary one. How, then, with me, writing of this Leviathan? Unconsciously my chirography expands into placard capitals. Give me a condor's quill! Give me Vesuvius' crater for an inkstand! Friends, hold my arms! For in the mere act of penning my thoughts of this Leviathan, they weary me, and make me faint with their outreaching comprehensiveness of sweep, as if to include the whole circle of the sciences, and all the generations of whales, and men, and mastodons, past, present, and to come, with all the revolving panoramas of empire on earth, and throughout the whole universe, not excluding its suburbs. Such, and so magnifying, is the virtue of a large and liberal theme! We expand to its bulk. To produce a mighty book, you must choose a mighty theme. No great and enduring volume can ever be written on the flea, though many there be who have tried it.

Ere entering upon the subject of Fossil Whales, I present my credentials as a geologist, by stating that in my miscellaneous time I have been a stone-mason, and also a great digger of ditches, canals and wells, wine-vaults, cellars, and cisterns of all sorts. Likewise, by way of preliminary, I desire to remind the reader, that while in the earlier geological strata there are found the fossils of monsters now almost completely extinct; the subsequent relics discovered in what are called the Tertiary formations seem the connecting, or at any rate intercepted links, between the antichronical creatures, and those whose remote posterity are said to have entered the Ark; all the Fossil Whales hitherto discovered belong to the Tertiary period, which is the last preceding the superficial formations. And though none of them precisely answer to any known species of the present time, they are yet sufficiently akin to them in general respects, to justify their taking rank as Cetacean fossils.

Detached broken fossils of pre-adamite whales, fragments of their bones and skeletons, have within thirty years past, at various intervals, been found at the base of the Alps, in Lombardy, in France, in England, in Scotland, and in the States of Louisiana, Mississippi, and Alabama. Among the more curious of such remains is part of a skull, which in the year 1779 was disinterred in the Rue Dauphine in Paris, a short street opening almost directly upon the palace of the Tuileries; and bones disinterred in excavating the great docks of Antwerp, in Napoleon's time. Cuvier pronounced these fragments to have belonged to some utterly unknown Leviathanic species.

But by far the most wonderful of all Cetacean relics was the almost complete vast skeleton of an extinct monster, found in the year 1842, on the plantation of Judge Creagh, in Alabama. The awe-stricken credulous slaves in the vicinity took it for the bones of one of the fallen angels. The Alabama doctors declared it a huge reptile, and bestowed upon it the name of Basilosaurus. But some specimen bones of it being taken across the sea to Owen, the English Anatomist, it turned out that this alleged reptile was a whale, though of a departed species. A significant illustration of the fact, again and again repeated in this book, that the skeleton of the whale furnishes but little clue to the shape of his fully invested body. So Owen rechristened the monster Zeuglodon; and in his paper read before the London Geological Society, pronounced it, in substance, one of the most extraordinary creatures which the mutations of the globe have blotted out of existence.

When I stand among these mighty Leviathan skeletons, skulls, tusks, jaws, ribs, and vertebrae, all characterized by partial resemblances to the existing breeds of sea-monsters; but at the same time bearing on the other hand similar affinities to the annihilated antichronical Leviathans, their incalculable seniors; I am, by a flood, borne back to that wondrous period, ere time itself can be said to have begun; for time began with man. Here Saturn's grey chaos rolls over me, and I obtain dim, shuddering glimpses into those Polar eternities; when wedged bastions of ice pressed hard upon what are now the Tropics; and in all the 25,000 miles of this world's circumference, not an inhabitable hand's breadth of land was visible. Then the whole world was the whale's; and, king of creation, he left his wake along the present lines of the Andes and the Himmalehs. Who can show a pedigree like Leviathan? Ahab's harpoon had shed older blood than the Pharaoh's. Methuselah seems a school-boy. I look round to shake hands with Shem. I am horror-struck at this antemosaic, unsourced existence of the unspeakable terrors of the whale, which, having been before all time, must needs exist after all humane ages are over.

But not alone has this Leviathan left his pre-adamite traces in the stereotype plates of nature, and in limestone and marl bequeathed his ancient bust; but upon Egyptian tablets, whose antiquity seems to claim for them an almost fossiliferous character, we find the unmistakable print of his fin. In an apartment of the great temple of Denderah, some fifty years ago, there was discovered upon the granite ceiling a sculptured and painted planisphere, abounding in centaurs, griffins, and dolphins, similar to the grotesque figures on the celestial globe of the moderns. Gliding among them, old Leviathan swam as of yore; was there swimming in that planisphere, centuries before Solomon was cradled.

Nor must there be omitted another strange attestation of the antiquity of the whale, in his own osseous post-diluvian reality, as set down by the venerable John Leo, the old Barbary traveller.

"Not far from the Sea-side, they have a Temple, the Rafters and Beams of which are made of Whale-Bones; for Whales of a monstrous size are often-times cast up dead upon that shore. The Common People imagine, that by a secret Power bestowed by God upon the temple, no Whale can pass it without immediate death. But the truth of the Matter is, that on either side of the Temple, there are Rocks that shoot two Miles into the Sea, and wound the Whales when they light upon 'em. They keep a Whale's Rib of an incredible length for a Miracle, which lying upon the Ground with its convex part uppermost, makes an Arch, the Head of which cannot be reached by a Man upon a Camel's Back. This Rib (says John Leo) is said to have layn there a hundred Years before I saw it. Their Historians affirm, that a Prophet who prophesy'd of Mahomet, came from this Temple, and some do not stand to assert, that the Prophet Jonas was cast forth by the Whale at the Base of the Temple."

In this Afric Temple of the Whale I leave you, reader, and if you be a Nantucketer, and a whaleman, you will silently worship there.

CHAPTER 105

Does the Whale's Magnitude Diminish?—
Will He Perish?

Inasmuch, then, as this Leviathan comes floundering down upon us from the head-waters of the Eternities, it may be fitly inquired, whether, in the long course of his generations, he has not degenerated from the original bulk of his sires.

But upon investigation we find, that not only are the whales of the present day superior in magnitude to those whose fossil remains are found in the Tertiary system (embracing a distinct geological period prior to man), but of the whales found in that Tertiary system, those belonging to its latter formations exceed in size those of its earlier ones.

Of all the pre-adamite whales yet exhumed, by far the largest is the Alabama one mentioned in the last chapter, and that was less than seventy feet in length in the skeleton. Whereas, we have already seen, that the tape-measure gives seventy-two feet for the skeleton of a large sized modern whale. And I have heard, on whalemen's authority, that Sperm Whales have been captured near a hundred feet long at the time of capture.

But may it not be, that while the whales of the present hour are an advance in magnitude upon those of all previous geological periods; may it not be, that since Adam's time they have degenerated?

Assuredly, we must conclude so, if we are to credit the accounts of such gentlemen as Pliny, and the ancient naturalists generally. For Pliny tells us of Whales that embraced acres of living bulk, and Aldrovandus of others which measured eight hundred feet in length—Rope Walks and Thames Tunnels of Whales! And even in the days of Banks and Solander, Cooke's naturalists, we find a Danish member of the Academy of Sciences setting down certain Iceland Whales (reydan-siskur, or Wrinkled Bellies) at one hundred and twenty yards; that is, three hundred and sixty feet. And Lacepede, the French naturalist, in his elaborate history of whales, in the very beginning of his work (page 3), sets down the Right Whale at one hundred metres, three hundred and twenty-eight feet. And this work was published so late as A.D. 1825.

But will any whaleman believe these stories? No. The whale of to-day is as big as his ancestors in Pliny's time. And if ever I go where Pliny is, I, a whaleman (more than he was), will make bold to tell him so. Because I cannot understand how it is, that while the Egyptian mummies that were buried thousands of years before even Pliny was born, do not measure so much in their coffins as a modern Kentuckian in his socks; and while the cattle and other animals sculptured on the oldest Egyptian and Nineveh tablets, by the relative proportions in which they are drawn, just as plainly prove that the high-bred, stall-fed, prize cattle of Smithfield, not only equal, but far exceed in magnitude the fattest of Pharaoh's fat kine; in the face of all this, I will not admit that of all animals the whale alone should have degenerated.

But still another inquiry remains; one often agitated by the more recondite Nantucketers. Whether owing to the almost omniscient look-outs at the mast-heads of the whaleships, now penetrating even through Behring's straits, and into the remotest secret drawers and lockers of the world; and the thousand harpoons and lances darted along all continental coasts; the moot point is, whether Leviathan can long endure so wide a chase, and so remorseless a havoc; whether he must not at last be exterminated from the waters, and the last whale, like the last man, smoke his last pipe, and then himself evaporate in the final puff.

Comparing the humped herds of whales with the humped herds of buffalo, which, not forty years ago, overspread by tens of thousands the prairies of Illinois and Missouri, and shook their iron manes and scowled with their thunder-clotted brows upon the sites of populous river-capitals, where now the polite broker sells you land at a dollar an inch; in such a comparison an irresistible argument would seem furnished, to show that the hunted whale cannot now escape speedy extinction.

But you must look at this matter in every light. Though so short a period ago—not a good lifetime—the census of the buffalo in Illinois exceeded the census of men now in London, and though at the present day not one horn or hoof of them remains in all that region; and though the cause of this wondrous extermination was the spear of man; yet the far different nature of the whale-hunt peremptorily forbids so inglorious an end to the Leviathan. Forty men in one ship hunting the Sperm Whales for forty-eight months think they have done extremely well, and thank God, if at last they carry home the oil of forty fish. Whereas, in the days of the old Canadian and Indian hunters and trappers of the West, when the far west (in whose sunset suns still rise) was a wilderness and a virgin, the same number of moccasined men, for the same number of months, mounted on horse instead of sailing in ships, would have slain not forty, but forty thousand and more buffaloes; a fact that, if need were, could be statistically stated.

Nor, considered aright, does it seem any argument in favor of the gradual extinction of the Sperm Whale, for example, that in former years (the latter part of the last century, say) these Leviathans, in small pods, were encountered much oftener than at present, and, in consequence, the voyages were not so prolonged, and were also much more remunerative. Because, as has been elsewhere noticed, those whales, influenced by some views to safety, now swim the seas in immense caravans, so that to a large degree the scattered solitaries, yokes, and pods, and schools of other days are now aggregated into vast but widely separated, unfrequent armies. That is all. And equally fallacious seems the conceit, that because the so-called whale-bone whales no longer haunt many grounds in former years abounding with them, hence that species also is declining. For they are only being driven from promontory to cape; and if one coast is no longer enlivened with their jets, then, be sure, some other and remoter strand has been very recently startled by the unfamiliar spectacle.

Furthermore: concerning these last mentioned Leviathans, they have two firm fortresses, which, in all human probability, will for ever remain impregnable. And as upon the invasion of their valleys, the frosty Swiss have retreated to their mountains; so, hunted from the savannas and glades of the middle seas, the whale-bone whales can at last resort to their Polar citadels, and diving under the ultimate glassy barriers and walls there, come up among icy fields and floes; and in a charmed circle of everlasting December, bid defiance to all pursuit from man.

But as perhaps fifty of these whale-bone whales are harpooned for one cachalot, some philosophers of the forecastle have concluded that this positive havoc has already very seriously diminished their battalions. But though for some time past a number of these whales, not less than 13,000, have been annually slain on the nor'-west coast by the Americans alone; yet there are considerations which render even this circumstance of little or no account as an opposing argument in this matter.

Natural as it is to be somewhat incredulous concerning the populousness of the more enormous creatures of the globe, yet what shall we say to Harto, the historian of Goa, when he tells us that at one hunting the King of Siam took 4,000 elephants; that in those regions elephants are numerous as droves of cattle in the temperate climes. And there seems no reason to doubt that if these elephants, which have now been hunted for thousands of years, by Semiramis, by Porus, by Hannibal, and by all the successive monarchs of the East—if they still survive there in great numbers, much more may the great whale outlast all hunting, since he has a pasture to expatiate in, which is precisely twice as large as all Asia, both Americas, Europe and Africa, New Holland, and all the Isles of the sea combined.

Moreover: we are to consider, that from the presumed great longevity of whales, their probably attaining the age of a century and more, therefore at any one period of time, several distinct adult generations must be contemporary. And what that is, we may soon gain some idea of, by imagining all the grave-yards, cemeteries, and family vaults of creation yielding up the live bodies of all the men, women, and children who were alive seventy-five years ago; and adding this countless host to the present human population of the globe.

Wherefore, for all these things, we account the whale immortal in his species, however perishable in his individuality. He swam the seas before the continents broke water; he once swam over the site of the Tuileries, and Windsor Castle, and the Kremlin. In Noah's flood he despised Noah's Ark; and if ever the world is to be again flooded, like the Netherlands, to kill off its rats, then the eternal whale will still survive, and rearing upon the topmost crest of the equatorial flood, spout his frothed defiance to the skies.

CHAPTER 106

Ahab's Leg

The precipitating manner in which Captain Ahab had quitted the Samuel Enderby of London, had not been unattended with some small violence to his own person. He had lighted with such energy upon a thwart of his boat that his ivory leg had received a half-splintering shock. And when after gaining his own deck, and his own pivot-hole there, he so vehemently wheeled round with an urgent command to the steersman (it was, as ever, something about his not steering inflexibly enough); then, the already shaken ivory received such an additional twist and wrench, that though it still remained entire, and to all appearances lusty, yet Ahab did not deem it entirely trustworthy.

And, indeed, it seemed small matter for wonder, that for all his pervading, mad recklessness, Ahab did at times give careful heed to the condition of that dead bone upon which he partly stood. For it had not been very long prior to the Pequod's sailing from Nantucket, that he had been found one night lying prone upon the ground, and insensible; by some unknown, and seemingly inexplicable, unimaginable casualty, his ivory limb having been so violently displaced, that it had stake-wise smitten, and all but pierced his groin; nor was it without extreme difficulty that the agonizing wound was entirely cured.

Nor, at the time, had it failed to enter his monomaniac mind, that all the anguish of that then present suffering was but the direct issue of a former woe; and he too plainly seemed to see, that as the most poisonous reptile of the marsh perpetuates his kind as inevitably as the sweetest songster of the grove; so, equally with every felicity, all miserable events do naturally beget their like. Yea, more than equally, thought Ahab; since both the ancestry and posterity of Grief go further than the ancestry and posterity of Joy. For, not to hint of this: that it is an inference from certain canonic teachings, that while some natural enjoyments here shall have no children born to them for the other world, but, on the contrary, shall be followed by the joy-childlessness of all hell's despair; whereas, some guilty mortal miseries shall still fertilely beget to themselves an eternally progressive progeny of griefs beyond the grave; not at all to hint of this, there still seems an inequality in the deeper analysis of the thing. For, thought Ahab, while even the highest earthly felicities ever have a certain unsignifying pettiness lurking in them, but, at bottom, all heartwoes, a mystic significance, and, in some men, an archangelic grandeur; so do their diligent tracings-out not belie the obvious deduction. To trail the genealogies of these high mortal miseries, carries us at last among the sourceless primo-genitures of the gods; so that, in the face of all the glad, hay-making suns, and soft cymballing, round harvest-moons, we must needs give in to this: that the gods themselves are not for ever glad. The ineffaceable, sad birth-mark in the brow of man, is but the stamp of sorrow in the signers.

Unwittingly here a secret has been divulged, which perhaps might more properly, in set way, have been disclosed before. With many other particulars concerning Ahab, always had it remained a mystery to some, why it was, that for a certain period, both before and after the sailing of the Pequod, he had hidden himself away with such Grand-Lama-like exclusiveness; and, for that one interval, sought speechless refuge, as it were, among the marble senate of the dead. Captain Peleg's bruited reason for this thing appeared by no means adequate; though, indeed, as touching all Ahab's deeper part, every revelation partook more of significant darkness than of explanatory light. But, in the end, it all came out; this one matter did, at least. That direful mishap was at the bottom of his temporary recluseness. And not only this, but to that ever-contracting, dropping circle ashore, who, for any reason, possessed the privilege of a less banned approach to him; to that timid circle the above hinted casualty—remaining, as it did, moodily unaccounted for by Ahab—invested itself with terrors, not entirely underived from the land of spirits and of wails. So that, through their zeal for him, they had all conspired, so far as in them lay, to muffle up the knowledge of this thing from others; and hence it was, that not till a considerable interval had elapsed, did it transpire upon the Pequod's decks.

But be all this as it may; let the unseen, ambiguous synod in the air, or the vindictive princes and potentates of fire, have to do or not with earthly Ahab, yet, in this present matter of his leg, he took plain practical procedures;—he called the carpenter.

And when that functionary appeared before him, he bade him without delay set about making a new leg, and directed the mates to see him supplied with all the studs and joists of jaw-ivory (Sperm Whale) which had thus far been accumulated on the voyage, in order that a careful selection of the stoutest, clearest-grained stuff might be secured. This done, the carpenter received orders to have the leg completed that night; and to provide all the fittings for it, independent of those pertaining to the distrusted one in use. Moreover, the ship's forge was ordered to be hoisted out of its temporary idleness in the hold; and, to accelerate the affair, the blacksmith was commanded to proceed at once to the forging of whatever iron contrivances might be needed.

CHAPTER 107

The Carpenter

Seat thyself sultanically among the moons of Saturn, and take high abstracted man alone; and he seems a wonder, a grandeur, and a woe. But from the same point, take mankind in mass, and for the most part, they seem a mob of unnecessary duplicates, both contemporary and hereditary. But most humble though he was, and far from furnishing an example of the high, humane abstraction; the Pequod's carpenter was no duplicate; hence, he now comes in person on this stage.

Like all sea-going ship carpenters, and more especially those belonging to whaling vessels, he was, to a certain off-handed, practical extent, alike experienced in numerous trades and callings collateral to his own; the carpenter's pursuit being the ancient and outbranching trunk of all those numerous handicrafts which more or less have to do with wood as an auxiliary material. But, besides the application to him of the generic remark above, this carpenter of the Pequod was singularly efficient in those thousand nameless mechanical emergencies continually recurring in a large ship, upon a three or four years' voyage, in uncivilized and far-distant seas. For not to speak of his readiness in ordinary duties:—repairing stove boats, sprung spars, reforming the shape of clumsy-bladed oars, inserting bull's eyes in the deck, or new tree-nails in the side planks, and other miscellaneous matters more directly pertaining to his special business; he was moreover unhesitatingly expert in all manner of conflicting aptitudes, both useful and capricious.

The one grand stage where he enacted all his various parts so manifold, was his vice-bench; a long rude ponderous table furnished with several vices, of different sizes, and both of iron and of wood. At all times except when whales were alongside, this bench was securely lashed athwartships against the rear of the Try-works.

A belaying pin is found too large to be easily inserted into its hole: the carpenter claps it into one of his ever-ready vices, and straightway files it smaller. A lost land-bird of strange plumage strays on board, and is made a captive: out of clean shaved rods of right-whale bone, and cross-beams of sperm whale ivory, the carpenter makes a pagoda-looking cage for it. An oarsman sprains his wrist: the carpenter concocts a soothing lotion. Stubb longed for vermillion stars to be painted upon the blade of his every oar; screwing each oar in his big vice of wood, the carpenter symmetrically supplies the constellation. A sailor takes a fancy to wear shark-bone ear-rings: the carpenter drills his ears. Another has the toothache: the carpenter out pincers, and clapping one hand upon his bench bids him be seated there; but the poor fellow unmanageably winces under the unconcluded operation; whirling round the handle of his wooden vice, the carpenter signs him to clap his jaw in that, if he would have him draw the tooth.

Thus, this carpenter was prepared at all points, and alike indifferent and without respect in all. Teeth he accounted bits of ivory; heads he deemed but top-blocks; men themselves he lightly held for capstans. But while now upon so wide a field thus variously accomplished and with such liveliness of expertness in him, too; all this would seem to argue some uncommon vivacity of intelligence. But not precisely so. For nothing was this man more remarkable, than for a certain impersonal stolidity as it were; impersonal, I say; for it so shaded off into the surrounding infinite of things, that it seemed one with the general stolidity discernible in the whole visible world; which while pauselessly active in uncounted modes, still eternally holds its peace, and ignores you, though you dig foundations for cathedrals. Yet was this half-horrible stolidity in him, involving, too, as it appeared, an all-ramifying heartlessness;—yet was it oddly dashed at times, with an old, crutch-like, antediluvian, wheezing humorousness, not unstreaked now and then with a certain grizzled wittiness; such as might have served to pass the time during the midnight watch on the bearded forecastle of Noah's ark. Was it that this old carpenter had been a life-long wanderer, whose much rolling, to and fro, not only had gathered no moss; but what is more, had rubbed off whatever small outward clingings might have originally pertained to him? He was a stript abstract; an unfractioned integral; uncompromised as a new-born babe; living without premeditated reference to this world or the next. You might almost say, that this strange uncompromisedness in him involved a sort of unintelligence; for in his numerous trades, he did not seem to work so much by reason or by instinct, or simply because he had been tutored to it, or by any intermixture of all these, even or uneven; but merely by a kind of deaf and dumb, spontaneous literal process. He was a pure manipulator; his brain, if he had ever had one, must have early oozed along into the muscles of his fingers. He was like one of those unreasoning but still highly useful, *multum in parvo*, Sheffield contrivances, assuming the exterior—though a little swelled—of a common pocket knife; but containing, not only blades of various sizes, but also screw-drivers, cork-screws, tweezers, awls, pens, rulers, nail-filers, countersinkers. So, if his superiors wanted to use the carpenter for a screw-driver, all they had to do was to open that part of him, and the screw was fast: or if for tweezers, take him up by the legs, and there they were.

Yet, as previously hinted, this omnitooled, open-and-shut carpenter, was, after all, no mere machine of an automaton. If he did not have a common soul in him, he had a subtle something that somehow anomalously did its duty. What that was, whether essence of quicksilver, or a few drops of hartshorn, there is no telling. But there it was; and there it had abided for now some sixty years or more. And this it was, this same unaccountable, cunning life-principle in him; this it was, that kept him a great part of the time soliloquizing; but only like an unreasoning wheel, which also hummingly soliloquizes; or rather, his body was a sentry-box and this soliloquizer on guard there, and talking all the time to keep himself awake.

Chapter 108

Ahab and the Carpenter

THE DECK—FIRST NIGHT WATCH
(Carpenter standing before his vice-bench, and by the light of two lanterns busily filing the ivory joist for the leg, which joist is firmly fixed in the vice. Slabs of ivory, leather straps, pads, screws, and various tools of all sorts lying about the bench. Forward, the red flame of the forge is seen, where the blacksmith is at work.)

Drat the file, and drat the bone! That is hard which should be soft, and that is soft which should be hard. So we go, who file old jaws and shinbones. Let's try another. Aye, now, this works better (*sneezes*). Halloa, this bone dust is (*sneezes*)—why it's (*sneezes*)—yes it's (*sneezes*)—bless my soul, it won't let me speak! This is what an old fellow gets now for working in dead lumber. Saw a live tree, and you don't get this dust; amputate a live bone, and you don't get it (*sneezes*). Come, come, you old Smut, there, bear a hand, and let's have that ferule and buckle-screw; I'll be ready for them presently. Lucky now (*sneezes*) there's no knee-joint to make; that might puzzle a little; but a mere shinbone—why it's easy as making hop-poles; only I should like to put a good finish on. Time, time; if I but only had the time, I could turn him out as neat a leg now as ever (*sneezes*) scraped to a lady in a parlor. Those buckskin legs and calves of legs I've seen in shop windows wouldn't compare at all. They soak water, they do; and of course get rheumatic, and have to be doctored (*sneezes*) with washes and lotions, just like live legs. There; before I saw it off, now, I must call his old Mogulship, and see whether the length will be all right; too short, if anything, I guess. Ha! that's the heel; we are in luck; here he comes, or it's somebody else, that's certain.

AHAB (*advancing*).
(*During the ensuing scene, the carpenter continues sneezing at times.*)

Well, manmaker!

Just in time, sir. If the captain pleases, I will now mark the length. Let me measure, sir.

Measured for a leg! good. Well, it's not the first time. About it! There; keep thy finger on it. This is a cogent vice thou hast here, carpenter; let me feel its grip once. So, so; it does pinch some.

Oh, sir, it will break bones—beware, beware!

No fear; I like a good grip; I like to feel something in this slippery world that can hold, man. What's Prometheus about there?—the blacksmith, I mean—what's he about?

He must be forging the buckle-screw, sir, now.

Right. It's a partnership; he supplies the muscle part. He makes a fierce red flame there!

Aye, sir; he must have the white heat for this kind of fine work.

Um-m. So he must. I do deem it now a most meaning thing, that that old Greek, Prometheus, who made men, they say, should have been a blacksmith, and animated them with fire; for what's made in fire must properly belong to fire; and so hell's probable. How the soot flies! This must be the remainder the Greek made the Africans of. Carpenter, when he's through with that buckle, tell him to forge a pair of steel shoulder-blades; there's a pedlar aboard with a crushing pack.

Sir?

Hold; while Prometheus is about it, I'll order a complete man after a desirable pattern. Imprimis, fifty feet high in his socks; then, chest modelled after the Thames Tunnel; then, legs with roots to 'em, to stay in one place; then, arms three feet through the wrist; no heart at all, brass forehead, and about a quarter of an acre of fine brains; and let me see—shall I order eyes to see outwards? No, but put a sky-light on top of his head to illuminate inwards. There, take the order, and away.

Now, what's he speaking about, and who's he speaking to, I should like to know? Shall I keep standing here? *(aside.)*

'Tis but indifferent architecture to make a blind dome; here's one. No, no, no; I must have a lantern.

Ho, ho! That's it, hey? Here are two, sir; one will serve my turn.

What art thou thrusting that thief-catcher into my face for, man? Thrusted light is worse than presented pistols.

I thought, sir, that you spoke to carpenter.

Carpenter? why that's—but no;—a very tidy, and, I may say, an extremely gentlemanlike sort of business thou art in here, carpenter;—or would'st thou rather work in clay?

Sir?—Clay? clay, sir? That's mud; we leave clay to ditchers, sir.

The fellow's impious! What art thou sneezing about?

Bone is rather dusty, sir.

Take the hint, then; and when thou art dead, never bury thyself under living people's noses.

Sir?—oh! ah!—I guess so;—yes—dear!

Look ye, carpenter, I dare say thou callest thyself a right good workman-like workman, eh? Well, then, will it speak thoroughly well for thy work, if, when I come to mount this leg thou makest, I shall nevertheless feel another leg in the same identical place with it; that is, carpenter, my old lost leg; the flesh and blood one, I mean. Canst thou not drive that old Adam away?

Truly, sir, I begin to understand somewhat now. Yes, I have heard something curious on that score, sir; how that a dismasted man never entirely loses the feeling of his old spar, but it will be still pricking him at times. May I humbly ask if it be really so, sir?

It is, man. Look, put thy live leg here in the place where mine once was; so, now, here is only one distinct leg to the eye, yet two to the soul. Where thou feelest tingling life; there, exactly there, there to a hair, do I. Is't a riddle?

I should humbly call it a poser, sir.

Hist, then. How dost thou know that some entire, living, thinking thing may not be invisibly and uninterpenetratingly standing precisely where thou now standest; aye, and standing there in thy spite? In thy most solitary hours, then, dost thou not fear eavesdroppers? Hold, don't speak! And if I still feel the smart of my crushed leg, though it be now so long dissolved; then, why mayst not thou, carpenter, feel the fiery pains of hell for ever, and without a body? Hah!

Good Lord! Truly, sir, if it comes to that, I must calculate over again; I think I didn't carry a small figure, sir.

Look ye, pudding-heads should never grant premises.—How long before the leg is done?

Perhaps an hour, sir.

Bungle away at it then, and bring it to me *(turns to go)*. Oh, Life! Here I am, proud as Greek god, and yet standing debtor to this blockhead for a bone to stand on! Cursed be that mortal inter-indebtedness which will not do away with ledgers. I would be free as air; and I'm down in the whole world's books. I am so rich, I could have given bid for bid with the wealthiest Praetorians at the auction of the Roman empire (which was the world's); and yet I owe for the flesh in the tongue I brag with. By heavens! I'll get a crucible, and into it, and dissolve myself down to one small, compendious vertebra. So.

CARPENTER

(Resuming his work.)

Well, well, well! Stubb knows him best of all, and Stubb always says he's queer; says nothing but that one sufficient little word queer; he's queer, says Stubb; he's queer—queer, queer; and keeps dinning it into Mr. Starbuck all the time—queer—sir—queer, queer, very queer. And here's his leg! Yes, now that I think of it, here's his bedfellow! has a stick of whale's jaw-bone for a wife! And this is his leg; he'll stand on this. What was that now about one leg standing in three places, and all three places standing in one hell—how was that? Oh! I don't wonder he looked so scornful at me! I'm a sort of strange-thoughted sometimes, they say; but that's only haphazard-like. Then, a short, little old body like me, should never undertake to wade out into deep waters with tall, heron-built captains; the water chucks you under the chin pretty quick, and there's a great cry for life-boats. And here's the heron's leg! long and slim, sure enough! Now, for most folks one pair of legs lasts a lifetime, and that must be because they use them mercifully, as a tender-hearted old lady uses her roly-poly old coach-horses. But Ahab; oh he's a hard driver. Look, driven one leg to death, and spavined the other for life, and now wears out bone legs by the cord. Halloa, there, you Smut! bear a hand there with those screws, and let's finish it before the resurrection fellow comes a-calling with his horn for all legs, true or false, as brewery-men go round collecting old beer barrels, to fill 'em up again. What a leg this is! It looks like a real live leg, filed down to nothing but the core; he'll be standing on this to-morrow; he'll be taking altitudes on it. Halloa! I almost forgot the little oval slate, smoothed ivory, where he figures up the latitude. So, so; chisel, file, and sand-paper, now!

CHAPTER 109

Ahab and Starbuck in the Cabin

next morning   into the cabin ˙

With his snow-white new ivory leg braced against the screwed leg of his table, and with a long pruning-hook of a jack-knife in his hand,

"Now that we are nearing Japan;"

"Thou art always prating to me, Starbuck, about those miserly owners, as if the owners were my conscience. But"

, with a daring so strangely respectful and cautious that it almost seemed not only every way seeking to avoid the slightest outward manifestation of itself, but within also seemed more than half distrustful of itself

(forming part of most South-Sea-men's cabin furniture)   "—"

half   rose   and

˙ In Sperm-whalemen with any considerable quantity of oil on board, it is a regular semiweekly duty to conduct a hose into the hold, and drench the casks with sea-water; which afterwards, at varying intervals, is removed by the ship's pumps. Hereby the casks are sought to be kept damply tight; while by the changed character of the withdrawn water, the mariners readily detect any serious leakage in the precious cargo.

CHAPTER 110

Queequeg in his Coffin

So, it being calm weather, they broke out deeper and deeper, disturbing the slumbers of the huge ground-tier butts; and from that black midnight sending those gigantic moles into the daylight above.   as if you were treading over empty catacombs,   Well was it that the Typhoons did not visit them then.

And like circles on the water, which, as they grow fainter, expand; so his eyes seemed rounding and rounding, like the rings of Eternity.   as strange things in his face, as any beheld who were bystanders when Zoroaster died. For whatever is truly wondrous and fearful in man, never yet was put into words or books. And   , which alike levels all, alike impresses all with a last revelation, which only an author from the dead could adequately tell. So that—let us say it again—no dying Chaldee or Greek had higher and holier thoughts than those, whose mysterious shades you saw creeping over the face of poor Queequeg, as he quietly lay in his swaying hammock, and the rolling sea seemed gently rocking him to his final rest, and the ocean's invisible flood-tide lifted him higher and higher towards his destined heaven

when the day was just breaking,   He added, that he shuddered at the thought of being buried in his hammock, according to the usual sea-custom, tossed like something vile to the death-devouring sharks. No: he desired a canoe like those of Nantucket, all the more congenial to him, being a whaleman, that like a whale-boat these coffin-canoes were without a keel; though that involved but uncertain steering, and much lee-way adown the dim ages.

, whatever it might include

Going to his vice-bench, the carpenter for convenience sake and general reference, now transferringly measured on it the exact length the coffin was to be, and then made the transfer permanent by cutting two notches at its extremities.

in that direction

, nor was there any denying him; seeing that, of all mortals, some dying men are the most tyrannical; and certainly, since they will shortly trouble us so little for evermore, the poor fellows ought to be indulged

, who had been slily hovering near by all this while,

"__"

"__   __   __"

, as if in a dream

; now that his coffin was proved a good fit   ,   —   , he averred

; and emptying into it his canvas bag of clothes, set them in order there

CHAPTER 111

The Pacific

CHAPTER 112

The Blacksmith

Availing himself of the mild, summer-cool weather that now reigned in these latitudes, and in preparation for the peculiarly active pursuits shortly to be anticipated, Perth,   , had not removed his portable forge to the hold again, after concluding his contributory work for Ahab's leg, but still retained it on deck, fast lashed to ringbolts by the foremast; being now almost incessantly invoked by the headsmen, and harpooneers, and bowsmen to do some little job for them; altering, or repairing, or new shaping their various weapons and boat furniture. Often he would be surrounded by an eager circle, all waiting to be served; holding boat-spades, pike-heads, harpoons, and lances, and jealously watching his every sooty movement, as he toiled. Nevertheless, this old man's was a patient hammer wielded by a patient arm. No murmur, no impatience, no petulance did come from him. Silent, slow, and solemn; bowing over still further his chronically broken back, he toiled away, as if toil were life itself, and the heavy beating of his hammer the heavy beating of his heart. And so it was.—Most miserable!

A peculiar walk in this old man, a certain slight but painful appearing yawing in his gait, had at an early period of the voyage excited the curiosity of the mariners. And to the importunity of their persisted questionings he had finally given in; and so it came to pass that every one now knew the shameful story of his wretched fate.

Belated, and not innocently, one bitter winter's midnight, on the road running between two country towns, the blacksmith half-stupidly felt the deadly numbness stealing over him, and sought refuge in a leaning, dilapidated barn. The issue was, the loss of the extremities of both feet. Out of this revelation, part by part, at last came out the four acts of the gladness, and the one long, and as yet uncatastrophied fifth act of the grief of his life's drama.

He was an old man, who, at the age of nearly sixty, had postponedly encountered that thing in sorrow's technicals called ruin. He had been an artisan of famed excellence, and with plenty to do; owned a house and garden; embraced a youthful, daughter-like, loving wife, and three blithe, ruddy children; every Sunday went to a cheerful-looking church, planted in a grove. But one night, under cover of darkness, and further concealed in a most cunning disguisement, a desperate burglar slid into his happy home, and robbed them all of everything. And darker yet to tell, the blacksmith himself did ignorantly conduct this burglar into his family's heart. It was the Bottle Conjuror! Upon the opening of that fatal cork, forth flew the fiend, and shrivelled up his home. Now, for prudent, most wise, and economic reasons, the blacksmith's shop was in the basement of his dwelling, but with a separate entrance to it; so that always had the young and loving healthy wife listened with no unhappy nervousness, but with vigorous pleasure, to the stout ringing of her young-armed old husband's hammer; whose reverberations, muffled by passing through the floors and walls, came up to her, not unsweetly, in her nursery; and so, to stout Labor's iron lullaby, the blacksmith's infants were rocked to slumber.

Oh, woe on woe! Oh, Death, why canst thou not sometimes be timely? Hadst thou taken this old blacksmith to thyself ere his full ruin came upon him, then had the young widow had a delicious grief, and her orphans a truly venerable, legendary sire to dream of in their after years; and all of them a care-killing competency. But Death plucked down some virtuous elder brother, on whose whistling daily toil solely hung the responsibilities of some other family, and left the worse than useless old man standing, till the hideous rot of life should make him easier to harvest.

Why tell the whole? The blows of the basement hammer every day grew more and more between; and each blow every day grew fainter than the last; the wife sat frozen at the window, with tearless eyes, glitteringly gazing into the weeping faces of her children; the bellows fell; the forge choked up with cinders; the house was sold; the mother dived down into the long church-yard grass; her children twice followed her thither; and the houseless, familyless old man staggered off a vagabond in crape; his every woe unreverenced; his grey head a scorn to flaxen curls!

Death seems the only desirable sequel for a career like this; but Death is only a launching into the region of the strange Untried; it is but the first salutation to the possibilities of the immense Remote, the Wild, the Watery, the Unshored; therefore, to the death-longing eyes of such men, who still have left in them some interior compunctions against suicide, does the all-contributed and all-receptive ocean alluringly spread forth his whole plain of unimaginable, taking terrors, and wonderful, new-life adventures; and from the hearts of in-finite Pacifics, the thousand mermaids sing to them—"Come hither, broken-hearted; here is another life without the guilt of intermediate death; here are wonders supernatural, without dying for them. Come hither! bury thyself in a life which, to your now equally abhorred and abhorring, landed world, is more oblivious than death. Come hither! put up *thy* grave-stone, too, within the churchyard, and come hither, till we marry thee!"

Hearkening to these voices, East and West, by early sunrise, and by fall of eve, the blacksmith's soul responded, Aye, I come! And so Perth went a-whaling.

CHAPTER 113

The Forge

"___"

"these are"

", then,"

"; these stubbs will weld together like glue from the melted bones of murderers   ,"

But, as Ahab looked up, he slid aside.

, to temper it,

" wincing for a moment with the pain; "

For a moment, the old blacksmith eyed the razors as though he would fain
not use them.

"Take them, man, I have no need for them; for I now neither shave, sup, nor
pray till—but here—to work!"

with the bark still investing it,

CHAPTER 114

The Gilder

These are the times, when in his whale-boat the rover softly feels a certain fil-
ial, confident, land-like feeling towards the sea; that he regards it as so much
flowery earth; and the distant ship revealing only the tops of her masts, seems
struggling forward, not through high rolling waves, but through the tall grass
of a rolling prairie: as when the western emigrants' horses only show their
erected ears, while their hidden bodies widely wade through the amazing
verdure.

The long-drawn virgin vales; the mild blue hill-sides; as over these there
steals the hush, the hum; you almost swear that play-wearied children lie
sleeping in these solitudes, in some glad May-time, when the flowers of the

woods are plucked. And all this mixes with your most mystic mood; so that fact and fancy, half-way meeting, interpenetrate, and form one seamless whole.

Oh, grassy glades! oh, ever vernal endless landscapes in the soul; in ye,— though long parched by the dead drought of the earthy life,—in ye, men yet may roll, like young horses in new morning clover; and for some few fleeting moments, feel the cool dew of the life immortal on them. Would to God these blessed calms would last. But the mingled, mingling threads of life are woven by warp and woof: calms crossed by storms, a storm for every calm. There is no steady unretracing progress in this life; we do not advance through fixed gradations, and at the last one pause:—through infancy's unconscious spell, boyhood's thoughtless faith, adolescence' doubt (the common doom), then scepticism, then disbelief, resting at last in manhood's pondering repose of If. But once gone through, we trace the round again; and are infants, boys, and men, and Ifs eternally. Where lies the final harbor, whence we unmoor no more? In what rapt ether sails the world, of which the weariest will never weary? Where is the foundling's father hidden? Our souls are like those orphans whose unwedded mothers die in bearing them: the secret of our paternity lies in their grave, and we must there to learn it.

—

And Stubb, fish-like, with sparkling scales, leaped up in that same golden light:—

"I am Stubb, and Stubb has his history; but here Stubb takes oaths that he has always been jolly!"

CHAPTER 115

The Pequod meets the Bachelor

And jolly enough were the sights and the sounds that came bearing down before the wind, some few weeks after Ahab's harpoon had been welded.

It was a Nantucket ship, the Bachelor, which had just wedged in her last cask of oil, and bolted down her bursting hatches; and now, in glad holiday apparel, was joyously, though somewhat vain-gloriously, sailing round among the widely-separated ships on the ground, previous to pointing her prow for home.

The three men at her mast-head wore long streamers of narrow red bunting at their hats; from the stern, a whale-boat was suspended, bottom down; and hanging captive from the bowsprit was seen the long lower jaw of the last whale they had slain. Signals, ensigns, and jacks of all colors were flying from her rigging, on every side. Sideways lashed in each of her three basketed tops were two barrels of sperm; above which, in her top-mast cross-trees, you saw slender breakers of the same precious fluid; and nailed to her main truck was a brazen lamp.

As was afterwards learned, the Bachelor had met with the most surprising success; all the more wonderful, for that while cruising in the same seas numerous other vessels had gone entire months without securing a single fish. Not only had barrels of beef and bread been given away to make room for the far more valuable sperm, but additional supplemental casks had been bartered for, from the ships she had met; and these were stowed along the deck, and in the captain's and officers' state-rooms. Even the cabin table itself had been knocked into kindling-wood; and the cabin mess dined off the broad head of an oil-butt, lashed down to the floor for a centrepiece. In the forecastle, the sailors had actually caulked and pitched their chests, and filled them; it was humorously added, that the cook had clapped a head on his largest boiler, and filled it; that the steward had plugged his spare coffee-pot and filled it; that the harpooneers had headed the sockets of their irons and filled them; that indeed everything was filled with sperm, except the captain's pantaloons pockets, and those he reserved to thrust his hands into, in self-complacent testimony of his entire satisfaction.

As this glad ship of good luck bore down upon the moody Pequod, the barbarian sound of enormous drums came from her forecastle; and drawing still nearer, a crowd of her men were seen standing round her huge try-pots, which, covered with the parchment-like *poke* or stomach skin of the black fish, gave forth a loud roar to every stroke of the clenched hands of the crew. On the quarter-deck, the mates and harpooneers were dancing with the olive-hued girls who had eloped with them from the Polynesian Isles; while suspended in an ornamented boat, firmly secured aloft between the foremast and mainmast, three Long Island negroes, with glittering fiddle-bows of whale ivory, were presiding over the hilarious jig. Meanwhile, others of the ship's company were tumultuously busy at the masonry of the try-works, from which the huge pots had been removed. You would have almost thought they were pulling down the cursed Bastille, such wild cries they raised, as the now useless brick and mortar were being hurled into the sea.

Lord and master over all this scene, the captain stood erect on the ship's elevated quarter-deck, so that the whole rejoicing drama was full before him, and seemed merely contrived for his own individual diversion.

And Ahab, he too was standing on his quarter-deck, shaggy and black, with a stubborn gloom; and as the two ships crossed each other's wakes—one all jubilations for things passed, the other all forebodings as to things to come—their two captains in themselves impersonated the whole striking contrast of the scene.

"Come aboard, come aboard!" cried the gay Bachelor's commander, lifting a glass and a bottle in the air.

"Hast seen the White Whale?" gritted Ahab in reply.

"No; only heard of him; but don't believe in him at all," said the other good-humoredly. "Come aboard!"

"Thou art too damned jolly. Sail on. Hast lost any men?"

"Not enough to speak of—two islanders, that's all;—but come aboard, old hearty, come along. I'll soon take that black from your brow. Come along, will ye (merry's the play); a full ship and homeward-bound."

"How wondrous familiar is a fool!" muttered Ahab; then aloud, "Thou art a full ship and homeward bound, thou sayst; well, then, call me an empty ship, and outward-bound. So go thy ways, and I will mine. Forward there! Set all sail, and keep her to the wind!"

And thus, while the one ship went cheerily before the breeze, the other stubbornly fought against it; and so the two vessels parted; the crew of the Pequod looking with grave, lingering glances towards the receding Bachelor; but the Bachelor's men never heeding their gaze for the lively revelry they were in. And as Ahab, leaning over the taffrail, eyed the homewardbound craft, he took from his pocket a small vial of sand, and then looking from the ship to the vial, seemed thereby bringing two remote associations together, for that vial was filled with Nantucket soundings.

CHAPTER 116

The Dying Whale

Not seldom in this life, when, on the right side, fortune's favorites sail close by us, we, though all adroop before, catch somewhat of the rushing breeze, and joyfully feel our bagging sails fill out. So seemed it with the Pequod. For after encountering the gay Bachelor

; then, such a sweetness and such plaintiveness, such inwreathing orisons curled up in that rosy air, that it almost seemed as if far over from the deep green convent valleys of the Manilla isles, the Spanish land-breeze, wantonly turned sailor, had gone to sea, freighted with these vesper hymns

Soothed again, but only soothed to deeper gloom, Ahab, who had sterned off from the whale, sat intently watching his final wanings from the now tranquil boat. For that strange spectacle observable in all sperm whales dying—the turning sunwards of the head, and so expiring—that strange spectacle, beheld of such a placid evening, somehow to Ahab conveyed a wondrousness unknown before.

"He turns and turns him to it,—how slowly, but how steadfastly, his homage-rendering and invoking brow, with his last dying motions. He too worships fire; most faithful, broad, baronial vassal of the sun!—Oh that these too-favoring eyes should see these too-favoring sights. Look! here, far water-locked; beyond all hum of human weal or woe; in these most candid and impartial seas; where to traditions no rocks furnish tablets; where for long Chinese ages, the billows have still rolled on speechless and unspoken to, as stars that shine upon the Niger's unknown source; here, too, life dies sunwards full of faith; but see! no sooner dead, than death whirls round the corpse, and it heads some other way.—

"Oh, thou dark Hindoo half of nature, who of drowned bones hast builded thy separate throne somewhere in the heart of these unverdured seas; thou art an infidel, thou queen, and too truly speakest to me in the wide-slaughtering Typhoon, and the hushed burial of its after calm. Nor has this thy whale sunwards turned his dying head, and then gone round again, without a lesson to me.

"Oh, trebly hooped and welded hip of power! Oh, high aspiring, rainbowed jet!—that one strivest, this one jettest all in vain! In vain, oh whale, dost thou seek intercedings with yon all-quickening sun, that only calls forth life, but gives it not again. Yet dost thou, darker half, rock me with a prouder, if a darker faith. All thy unnamable imminglings float beneath me here; I am buoyed by breaths of once living things, exhaled as air, but water now.

"Then hail, for ever hail, O sea, in whose eternal tossings the wild fowl finds his only rest. Born of earth, yet suckled by the sea; though hill and valley mothered me, ye billows are my foster-brothers!"

CHAPTER 117

The Whale Watch

'

'

, face to face,

"—"

", old man"

"—"

.

in the gloom

"—"   —

CHAPTER 118

The Quadrant

The season for the Line at length drew near; and every day when Ahab, coming from his cabin, cast his eyes aloft, the vigilant helmsman would ostentatiously handle his spokes, and the eager mariners quickly run to the braces, and would stand there with all their eyes centrally fixed on the nailed doubloon; impatient for the order to point the ship's prow for the equator. In good time the order came.

That unblinkingly vivid Japanese sun seems the blazing focus of the glassy ocean's immeasurable burning-glass.   "This instant thou must be eyeing him."

and handling, one after the other, its numerous cabalistical contrivances,

mute,   Unobserved he rose and glided away; while, awestruck by the aspect of their commander, the seamen clustered together on the forecastle, till Ahab, troubledly pacing the deck, shouted out—"To the braces! Up helm!— square in!"

In an instant the yards swung round; and as the ship half-wheeled upon her heel, her three firm-seated graceful masts erectly poised upon her long, ribbed hull, seemed as the three Horatii pirouetting on one sufficient steed.

Standing between the knight-heads, Starbuck watched the Pequod's tumultuous way, and Ahab's also, as he went lurching along the deck.

"I have sat before the dense coal fire and watched it all aglow, full of its tormented flaming life; and I have seen it wane at last, down, down, to dumbest dust. Old man of oceans! of all this fiery life of thine, what will at length remain but one little heap of ashes!"

"Aye," cried Stubb, "but sea-coal ashes—mind ye that, Mr. Starbuck—sea-coal, not your common charcoal. Well, well; I heard Ahab mutter, 'Here some one thrusts these cards into these old hands of mine; swears that I must play them, and no others.' And damn me, Ahab, but thou actest right; live in the game, and die in it!"

CHAPTER 119

The Candles

"Stubb, for one, can't fight it. You see, Mr. Starbuck, a wave has such a great long start before it leaps, all round the world it runs, and then comes the spring! But as for me, all the start I have to meet it, is just across the deck here. But never mind; it's all in fun: so the old song says;"—*(sings.)*

> *Oh! jolly is the gale,*
> *And a joker is the whale,*
> *A' flourishin' his tail,—*

Such a funny, sporty, gamy, jesty, joky, hoky-poky lad, is the Ocean, oh!

> *The scud all a flyin',*
> *That's his flip only foamin';*
> *When he stirs in the spicin',—*

Such a funny, sporty, gamy, jesty, joky, hoky-poky lad, is the Ocean, oh!

> *Thunder splits the ships,*
> *But he only smacks his lips,*
> *A tastin' of this flip,—*

Such a funny, sporty, gamy, jesty, joky, hoky-poky lad, is the Ocean, oh!

"Avast Stubb," cried Starbuck, "let the Typhoon sing, and strike his harp here in our rigging; but if thou art a brave man thou wilt hold thy peace."

"But I am not a brave man; never said I was a brave man; I am a coward; and I sing to keep up my spirits. And I tell you what it is, Mr. Starbuck, there's no way to stop my singing in this world but to cut my throat. And when that's done, ten to one I sing ye the doxology for a wind-up."

"Madman! look through my eyes if thou hast none of thine own."

"What! how can you see better of a dark night than anybody else, never mind how foolish?"

seizing Stubb by the shoulder, and pointing his hand towards the weather bow, "now mark his boat there; where is that stove? In the stern-sheets, man; where he is wont to stand—his stand-point is stove, man! Now jump over-board, and sing away, if thou must!

"I don't half understand ye: what's in the wind?"

"Yes, yes, round the Cape of Good Hope is the shortest way to Nantucket," soliloquized Starbuck suddenly, heedless of Stubb's question. " to stave us
—I"

following the flashes,

, ; and as moreover, if kept constantly towing there, it would be liable to many mishaps, besides interfering not a little with some of the rigging, and more or less impeding the vessel's way in the water; because of all this

"Blast the boat! let it go!" cried Stubb at this instant, as a swashing sea heaved up under his own little craft, so that its gunwale violently jammed his hand, as he was passing a lashing. "Blast it!"—but slipping backward on the deck, his uplifted eyes caught the flames; and immediately shifting his tone he cried— "The corpusants have mercy on us all!"

To sailors, oaths are household words; they will swear in the trance of the calm, and in the teeth of the tempest; they will imprecate curses from the topsail-yard-arms, when most they teeter   to   ; but in all my voyagings   seldom have I heard a common oath when ; when His "Mene, Mene, Tekel Upharsin" has been woven into the shrouds and the cordage.

"What thinkest thou now, man; I heard thy cry; it was not the same in the song."

"No, no, it wasn't; I said the corpusants have mercy on us all; and I hope they will, still. But do they only have mercy on long faces?—have they no bowels for a laugh? And"

like the standing, or stepping, or running skeletons in Herculaneum,

"In the midst of the personified impersonal, a personality stands here. Though but a point at best; whencesoe'er I came; wheresoe'er I go; yet   But war is pain, and hate is woe. Come in thy lowest form of love, and I will kneel and kiss thee; but at thy highest, come as mere supernal power; and though thou launchest navies of full-freighted worlds, there's that in here that still remains indifferent."

"Take the homage of these poor eyes, and shutter-hands. I would not take it.   The javelins cease; open eyes; see, or not? There burn the flames! Oh, thou magnanimous! now I do glory in my genealogy. But thou art but my fiery father; my sweet mother, I know not. Oh, cruel! what hast thou done with her? There lies my puzzle; but thine is greater. Thou knowest not how came ye, hence callest thyself unbegotten; certainly knowest not thy beginning, hence callest thyself unbegun. I know that of me, which thou knowest not of thyself, oh, thou omnipotent. There is some unsuffusing thing beyond thee, thou clear spirit, to whom all thy eternity is but time, all thy creativeness mechanical. Through thee, thy flaming self, my scorched eyes do dimly see it.   thou hermit immemorial, thou too hast thy incommunicable riddle, thy unparticipated grief. Here again with haughty agony, I read my sire"

"the boat!"

For the moment all the aghast mate's thoughts seemed theirs; they raised a half mutinous cry.   —

CHAPTER 120

The Deck towards the End of the First Night Watch

(Ahab standing by the helm. Starbuck approaching him.)

"We must send down the main-top-sail yard, sir. The band is working loose and the lee lift is half-stranded. Shall I strike it, sir?"

"Strike nothing; lash it. If I had sky-sail poles, I'd sway them up now."

"Sir!—in God's name!—sir?"

"Well."

"The anchors are working, sir. Shall I get them inboard?"

"Strike nothing, and stir nothing, but lash everything. The wind rises, but it has not got up to my table-lands yet. Quick, and see to it.—By masts and keels! he takes me for the hunch-backed skipper of some coasting smack.

Send down my main-top-sail yard! Ho, gluepots! Loftiest trucks were made for wildest winds, and this brain-truck of mine now sails amid the cloud-scud. Shall I strike that? Oh, none but cowards send down their brain-trucks in tempest time. What a hooroosh aloft there! I would e'en take it for sub-lime, did I not know that the colic is a noisy malady. Oh, take medicine, take medicine!"

CHAPTER 121

Midnight—The Forecastle Bulwarks

(Stubb and Flask mounted on them, and passing additional lashings over the anchors there hanging.)

"No, Stubb; you may pound that knot there as much as you please, but you will never pound into me what you were just now saying. And how long ago is it since you said the very contrary? Didn't you once say that whatever ship Ahab sails in, that ship should pay something extra on its insurance policy, just as though it were loaded with powder barrels aft and boxes of lucifers forward? Stop, now; didn't you say so?"

"Well, suppose I did? What then? I've part changed my flesh since that time, why not my mind? Besides, supposing we *are* loaded with powder barrels aft and lucifers forward; how the devil could the lucifers get afire in this drench-ing spray here? Why, my little man, you have pretty red hair, but you couldn't get afire now. Shake yourself; you're Aquarius, or the water-bearer, Flask; might fill pitchers at your coat collar. Don't you see, then, that for these extra risks the Marine Insurance companies have extra guarantees? Here are hydrants, Flask. But hark, again, and I'll answer ye the other thing. First take your leg off from the crown of the anchor here, though, so I can pass the rope; now listen. What's the mighty difference between holding a mast's lightning-rod in the storm, and standing close by a mast that hasn't got any lightning-rod at all in a storm? Don't you see, you timber-head, that no harm can come to the holder of the rod, unless the mast is first struck? What are you talking about, then? Not one ship in a hundred carries rods, and Ahab,—aye, man, and all of us,—were in no more danger then, in my poor opinion, than all the crews in ten thousand ships now sailing the seas. Why, you King-Post, you, I suppose you would have every man in the world go about with a small lightning-rod running up the corner of his hat, like a militia officer's skewered feather, and trailing behind like his sash. Why don't ye be sensible, Flask? it's easy to be sensible; why don't ye, then? any man with half an eye can be sensible."

"I don't know that, Stubb. You sometimes find it rather hard."

"Yes, when a fellow's soaked through, it's hard to be sensible, that's a fact. And I am about drenched with this spray. Never mind; catch the turn there, and pass it. Seems to me we are lashing down these anchors now as if they were never going to be used again. Tying these two anchors here, Flask, seems like tying a man's hands behind him. And what big generous hands they are, to be sure. These are your iron fists, hey? What a hold they have, too! I wonder, Flask, whether the world is anchored anywhere; if she is, she swings with an uncommon long cable, though. There, hammer that knot down, and we've done. So; next to touching land, lighting on deck is the most satisfactory. I say, just wring out my jacket skirts, will ye? Thank ye. They laugh at long-togs so, Flask; but seems to me, a long tailed coat ought always to be worn in all storms afloat. The tails tapering down that way, serve to carry off the water, d'ye see. Same with cocked hats; the cocks form gable-end eave-troughs, Flask. No more monkey-jackets and tarpaulins for me; I must mount a swallow-tail, and drive down a beaver; so. Halloa! whew! there goes my tarpaulin overboard; Lord, Lord, that the winds that come from heaven should be so unmannerly! This is a nasty night, lad."

CHAPTER 122

Midnight Aloft—
Thunder and Lightning

(The main-top-sail yard.—Tashtego passing new lashings
around it.)

"Um, um, um. Stop that thunder! Plenty too much thunder up here. What's the use of thunder? Um, um, um. We don't want thunder; we want rum; give us a glass of rum. Um, um, um!"

CHAPTER 123

The Musket

, at intervals,   at almost every shock the helmsman had not failed to notice the whirling velocity with which they revolved upon the cards;

, like the feathers of an albatross, which sometimes are cast to the winds when that storm-tossed bird is on the wing

Instantly the yards were squared, to the lively song of "*Ho! the fair wind! oh-ye-ho, cheerly men!*" the crew singing for joy, that so promising an event should so soon have falsified the evil portents preceding it.

, ,

burning fitfully, and   ,   The isolated subterraneousness of the cabin made a certain humming silence to reign there, though it was hooped round by all the roar of the elements.   when he saw the muskets   strangely

"—that one with the studded stock;   — — , — — Does he not
say he will not strike his spars to any gale?   ; and come to deadly harm, my
soul swears this ship will, if Ahab have his way.   ,   ; all this thou scornest
—   Say he were pinioned even; knotted all over with ropes and hawsers;
chained down to ring-bolts on this cabin floor; he would be more hideous
than a caged tiger, then. I could not endure the sight; could not possibly fly
his howlings; all comfort, sleep itself, inestimable reason would leave me on
the long intolerable voyage.   —   —Is heaven a murderer when its lightning
strikes a would-be murderer in his bed, tindering sheets and skin together?—
And"   and half sideways looking,

CHAPTER 124

The Needle

Emblazonings, as of crowned Babylonian kings and queens, reigned over everything. The sea was as a crucible of molten gold, that bubblingly leaps with
light and heat.

; and every time the tetering ship loweringly pitched down her bowsprit,
he turned to eye the bright sun's rays produced ahead; and when she profoundly settled by the stern, he turned behind, and saw the sun's rearward
place, and how the same yellow rays were blending with his undeviating
wake

"Ha, ha, my ship! thou mightest well be taken now for the sea-chariot of the
sun. Ho, ho! all ye nations before my prow, I bring the sun to ye! Yoke on the
further billows; hallo! a tandem, I drive the sea!"

reined back by some counter thought,

; but its very blinding palpableness must have been the cause

Here, it must needs be said, that accidents like this have in more than one case occurred to ships in violent storms. The magnetic energy, as developed in the mariner's needle, is, as all know, essentially one with the electricity beheld in heaven; hence it is not to be much marvelled at, that such things should be. Instances where the lightning has actually struck the vessel, so as to smite down some of the spars and rigging, the effect upon the needle has at times been still more fatal; all its loadstone virtue being annihilated, so that the before magnetic steel was of no more use than an old wife's knitting needle. But in either case, the needle never again, of itself, recovers the original virtue thus marred or lost; and if the binnacle compasses be affected, the same fate reaches all the others that may be in the ship; even were the lowermost one inserted into the kelson.

, for the supposed fair one had only been juggling her

in some small degree   ; or if impressed, it was only with a certain magnetism shot into their congenial hearts from inflexible Ahab's

,

CHAPTER 125

The Log and Line

While now the fated Pequod had been so long afloat this voyage, the log and line had but very seldom been in use. Owing to a confident reliance upon other means of determining the vessel's place, some merchantmen, and many whalemen, especially when cruising, wholly neglect to heave the log; though at the same time, and frequently more for form's sake than anything else, regularly putting down upon the customary slate the course steered by the ship, as well as the presumed average rate of progression every hour. It had been thus with the Pequod. The wooden reel and angular log attached hung, long untouched, just beneath the railing of the after bulwarks. Rains and spray had damped it; sun and wind had warped it; all the elements had combined to rot a thing that hung so idly. But heedless of all this, his mood seized Ahab, as he happened to glance upon the reel, not many hours after the magnet scene, and he remembered how his quadrant was no more, and recalled his frantic oath about the level log and line. The ship was sailing plungingly; astern the billows rolled in riots.

"Forward, there! Heave the log!"

Two seamen came. The golden-hued Tahitian and the grizzly Manxman. "Take the reel, one of ye, I'll heave."

They went towards the extreme stern, on the ship's lee side, where the deck, with the oblique energy of the wind, was now almost dipping into the creamy, sidelong-rushing sea.

The Manxman took the reel, and holding it high up, by the projecting handle-ends of the spindle, round which the spool of line revolved, so stood with the angular log hanging downwards, till Ahab advanced to him.

Ahab stood before him, and was lightly unwinding some thirty or forty turns to form a preliminary hand-coil to toss overboard, when the old Manxman, who was intently eyeing both him and the line, made bold to speak.

"Sir, I mistrust it; this line looks far gone, long heat and wet have spoiled it."

"'Twill hold, old gentleman. Long heat and wet, have they spoiled thee? Thou seem'st to hold. Or, truer perhaps, life holds thee; not thou it."

"I hold the spool, sir. But just as my captain says. With these grey hairs of mine 'tis not worth while disputing, 'specially with a superior, who'll ne'er confess."

"What's that? There now's a patched professor in Queen Nature's granite-founded College; but methinks he's too subservient. Where wert thou born?"

"In the little rocky Isle of Man, sir."

"Excellent! Thou'st hit the world by that."

"I know not, sir, but I was born there."

"In the Isle of Man, hey? Well, the other way, it's good. Here's a man from Man; a man born in once independent Man, and now unmanned of Man; which is sucked in—by what? Up with the reel! The dead, blind wall butts all inquiring heads at last. Up with it! So."

The log was heaved. The loose coils rapidly straightened out in a long dragging line astern, and then, instantly, the reel began to whirl. In turn, jerkingly raised and lowered by the rolling billows, the towing resistance of the log caused the old reelman to stagger strangely.

"Hold hard!"

Snap! the overstrained line sagged down in one long festoon; the tugging log was gone.

"I crush the quadrant, the thunder turns the needles, and now the mad sea parts the log-line. But Ahab can mend all. Haul in here, Tahitian; reel up, Manxman. And look ye, let the carpenter make another log, and mend thou the line. See to it."

"There he goes now; to him nothing's happened; but to me, the skewer seems loosening out of the middle of the world. Haul in, haul in, Tahitian! These lines run whole, and whirling out: come in broken, and dragging slow. Ha, Pip? come to help; eh, Pip?"

"Pip? whom call ye Pip? Pip jumped from the whale-boat. Pip's missing. Let's see now if ye haven't fished him up here, fisherman. It drags hard; I guess he's holding on. Jerk him, Tahiti! Jerk him off; we haul in no cowards here. Ho! there's his arm just breaking water. A hatchet! a hatchet! cut it off—we haul in no cowards here. Captain Ahab! sir, sir! here's Pip, trying to get on board again."

"Peace, thou crazy loon," cried the Manxman, seizing him by the arm. "Away from the quarter-deck!"

"The greater idiot ever scolds the lesser," muttered Ahab, advancing. "Hands off from that holiness! Where sayest thou Pip was, boy?"

"Astern there, sir, astern! Lo! lo!"

"And who art thou, boy? I see not my reflection in the vacant pupils of thy eyes. Oh God! that man should be a thing for immortal souls to sieve through! Who art thou, boy?"

"Bell-boy, sir; ship's-crier; ding, dong, ding! Pip! Pip! Pip! One hundred pounds of clay reward for Pip; five feet high—looks cowardly—quickest known by that! Ding, dong, ding! Who's seen Pip the coward?"

"There can be no hearts above the snow-line. Oh, ye frozen heavens! look down here. Ye did beget this luckless child, and have abandoned him, ye creative libertines. Here, boy; Ahab's cabin shall be Pip's home henceforth, while Ahab lives. Thou touchest my inmost centre, boy; thou art tied to me by cords woven of my heart-strings. Come, let's down."

"What's this? here's velvet shark-skin," intently gazing at Ahab's hand, and feeling it. "Ah, now, had poor Pip but felt so kind a thing as this, perhaps he had ne'er been lost! This seems to me, sir, as a man-rope; something that weak souls may hold by. Oh, sir, let old Perth now come and rivet these two hands together; the black one with the white, for I will not let this go."

"Oh, boy, nor will I thee, unless I should thereby drag thee to worse horrors than are here. Come, then, to my cabin. Lo! ye believers in gods all goodness, and in man all ill, lo you! see the omniscient gods oblivious of suffering man; and man, though idiotic, and knowing not what he does, yet full of the sweet things of love and gratitude. Come! I feel prouder leading thee by thy black hand, than though I grasped an Emperor's!"

"There go two daft ones now," muttered the old Manxman. "One daft with strength, the other daft with weakness. But here's the end of the rotten line— all dripping, too. Mend it, eh? I think we had best have a new line altogether. I'll see Mr. Stubb about it."

CHAPTER 126

The Life-Buoy

like the carved Roman slave,   ,

"_"

"I make a leg for Captain Ahab, and he wears it like a gentleman; but I make a bandbox for Queequeg, and he won't put his head into it. Are all my pains to go for nothing with that coffin? And now I'm ordered to make a life-buoy of it. It's like turning an old coat; going to bring the flesh on the other side now. I don't like this cobbling sort of business—   ; it's undignified; it's not my place. Let tinkers' brats do tinkerings; we are their betters. I like to take in hand none but clean, virgin, fair-and-square mathematical jobs, something that regularly begins at the beginning, and is at the middle when midway, and comes to an end at the conclusion; not a cobbler's job, that's at an end in the middle, and at the beginning at the end. It's the old woman's tricks to be giving cobbling jobs. Lord! what an affection all old women have for tinkers. I know an old woman of sixty-five who ran away with a bald-headed young tinker once. And that's the reason I never would work for lonely widow old women ashore, when I kept my job-shop in the Vineyard; they might have taken it into their lonely old heads to run off with me   there are no caps at sea but snow-caps. Let me see. Nail down the lid; caulk the seams; pay over the same with pitch; batten them down tight, and hang it with the snap-spring over the ship's stern. Were ever such things done before with a coffin? Some superstitious old carpenters, now, would be tied up in the rigging, ere they would do the job. But I'm made of knotty Aroostook hemlock; I don't budge. Cruppered with a coffin! Sailing about with a grave-yard tray! But never mind. We workers in woods make bridal-bedsteads and card-tables, as well as coffins and hearses. We work by the month, or by the job, or by the profit; not for us to ask the why and wherefore of our work, unless it be too confounded cobbling, and then we stash it if we can. Hem!   Come hammer, caulking-iron, pitch-pot, and marling-spike! Let's to it."

CHAPTER 127

The Deck

(The coffin laid upon two line-tubs, between the vice-bench and the open hatchway; the Carpenter caulking its seams; the string of twisted oakum slowly unwinding from a large roll of it placed in the bosom of his frock.—Ahab comes slowly from the cabin-gangway, and hears Pip following him.)

"Back, lad; I will be with ye again presently. He goes! Not this hand complies with my humor more genially than that boy.—Middle aisle of a church! What's here?"

"Life-buoy, sir. Mr. Starbuck's orders. Oh, look, sir! Beware the hatchway!"

"Thank ye, man. Thy coffin lies handy to the vault."

"Sir? The hatchway? oh! So it does, sir, so it does."

"Art not thou the leg-maker? Look, did not this stump come from thy shop?"

"I believe it did, sir; does the ferrule stand, sir?"

"Well enough. But art thou not also the undertaker?"

"Aye, sir; I patched up this thing here as a coffin for Queequeg; but they've set me now to turning it into something else."

"Then tell me; art thou not an arrant, all-grasping, intermeddling, monopolising, heathenish old scamp, to be one day making legs, and the next day coffins to clap them in, and yet again life-buoys out of those same coffins? Thou art as unprincipled as the gods, and as much of a jack-of-all-trades."

"But I do not mean anything, sir. I do as I do."

"The gods again. Hark ye, dost thou not ever sing working about a coffin? The Titans, they say, hummed snatches when chipping out the craters for volcanoes; and the grave-digger in the play sings, spade in hand. Dost thou never?"

"Sing, sir? Do I sing? Oh, I'm indifferent enough, sir, for that; but the reason why the grave-digger made music must have been because there was none in his spade, sir. But the caulking mallet is full of it. Hark to it."

"Aye, and that's because the lid there's a sounding-board; and what in all things makes the sounding-board is this—there's naught beneath. And yet, a coffin with a body in it rings pretty much the same, Carpenter. Hast thou ever helped carry a bier, and heard the coffin knock against the churchyard gate, going in?"

"Faith, sir, I've———"

"Faith? What's that?"

"Why, faith, sir, it's only a sort of exclamation-like—that's all, sir."

"Um, um; go on."

"I was about to say, sir, that———"

"Art thou a silk-worm? Dost thou spin thy own shroud out of thyself? Look at thy bosom! Despatch! and get these traps out of sight."

"He goes aft. That was sudden, now; but squalls come sudden in hot latitudes. I've heard that the Isle of Albemarle, one of the Gallipagos, is cut by the Equator right in the middle. Seems to me some sort of Equator cuts yon old man, too, right in his middle. He's always under the Line—fiery hot, I tell ye! He's looking this way—come, oakum; quick. Here we go again. This wooden mallet is the cork, and I'm the professor of musical glasses—tap, tap!"

(Ahab to himself.)

"There's a sight! There's a sound! The grey-headed woodpecker tapping the hollow tree! Blind and dumb might well be envied now. See! that thing rests on two line-tubs, full of tow-lines. A most malicious wag, that fellow. Rat-tat! So man's seconds tick! Oh! how immaterial are all materials! What things real are there, but imponderable thoughts? Here now's the very dreaded symbol of grim death, by a mere hap, made the expressive sign of the help and hope of most endangered life. A life-buoy of a coffin! Does it go further? Can it be that in some spiritual sense the coffin is, after all, but an immortality-preserver! I'll think of that. But no. So far gone am I in the dark side of earth, that its other side, the theoretic bright one, seems but uncertain twilight to me. Will ye never have done, Carpenter, with that accursed sound? I go below; let me not see that thing here when I return again. Now, then, Pip, we'll talk this over; I do suck most wondrous philosophies from thee! Some unknown conduits from the unknown worlds must empty into thee!"

CHAPTER 128

The Pequod meets the Rachel

as it shortly turned out,   ,   the circumstance,   not only was one of
            sons among the number of the missing boat's crew; but among the number of the other boat's crews, at the same time, but on the other hand, separated from the ship during the dark vicissitudes of the chase, there had been still another   ; as that for a time, the wretched father was plunged to the bottom of the cruellest perplexity; which was only solved for him by his chief mate's instinctively adopting the ordinary procedure of a whale-ship in such emergencies, that   , when placed between jeopardized but divided boats, always to pick up the majority first. But the captain, for some unknown constitutional reason, had refrained from mentioning all this, and not till forced to it by Ahab's iciness did he allude to his one yet missing boy;   ,

CHAPTER 129

The Cabin

(Ahab moving to go on deck; Pip catches him by the hand to follow.)

"Lad, lad, I tell thee thou must not follow Ahab now. The hour is coming when Ahab would not scare thee from him, yet would not have thee by him. There is that in thee, poor lad, which I feel too curing to my malady. Like cures like; and for this hunt, my malady becomes my most desired health. Do thou abide below here, where they shall serve thee, as if thou wert the captain. Aye, lad, thou shalt sit here in my own screwed chair; another screw to it, thou must be."

"No, no, no! ye have not a whole body, sir; do ye but use poor me for your one lost leg; only tread upon me, sir; I ask no more, so I remain a part of ye."

"Oh! spite of million villains, this makes me a bigot in the fadeless fidelity of man!—and a black! and crazy!—but methinks like-cures-like applies to him too; he grows so sane again."

"They tell me, sir, that Stubb did once desert poor little Pip, whose drowned bones now show white, for all the blackness of his living skin. But I will never desert ye, sir, as Stubb did him. Sir, I must go with ye."

"If thou speakest thus to me much more, Ahab's purpose keels up in him. I tell thee no; it cannot be."

"Oh good master, master, master!"

"Weep so, and I will murder thee! have a care, for Ahab too is mad. Listen, and thou wilt often hear my ivory foot upon the deck, and still know that I am there. And now I quit thee. Thy hand!—Met! True art thou, lad, as the circumference to its centre. So: God for ever bless thee; and if it come to that,—God for ever save thee, let what will befall."

(Ahab goes; Pip steps one step forward.)

"Here he this instant stood; I stand in his air,—but I'm alone. Now were even poor Pip here I could endure it, but he's missing. Pip! Pip! Ding, dong, ding! Who's seen Pip? He must be up here; let's try the door. What? neither lock, nor bolt, nor bar; and yet there's no opening it. It must be the spell; he told me to stay here: Aye, and told me this screwed chair was mine. Here, then, I'll seat me, against the transom, in the ship's full middle, all her keel and her three masts before me. Here, our old sailors say, in their black seventy-fours great admirals sometimes sit at table, and lord it over rows of captains and lieuten-ants. Ha! what's this? epaulets! epaulets! the epaulets all come crowding! Pass round the decanters; glad to see ye; fill up, monsieurs! What an odd feeling, now, when a black boy's host to white men with gold lace upon their coats!— Monsieurs, have ye seen one Pip?—a little negro lad, five feet high, hang-dog look, and cowardly! Jumped from a whale-boat once;—seen him? No! Well then, fill up again, captains, and let's drink shame upon all cowards! I name no names. Shame upon them! Put one foot upon the table. Shame upon all cowards.—Hist! above there, I hear ivory—Oh, master! master! I am indeed down-hearted when you walk over me. But here I'll stay, though this stern strikes rocks; and they bulge through; and oysters come to join me."

Chapter 130

The Hat

, ,   —   It domineered above them so, that all their bodings, doubts, misgivings, fears, were fain to hide beneath their souls, and not sprout forth a single spear or leaf.

In this foreshadowing interval too, all humor, forced or natural, vanished. Stubb no more strove to raise a smile; Starbuck no more strove to check one.

But did you deeply scan him in his more secret confidential hours; when he thought no glance but one was on him; then you would have seen that even as Ahab's eyes so awed the crew's, the inscrutable Parsee's glance awed his; or somehow, at least, in some wild way, at times affected it. Such an added, gliding strangeness began to invest the thin Fedallah now; such ceaseless shudderings shook him; that the men looked dubious at him; half uncertain, as it seemed, whether indeed he were a mortal substance, or else a tremulous shadow cast upon the deck by some unseen being's body. And that shadow was always hovering there. For not by night, even, had Fedallah ever certainly been known to slumber, or go below. He would stand still for hours: but never sat or leaned; his wan but wondrous eyes did plainly say—We two watchmen never rest.

either standing in his pivot-hole, or exactly pacing the planks between two undeviating limits,—the main-mast and the mizen; or else they saw him standing in the cabin-scuttle,—his living foot advanced upon the deck, as if to step;

that is, his two only meals,—breakfast and dinner: supper   touched; nor   , which still grow idly on at naked base, though perished in the upper verdure   mystic   Though such a potent spell seemed secretly to join the twain; openly, and to the awe-struck crew, they seemed pole-like asunder. If by day they chanced to speak one word; by night, dumb men were both, so far as concerned the slightest verbal interchange. At times, for longest hours, without a single hail, they stood far parted in the starlight; Ahab in his scuttle, the Parsee by the mainmast;   still fixedly gazing upon each other; as if in the Parsee Ahab saw his forethrown shadow, in Ahab the Parsee his abandoned substance.

And yet, somehow, did   —in his own proper self, as daily, hourly, and every instant, commandingly revealed to his subordinates   —Ahab seemed an independent lord; the Parsee but his slave. Still again both seemed yoked together, and an unseen tyrant driving them; the lean shade siding the solid rib. For be this Parsee what he may, all rib and keel was solid Ahab.

,

But if these suspicions were really his, he sagaciously refrained from verbally expressing them, however his actions might seem to hint them.

— — , ,

When in working with his hands at some lofty almost isolated place in the rigging, which chances to afford no foothold, the sailor at sea is hoisted up to that spot, and sustained there by the rope; under these circumstances, its fastened end on deck is always given in strict charge to some one man who has the special watch of it. Because in such a wilderness of running rigging, whose various different relations aloft cannot always be infallibly discerned by what is seen of them at the deck; and when the deck-ends of these ropes are being every few minutes cast down from the fastenings, it would be but a natural fatality, if, unprovided with a constant watchman, the hoisted sailor should by some carelessness of the crew be cast adrift and fall all swooping to the sea. So Ahab's proceedings in this matter were not unusual; the only strange thing about them seemed to be, that Starbuck, almost the one only man who had ever ventured to oppose him with anything in the slightest degree approaching to decision—one of those too, whose faithfulness on the look-out he had seemed to doubt somewhat;—it was strange, that this was the very man he should select for his watchman; freely giving his whole life into such an otherwise distrusted person's hands.

An eagle flew thrice round Tarquin's head, removing his cap to replace it, and thereupon Tanaquil, his wife, declared that Tarquin would be king of Rome. But only by the replacing of the cap was that omen accounted good.

CHAPTER 131

The Pequod meets the Delight

CHAPTER 132

The Symphony

It was a clear steel-blue day. The firmaments of air and sea were hardly separable in that all-pervading azure; only, the pensive air was transparently pure and soft, with a woman's look, and the robust and man-like sea heaved with long, strong, lingering swells, as Samson's chest in his sleep.

Hither, and thither, on high, glided the snow-white wings of small, unspeckled birds; these were the gentle thoughts of the feminine air; but to and fro in the deeps, far down in the bottomless blue, rushed mighty leviathans, swordfish, and sharks; and these were the strong, troubled, murderous thinkings of the masculine sea.

But though thus contrasting within, the contrast was only in shades and shadows without; those two seemed one; it was only the sex, as it were, that distinguished them.

Aloft, like a royal czar and king, the sun seemed giving this gentle air to this bold and rolling sea; even as bride to groom. And at the girdling line of the horizon, a soft and tremulous motion—most seen here at the Equator—

denoted the fond, throbbing trust, the loving alarms, with which the poor bride gave her bosom away.

Tied up and twisted; gnarled and knotted with wrinkles; haggardly firm and unyielding; his eyes glowing like coals, that still glow in the ashes of ruin; un-tottering Ahab stood forth in the clearness of the morn; lifting his splintered helmet of a brow to the fair girl's forehead of heaven.

Oh, immortal infancy, and innocency of the azure! Invisible winged creatures that frolic all round us! Sweet childhood of air and sky! how oblivious were ye of old Ahab's close-coiled woe! But so have I seen little Miriam and Martha, laughing-eyed elves, heedlessly gambol around their old sire; sporting with the circle of singed locks which grew on the marge of that burnt-out crater of his brain.

"Forty—forty—forty years ago!—ago!   for forty years has Ahab forsaken the peaceful land, for forty years to make war on the horrors of the deep! Aye and yes, Starbuck, out of those forty years I have not spent three ashore. When I think of this life I have led; the desolation of solitude it has been; the masoned, walled-town of a Captain's exclusiveness, which admits but small entrance to any sympathy from the green country without—oh, weariness! heaviness! Guinea-coast slavery of solitary command!—when I think of all this; only half-suspected, not so keenly known to me before—and how fool—fool—old   ,   Why this strife of the chase? why weary, and palsy the arm at the oar, and the iron, and the lance? how the richer or bet-ter is Ahab now? Behold. Oh, Starbuck! is it not hard, that with this weary load I bear, one poor leg should have been snatched from under me? Here, brush this old hair aside; it blinds me, that I seem to weep. Locks so grey did never grow but from out some ashes! But do I look very old, so very, very old, Starbuck? I feel deadly faint, bowed, and humped, as though I were Adam, staggering beneath the piled centuries since Paradise. God! God! God!—crack my heart!—stave my brain!—mockery! mockery! bitter, biting mockery of grey hairs, have I lived enough joy to wear ye; and seem and feel thus intolerably old?"

"But if the great sun move not of himself; but is as an errand-boy in heaven; nor one single star can revolve, but by some invisible power; how then can this one small heart beat; this one small brain think thoughts; unless God does that beating, does that thinking, does that living, and not I. By heaven, man, we are turned round and round in this world, like yonder windlass, and Fate is the handspike.   Look! see yon Albicore! who put it into him to chase and fang that flying-fish? Where do murderers go, man! Who's to doom, when the judge himself is dragged to the bar?"

CHAPTER 133

The Chase—First Day

when   —as his wont at intervals—stepped forth from the scuttle in which he leaned, and went to his pivot-hole, he

,

at every roll of the sea

"I saw him almost that same instant, sir, that Captain Ahab did, and I cried out," said Tashtego.

"Not the same instant; not the same—   —   —"

"—   —"

as if an isolated thing,

. Not the white bull Jupiter swimming away with ravished Europa clinging to his graceful horns; his lovely, leering eyes sideways intent upon the maid; with smooth bewitching fleetness, rippling straight for the nuptial bower in Crete; not Jove, not that great majesty Supreme! did surpass the glorified White Whale so divinely

On each soft side—coincident with the parted swell, that but once leaving him, then flowed so wide away—on each bright side, the whale shed off enticings.

*

›

! ,

" __ "

" __ "

.

" __ "

"›"
›

" __ " __

---

* This motion is peculiar to the sperm whale. It receives its designation (pitchpoling) from its being likened to that preliminary up-and-down poise of the whale-lance, in the exercise called pitchpoling, previously described. By this motion the whale must best and most comprehensively view whatever objects may be encircling him.

CHAPTER 134

The Chase—Second Day

";"

Here be it said, that this pertinacious pursuit of one particular whale, continued through day into night, and through night into day, is a thing by no means unprecedented in the South sea fishery. For such is the wonderful skill, prescience of experience, and invincible confidence acquired by some great natural geniuses among the Nantucket commanders; that from the simple observation of a whale when last descried, they will, under certain given circumstances, pretty accurately foretell both the direction in which he will continue to swim for a time, while out of sight, as well as his probable rate of progression during that period. And, in these cases, somewhat as a pilot, when about losing sight of a coast, whose general trending he well knows, and which he desires shortly to return to again, but at some further point; like as this pilot stands by his compass, and takes the precise bearing of the cape at present visible, in order the more certainly to hit aright the remote, unseen headland, eventually to be visited: so does the fisherman, at his compass, with the whale; for after being chased, and diligently marked, through several hours of daylight, then, when night obscures the fish, the creature's future wake through the darkness is almost as established to the sagacious mind of the hunter, as the pilot's coast is to him. So that to this hunter's wondrous skill, the proverbial evanescence of a thing writ in water, a wake, is to all desired purposes well nigh as reliable as the steadfast land. And as the mighty iron Leviathan of the modern railway is so familiarly known in its every pace, that, with watches in their hands, men time his rate as doctors that of a baby's pulse; and lightly say of it, the up train or the down train will reach such or such a spot, at such or such an hour; even so, almost, there are occasions when these Nantucketers time that other Leviathan of the deep, according to the observed humor of his speed; and say to themselves, so many hours hence this whale will have gone two hundred miles, will have about reached this or that degree of latitude or longitude. But to render this acuteness at all successful in the end, the wind and the sea must be the whaleman's allies; for of what present avail to the becalmed or windbound mariner is the skill that assures him he is exactly ninety-three leagues and a quarter from his port? Inferable from these statements, are many collateral subtile matters touching the chase of whales.

""
,

,

—

; — ,

"The ferrule has not stood, sir," said the carpenter, now coming up; "I put good work into that leg."

"—"

" "
, ,

"— "
,

"— "
,

"— —"

CHAPTER 135

The Chase—Third Day

";   ;"

,

,   ,   —   —"

"—"

,

"—"

,

""
,

"—"

""
,

;

;

Epilogue

CONTRIBUTORS

HERMAN MELVILLE was born in New York, the son of a merchant, and was largely self-educated. He started writing after having first sailed to Liverpool in 1839, where he joined a whaler bound for the Pacific Ocean. Deserting the ship the following year in the Marquesas, he made his way to Tahiti and Honolulu, returning as an ordinary seaman to Boston, where he was discharged in October 1844. Books based on these adventures won him immediate success. This literary attention soon faded, however, as his prose became more ambitious, culminating in his final, and many would say greatest, novel *The Confidence-Man*. He died virtually unknown in 1891, and it was not until the 1920s that he received recognition as a key figure in American literature.

DAMION SEARLS was also born in New York but the similarities end there. He is the author of two books, *Everything You Say Is True* and *What We Were Doing and Where We Were Going*, and his abridgment (produced with traditional methods) of Thoreau's 7,000-page *Journal* will be published by NYRB Classics in 2009. He is also an award-winning translator from German, Norwegian, French, and Dutch, of writers including Marcel Proust and Rainer Maria Rilke. For more information, see www.damionsearls.com.

BOOK REVIEWS

Gérard Gavarry. *Expérience d'Edward Lee, Versailles*. P.O.L, 2009. 234 pp. Paper: €21.00.

Édouard Levé was a brilliant and extremely promising French writer and photographer who committed suicide at the age of forty-two in 2007. Three years before that event, he had taken a series of photographs during a trip to the United States, in American towns and small cities whose curious names— Berlin, Oxford, Amsterdam, Paris, Versailles, and so forth—appealed to him. In *Expérience d'Edward Lee, Versailles*, Gérard Gavarry meditates upon one hundred of those photos. Each meditation puts on offer three very brief passages that seem to lack both beginning and end, as if they had been abstracted from some vaster and more detailed discourse. The collection is colored by absence, from first page to last. Most obviously, the photos themselves are absent. We "see" them only through the titles that Levé assigned to them ("Fireman in Oxford," for instance, "Jehovah's Witness in Paris," or "Restaurant in Berlin"), or through Gavarry's prose. Gavarry's evocation of the photos plays out in long focus at best, ensuring that those images remain out of our grasp, and suggesting perhaps, too, that Gavarry himself has yet to come to satisfactory terms with them. Just as these fragments have neither beginning nor end, so does Gavarry intimate that the writing of mourning has neither beginning nor end, but rather adopts as its characteristic mode a shattered, painful *now* situated in the very middle of things. Death and the trappings that adorn it abound, for Gavarry reads the photos as Levé's comments upon his own mortality. That doubled, layered reading is fragile of course, relying as it does upon hindsight, yet it is admirably rich as well. Even those readers most familiar with Gavarry's previous work will not fail to be astonished by the freshness of tone and technique here. Like Georges Perec before him, it seems that Gérard Gavarry approaches each of his books anew, unfettered by what he has done in the past, making him one of the most pleasingly unpredictable writers in our midst. [Warren Motte]

Christopher Miller. *The Cardboard Universe*. Harper Perennial, 2009. 522 pp. Paper: $14.99.

The Cardboard Universe is an encyclopedic guide to the life work of an imaginary, reclusive sci-fi author whose initials are PKD. That should raise a few alarms with anyone, but don't worry: Christopher Miller handles his book with grace and ingenuity. Although decidedly metafictional, *The Cardboard Universe* is also deeply character-driven: one of the book's many pleasures is determining exactly who Phoebus K. Dank is and whether he's a hack or not. This is not easy, as the encyclopedia is written by two heavily biased critics (one a sycophantic academic that lived with Dank for years, the other a haughty poet that finds joy in tearing Dank down), and we get precious few glimpses of the author's writing by which to judge firsthand. Paralleling this literary mystery is a criminal one: Who murdered Dank and why? Miller capably strings this out to the end, and the question is far more than an idle one in the context of the book. Even if you choose to hopscotch through *The Cardboard Universe* (it is a reference book, after all) it's hard to spoil the plot, and such a reading sustains interest because the book is resplendent with scores of premises from the prolific Dank's work. For every jarringly stupid plot (a story narrated by a "sentient washing machine") there's something almost brilliant (the consequences of a world where everyone has the same dream), and even when the conceit stinks we gain insight into the character of the heavily autobiographical author. There's even an entry for Dank's fictional character

"Philip K. Dick," wherein we learn "Dick seems at times to realize that he is nothing but a fictional character." Happily, *The Cardboard Universe* can attend to such fine moments without beating us over the head with its glorious meta-fictionality, which is to say *The Cardboard Universe* has enough grist for the grad students and enough life for a satisfying story. [Scott Esposito]

Donald Breckenridge. *You Are Here.* Starcherone Books, 2008. 144 pp. Paper: $16.00.

Most 9/11 novels fall into the trap of attempting to narrate that day or manipulate its consequences. Donald Breckenridge's slim, stylish, and seductive third novel, *You Are Here*, never directly mentions 9/11, but rather confronts the fundamental problem of composing a 9/11 novel—that doing so turns events into just another story. Its premise is deceptively simple: A married architect has an affair with a younger, unemployed woman in New York in the months leading up to 9/11; later, a middle-aged woman, Janet, begins a relationship with a twenty-four-year-old writer she meets while shopping for used books. Both forms of the May–September romance are doomed, as predicted by major twenty-first century news items buzzing in the background—presidential elections, a battle in Iraq, the disappearance of a congressman's mistress. What makes this novel particularly innovative is Breckenridge's clever dialogue, which he interpolates into description so that the two occur simultaneously, even when they are at a chronological distance. For example, a casual conversation between Janet and her lover is interrupted by memories of her former marriage: " 'Have you been?' Mark was of average intelligence, 'in Beacon . . .' dishonest and manipulative, 'no I haven't,' and often believed his own lies, 'I hear it's very impressive.' " The young writer documents Janet, who then becomes a character both in the novel we are reading and in the text he is composing. Meticulously tracking the vintages of the wines characters drink and alluding to New York-specific sites like Pete's Candy Store and The Strand, Breckenridge emphasizes that every layer of personal experience—including the shops in which we buy our books—is another composition.

A first-person narrator, Donald, presents himself as the writer composing the characters as we read them, a further reminder of the fictionality of fiction. As the architect claims, people behave "[i]n the roles they're expected to perform." In the end, his ill-fated girlfriend escapes their affair through a job that links her story to the headlines. The intimacy of her portrayal shows Breckenridge's finesse in handling both the imperative to reconcile personal and public tragedy through writing, and the impossibility of its fulfillment. [Stefanie Sobelle]

Amina Cain. *I Go To Some Hollow.* Intro. Bhanu Kapil. Les Figues Press, 2009. 108 pp. Paper: $15.00.

Cain's first book presents fifteen stories that veer between the realist and the absurd. None of them form complete narratives, and nearly all of them end abruptly, just as they seem to be starting—but in Cain's hands, such open-endedness quickly becomes a strength. These are stories that express wonder at the world, and the author makes no pretense about being able to see things clearly, or in their entirety. Her voice, rather, delights in naivety: "Sometimes people die when they build houses. They fall off roofs or accidentally shock themselves when it rains on a drill." At times her tone juxtaposes subjects in a manner not unlike Donald Barthelme; at other times it leans more toward Amy Hempel, estranging by means of brevity. Meanwhile, the characters speak like refugees from a Nicholas Mosley novel: "'How is he?' she asked. / 'He's hauling lumber on the farm,' the doctor said. 'He's forgotten about you.'" Binding the stories together is a small list of recurring subjects—relationships, animals, concentration, the way bodies move through space—all rendered in a clear, penetrating language that routinely settles on incisive images: "The moon shone on Rosita's lobster." "That night a large hole opened up next to the cabin." "Our grandfather lives in a hospital in Montana where the snow is heavy and disastrous to small cars and women riding horses." Cain's debut demonstrates that when the clichéd expectations of traditional narrative are gently omitted, what's left is a calming stillness, and startling language—a welcome relief from the ironic realism that characterizes so much young contemporary fiction. We need more writing like this. [A D Jameson]

Robert Walser. *The Tanners.* Intro. W. G. Sebald. Trans. and afterword Susan Bernofsky. New Directions, 2009. 368 pp. Paper: $15.95.

Robert Walser's early (1907) novel *The Tanners* concerns the autodidactic rebel Simon Tanner and his family. A coming-of-age story, it details Simon's intense and illuminating relationships with his brothers Klaus (an academic) and Kaspar (an artist), as well as his sister Hedwig (a school teacher). It's a curious sort of bildungsroman, however: there is little character development and Simon is never successfully integrated into society. Between odd jobs, Simon contemplates nature, engages in homespun (though insightful) philosophy, and is a student of human society (always from the position of a resolutely, almost absurdly cheerful outsider). But Simon is a young man of ability: he is articulate, bold, and engages the interest of powerful people. He talks his way guilelessly into the home of the wealthy and sympathetic Klara, who falls in love with Simon's brother Kaspar. There they live together, Simon and Kaspar, unemployed, violating social norms (thought not sexual mores: *The Tanners* is a chaste novel). And class relations here are always clear. In fact, Simon works briefly as a servant for an overtly cruel mistress. These relationships are dynamic, however: characters rise and fall from riches as in Smollett, including, ultimately, and most movingly, Klara herself. This is one indicator of modernity: social fluidity as opposed to a vestigial aristocracy; any other markers for modernism in *The Tanners* are more thematic than formal, as the novel is episodically structured, and its prose, while beautifully rendered (as translated by Susan Bernofsky), poses no real formal challenges. In the final analysis, Simon's cheerful refusal to acknowledge the pain and suffering inherent in human social life is a refusal to assume the emotional and spiritual burdens of life as officially constituted, framing these burdens as normative rather than intrinsic to human experience. Simon is in his way courageous: the unassuming hero of a remarkable and compelling novel. [Gary Lain]

Nawal El Saadawi. *The Novel.* Trans. Omnia Amin and Rick London. Interlink Books, 2009. 236 pp. Paper: $15.00.

It's probably odd and not a little insulting to say that with *The Novel*, Nawal El Saadawi (b. 1931), one of the leaders of Egypt's feminist movement and author of over thirty other books of fiction and nonfiction, has reached maturity as a novelist. Much of her earlier fictive work was characterized by a bluntness that worked well to convey outrage—El Saadawi has endured imprisonment, death threats, and exile, among other indignities far beyond what most of us will ever contend with, much of which features prominently in her work—but which made for less-than-graceful narrative art. *The Novel*, by contrast, may be the most elegant and ambitious of her ten novels. A mysteriously nameless young woman, with "no family, no university degree, no national identity card," writes a novel in spite of herself, having little idea of what she wants to write or how to do so. Once published, we're told twice, the novel causes tremendous outrage (as *The Novel* evidently did in the real world, though it's tame by Western standards). Its protagonist is an affluent politician named Roustum, who seems to be at the center of both the young woman's novel and *The Novel*. Lest it seem like El Saadawi is coming late to the metafiction party, she downplays standard self-referentiality in favor of a dreamy, disorienting landscape in which the relationships between characters are never quite clear, nor their motivations or abilities, as the young woman's novel appears and spreads surreptitiously, yet loudly, through Cairo like uncertain magic. Unlike the hard-charging bleakness of some of her early work, here El Saadawi creates an impressionistic Cairo full of writers and poets, all more prosperous than many of her earlier characters but not at all the better for it. [Tim Feeney]

Carla Harryman. *Adorno's Noise.* Essay Press, 2008. 181 pp. Paper: $14.95.

Carla Harryman's Adorno is the Adorno of negative dialectics, but is not: is also Adorno, composer and music critic, he who said that poetry should end at Auschwitz, but then said not: "the tortured have [the right] to scream." Harryman begins her howling prose piece with a collision of word and tone: "*A might be an abbreviation. . . . It may insinuate itself into a frequency or the touch of A.*"; she then crashes non-identity into the individual: "The person had revealed something at a vulnerable moment and now that thing is known to be what goes on in the person's head. . . . [I]t grew out of proportion to the language . . . and now it is mushrooming." Invoking the Latin root of "noise" (nausea), she articulates her concern thusly: ". . . we have been known to get sick of . . . our own subjectivity." But as Adorno wrote, humans will be liberated not by reason, but by not "always-the-same" art, a language/music "praxis," as Bruce Andrews put it, that expresses meaningful dissonance. Thus the backbone of this work obliterates the hierarchy of pitches, thereby obliterating hierarchy and out-Adorno-ing Adorno. "Beware of Seeking out the Mighty" *does* Adorno's gap between identity and false identity with a diatribe structured as a negative series of positives. "[I]n writing a poem she is not writing a novel in writing a novel she is not writing an essay in writing an essay she is not writing a diatribe." The beauty of this piece—its dissonance—resides in selection/serialization of juxtaposition ("amending [a] statement" follows "crossing a river" follows "taking dictation" follows "punctuating time"); but also in asymmetrical sound, a refusal to scan "well." This narrator is/is not filching, repellent, basking in the sunlight in the aftermath of a natural disaster, creating social anarchy, drowning in sorrow—and writing a novel. To understate, then, this expression of Adorno's atonality is doing what the great man only said. [Kass Fleisher]

Jessica Treat. *Meat Eaters & Plant Eaters.* BOA Editions, Ltd., 2009. 160 pp. Paper: $14.00.

Animals—domesticated, wild, and extinct—figure prominently in Jessica Treat's third collection of stories, *Meat Eaters & Plant Eaters*. Taking on familiar functions as sources of comfort, custodians of intuitive knowledge, and symbols of single-track simplicity, Treat's dogs, cats, and birds become the objects of human projection in a book filled with dissatisfied protagonists who long for and sometimes embark on lives not their own. In "Listing," a man who has lost a battle for emotional primacy with his now ex-girlfriend's dog regrets that someone's discarded shopping list does not convey a more portentous message. The excellent "Make a Nest" uses the bird's nest not only as figure for the stable family but also, in the egg that falls from the nest, the violent wild in the longed-for life outside the nest's confines. Treat's mix of flash-sized and mid-length stories contain simple, meticulous sentences, and her characters don't pontificate on big ideas. In a book that forces the reader to work between the lines and beyond the page, however, the extreme compression of plot and emotion can be both blessing and curse. While the hazy weight of meaning, evident in the finest pieces, balances delicately between abstruseness and melodrama, one telegraphed word can and sometimes does push the writing towards the banal or the sappy, and occasionally Treat's final, diminishing note unnecessarily overloads the conclusion with a sense of indeterminacy. At best, as in "Waiting," where a woman pretends to be a man's absentee blind date, the closing detail—a twisted, shredded napkin—is powerful enough to hold the ambiguity and volatility of the chance encounter without waterlogging the story. Characters and reader come together to share the charged moment before setting off in search of fulfillment elsewhere. [Robert Glick]

Breyten Breytenbach. *Mouroir: Mirror Notes of a Novel.* Archipelago Books, 2009. 279 pp. Paper: $15.00. (Reprint)

Breyten Breytenbach. *Voice Over: A Nomadic Conversation with Mahmoud Darwish.* Archipelago Books, 2009. 45 pp. Paper: $9.00.

Long out of print (it was originally published in 1984), *Mouroir* might be seen as a novel, a series of stories, essays, prose poems, philosophical reflections, notes, or fragments, but is at the same time none of these things. Indeed, the power of this book, written by South African writer Breytenbach when he was imprisoned for seven years, lies in just that: these are pieces that cannot be pinned down. Here, the boundaries between the real and the magical are blurry, here the poetic and the lyrical can draw abruptly up into something painfully real. They are flights of the imagination written during a time of physical immobility. Though a few don't amount to much, the majority of them develop in surprising and satisfying ways. Breytenbach's English, inflected as it is by the logic of poetry and dream, by his native Afrikaans, and by French, is surprising as well: a mortal wound, for instance, might be described as having "an odd odor, the dank and yet distant smell of a wing." At its best (in, for instance, pieces such as "G?," "Wiederholen," and "A Pattern of Bullets"), *Mouroir* is replete with stunning gestures and startling imagery. Often too, Breytenbach has a way of folding reality back on itself that makes the metafictional seem deadly serious and engaged while still remaining playful. *Mouroir* is a complex, important book.

Voice Over, published simultaneously, is a twelve-section poem written as an homage to Mahmoud Darwish. It converses with Darwish after his death, continuing to wrestle with his presence and his poetry. Whereas *Mouroir* makes the most of ambiguity and shapelessness, *Voice Over* shows Breytenbach to be equally talented when working in a more directed and formal space. [Brian Evenson]

Yuri Andrukhovych. *The Moscoviad.* Trans. Vitaly Chernetsky. Spuyten Duyvil, 2008. 186 pp. Paper: $14.00.

Drunken, dissolute Ukrainian poet Otto von F., whose adventures in and out of the writer's dormitory in Moscow in the waning days of the USSR comprise this ribald novel, takes Baudelaire's bibulous counsel to heart, despite occasional pangs of conscience and the knowledge that there are far more profitable associates, in terms of getting his latest effusions into print, than a bunch of old cronies out to raise hell. Here, style mimics substance with a vengeance, as the episodes through which Andrukhovych leads us each arrive in a boozy haze, the decadent sway of dying communism lending an arch sense of twisted ritual to the intricacies of Otto's quest for self-justification. No *samizdat* rebel, Otto enjoys the privileges of the authorized intelligentsia, but knows no limits to his behavior, measuring all progress by the strata of booze in his gut. Much of the book recounts the events of a single day, all conspiring to ruin Otto's plans to see his publisher and buy presents for friends' children. Otto's account of his antics—shagging a fetching female in the shower, barely eluding the detonation of a grenade in a louche bar, tracking a pickpocket into the depths of a building only to discover a subterranean bacchanal stoking the passions of Soviet apparatchiks, all declaiming perpetual hegemony in the dregs of their toppling regime—displays how much Andrukhovych's art relies on contingency. One overwrought lover, a snake-venom expert, appears as if by magic to spring Otto from a KGB jail where he awaits death for killing the pickpocket—an agent, naturally. Falling in a hail of bullets while trying to escape, Otto does a double take and lives again. His true poetry is unleashed in action, his words only an extension of his riotous nature. Andrukhovych's overheated imagination, like that of his protagonist, knows no restraint in this wild spree of a novel, merrily stomping on the grave of socialist realism. [Michael Pinker]

Ana María Shua. *Microfictions*. Trans. Steven J. Stewart. University of Nebraska Press, 2009. 196 pp. Paper: $19.95.

It's tempting to describe Ana María Shua as a writer of flash fiction; the longest piece in her *Microfictions* runs four pages, novelistic compared with many of the other selections, which can be as short as a few lines. But the more one delves into Shua's alternate realities, the more one realizes how inappropriate the flash designation is, not just for the strongest pieces in this collection, but also for standouts by other practitioners of the genre. Shua's fictions often work like Zen koans, compelling the reader to mull over paradoxes dramatized in a handful of suggestive sentences. In "Genie," the insomniac narrator wishes that the genie at his command could make his unsettling dreams *not* come true. In "Cast Out," Adam and Eve are punished for their disobedience by being woken up from a shared dream. Divided into sections that coalesce around a different theme—such as "Monsters," "Dreams," "Men and Women"—*Microfictions* has the atmospheric unity of miscellanies such as Julio Cortázar's *Cronopios and Famas* or Barry Yourgrau's *Wearing Dad's Head*. The connection to Cortázar is particularly strong in the absurdist instructions of a piece like "Bad Manners," which consists in its entirety of two sentences: "If your chicken champignon takes off, leaving a trail of sauce on the tablecloth in its wake, don't blame your guests. You can't expect such an exquisite dish to tolerate your table manners." The suppleness of the short prose form is further demonstrated in the section devoted to "Literature," in which Shua reimagines elements of mythology, fairy tales, the Western, and other genres. Arguably, Shua also makes strides in genre theory. In designating her creations "microfictions," she suggests their remarkable scale while hinting at the layers beyond the visible afforded by the possibilities of this still-emerging form. [Pedro Ponce]

Petre M. Andreevski. *Pirey*. Trans. Will Firth and Mirjana Simjanovska. Pollitecon, 2009. 288 pp. Paper: $40.00.

Petre M. Andreevski's novel *Pirey* begins with its end—the death of Velika Meglenoska, during the Second World War. Her only surviving child, Roden, returns to the village for his mother's funeral. In the course of that day, Roden is told the life stories of his parents Velika and Ion by their friend, Duko Vendiya. Duko tells Velika's and Ion's stories as he himself heard it from them, so they serve as our narrators, taking turns, chapter by chapter. The couple is separated at the beginning of the First World War, with Ion being mobilized and Velika staying behind in the village to look after their children, who she nevertheless loses one by one. When Ion returns, he's a changed man, and severely tortures his wife, whom he's already gotten pregnant one last time. On the day he dies, Velika gives birth to Roden. With her stoicism and high ethical ideals, Velika stands as a positive counterbalance to her husband's brutality, but is also an archetypical representation of the pre-modern Macedonian woman—and *Pirey*'s focus on war, epidemics, births, deaths, and its characters' fatalism, makes this twentieth-century novel very much an echo of classical tragedy. At the same time, however, with its mixture of magical logic and political realities, *Pirey* comes close to the poetics of Gabriel García Márquez and Salman Rushdie: full of wordplay, puns, and alliteration, it's a novel calling for brave translators. Will Firth and Mirjana Simjanovska's wonderful work retains the peculiar rhythms of Andreevski's prose, giving English-readers an excellent approximation of the experience of the original. "Pirey," by the way, means "couch grass," and in the context of this work, it symbolizes human persistence—the translators decided to leave the word as is, with its foreign sonorities intact . . . and it, and the whole novel, sings. [Goce Smilevski]

Jeremy M. Davies. *Rose Alley.* Counterpath Press, 2009. 178 pp. Paper: $15.95.

Jeremy M. Davies, a veteran of narrative excavations, knows there is something provocatively heroic—and audaciously ironic—in the idea of design. The premise here is delightfully appealing: during the height of the 1968 Paris student riots, an avant-garde film crew makes an experimental movie about a 1679 London back-alley attack on John Dryden—arranged, historians conjecture, by a rival poet, the darkly lecherous Earl of Rochester. With riveting clarity, characters emerge chapter by chapter—the screenwriter, the set designer, the actors, the producer—threaded by the voice-over of the British director-as-archivist assembling an account of this long-ago cinematic endeavor. The premise allows Davies to interrogate with confident coolness the fascinating dynamic between art and chaos, messy fact rescued into form ironically by artists with wild libertine tastes and a relish of anarchy. Davies ingeniously reminds us that art is forever contested, any edifice-text, film or narrative or poem, constructed against and amid riots, personal or cultural, Davies deftly juxtaposes the volcanic hormones of the film's creators, the growing menace of the violence in the streets, and the Restoration squabble between Dryden and Rochester, each a pitched contest between anarchy and art. Each chapter is given over to the controlling awareness of another member of the film team; thus, what emerges is context, dense and yielding, not the fascist buzzkill of narrative. That such cumulative evidence cannot yield tidiness gives creativity its delight. Davies' narrative is engaging, subtle, at times mordantly funny— the closing chapter recounts the sheer number of versions of the film that survived, how those fragments become a coaxing, suasive (w)hole. With a pitch-perfect prose line, at once sinuous, witty, and stylish, that coins the most striking metaphors with the understated offhandedness that recalls vintage DeLillo, *Rose Alley* gathers us within its enthralling premise and leaves us content within its illusion of completeness. [Joseph Dewey]

Carlo Emilio Gadda. *The Philosophers' Madonna*. Trans. and intro. Antony Melville. Atlas Press, 2008. 78 pp. Paper: £12.00.

One of the most engaging things about Gadda's fiction and the one most difficult to translate is his use of dialect and syntax. Those things become apparent in such works as *That Awful Mess on the Via Merulana*. The difficulty in translating Gadda is significant: his work *Eros and Priapus* has yet to be translated into English primarily because of the linguistic knots it presents. To that end, one must be thankful to Antony Melville for translating *The Philosophers' Madonna*, Gadda's first novella. Though brief, it bears the seeds of the greatness that will follow. The opening line is brilliant in its simplicity: "I'm sorry if I get a bit conventional, but it really did happen like this." Like Camus's opening line in *The Stranger*, Gadda's first sentence compels a reader to continue by virtue of that simplicity. But even in this novella, one is exposed to syntactical gambols that may cause a reader to stutter or stop, but never to quit. Written in 1931, thirteen years before Borges's *Ficciones*, *The Philosophers' Madonna* could easily have been the precursor to Borges's work, as Gadda's narrative often becomes "surreptitiously sinister," leading his readers into labyrinth upon labyrinth. That is, he tends to interrupt the main line of the narrative as the subject he's just begun to introduce suddenly becomes a transition into yet another subject, which may or may not conclude with its own subjectivity being called into question, leaving one to wonder just where the narrative is: where it's been and where it might be going. Stylistically, Gadda uses a number of rhetorical techniques that manifest in his later works, but to attempt a summary of *The Philosophers' Madonna* would be difficult indeed. Suffice it to say, it blends rhetoric, lyricism, and black humor into an amalgam well worth reading. [Mark Axelrod]

Brian Evenson. *Last Days.* Intro. Peter Straub. Underland Press, 2009. 201 pp. Paper: $12.95.

Imagine Raymond Chandler's Philip Marlowe stumbling into an entirely dystopic, nihilistic, and somewhat surreal universe co-directed by Quentin Tarantino and David Lynch. If you can conjure this, you might begin to get an idea of what to expect in Evenson's new novel (or interconnected novellas). The work includes the flat, deadpan, "noir voice" of the potboiler detective story, but one that is filtered through an entirely deranged, depraved, and often bizarre narrative. Evenson presents violence with an unsurprising tone that becomes absurd. Mutilation and bodily disfigurement are simply status quo in this particular universe, and the bizarre brutality of the Brotherhood of Mutilation—a cult that finds amputation of various extremities to be a sacred act—is alarming but somehow easy to believe. In fact, the violence is so extreme and the voice so deliberate, yet ironically detached, that the contrast is disorienting. The seeming lack of any moral ground and the challenge to any logical or reasonable vision of reality creates a bizarre and irrational atmosphere that dislocates the fiction itself. In other words, as Borchert, one of the main characters notes, "surely you're enough of an armchair philosopher to realize that everything is a reconstruction of something else? Reality is a desperate and evasive creature." This is a story of extremity in every sense of the word. It begins with amputation and spirals into a world of murder surrounding the activities of the main character, Kline, and his involvement with two religious cults. Both sections of the book reveal a vehement and satirical critique of religion and fanaticism, especially the way in which prophets or messiahs are constructed, ostensibly, via utter lunacy and insane power relationships. But, it is also a viciously funny pastiche of detective fiction and horror stories, as well as a stinging and relentless critique of human depravity and irrationality. [Mark Tursi]

Mac Wellman. *A Chronicle of the Madness of Small Worlds*. Trip Street, 2008. 125 pp. Paper: $15.00.

Wellman, long known on the New York scene as an innovative dramatist, here provides a series of narratives discontinuous in both subject and meaning, yet undergirded by a vertebral jauntiness in the ability of language to still matter after all its customary props have been denied it. By writing coherent sentences that yet use phony, concocted, or deliberately absurd referents, which in turn do not carry over even from paragraph to paragraph, Wellman satisfies both our urge to read along and our dissatisfaction with merely mimetic or illusionistic tableaux. Citing "bong farmers" and "postmodern critical theory" on the same page, Wellman's travesty of reference sends up the many books that are bolstered by such reference—from three-dimensional realism to encyclopedic experimentalism. Wellman's ways of worldmaking exult in the way the writer creates new worlds without regard to whether or not they "really" exist, but also mocking the allure of preferentiality for writers who use it to fix reality and provide pleasing detail in a way that short-circuits the imaginative reach of their texts—e.g. "The Name That Was Too Much." He is a sensible, forthright game-player with a subversive if stalwart temperament. As names, Z'hung, El Pez de Fuma, and Twin Donuts all jangle together, and the sound-clusters that lie beneath customary usage but that we usually actively resist are allowed full play—"Another lemma of Gemma's dilemma" or calques of phrases, such as, not World War Two (or World Wide Web), but "Wu World

Woo." Science fiction, exoticism, and parody are used to defamiliarize, yet are also defamiliarized, as Wellman makes them no less solid or more preposterous than that which is usually taken as reality. The third world from the sun is one of many worlds whose madness Wellman congenially and steadily reveals. [Nicholas Birns]

Pierre Michon. *Small Lives*. Trans. Jody Gladding and Elizabeth Deshays. Archipelago Books, 2008. 250 pp. Paper: $15.00.

Rarely have I encountered a writer whose work felt so rewarding upon a first reading. Pierre Michon, the French novelist, is such a writer. In his novel, *Small Lives*, Michon takes us on a journey, tracking the lives of eight people in his search for his roots and place in his own family history. The stories span two centuries, but really they are timeless. In exploring these interconnected lives, Michon is on a journey to discover himself, and within this framework constantly asks the questions: What if? What might have been? What could be? In other words, Michon imagines what is possible within the human framework. Though stylistically challenging, the writing is textured and layered with singular depth and insight, poetry and profundity: so much so that it is difficult to single out any of the lives explored. Still, the life of Father Bandy, even though he is little more than a priest in a small French village, resonated with me as not only profound and timeless, but very much true to the contemporary blight we ourselves are experiencing on the human condition—with all the limitations, complexities, contradictions, and self-interest we see in so many of our corporate and world leaders today. In any given sentence Michon can take off from the prosaic and pedestrian on a flight that smacks of the visionary and aboriginally imaginative. Indeed, the real and imagined become interfused and interconnected and are more often than not indistinguishable for this author. If there is one leitmotif in these superlative stories, it is that of Michon himself, the man and the writer: learning, finding, evolving, becoming himself, relating his impotence, rage, regret, transfigured loss, aspiration, poetic glimmers, grandiosity, unbridled hopes and dreams, and ultimately finding his own voice—in short, all that being a writer is. Reading *Small Lives*, I felt profoundly that Michon was carrying the mark of a true writer: one who speaks in his own voice while conveying with all its immediacy and flesh and blood-possibility what it means to be human. [Richard Kalich]

Eckhard Gerdes. *My Landlady the Lobotomist.* Raw Dog Screaming Press, 2008. 113 pp. Paper: $12.95.

This is the eighth novel by Eckhard Gerdes, the editor of *Journal of Experimental Fiction*. The title refers to a boarding house where the landlady preserves the frontal lobes of former guests in jars around the building, a scenario that confirms Gerdes's connections with the Bizarro school of fiction. The containing frame of the boarding house gives way to an open, outdoor location in chapter two, "The Running of the Rapids." Here, a local swimming competition offers a pretext for thumbnail character sketches, including one man who has "built his life on liquid structures." While the first chapter suggests containment, the second evokes the flux of Gerdes's text, which is partly held together by a central figure whose unfulfilled desires are enacted through a series of personas ranging from Werther to the Japanese movie monster Godzilla. Drawing on the whimsical humor of writers like Richard Brautigan, Gerdes never allows a fictional illusion to take form without disrupting it through wordplay, textual breaks, and numbered statements addressed to an unnamed second person. The resulting rapid sequence of tones and situations reaches its grotesque climax in the narrator's skull being opened and his brain extracted to complete his landlady's collection. [David Seed]

Blake Butler. *EVER.* Calamari Press, 2009. 104 pp. Paper: $12.00.

Butler's debut novella is, above all, a playful text that repeatedly mines the tension between repression and expulsion. Superfluous brackets contain every paragraph, visually constraining the words, giving the proceedings a whispered, aside-like quality. Meanwhile, these snatches of subdued text are arranged seemingly randomly around the page, at times overlapping collage illustrations by publisher Derek White, imparting a restlessness that is amplified by sudden shifts in tone. Much of the narrative itself remains opaque, the writing for the most part consisting of stretches of abstract prose propped up by regular meter, alliteration, repetition, and wordplay: "The wind would wind my hair. . . . ripped with rashing." The female narrator relates a fragmented list of details about herself and her surroundings, some prosaic, others horrific: "The door in the floor in the sunroom changes colors with the weather. . . . Sometimes at night I hear certain doors open and people come into my house." Her creepily indifferent tone lurches from singsong ("At first our local leaders tried to zone around the madness") to flat, mundane sentences ("Some weeks, I should mention, I would live off candy bars"). Something here, obviously, is very much not right. The obscure plot (as I interpret it) involves a supernatural kind of "fold" or "yawning" that appears in a neighborhood, distorting reality, and forcing the narrator to retreat inside her house, then deeper and deeper within the architecture that is herself—although her patchy evasiveness renders all related information and events questionable. The gothic/sci-fi angle and typographic experimentation ultimately births a text that falls somewhere between FC2's former Black Ice imprint and a grungier *House of Leaves*. A deceptively brief read, *EVER* proves ever disquieting. [A D Jameson]

Cesare Pavese. *This Business of Living: Diaries 1935–1950.* Trans. A. E. Murch. Intro. John Taylor. Transaction, 2009. 350 pp. Paper: $29.95. (Reprint)

Natalia Ginzburg once wrote that Cesare Pavese's "conversation could be pointed and invigorating like nobody else's." The observation will strike one as all too true after reading his extraordinary diaries. Whether meditating on matters aesthetic, philosophical, or romantic, Pavese brings to bear a metaphysical yearning and a dry, compressed expressiveness to rival that of Kafka,

Weil, and Cioran. The journal begins with the aspiring poet eagerly parsing the distinction between the "material unity" and "spiritual unity" of his work and claiming "how allusive, how *all-pervading*, every future subject must be to me . . ." Soon, though, whatever hope that might underlay his passionate purposefulness is crushed by self-flagellation: "Have I really ever asked myself what I ought to do according to conscience? . . . And even where my work is concerned, have I ever been anything but a hedonist?" Pavese translated Defoe, Melville, and Joyce, and he studs his diaries with provocative reflections on a startling array of authors, including Horace, Murasaki, and Flaubert, about whom he admonishes, "Be careful not to take seriously Flaubert's reviews of reality. They are based on no other principle but this: all is filth, except the conscientious artist." He treats the war years in largely abstract terms: Pavese was one for whom, though he lived a fairly colorful life (confined for antifascist activities, lover to the American actress Constance Dowling), emotional fibrillations took precedence over exterior circumstances. He aspired to an existence that would be utterly inaugural, suffused with a sense of revelation. His suffering stemmed from his inability to carry out the impossible task of raising his life and work to the level of myth. A year before his suicide, he mourned, "I wanted to go on, take it further, absorb another generation, become everlasting, like a hill." These journals are a bracing testament to that struggle. [Tayt J. Harlin]

Guy Debord. *Correspondence: The Foundation of the Situationist International (June 1957–August 1960)*. Trans. Stuart Kendall and John McHale. Intro. McKenzie Wark. Semiotexte, 2009. 397 pp. Paper: $19.95.

The Situationist International had its moment—its brief moment—in the streets of Paris in May, 1968, when French students took for their slogan the Situationist cry, "Beneath the Paving Stones, the Beach!" to emphasize the need to discard old ways of doing business in order to find ways to live that were free, just, total. Its revolution, Greil Marcus writes, "was to begin and end in the realm of everyday life." The Situationists sought to turn history around, re-inscribe it so that it could not be read as it had been read. What was crucial was not the goal but the trip; those moments, however spectral, that each of us has, blotting out history books. There—we were alive, more ourselves than we had ever been. Thus, though the Situationists were influenced by surrealism and Dada, their interest in art was to end it. Art, as we understand it, is not transcendence, but a substitute for transcendence. "We are artists insofar as we are no longer artists," wrote Guy Debord—himself influenced by Hegel, Marx, and Lukács—further arguing that philosophy—doctrine—must disappear in *praxis*. We must walk the streets until the streets make themselves known to us. It was war, and this correspondence, written between 1957, at the founding of the Situationist International in Italy, and 1960, reflects the strategy and practice of the revolutionary. "The most rigorous secrecy must be maintained," Debord advises one correspondent. He issues directives, positions the Situationists in relation to the war in Algeria and DeGaulle, expels those who fail to follow the party line (seven of the original eight founders are dismissed, leaving only Debord). They are seen to be a clandestine political organization. Police question Debord. Their publications are held up by customs. It is no accident that Debord, along with his second wife, Alice Ho, design a board game, *A Game of War*.

Of course, the Situationists were doomed to failure. Of course, their moment never disappears. We conjure it up in the Paris Commune (a seminal influence for Debord); hear it in Johnny Rotten's "NO FUTURE NO FUTURE" and Pere Ubu's "30 Seconds Over Tokyo"; see it in the riots of Watts; follow it in Bernadette Corporation's *detournement* of Michelle Bernstein's novel, *All the King's Horses,* written at the same time as these letters (Bernstein was Debord's first wife). The No that swallows lives. [Robert Buckeye]

Books Received

Adnan, Etel. *Master of the Eclipse*. Interlink Books, 2009. Paper: $15.00. (F)

Baker, Larry. *A Good Man*. ICP Books, 2009. Cloth: $24.95. (F)

Barone, Dennis and James Finnegan, eds. *Visiting Wallace: Poems Inspired by the Life and Work of Wallace Stevens*. Univ. of Iowa Press, 2009. Paper: $18.00. (F)

Berry, R.M., ed. *Forms at War: FC2 1999–2009*. FC2, 2009. Paper: $25.95. (F)

Biller, Maxim. *Love Today*. Trans. Anthea Bell. Simon & Schuster, 2009. Paper: $15.00. (F)

Botsford, Keith. *Józef Czapski: A Life in Translation*. Sylph Editions, 2009. Paper: £10.00. (NF)

Bradley, Alan. *The Sweetness at the Bottom of the Pie*. Delacorte Press, 2009. Cloth: $23.00. (F)

Broner, E.M. *The Red Squad*. Pantheon, 2009. Cloth: $24.00. (F)

Buckeye, Robert. *Left*. Amandla Publishing, 2009. Paper: $15.00. (F)

Byatt, A. S. *The Children's Book*. Knopf, 2009. Cloth: $26.95. (F)

Caputo, Philip. *Crossers*. Knopf, 2009. Cloth: $27.95. (F)

Carter, Stephen L. *Jericho's Fall*. Knopf, 2009. Cloth: $25.95. (F)

Christensen, Inger. *Azorno*. Trans. Denise Newman. New Directions, 2009. Paper: $13.95. (F)

Christie, Jackie. *Proud to be a Colored Girl*. Infinite Love Publishing, 2008. Paper: $14.95. (F)

Crucet, Jennine Capó. *How to Leave Hialeah*. Univ. of Iowa Press, 2009. Paper: $16.00. (F)

Daudet, Alphonse. *Artists' Wives*. Trans. Laura Ensor. Intro. Olivier Bernier. Turtle Point Press, 2009. Paper: $14.95. (F)

Defoe, Gideon. *The Pirates! In an Adventure with Napoleon*. Pantheon, 2008. Cloth: $16.95. (F)

De Robertis, Carolina. *The Invisible Mountain*. Knopf, 2009. Cloth: $24.95. (F)

Economou, George. *Ananios of Kleitor: Poems & Fragments and Their Reception from Antiquity to the Present*. Shearsman Books, 2009. Paper: $17.00. (F)

Fanailova, Elena. *The Russian Version*. Trans. Genya Turovskaya and Stephanie Sandler. Intro Aleksandr Skidan. Ugly Duckling Press, 2009. Paper: $15.00. (F)

Finger, Anne. *Call Me Ahab*. Univ. of Nebraska Press, 2009. Paper: $17.95. (F)

Gerdes, Eckhard, ed. *Journal of Experimental Fiction 35*. Depth Charge Publishing, 2009. Paper: $23.99. (F)

Guida, James. *Marbles*. Turtle Point Press, 2009. Paper: $14.95. (F)

Guignery, Vanessa and Ryan Roberts. *Conversations with Julian Barnes*. Univ. Press of Mississippi, 2009. Cloth: $50.00. Paper: $22.00. (NF)

Hart, Josephine. *The Truth About Love*. Knopf, 2009. Cloth: $24.95.

Hecht, Julie. *Happy Trails to You*. Simon & Schuster, 2009. Paper: $14.00. (F)

Herman, Arthur. *Gandhi & Churchill: The Epic Rivalry That Destroyed an Empire and Forged Our Age*. Bantam, 2009. Paper: $20.00. (NF)

Hoffmann, Yoel. *Curriculum Vitae*. Trans. Peter Cole. New Directions, 2009. Paper: $14.95. (F)

Hopper, Keith. *Flann O'Brien: A Portrait of the Artist as a Young Post-Modernist (Second Edition)*. Foreword J. Hillis Miller. Cork Univ. Press, 2009. Cloth: £35.00. (NF)

Howard, Joanna. *On the Winding Stair*. BOA Editions, Ltd., 2009. Paper: $14.00. (F)

Johnston, Devin. *Creaturely and Other Essays*. Turtle Point Press, 2009. Paper: $14.95. (F)

Kabdebo, Thomas. *Tracking Giorgione*. Brandon Books / Dufour Editions, 2009. Paper: $19.95. (F)

Kolm, Ron, Carol Wierzbicki, Alfrad Vitale, Shalom Neuman, and Jim Feast, eds. *The Worst Book I Ever Read*. Unbearables Books / Autonomedia, 2009. Paper: $16.95. (NF)

Leviant, Curt. *A Novel of Klass*. Livingston Press, 2008. Paper: $16.95. (F)

Ma, Kathryn. *All That Work and Still No Boys*. Univ. of Iowa Press, 2009. Paper: $16.00. (F)

McKoy, Sheila Smith. *Obsidian: Literature in the African Diaspora. Zora Neale Hurston Special Edition: Volume 9, Issue 1. Spring/Summer 2008*. North Carolina State Univ., 2008. Paper: $8.00. (F)

Osborn, Susan, ed. *Elizabeth Bowen: New Critical Perspectives*. Cork Univ. Press, 2009. Cloth: £35.00. (NF)

Phillips, Thomas. *Long Slow Distance*. Object Press, 2009. Paper: $13.00. (F)

Piatigorsky, Anton. *Eternal Hydra*. Coach House Books, 2009. Paper: $14.95. (F)

Roberson, Matthew. *Impotent*. FC2, 2009. Paper: $13.95. (F)

Roncagliolo, Santiago. *Red April*. Trans. Edith Grossman. Pantheon, 2009. Cloth: $24.95. (F)

Schami, Rafik. *The Dark Side of Love*. Trans. Anthea Bell. Interlink Books, 2009. Paper: $24.00. (F)

Schell, Adam. *Tomato Rhapsody*. Delacorte Press, 2009. Cloth: $25.00. (F)

Shaffer, Mary Ann and Annie Barrows. *The Guernsey Literary and Potato Peel Pie Society*. Dial Press, 2009. Paper: $14.00. (F)

Sutin, Lawrence. *When to Go into the Water*. Sarabande Books, 2009. Paper: $15.95. (F)

Thompson, Jean. *Do Not Deny Me*. Simon & Schuster, 2009. Paper: $14.00. (F)

Thornton, Tim. *The Alternative Hero*. Knopf, 2009. Cloth: $24.95. (F)

Tomasula, Steve. *TOC: A New Media Novel*. Univ. of Alabama Press, 2009. $16.95. (DVD-ROM)

Weldt-Basson, Helen Carole. *Subversive Silences: Nonverbal Expression and Implicit Narrative Strategies in the Works of Latin American Women Writers*. Farleigh Dickinson Univ. Press, 2009. Cloth: $58.50. (NF)

Zhang, Lijia. *"Socialism is Great!" A Worker's Memoir of the New China*. Anchor Books, 2009. Paper: $14.95. (NF)

DELILLO FIEDLER GASS PYNCHON
University of Delaware Press
Collections on Contemporary Masters

UNDERWORDS
Perspectives on Don DeLillo's *Underworld*

Edited by Joseph Dewey, Steven G. Kellman, and Irving Malin

Essays by Jackson R. Bryer, David Cowart, Kathleen Fitzpatrick, Joanne Gass, Paul Gleason, Donald J. Greiner, Robert McMinn, Thomas Myers, Ira Nadel, Carl Ostrowski, Timothy L. Parrish, Marc Singer, and David Yetter

$39.50

LESLIE FIEDLER AND AMERICAN CULTURE

Edited by Steven G. Kellman and Irving Malin

Essays by John Barth, Robert Boyers, James M. Cox, Joseph Dewey, R.H.W. Dillard, Geoffrey Green, Irving Feldman, Leslie Fiedler, Susan Gubar, Jay L. Halio, Brooke Horvath, David Ketterer, R.W.B. Lewis, Sanford Pinsker, Harold Schechter, Daniel Schwarz, David R. Slavitt, Daniel Walden, and Mark Royden Winchell

$36.50

INTO *THE TUNNEL*
Readings of Gass's Novel

Edited by Steven G. Kellman and Irving Malin

Essays by Rebecca Goldstein, Donald J. Greiner, Brooke Horvath, Marcus Klein, Jerome Klinkowitz, Paul Maliszewski, James McCourt, Arthur Saltzman, Susan Stewart, and Heide Ziegler

$35.00

PYNCHON AND *MASON & DIXON*

Edited by Brooke Horvath and Irving Malin

Essays by Jeff Baker, Joseph Dewey, Bernard Duyfhuizen, David Foreman, Donald J. Greiner, Brian McHale, Clifford S. Mead, Arthur Saltzman, Thomas H. Schaub, David Seed, and Victor Strandberg

$39.50

ORDER FROM ASSOCIATED UNIVERSITY PRESSES
2010 Eastpark Blvd., Cranbury, New Jersey 08512
PH 609-655-4770   FAX 609-655-8366   E-mail AUP440@ aol.com

EDWARD DORN
LOUIS ZUKOFSKY
LISA ROBERTSON
KENNETH REXROTH
CHRISTOPHER MIDDLETON

CHICAGO REVIEW

5801 SOUTH KENWOOD AVENUE • CHICAGO ILLINOIS 60637

visit humanities.uchicago.edu/review to subscribe and order special issues

Dalkey Archive
Scholarly Series

Available Now

Phantasms of Matter
in Gogol (and Gombrowicz)
MICHAL OKLOT

Fiction Now:
The French Novel in the Twenty-First Century
WARREN MOTTE

Intersections:
Essays on Richard Powers
STEPHEN J. BURN AND PETER DEMPSEY, EDS.

Energy of Delusion:
A Book on Plot
VIKTOR SHKLOVSKY

Life Itself:
Louis Paul Boon as Innovator of the Novel
ANNIE VAN DEN OEVER

Rayner Heppenstall:
A Critical Study
G. J. BUCKELL

Reading Games:
An Aesthetics of Play in
Flann O'Brien, Samuel Beckett, and Georges Perec
KIMBERLY BOHMAN-KALAJA

I Am Otherwise:
The Romance between Poetry and
Theory after the Death of the Subject
ALEX E. BLAZER

Don't Ever Get Famous:
Essays on New York Writing
after the New York School
DANIEL KANE, ED.

An investigation into the problem of art and matter in the work of Nikolai Gogol, and, indirectly, into the Neoplatonic tradition in Russian literature, *Phantasms of Matter* constitutes a rigorous examination of Gogol's "image of matter," as well as an attempt to enumerate the rules of its construction. After developing an artistic language corresponding to the Neoplatonic discourse on matter, Gogol subsequently abandoned literature; yet this transposition of the Neoplatonic problem has recurred frequently in Russian and Slavic literature following his death. Oklot therefore extends this investigation into the work of the Polish author Witold Gombrowicz, allowing unique parallels to be drawn between the writings of these two giants of world literature.

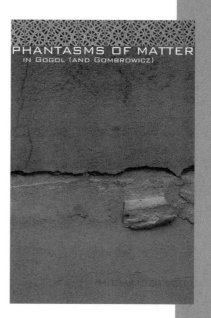

Phantasms of Matter
in Gogol (and Gombrowicz)

MICHAL OKLOT

Dalkey Archive Scholarly Series
Literary Criticism
$34.95 / paper
ISBN: 978-1-56478-494-0

"Combining complex philosophical analysis with uncannily intelligent close readings, Oklot provides strikingly new interpretations of the work of Gogol and Gombrowicz while simultaneously focusing attention on literary manifestations of new-Platonic thought. *Phantasms of Matter* is a tour de force."
—Andrew Wachtel, Northwestern University

Fiction Now reports on the current states of the novel in France, taking a series of soundings within the compass of innovative French writing since 2001. Chapters focus closely upon Jean Echenoz, Marie Redonnet, Christian Gailly, Lydie Salvayre, Gérard Gavarry, Hélène Lenoir, Patrick Lapeyre, and Christine Montalbetti. Each of the authors invoked exemplifies in his or her work a different set of strategies, concerns, and approaches: one of them transposes the Book of Judith to the Parisian suburbs; another imagines the most taciturn of cowboys in the American West; still another goes well beyond death, into the afterlife of a concert pianist. Despite their diversity of theme and technique, these writers share a will to make French fiction new, and demonstrate compellingly that the novel as it is practiced today in France is a vigorous, enthralling, and richly plural cultural form.

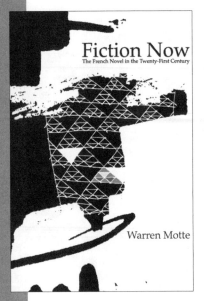

Fiction Now:
The French Novel in the
Twenty-First Century

WARREN MOTTE

Dalkey Archive Scholarly Series
Literary Criticism
$29.95 / paper
ISBN: 978-1-56478-503-9

Warren Motte is chair of the Department of French and Italian at the University of Colorado, Boulder. He has written several studies of contemporary French literature, including *Fables of the Novel: French Fiction since 1990,* and is translator and editor of *Oulipo: A Primer of Potential Literature*—both available from Dalkey Archive Press.

Since his first novel was published in 1985, Richard Powers
has assembled a body of work whose intellectual breadth and
imaginative energy bears comparison with that of any writer
working today. *Intersections: Essays on Richard Powers* pays tribute to that achievement by collecting seventeen essays—by
leading literary critics, philosophers, and a novelist—each
of which offers important insights into Powers's narrative
craft and the intellectual grids that underlie his work. Powers's novels are distinguished by both their multiple narrative forms and their sophisticated synthesis of diverse fields
of knowledge; to attempt to adequately address this range,
the contributors to this volume mix their study of Powers's
narrative innovations with eclectic interdisciplinary perspectives, which range from photography and systems theory, to
ecocriticism and neuroscience. The volume concludes with
an essay by Powers himself.

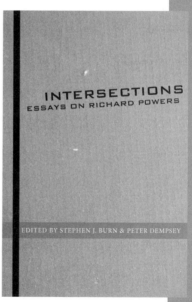

Intersections:
Essays on Richard Powers

STEPHEN J. BURN
& PETER DEMPSEY, EDS.

Dalkey Archive Scholarly Series
Literary Criticism
$29.95 / paper
ISBN: 978-1-56478-508-4

Contributors: Jon Adams, Sven Birkerts, Stephen J. Burn,
David Cowart, Anca Cristofovici, Daniel C. Dennett, Joseph
Dewey, Charles B. Harris, Scott Hermanson, Jenell Johnson,
Bruno Latour, Barry Lewis, Paul Maliszewski, Richard Powers,
Carter Scholz, Trey Strecker, Joseph Tabbi, and Patti White.

One of the greatest literary minds of the twentieth century, Viktor Shklovsky writes the critical equivalent of what Ross Chambers calls "loiterature"—writing that roams, playfully digresses, moving freely between the literary work and the world. In *Energy of Delusion*, a masterpiece that Shklovsky worked on over thirty years, he turns his unique critical sensibility to Tolstoy's life and novels, applying the famous "formalist method" he invented in the 1920s to Tolstoy's massive body of work, and at the same time taking Tolstoy (as well as Boccaccio, Pushkin, Chekhov, Dostoevsky, and Turgenev) as a springboard to consider the devices of literature—how novels work and what they do.

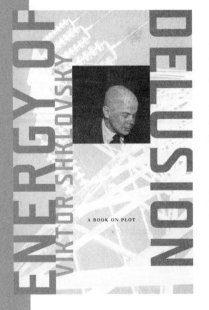

A BOOK ON PLOT

Energy of Delusion:
A Book on Plot

VIKTOR SHKLOVSKY
TRANSLATION BY
SHUSHAN AVAGYAN

Dalkey Archive Scholarly Series
Literary Criticism
$14.95 / paper
ISBN: 978-1-56478-426-1

"A rambling, digressive stylist, Shklovsky throws off brilliant aperçus on every page ... Like an architect's blueprint, [he] lays bare the joists and studs that hold up the house of fiction."
—Michael Dirda, *Washington Post*

"Perhaps because he is such an unlikely Tolstoyan, Viktor Shklovsky's writing on Tolstoy is always absorbing and often brilliant."
—*Russian Review*

Life Itself is the first book-length study in English of the great Flemish writer Louis Paul Boon. Annie van den Oever begins by questioning the paradox between Boon's international reputation as a significant innovator of the novel, and the peculiarly reductive biographical interpretations regularly uttered by some of his fellow countrymen and contemporaries. She looks for answers in Boon's misinterpreted "primitive" Flemish and analyzes the so-called refined pseudo-primitive style within both the grotesque tradition (Kafka, van Ostajien, Gogol) and the skeptical, radical tradition of Nietzsche. In addition, she offers fresh insight into Boon's character Boontje, seen by many as a diminutive for the writer himself, outlining the sublime and slightly sinister relation of this quasi-comical character to its mighty creator.

Life Itself:
Louis Paul Boon as Innovator of the Novel

ANNIE VAN DEN OEVER

Dalkey Archive Scholarly Series
Literary Criticism
$29.95 / paper
ISBN: 978-1-56478-507-7

Annie van den Oever is a senior researcher at the State University of Groningen and the University of Utrecht, and is part of the community of Boon specialists within the Netherlands and Flanders.

This book examines the first five novels of Rayner Heppenstall (1911–1981). During his lifetime, many critics cited Heppenstall as the founder of the nouveau roman, believing his debut novel *The Blaze of Noon* (1939) anticipated the postwar innovations of French writers such as Alain Robbe-Grillet and Nathalie Sarraute. Since his death, however, Heppenstall's reputation has faded, and his fiction is out of print. His final novels were structurally simplistic and politically unpalatable, and their disastrous critical reception clouded critical judgment of his previous novels. G. J. Buckell examines the importance of technical experimentation, rather than the ideological content, within Heppenstall's earlier works, and seeks a more favorable standing for him within our critical and cultural memory.

Rayner Heppenstall:
A Critical Study

G. J. BUCKELL

Dalkey Archive Scholarly Series
Literary Criticism
$29.95 / paper
ISBN: 978-1-56478-471-1

"Heppenstall's novels were poetic, considered, and intelligently realised engagements with literary form, and, regardless of the sub-discourses of Modernist writing they can justifiably be situated within, they deserve a far better reputation."

—G. J. Buckell

"It was the historian Johan Huizinga who first elaborated a theory of play. Martin Heidegger, Ludwig Wittgenstein, Roger Caillot and other luminaries have also been drawn to the subject. Now, Kimberly Bohman-Kalaja has applied play-theory to the works of three authors—Flann O'Brien, Samuel Beckett and Georges Perec, with illuminating, sometimes startling results. I was in turn bemused, enlightened and exhilarated by the realization of what adept game-players these authors were."

—Anthony Cronin, author of *Samuel Beckett: The Last Modernist* and *No Laughing Matter: The Life and Times of Flann O'Brien*

Reading Games:
An Aesthetics of Play in Flann O'Brien, Samuel Beckett, and Georges Perec

KIMBERLY BOHMAN-KALAJA

Dalkey Archive Scholarly Series
Literary Criticism
$34.95 / paper
ISBN: 978-1-56478-473-5

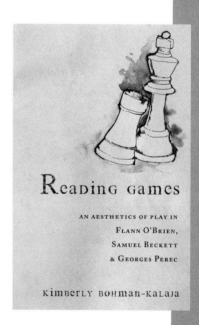

"We all know that there's more to games than fun. Bohman-Kalaja's remarkable study of O'Brien, Beckett and Perec is the first to get to grips with the deeper issues involved in the ludic practices of these post-modern masters. It also teaches us a great deal about what kind of games can be played with and through words. Learned, illuminating, original and profound, this is a study that should transform the teaching of modern literature—and bring back some of the fun!"

—David Bellos

I Am Otherwise: The Romance between Poetry and Theory after the Death of the Subject examines the contemporary poet's relationship with language in the age of theory. As the book works through close readings and interpretations of Adrienne Rich and Harold Bloom, John Ashbery and Paul de Man, Jorie Graham and Maurice Blanchot, and Barrett Watten and Jacques Lacan, it shows how the main psychological modes of contemporary poetry and the postmodern poet are anxiety, irony, abjection, and destitution. The book ultimately concludes that the new theoretical poetry self-consciously renders the effect of critical theory in its own construction. Whereas poets of the past tarried with nature, self, or philosophy, poets of our time unite lyric feeling with literary theory itself.

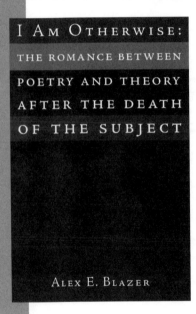

I AM OTHERWISE:

THE ROMANCE BETWEEN

POETRY AND THEORY

AFTER THE DEATH

OF THE SUBJECT

ALEX E. BLAZER

I Am Otherwise:

The Romance between Poetry and Theory after the Death of the Subject

ALEX E. BLAZER

Dalkey Archive Scholarly Series
Literary Criticism
$34.95 / paper
ISBN: 978-1-56478-458-2

"Like Ashbery, I too am nostalgic for an understanding of subjectivity—replete with inner being, in control of the outer language—which current thinking does not afford."
—Alex E. Blazer

The essays in this book focus attention on the vibrant New York poetry scene of the 1960s and '70s, on the poets who came after what is now known as the New York School. Amiri Baraka, Bernadette Mayer, Hannah Weiner, Clark Coolidge, Anne Waldman, and Ron Padgett are just some of the poets who extended the line that John Ashbery, Frank O'Hara, Kenneth Koch, and James Schuyler started. In *Don't Ever Get Famous*, a range of writers and scholars examine the cultural, sociological, and historical contexts of this wildly diverse group of writers. These poets, many of whom are still writing today, changed American poetry forever, and this book provides the first large-scale consideration of their work.

Don't Ever Get Famous:
Essays on New York Writing after the New York School

DANIEL KANE, ED.

Dalkey Archive Scholarly Series
Literary Criticism
$34.95 / paper
ISBN: 978-1-56478-460-5

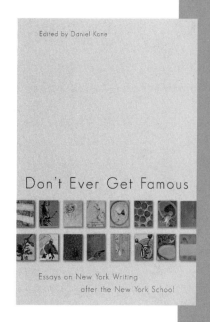

Edited by Daniel Kane

Don't Ever Get Famous

Essays on New York Writing after the New York School

"Kane's volume is the first to tackle the period in New York's downtown literary history most closely tied to the group of poets known as the 'Second Generation New York School.' . . . [It] is a must-have for historians of American poetry in the 20th century."
—*Publishers Weekly*

ORDER FORM

Individuals may use this form to subscribe to the *Review of Contemporary Fiction* or to order back issues of the *Review* and Dalkey Archive titles at a discount (see below for details).

Title   ISBN   Quantity   Price

_____

_____

_____

_____

_____

_____

                                        Subtotal   _____

                                   Less Discount   _____
(10% for one book, 20% for two or more books, and
25% for Scholarly titles advertised in this issue)
                                        Subtotal   _____

                                    Plus Postage   _____
(U.S. $3 + $1 per book; foreign $5 + $3 per book)

1 Year Individual Subscription to the **Review**   _____
($17 U.S.; $22.60 Canada; $32.60 all other countries)
                                           Total   _____

        Mailing Address   _____

                            _____

                            _____

                            _____

---

xxix/2

Credit card payment   ☐ Visa   ☐ Mastercard

Acct. # _____   Exp. Date _____

Name on card _____   Phone # _____

Please make checks (in U.S. dollars only) payable to *Dalkey Archive Press.*

mail or fax this form to: Dalkey Archive Press, University of Illinois,
1805 S. Wright Street, MC-011, Champaign, IL 61820
fax: 217.244.9142 tel: 217.244.5700